A sudden curtain of silence fell over the burning city. All that could be heard was the steady crackling of the flames, and now and then the sound of falling masonry as yet another building collapsed. The Place Wilson, so lately filled with tanks and soldiers, was now deserted. Blackened fragments of paper fell gently to rest on the burnt-out hulk of a tank where the remains of a German soldier sprawled, half in, half out of the turret.

Down in our basement, we crouched in primitive terror as the wall of silence built up round the city. The sound of warfare we could understand, but no sound at all filled us with a nameless dread . . .

Reign of Hell

Sven Hassel

CORGI BOOKS

REIGN OF HELL

A CORGI BOOK 0 552 09178 2

First publication in Great Britain

PRINTING HISTORY
Corgi edition published 1973
Corgi edition reprinted 1973 (twice)
Corgi edition reprinted 1974
Corgi edition reprinted 1975
Corgi edition reprinted 1976 (twice)
Corgi edition reprinted 1977
Corgi edition reprinted 1978 (twice)
Corgi edition reprinted 1979
Corgi edition reprinted 1980
Corgi edition reprinted 1981
Corgi edition reprinted 1983
Corgi edition reprinted 1985
Corgi edition reprinted 1986
Corgi edition reprinted 1987

Corgi Books are published by Transworld Publishers Ltd.,
61–63 Uxbridge Road, Ealing, London W5 5SA,
in Australia by Transworld Publishers (Aust.) Pty. Ltd.,
15–23 Helles Avenue, Moorebank, NSW 2170, and in New
Zealand by Transworld Publishers (N.Z.) Ltd., Cnr. Moselle
and Waipareira Avenues, Henderson, Auckland.

Printed and bound in Great Britain by
Hazell Watson & Viney Limited,
Member of the BPCC Group,
Aylesbury, Bucks

REIGN OF HELL

*'Why does the Vistula heave and swell, like the breast
    of a hero
Breathing his last on a wild sea shore?
Why does the waves' lament, from the dark of the deep
    abyss,
Resound like the sigh of a dying man?*

*'From out of the depths of the cold river bed, like a sad
    dream of death
The song is sung.
From rain-washed fields the silver willows weep in
    chorus of sorrow ...
The young girls of Poland have forgotten how to smile.'*

*'The Germans are without any doubt marvellous sol-
diers'—*

> These words were written in his notebook on
> 21st May 1940 by the future Field Marshal
> Lord Alanbrooke.

THIS book is dedicated to the Unknown Soldier and to all
the victims of the Second World War, in the hope that never
again will politicians plung us into the irresponsible lunacy of
mass murder.

*'What we want is power. And we have it, we shall keep
it. No one shall wrest it from us'—*

> Speech by Hitler at Munich, 30th November
> 1932.

NONE of the men of the 5th Company wanted to become a
guard Sennelager. But what does it matter what a soldier may
or may not want? A soldier is a machine. A soldier is there
for the sole purpose of executing orders. Let him make only

one slip and he would very soon find himself transferred to the infamous punishment battalion, number 999, the general rubbish tip for all offenders.

Examples are legion. Take, for instance, the tank commander who refused to obey an order to burn down a village and all its inhabitants: court martial, reduction to the ranks, Germersheim, 999 ... The sequence was swift and inevitable.

Or there again, take the SS Obersturmführer who stood out against his transfer to the security branch: court martial, reduction to the ranks, Torgau, 999 ...

All examples have a certain dreary monotony. The pattern, once established, could never be altered, although after a time they did begin swelling the ranks of the punishment battalions by transferring criminals as well as military offenders.

In Section I, Paragraph 1, of the German Army Regulations can be read the following: 'Military service is a service of honour' ...

And in Paragraph 13: 'Anyone who receives a prison sentence of more than five months shall be deemed no longer fit for military service and shall henceforth be debarred from serving in any of the armed forces of land, sea or air' ...

But in Paragraph 36: 'In exceptional circumstances Paragraph 13 may be disregarded and men serving prison sentences of more than five months may be enlisted in the Army provided they are sent to special disciplinary companies. Certain of the worst classes of offenders shall be drafted into squads occupied solely with mine disposal or burial duties; such squads not to be supplied with firearms. After six months' satisfactory service, such men may be transferred to 999 Battalion at Sennelager, along with soldiers who have been charged with offences on the field of battle. In time of war, non-commissioned officers must have spent at least twelve months on active service in the front line; in time of peace, ten years. All officers and non-commissioned officers shall be severely reprimanded if found guilty of showing undue leniency towards the men under their command. Any recruit who endures severe discipline without complaint and shows himself fit for military service may be transferred into an ordinary Army regiment and will there be eligible for promotion in the normal way. Before such transfer shall be approved, however, a man must have been recommended for the Cross on at least four occasions following action in the field.'

The number 999 (the three nines, as it was known) was a joke. Or at any rate, supposed to be joke. It must be admitted that Supreme Command at first totally failed to see the humour of it, for the nine hundreds had always been reserved for the special crack regiments. And then someone kindly explained to them that treble nine was the telephone number of Scotland Yard in London. And what could possibly be more subtle or amusing to the Nazi mind than to give the very same number to a battalion composed entirely of criminals? Supreme Command allowed itself a tight bureaucratic smile and nodded its head in sage approval. Let nine-nine-nine be the number; and just for a bit of further fun, why not preface it with a large V with a red line slashed across it? Signifying: annulled. Cancelled. Wipe out ... Which could, of course, have referred either to Scotland Yard or the battalion itself. But that was the joke of it. That was what was so excruciatingly funny. Either way, it was enough to make you split your sides laughing. For let's face it, the swine who served in 999 battalion were scarcely what you could call desirables. Thieves and cut-throats and petty criminals; traitors and cowards and religious maniacs; the lowest scum of the earth and fit only to die.

Those of us sweating our guts out on the front line, didn't look at it quite like that. We couldn't afford to. Dukes or dustmen, saints or swindlers, all we cared about was whether a chap would share his last fag with you in times of need. To hell with what a man had done before: it was what he did now, right here and now, that mattered to us. You can't exist on your own when you're in the Army. It's every man for another, and the law of good comradeship takes precedence over all else.

THE CAMP AT SENNELAGER

An ancient locomotive grunted slowly up the line, dragging behind it a row of creaking goods wagons.

On the platform, waiting passengers glanced up curiously as the train drew to a halt. In one of the wagons was a party of armed guards, hung about with enough weaponry to wipe out an entire regiment.

We were sitting on one of the departure platforms, playing a game of pontoon with some French and British prisoners of war. Porta and a Scottish sergeant had between them practically cleared the rest of us out, and Tiny and Gregor Martin had for the past hour been gambling on rather dubious credit. The sergeant was already in possession of four of their IOUs.

We were in the middle of a deal when Lieutenant Löwe, our company commander, suddenly broke up the game with one of his crude interruptions.

'All right, you lads! Come on, look alive, there! Time to get moving!'

Porta flung down his cards in disgust.

'Bloody marvellous,' he said, bitterly. 'Bloody marvellous, ain't it? No sooner get stuck into a decent game of cards than some stupid sod has to go and start the flaming war up again. It's enough to make you flaming puke.'

Löwe shot out his arm and pointed a finger at Porta.

'I'm warning you,' he said. 'Any more of your bloody lip and I'll——'

'Sir!' Porta sprang smartly to his feet and saluted. He never could resist having the last word. He'd have talked even the Führer himself to a standstill. 'Sir,' he said, earnestly. 'I'd like you to know that if you find the sound of my voice in any way troublesome I shall be only too happy for the future not to speak unless I am first spoke to.'

Löwe made an irritable clicking noise with his tongue and wisely walked off without further comment. The Old Man rose painfully to his feet and kicked away the upturned bucket on which he had been sitting. He settled his cap on his head and picked up his belt, with the heavy Army revolver in its holster.

'Second Section, stand by to move off!'

Reluctantly, we shuffled to our feet and looked with distaste at the waiting locomotive and its depressing string of goods wagons. Why couldn't the enemy have destroyed the wretched thing with their bombs? The prisoners of war, still sprawling at their ease on the ground, laughed up at us.

'Your country needs you, soldier!' The Scots sergeant took his half smoked cigarette from his lips and pinched the end between finger and thumb. 'I'll not forget you,' he promised. He waved Tiny's IOUs in a farewell gesture. 'I'll be waiting to greet you when you come back.'

'You know what?' said Tiny, without rancour. 'We should have polished your lot off once and for all at Dunkirk.'

The Sergeant shrugged, amiably.

'Don't you worry, mate. There'll be plenty of other opportunities ... I'll reserve a place for you when I get to heaven. We'll pick up the game where we left off.'

'Not in heaven we won't,' said Tiny. 'Not bleeding likely!' He jerked a thumb towards the ground. 'It's down there for me, mush! You can go where you like, but you're not getting me up there to meet St Flaming Peter and his band of bleeding angels!'

The Sergeant just smiled and stuffed the IOUs into his pocket. He took out the Iron Cross which he had won from Tiny and thoughtfully polished it on his tunic.

'Man, just wait till the Yanks get here! It'll go down a fair treat ...'

He held the Cross admiringly before him, in joyous anticipation of the price it would fetch. The Americans were great ones for war souvenirs. There was already a roaring trade in bloodstained bandages and sweaty scraps of uniform. Porta

11

had a large box crammed full with gruesome mementoes, ready for the time when the market would be most favourable. A grisly business, but at least it spelt the beginning of the end as far as the war was concerned.

The locomotive heaved itself and its trail of open wagons to a slow, creaking halt, and we trundled sullenly and resentfully up the platform and into the rain. It had been raining non-stop for four days and by now we were almost resigned to it. We turned up our coat collars and stuck our hands in our pockets and stood with hunched shoulders in a sodden silence. We had recently been issued new uniforms, and the stench of naphthalene was appalling. It could be smelt a mile off on a fine day, and in enclosed quarters it was enough to suffocate you. Fortunately, the lice enjoyed it no more than we did, and they had deserted us *en masse* in favour of the unsuspecting prisoners of war. So at least we were now saved the trouble of constantly having to take a hand out of a pocket to scratch at some inaccessible part of the body.

Painted on the sides of the leading wagons were the already half-forgotten names of Bergen and Trondheim. The wagons were being used for a transport of sturdy little mountain ponies. We paused for a moment to watch them. They all looked quite absurdly alike, with a dark line along the ridge of the back and soft black muzzles. One of them took a fancy to Tiny and began licking his face like a dog, whereupon Tiny, ever ready to adopt the first animal or child that showed him the least affection, instantly decided that the pony was his own personal property and should henceforth travel everywhere with him. He was attempting to separate it from the rest of the herd and lead it out of the wagon, when a couple of armed guards arrived, waving revolvers and yelling at the top of their voices. Seconds later, the combined noise of apoplectic guards, skittish ponies and a viciously swearing Tiny brought Lieutenant Löwe angrily on to the scene.

'What the hell's going on here?' He pushed the guards out of the way, striding into the midst of the mêlée with Danz, the chief guard at Sennelager and the ugliest brute on earth, striding self-importantly at his elbow. Löwe stopped in amazement at the sight of Tiny and his pony. 'What the devil do you think you're doing with that horse?'

'I'm taking him,' said Tiny. 'He wants to be with me. He's my mascot.' The pony licked him ecstatically, and Tiny placed a proprietary hand about its neck. 'He's called Jacob,' he said. 'He won't be any bother. He can travel about with me from place to place. I reckon he'll soon take to Army life.'

'Oh, you do, do you?' Löwe breathed heavily through dilated nostrils. 'Put that bloody horse back where it belongs! We're supposed to be fighting a war, not running a circus!'

He stormed off again, followed by Danz, and Tiny stood scowling after him.

'Sod the lot of 'em!' said Porta, cheerfully. He took a hand from his pocket and gesticulated crudely in the direction of Löwe's departing back. 'Don't you worry, mate, they'll be laughing the other side of their ugly officers' mugs when this little lot's over ... whole bloody lot of 'em, they'll be for the high jump all right and no mistake.' He turned and cocked an eyebrow at Julius Heide, who was without any doubt at all the most fanatical NCO in the entire German Army. 'Don't you reckon?' he said.

Heide gave him a cold, repressive frown. He disliked all talk of that nature. It gave him shivers up his rigid Nazi spine.

'More likely the corporals,' he said, looking hard at Porta's stripes. 'More likely the corporals will find their heads rolling.'

'Oh yeah?' jeered Porta. 'And who's going to round 'em all up, then? Not the bleeding officers, I can tell you that for a start. How many of us corporals do you reckon there are in this bleeding Army? A damn sight too many to let themselves be put upon, I can tell you that much.' He poked his finger into the middle of Heide's chest. 'You want to get your facts right,' he said. 'You want to open your eyes and have a look round some time. The cooking pots are already being put on to boil, mate—and it's us what's going to be doing all the cooking, not you and your load of rat-faced officers.'

Heide squared his narrow shoulders.

13

'Continue,' he said, coldly. 'Go on and hang yourself. I'm making a note of it all.'

Very casually, behind his back, Tiny took a kick at a stray oil drum and lobbed it through the air towards a passing military policeman. The oil drum caught the man on the shoulder, and he spun round in an instant. Silently, Tiny jerked his head towards Heide. The policeman charged forward like a bull elephant. A few years ago, he had probably been directing traffic eight hours a day, out for the blood of parking offenders and careless pedestrians. The war had given him his chance, and now his little moment of glory had come. Before he knew what was happening, Heide found himself up on a charge, with Porta sniggering like a cretin and Tiny droning on and on like a tiresome parrot in the background:

'I saw it with my own eyes. I saw him do it. I saw him.'

Lieutenant Löwe dismissed the whole affair with a few short sharp words and an irritable wave of the hand.

'What do you mean, this man attacked you? I don't believe a word of it. I never heard anything so far-fetched in all my life! Sergeant Heide is an excellent soldier. If he'd attacked you, I can assure you that you would not now be alive to tell the tale ... Get out of my sight before I lose my temper. Go and find something better to do and stop wasting my time.' He screwed up the charge sheet, tossed it contemptuously on to the railway line and turned to look at the Old Man. 'Frankly, I've just about had a bellyful of your section today, Sergeant Beier. We are, I would remind you, supposed to be a tank regiment: not a pack of squabbling half-wits. If you can't keep your men under better control, I shall have to get you transferred elsewhere. Do I make myself quite clear?'

The officer in charge of the convoy which had just arrived now approached the Lieutenant and nonchalantly saluted him with two fingers raised to his cap. He held out a sheaf of papers. He was a busy man. He had a delivery to make—five hundred and thirty prisoners destined for number 999 battalion, Sennelager—and he was anxious to empty the wagons as soon as possible and be on his way. He was already behind

14

schedule, and his next port of call was Dachau, where he had a new load to pick up. Löwe accepted the papers and glanced through them.

'Any casualties *en route*?'

The man hunched a shoulder.

'No way of telling until we get them out and have a look at them ... We've been travelling for almost a fortnight, so one wouldn't be altogether surprised.'

Löwe raised an eyebrow.

'Where have they come from?'

'Just about everywhere. Fuhlsbüttel, Struthof, Torgau, Germersheim ... The last lot were picked up from Buchenwald and Borge Moor. If you'll just sign the receipt and let me have it, I'll be getting on my way.'

'Sorry,' said Löwe. 'Quite out of the question.' He smiled rather grimly. 'It's a habit of mine never to sign a receipt until I've checked up on the goods ... Get the prisoners unloaded and have them lined up on the platform. I'll take a count of heads. Produce for me the correct number and you can have your receipt. But mind this: I don't sign for dead bodies.'

The officer pulled an irritable face.

'Alive or dead, where's the difference? You can't be too fussy after five years of war. You want to see the way we make a delivery to the Waffen SS. Short and snappy. No trouble at all. A nice quick bullet through the back of the neck, and Bob's your uncle! Finished for the day.'

'Very likely,' said Löwe, with his top lip curling distastefully. 'But we are not the Waffen SS. We are a tank regiment and are supposed to be taking delivery of five hundred and thirty volunteers for the front. Dead men are therefore of no possible use to us. You'll get a receipt for the actual number of live prisoners handed over to my sergeants, and if you wish to raise any objections you are quite at liberty to take matters up with the camp commander, the Count von Gernstein. It is entirely up to you.'

The officer pursed his mouth into a thin line and said nothing. Gernstein was not a man anyone in his right senses would ever choose to take matters up with. Rumour had it that he communed with Satan every night from twelve o'clock till four, and he had a reputation for wanton cruelty and viciousness which struck terror to the heart even after five years of bloodshed and slaughter.

The wagons were opened and they vomited out their load of tortured humanity. The guards stood by with dogs and guns, ready to club senseless the first man who stumbled or fell. One poor devil, palsied and trembling, caught up in the general panic yet not strong enough to keep his footing, disappeared beneath a flood of bodies and emerged at the end of the stampede a bloodied mass, his throat torn open by the snarling hounds.

We stood watching as the trembling figures were lined up in three columns. We saw the dead bodies being tossed back into the wagons. The officer in charge strutted down the columns and briskly saluted Löwe.

'All present and correct, Lieutenant. I think you'll find there's no need to waste time on a roll-call.'

Löwe made no reply. He walked in silence the length of the ragged cortège of men, who had been collected from some of the worst hells on earth and confined in communal suffering for the past fourteen days. He waited while a count was taken. Three hundred and sixty-five men out of the five hundred and thirty who had set out on the journey were still alive.

Löwe stood a moment with bent head. He turned at last to the waiting officer.

'I will sign for three hundred and sixty-five men,' he said.

There was a pause. We could feel the tension mounting.

'I beg your pardon,' said the officer, through clenched teeth. 'I believe I have delivered my full quota. The condition of the goods is immaterial. It is the quantity which concerns us.'

Löwe raised an eyebrow.

'Do we deal in human flesh?' he said. 'What is your merchandise? Men or meat?'

Another silence fell. It was broken, none too soon, by the arrival of Gernstein's aide-de-camp, Captain von Pehl. His car

16

came to a flamboyant halt a few yards away, and the Captain leapt out, smiling benignly upon one and all. He adjusted his monocle and swayed up to the two disputing officers, spurs jingling and gold braid flashing. He clicked his heels together and tapped his polished boots with his riding crop.

'What news on the Rialto, dear sirs? The end of the war? Or merely another bomb in the Führer's bunker?'

Gravely, Löwe explained the situation. The Captain brought his riding crop up to his face and thoughtfully scratched his beautifully-shaven chin with it.

'A slight question of numbers,' he murmured. 'One is expecting a battalion, and one receives scarcely three companies. One can understand the predicament.' He turned pleasantly to the convoy officer. 'How, if the question is not too impertinent, dear sir, could you possibly manage to mislay so many men?'

He strolled across to the wagon containing the corpses. He inspected for a moment the top layer, then motioned with his riding crop towards one of the bodies. A couple of guards stepped forward and heaved it on to the platform where it lay in a sawdust heap, a dead man without a head. Von Pehl readjusted his monocle. Gingerly, with a handkerchief held to his nose, he bent over the body and examined it. He straightened up and beckoned to the officer.

'Perhaps you would be so kind as to show me the point of entry of the bullet, dear sir?'

The indignant officer slowly turned crimson. All this absurd amount of fuss over one dead prisoner with a bullet through the back of the head! Did they live in a fool's paradise, out here at Sennelager?

'The point of entry,' gently insisted von Pehl. 'Purely as a matter of interest, I assure you.'

Behind von Pehl stood his ordnance officer, Lieutenant Althaus, with a sub-machine-gun under his arm. Behind Althaus stood a lieutenant of the military police, rocklike and immovable. They were mad, of course. They were all mad. No one in his right mind would have made such a song and dance over one dead prisoner. One dead prisoner, a hundred dead

17

prisoners, what the devil did it matter? There were plenty more where that lot had come from.

'There was a revolt.' The officer tilted his chin, in sullen defiance. 'There was a revolt. The guards had to fire.'

Von Pehl stretched out a languid hand.

'Report?'

'I—I haven't had time to write one out yet.'

Von Pehl tapped his teeth with the handle of his riding crop.

'So tell me, dear sir—where, exactly, did this—ah—revolt take place?'

'Just outside Eisenach.'

Eisenach.

It was far enough away, in all conscience. Perhaps now the man would stop poking his interfering Prussian nose into other people's business and let him get on his way to Dachau for the next batch of human misery.

'You know, my dear sir,' murmured von Pehl, 'that the regulations quite plainly state that any such incident as the one you have mentioned should be reported immediately? Without fail? No matter what?' He turned to Althaus, standing at his shoulder. 'Lieutenant, perhaps you would be so good as to telephone at once to the station master at Eisenach?'

We stood patiently waiting in the rain, while von Pehl amused himself by walking up and down looking like a mannequin with a hand on his hip, jangling his spurs and tapping himself with his crop. The officer of the convoy ran a finger round the inside of his collar. Discreetly, his men began to edge away from him. One of the guards, finding himself at my side, spat on the floor and spoke to me out of the side of his mouth.

'I always said he was riding for a fall. Over and over again I've said it. The way he treats those prisoners is disgraceful. Absolutely bloody disgraceful. I've said so all along.'

Lieutenant Althaus returned, accompanied by the station master, a small squat man wearing a steel helmet just in case things should turn nasty. He held out a jovial plump hand,

18

which von Pehl adroitly managed not to notice without giving any offence. The convoy officer made a rasping sound in the back of his throat.

'I trust Colonel von Gernstein is keeping well?' he said.

His attempt at polite conversation fell into a void of stony silence. The station master dropped his hand to his side. Lieutenant Althaus fingered his sub-machine-gun. Von Pehl examined his filbert fingernails. The convoy officer took a step backwards. He should have remained where he belonged, in Budapest, in the Hungarian Army. It was a dangerous game he was playing, gambling on fame and fortune in Nazi Germany.

Von Pehl turned casually to his aide.

'Well, Lieutenant? What news from Eisenach?'

Eisenach, it seemed, not only had no knowledge of the alleged revolt: they had not even heard of the convoy. I saw a frosty sparkle appear in von Pehl's cold Prussian eyes. He beckoned to Danz, who charged up like an eager rhinoceros. The Hungarian was arrested on the spot on charges of murder, submitting a false report and sabotaging a convoy. He was promptly manhandled into a waiting truck and driven off to Sennelager. Lieutenant Löwe duly signed a receipt for the delivery of three hundred and sixty-five volunteers, and the guards, cowed and nervous since the arrest of their officer, withdrew in some disorder. Von Pehl unscrewed his monocle, nodded affably at the assembled volunteers, gave himself one last hearty thwack with his riding crop and mercifully disappeared.

Relief was instantaneous. The tension went out of the atmosphere, cigarettes were lighted, men breathed more easily. Some of the MPs even went so far as to pass round bottles of booze they had recently brought back from France with them, and under the comfortable influence of alcohol we all became blood brothers and rolled off arm in arm to the station canteen to drink each other's health.

The prisoners were given permission to sit down, and some food was passed out. Only dry bread. But even dry bread can be a luxury to a man who has seen the inside of Torgau or Glatz—to anyone who has lived for days on a diet of water in the dark hell of Germersheim, where more people go in than have ever come out.

Germersheim ... It's a name that conjures up fear. It's a place not marked on the map, yet it's easy enough to find your way there. Just leave the motorway near Bruchsal, between Mannheim and Karlsruhe, and drive straight on towards the Rhine. Anyone will tell you the road. It's not difficult to follow. You go through a pretty little village full of jolly cottages with roses round their doors. You take the first turning to the left, and you leave the little village with its cheery cottages and you drive into the cold dark midnight of the forest. And there, on a large signboard, is your first introduction to Germersheim: ENTRY FORBIDDEN, it says, in capital letters a foot high. ENTRY FORBIDDEN: MILITARY ZONE. You can drive on for only another half mile or so before the road narrows to a mere track. And that's where you stop, and you thank God and your lucky stars that you're only a sightseer. You can get a good view of the prison from there. A vast grey block of stone straddling like a colossus among the trees. Military Correction Centre, that's what they call it. And if you care to advance any further along the narrow road, and if you manage to escape the armed guards and the dogs, and if you can safely pick your way through the minefield beyond, then they'll no doubt welcome you with open arms, and Germersheim will be your last resting place. Because once you're in, the chances are that you're in to stay. Between 1933 and 1945, one hundred and thirty-three thousand men were swallowed up by Germersheim and never seen again ...

While the prisoner-volunteers sat smacking the edges of their ragged lips over hunks of bone-hard bread, and while the rest of us lounged about drinking and smoking, Lieutenant Löwe was being regaled by the station master with roast hare. But even eating that delicacy did not put him in a good humour. He marched us out of the station on the double, and not even Porta, dragged away from a pleasant drinking session, saw fit to do more than make an obscene gesture and mutter under his breath.

The arrest of the convoy officer was likely to have tiresome repercussions for Löwe. It would have been simpler by far if the man had accepted a receipt for only three hundred and sixty-five prisoners and there let the matter rest. As it was, the wheels of the military machine had been set in motion and there could be no stopping them now. Colonel von Gernstein was at the moment absent from camp, hunting in the mountains. It was common knowledge that whenever he returned from a hunting trip he was in an even more satanic frame of mind than usual. God help the officer who had the temerity to trouble him with affairs such as this present one. And it would certainly be Löwe who was left to lay the matter before him. Everyone else could disclaim responsibility, but in the final analysis it was Löwe's affair and no one else's. He could expect no support from within the camp. Gernstein's second-in-command, who had lost an arm during the early years of the war and tended to make capital out of it, always took the opportunity to report sick on such occasions; and the next in the chain inevitably managed to put in a few days' leave at the right moment. All in all, it would have been far less bother if the Lieutenant had followed normal Sennelager procedure and shot the wretched Hungarian on the spot.

We marched mutinously, infected by the Lieutenant's ill-humour and harangued on all sides by bawling NCOs. Non-commissioned officers in the Prussian Army spent their entire lives, from the cradle to the grave, shouting themselves hoarse on the principle that the more noise one makes, the more likely one is to be obeyed. On the whole, men grew so accustomed that they never even noticed it any more, but still the NCOs went on shouting. It was, by this time, probably a reflex action. Not even the prisoners, straggling and stumbling in our midst, took any notice of the threats and curses that accompanied us.

About six miles off from camp, some of them began to flag pretty badly. Löwe yelled at them to keep in line, but they

21

were past it, they were dropping down like flies and lying in heaps at the side of the road. Not even the frenzied clubbing of the guards could bring them to their feet. Löwe was forced to call a halt and give them a breathing space. He stood before them in the pouring rain and delivered one of his pep talks, to which I listened with growing fascination.

'You are all volunteers, you men. No one has forced you to come here—but now that you are here, by God, you're going to be treated like soldiers!'

The volunteers, beaten, starved and systematically brutalised, shivered in their prison garb and kept their heads bent low and their shoulders hunched. I wondered if the Lieutenant really could be so naïve as to believe what he was saying. Or whether for the sake of his conscience he had had to force himself to believe it. I wondered what his definition of a volunteer was. When threatened with execution on the one hand or 999 battalion on the other, could any man really be said to have had freedom of choice?

The column formed up once again. We set off in good marching order along the asphalt road, with Löwe at the head and Lieutenant Komm at his side. Komm had lost an arm at the front, and now marched with the thumb of his false hand tucked into his belt. We had barely covered half a mile when the prisoners began to falter again. They were whipped on from behind by the prison guards, encouraged by the manic vociferations of Danz, who I swear could have made a corpse stand up and dance if he had been so inclined. Inside the column, Tiny lumbered up and down his section like a sheepdog with a herd of stupid sheep, exhorting them to keep in line and not to drop down dead before they reached Sennelager. I suddenly saw him pause, and give a joyous shout, and club one of the prisoners affectionately in the chest. I thought at first that he'd met up with one of his old mates from days gone by, but the prisoner, an ugly giant of a man almost as large as Tiny himself, appeared not to know him. He screwed up his little piggy eyes in puzzlement.

'Corporal?'

'You remember me!' roared Tiny, giving him another affec-
tionate punch in the middle of the chest. The man staggered
slightly. 'Lutz!' shouted Tiny. 'It's my old friend Lutz!'

'I think,' said the man, nervously, 'that you must be mistaken. Perhaps you may have confused me with another——'

'Paris!' bawled Tiny, throwing open his arms. 'Paris, that's
where it was! Gay Paree and all the rest of it, and you having
the time of your life, shafting a different bird every night of
the week ... It had to be a different bird, didn't it, Lutz? Do
you remember that? It always had to be a different one on
account of they was never there the next day ... A quick jump
with a nice bit of Jewish cunt before popping her into the oven
to roast ... That's what it used to be, didn't it, Lutz? You
remember that, don't you, Lutz? Those were the days, eh?
Those were the days, weren't they, Lutz? When you was in
the Gestapo and all the rest of us had to bow and scrape and
lick your bleeding arsehole——'

'Corporal, you're making a terrible mistake!' said the man,
with the sweat pouring in glistening grey drops off his forehead. 'I've never been to Paris—never in my life—never, I
swear it!'

'Next you'll be telling me you've never had a woman!'
jeered Tiny. He suddenly whipped his knife out of his boot
and held it within centimetres of the man's throat, half choking him with an arm tight round his neck as they marched.
'I'm going to make a soldier out of you, Lutz. From now on,
I'm going to take you under my wing. I'm going to see to it
that you're the best bleeding soldier in the whole bleeding
Army. I'm not going to know a moment's peace until I've got
you right out there at the front, fighting mad with half your
head blown off ... You understand me, Lutz? You understand
me, do you?' The terrified man nodded his head and almost
slit his throat open on the gleaming edge of Tiny's knife. Tiny
slowly relaxed. He slipped the knife back into his boot. 'All
right, so tell me, Lutz,' he said, sounding quite affable once
again. 'Tell me how much you weigh?'

Lutz swallowed so hard I thought his Adam's apple was

going to come shooting out the top of his head.

'A hundred and twenty-five kilos, Corporal.'

'A hundred and twenty-five kilos?' said Tiny, horrified. 'Christ almighty, you're lucky you're alive. They been feeding you rich food, have they?' He gripped the man's arm, affectionately. 'Don't you worry, mate, we'll soon shift that lot for you. Good stiff diet of bread and water and lots of nice healthy exercise round and round the courtyard ... You'll be all right, chum, we'll have you down to thirty in next to no time. The Sylph of Sennelager, that's what you'll be known as by the time I've finished with you ...'

About half a mile off camp, Löwe ordered another short rest. The prisoners collapsed on to the waterlogged ground. The rest of us squatted on our haunches or tried to find a bit of shelter in the ditch at the side of the road. From now on we should be under constant observation from the camp, and it was essential we finish the march in good order. We were whipped back into line and set off yet again.

'Sing!' ordered Löwe, and obediently we sang.

We swung into camp like a crack Prussian regiment rather than the rough vagabond mob that we were. There was always an unpleasant possibility, with Colonel von Gernstein, that he would sneak back unexpectedly twenty-four hours before he was due and start poking and prying and generally pushing his nose in where it was least wanted. For all we knew, he could be spying on us at that very moment with his field-glasses. He had done it before, and we had learned through harsh experience that he had an eagle eye for spotting even the smallest disciplinary shortcoming.

We came to a halt outside First Company block and the new recruits were left to freeze in the open air and the lashing rain for a further two hours. At that point Staff-Sergeant Hofmann decided to wander out and take a look at them.

Hofmann wore the black uniform of the tank corps, though to our knowledge had never set foot in a tank in his life. His bible was the Staff Sergeants' Manual, which he carried with him everywhere. He was so attached to it that to have removed it from him would have been tantamount to putting a bullet through the man's heart. He now moved slowly down the straggling column of volunteers, taking his time, subjecting each man to a long, penetrating stare. As he reached the last of the line, he sorrowfully shook his head with the air of one who has the cares of the entire world upon his shoulders.

'Monkeys!' he said, witheringly. 'They send me a load of gibbering monkeys and expect me to make men out of them!'

He trod heavily up the steps and planted himself at the top of the flight, legs apart and flanked on either side by a respectful minion. He looked down, kinglike, upon his miserable band of victims.

'All right,' he said. 'All right, I've been lumbered with you, so that's my hard luck. It's enough to make a cat puke, but I'm not complaining—and neither are you, if you know what's good for you. Open your mouths too wide and it could start growing very unhealthy round here. Very unhealthy.' He swayed slightly forward and tried a balancing act on the balls of his feet. He had seen the Colonel do it many times, but it turned out to be not quite as easy as it looked. He rocked back heavily on to his heels and jarred his spine. 'From now on,' he bellowed, 'you've only got one guardian angel round here, and that's me ... Your lives are in my hands, and don't you ever forget it. If I decide you're not worth the air you're breathing, then that's that. That's your lot. You've had it. OK?' He placed his hands on his hips. 'You with me?'

His flock bleated in chorus, nodding their weary heads in acknowledgment of his absolute power. What else, poor sheep, could they do? Many of them had been soldiers before—some among them had even been generals—and not even in their most hideous dreams could they have imagined a reception such as this. The nine-nine-nine battalion was notorious, but never before had a reality turned out to be so much more ghastly than the anticipation. It must have seemed to them at that moment that this, after all, was the meaning of the phrase, a fate worse than death.

Hofmann swept on with his speech of welcome.

'As from today, Company 15 will be attached to the Seventh Tank Regiment—and all I can say is, God help the lot of us. It makes me sick to my stomach, it gives me a pain right down in the guts to think that the German Army is going to be contaminated by vermin like you lot.' He shifted his position and glared down at them scornfully. 'I'm not complaining,' he said. 'I'm just letting you know how I feel. I shouldn't like there to be any misunderstanding in the future.'

Gratefully, they mouthed their thanks for this act of generosity.

'Here in Sennelager,' Hofmann went on, 'it doesn't matter what you've done in the past, it doesn't matter who you were or what you were, a bleeding general of a bleeding road-sweeper. From this moment on you're all equal. You're all scum. You're all grovelling in the same patch of mud together, and you can consider yourselves lucky that the Führer's a damn sight more soft-hearted than I am, 'cos if I had my way you'd go straight off to the slaughterhouse where you belong.' He glanced down at a sheet of paper he was holding. 'I see we have two generals among us—two generals, one colonel and a couple of cavalry captains. That's nice. That's really nice. I like a bit of quality. It raises the tone of the establishment. It makes me feel good when I see a general down on his hands and knees cleaning out the shithouse. It makes me feel really gratified. It——'

Hofmann suddenly broke off in mid-sentence. From the corner of his eye he had caught sight of Sergeant Wolf leaning against a lamp-post, with his dogs, listening to his discourse. Wolf had an ironical smile on his face. Even the dogs seemed to be grinning. Hofmann's cheeks began to mottle. Wolf was one of his biggest bugbears. He could never quite decide which one he hated most, Porta or Wolf. Generally it was Porta, but at this moment it was Sergeant Wolf. He turned to him irritably.

'What are you lounging about for? Can't you find anything better to do with your time?'

Wolf's smile broadened into a grin. One of the dogs began

to slowly thump its tail.

'I'm just enjoying myself,' said Wolf. 'I always appreciate a good comedy show.' He prised himself apart from the lamp-post. 'Who writes your scripts?' he inquired. 'They'd pay you good money for them in civvy street. Have 'em laughing till the tears ran down their legs.'

Hofmann's face swelled up like an overripe tomato. To humiliate a Prussian sergeant before a group of reprieved criminals! What on earth was the war coming to?

'Sergeant Wolf,' he said, with as much dignity as he was still able to muster. 'I shall make it my business to report those remarks. You have gone out of your way deliberately to insult the honour of a non-commissioned officer.'

'Honour?' said Wolf. 'What honour?' He shook his head. 'Forget it, chum, you don't have a leg to stand on. Remember what Ludendorff said? Honour doesn't exist below the rank of lieutenant . . . so stick that up your backside and chew it over!'

He wandered amiably away, with his two hounds ambling at his heels. Hofmann turned angrily back to his flock. He surveyed them through slatted lids, searching their faces for the least sign of a grin or a smirk, but they stared back at him with bleak, blank-eyed devotion. Their guardian angel. Their lives were in his hands. They could not afford to be amused.

'Right,' said Hofmann. 'All right. That brings me to my next point. Chalked up on a slate in my office there's a list of rules and regulations. Do's and don'ts. Mostly don'ts. Learn them by heart. Your life depends on them. I got eyes in the back of my head and I got eyes in the cheeks of my arse. Nothing goes on round here what I don't know about. Anyone tries stepping out of line and he's a dead man. Do I make myself clear?'

The choir hastened to assure him that he did, and Hofmann seemed satisfied at last that he had sufficiently bent them to his will. He dismissed them contemptuously and they stumbled inside, out of the rain, and collapsed in sodden heaps of bone-less flesh on to their mattresses. There they stayed, unfed, unwashed, in their soaking clothes until morning.

Life at Sennelager, if it could properly be called life, began at four a.m. with jackboots crashing down the corridors. Piercing whistles and raucous shouts completed the awakening of anyone who could manage to sleep through the sound of endless doors being kicked open. A German NCO never approaches a door in the usual way. He never turns a handle and walks into a room as any normal, sane person might do. To him, a door represents an irresistible challenge. It is kicked, it is battered, it is assaulted with venom. That is what a door is there for. The greatest ambition of every NCO worth his salt is to kick a door right off its hinges at one blow. As Porta always used to say, 'In the eyes of God and the Prussian Army, nothing is impossible' . . .

At four o'clock in the morning, therefore, Sennelager's very foundations trembled and shook beneath the onslaught. Not even Porta could train himself to sleep through it. Soldiers everywhere were hurled to the floor, and barely five minutes later every bed was a model of perfection. Such was the discipline of the place.

In the officers' quarters, the Colonel could be seen each morning doing his exercises to the strains of military music. He had a regular set of rigorous movements which were followed with Prussian precision day after day. He always ended up with a ride on the mechanical horse accompanied by the 'March of the 18th Hussars.'

For us, the common riff-raff fighting for existence in the overcrowded barrack rooms, it was a somewhat different picture. Splayed feet attached to skeletal legs wavered across the stone floor in search of a square inch of standing space at the washbasins. Bare toes were crushed underfoot. Men jostled and swore, and NCOs strode about in their midst adding to the confusion.

Everything was always in confusion. Too many men trying to be in too many places at exactly the same time, and everything done at the double. I think I scarcely ever saw anyone walk anywhere at Sennelager. Wherever you went, you went at the trot. After a while, it became instinctive. It was a race for survival, and the slowest went to the wall.

'Get a move on, there! Pick those bloody feet up! What do you think this is, Spastic bloody Sunday?'

It went on all the time. It got to be so ingrained in a man that after a while he'd find he was even disciplining himself in the same way as he went about his business:

'Get a move on, there! Pick those bloody feet up! What do you think this is, Spastic bloody Sunday?'

One of the worst of the NCOs at Sennelager was Helmuth, the Fifth Company cook. He was one of the world's natural bullies and arsehole creepers. What trash the Gestapo recruited for their stool pigeons. It was Helmuth who quite gratuitously threw a can of boiling coffee over Fischer, one of the mildest, softest-spoken and best-intentioned men ever to arrive in 999 battalion. It was probably this very mildness that provoked the attack. I've noticed before that people of Helmuth's ilk can't stand the meek and the humble. Poor Fischer. He'd been a minister before coming to the hell at Sennelager. He had innocently imagined that being a servant of God would afford him some kind of divine protection, and he had stood up in the pulpit and denounced Adolf Hitler and the Nazi régime to a congregation which had discreetly vanished before the end of the sermon. That same night, the bogey-men in their leather coats had come and taken him away. Parson Fischer had then commenced upon a series of experiences for which none of his bible reading could possibly have prepared him. It had begun at Bielefeldt and it had continued at Dachau, in the special torture wing reserved for men of God. The worst of it all had been when they arrested his wife and three children and held them as hostages. Dachau had been nothing compared to that.

Now they had sent him to Sennelager and men like Helmuth were pouring boiling coffee over his fingers for the sheer joy of hearing him scream. Fischer, not unnaturally, jerked his scalded hands away, dropping his tin mug as he did so. A torrent of liquid cascaded on to the brightly shining boots of Sergeant Helmuth. Poor Fischer. With a little more experience he would have stood his ground and let himself be scalded to the very bone, if necessary. It would have been worth it, for the days of blessed peace and quiet it would have earned him in the infirmary. But Fischer was green. He had not yet learnt how to control his reflexes. He acted exactly as Helmuth had predicted. In the startled silence which followed, Helmuth picked up one of his big iron coffee pots and brought it crashing down on Fischer's head. We stood and watched, and none of us said a word. It was typical Sennelager behaviour. Hold your tongue at all times. There was nothing to be gained by speaking out. We might have hated Helmuth, but who after all was Parson Fischer? Merely one new arrival among three hundred others. No one was going to risk his life for an unknown preacher.

Helmuth banged down the coffee pot. He came out from behind his table and indicated his spattered footwear.

'Come on, parson! Down on your knees and do a bit of praying! Lick my boots with your holy tongue and let's have a bit of real humility for a change ...'

Fischer sank slowly to the ground, and I found it difficult to imagine how he was ever going to get up again. He was an old man of sixty, broken and bent by the treatment meted out to him at Bielefeldt and Dachau, and his will to live must have been strong indeed to have carried him this far. He craned his skinny neck forward. It looked like a length of perished hose-pipe. Slowly and painfully, his tongue approached the toe of Helmuth's right boot. It was a spectacle we had witnessed so many times before that we had ceased to find it degrading. We had all been put through it at some stage or another in our Army careers. You soon learned how to swallow your disgust. You had to if you wanted to survive. But it was always difficult, the first time. I hadn't found it too easy myself, as a raw recruit in the 7th Uhlans, ordered to lick a horse's hooves every morning for a week. It wasn't surprising that Fischer was making such heavy weather of it. He wasn't helped any by a kick in the teeth from Helmuth. He fell backwards, spitting out blood and pieces of bone, and as he did so Helmuth brought the heavy coffee pot crashing down again on his skull.

That was the end of the fun for that morning. Helmuth had overdone things as usual, and yet another victim was carted off unconscious to the infirmary to live or die as the doctors saw fit. Die, in all probability. An old man like that wasn't much use to anyone. 'Fell down a flight of stone steps due to under-nourishment in previous place of detention' … By the time the report reached the previous place of detention, and by the time they had self-righteously denied the charge and the papers had been rubber-stamped and copied in duplicate and triplicate and finally mislaid in the bowels of some conveniently far-flung cabinet, the victim would have been dead and dumped so long ago that no one would have been able to remember what he looked like.

After the music-hall comedy of Helmuth and Fischer, we turned out for the euphemistically labelled 'Morning Sports Session'. Never a day passed but some unfortunate devil who couldn't stand the pace was kicked or punched to death and carried off on a stretcher. Sports session at Sennelager was an endurance test that would have defeated most Olympic athletes in full training. But when death is the only alternative, it's amazing what feats a half-starved body can be forced to perform.

At the end of an hour, with black spots leaping in crazy patterns before the eyes, blood like a cataract pounding in the ears, lungs heaving and ribs strained to breaking point, the survivors were sent off at the double to pick up their uniforms and arms from a communal dump. Boots, jackets, trousers, caps, they were flung about at random and it was each man for himself to grab what he could. The idea was to get one of everything in as short a time as possible and to hell whether or not it was the right size. It was the boots that were the most important. A man could survive with a jacket which scarcely met across the chest, he could hitch his trousers up under the armpits, but if he found himself with a boot a couple of sizes too small, he was really in trouble. One poor bastard I knew once found himself with two right feet. After only half an hour on the march, he passed out, while some silly sod somewhere

31

must have been tramping about quite happily with a big left boot on a small right foot and never even noticed the difference.

The same morning that Parson Fischer fell foul of Helmuth, we had another bit of excitement with a Jehovah's Witness. It was his first day in camp and he caused quite a pleasurable stir when he refused point-blank to put on a uniform. His mate—an ex-housebreaker, as I subsequently discovered—did his best to coax him into it, but the chap stood his ground and they couldn't budge him. It seemed he had some sort of religious objections to uniforms in general and the German Army uniform in particular. Someone asked him why he'd come to Sennelager in the first place if he had no intention of becoming a soldier. It turned out that like so many others he'd had no alternative. It was either volunteering to fight for the Fatherland or standing by to watch while they strung up his crippled brother. Not unnaturally, he volunteered. But now that he was here, not wild dogs nor Prussian NCOs could force him into wearing that uniform.

They threw a pile of clothes at him, but he let it fall to the ground, only picking up the green working overalls. The rest of it, the grey overcoat, the steel helmet, the cap, the cartridge belt, the rifle, the gas mask and all the other thousand and one bits and pieces we were supposed to hump about with us, he left in a heap where they had fallen. Simply rolled up the overalls, stuffed them under his arm and set off towards the stairs. The Quartermaster-Sergeant stuck his big red head through the hatch and stared with bulldog eyes at the discarded pile of arms and uniform. I thought for one delightful moment that he was about to burst a main artery. He caught my hopeful gaze upon him, and sadly tapped his head with a finger.

'Now I've seen the lot,' he said. 'So help me, I never thought the day would come when they'd start opening up the bleeding loony bins and recruiting the nuts.'

He came to the door and bawled across the room at the legs of the Jehovah's Witness as they disappeared up the stairs.

'Hey, you! You with the bleeding halo! Where in hell's name do you think you're going?'

The man paused at the head of the stairs. Slowly, he turned back to look at the outraged sergeant. Before he could say anything in reply, Sergeant-Major Matho came lumbering up with all his usual doglike devotion. Any duty which might possibly involve a few quick karate chops or a kick in the guts delighted him.

'What's going on, Sergeant? What's all the noise about? Who's making trouble?'

The Sergeant pointed an accusing finger.

'We've got a bleeding nutter on our hands. Thinks he's already flapping about heaven playing pat-a-cake with the angels. Says he doesn't want to put his uniform on.'

The Jehovah's Witness clicked his heels together.

'Only the overalls,' he said. 'I have no objections to wearing the overalls.'

'No objections to wearing the OVERalls?' repeated Sergeant-Major Matho, outraged.

The whole room had by now come to a standstill. In all my years in the German Army, I had never met anything quite like it. I began to have a sneaking respect for Jehovah's Witnesses. They might have belonged to the lunatic fringe, but it seemed they could hold their own with a Prussian NCO.

'No objections to the OVERalls, did you say?' Matho suddenly picked up the discarded greatcoat and shook it as he would a rat. 'What's the matter with the rest of the uniform? Don't you like the colour or something? Don't you care for the cut of it? Great balls of fire!' He tossed the coat back to the floor and sent it flying across the room with one almighty kick. 'What do you think this is, a Paris bleeding fashion show? You're here to fight a war, not ponce about the place complaining the clothes don't suit you! You're willing enough to sit on your great fat arse all day long, guzzling the Führer's bread and sausages, and then you have the bloody nerve to start grizzling and bloody moaning because you don't like the look of the bloody uniform!'

'Sergeant, it's not the look of it. It's the whole principle of warfare.' The Jehovah's Witness turned earnestly to face the enraged Matho. 'I happen to be a Christian. Thou shalt not kill ... I am forbidden by my faith to take up arms or to wear a uniform. It is as simple as that.'

The man turned to go. Matho was up those stairs behind him so fast his hair started to singe. He grabbed him by the shoulder, spun him round and gave him a kick in the backside which sent him crashing over the railings and headfirst to the ground. Swiftly and silently, the room was vacated. We knew only too well what was coming next. We had no desire to stand and watch. We herded like cattle into the corridor outside. Behind that closed door, in the room that stank of musk and dust and human sweat, the grim scene was played to its inevitable conclusion. We heard Matho's voice rising to an hysterical shriek, cursing the bible, the Jehovah's Witnesses and the church in general. We heard his victim's replies, low but clear:

'I cannot help it. I am a Christian. I will not take up arms, I would rather die.'

And we knew, and he knew that he would never come out of that room alive.

We heard Matho unclasping his heavy leather belt and doubtless shoving the buckle under the man's nose as he said the familiar, meaningless words: 'Gott mit uns.'

God was with us. The Holy German Army and the Sainted Führer fed his ungrateful children on bread and sausages, and still this maniac stood his weak snivelling ground and refused to fight.

We heard the first loud crack of leather as the belt whipped out and lashed its buckle across the victim's face. It wasn't only Matho, there were half a dozen other sergeants there to help him in his task. They took it in turns, competing among themselves to see who could cause the most damage, or who could produce the longest and the loudest scream of agony. It took almost thirty minutes before a blessed silence fell at last over the room and we knew that the suffering had finished.

There was only a lifeless form left for them to kick around the floor. Now they could not inflict any more of their insane tortures. They opened the doors and called us in to dispose of the body. There was an eye hanging out of its socket half-way down a cheek. There was a scarlet pulp where the nose had been. The mouth was torn to shreds and the gums split open. We picked up the remnants of vainglorious humanity and threw it out of the window. After the floor was mopped, we continued with the business of the day.

It was all quite normal and in order. Just one more dead body to be picked up and buried in a nameless grave. He probably died under the influence of drink. Fell out of the window in an alcoholic stupor. It was amazing the number of inmates at Sennelager who fell out of windows in alcoholic stupors. It happened every day of the week—nothing to write home about. His wife, if he had a wife, would wear out her shoe leather traipsing from one bureaucratic blimp to another. But no one would be able to give her any satisfactory answers. Probably no one would even try. People were disappearing all the time in the German Army. Who should trouble his head about one murdered Jehovah's Witness?

We put the matter from our minds and went along to hear the Captain make his traditional speech of welcome to the newcomers—or what was left of the newcomers. Fischer was in the infirmary and the Jehovah's Witness was dead, and God knows how many more had expired during the night or would vanish during the course of the day.

'You are here,' said the Captain, with his pleasant smile, 'by the grace of God and the Führer. This is your chance to repent and be forgiven. To wipe out the sins of the past and to start again with a clean slate. It is our job, here at Sennelager, to train you to be good and useful soldiers: it is your job to co-operate with us and to show your willingness to serve the Führer as loyal citizens of the Fatherland. There are several ways in which you can do this. Just to give you one example, you may volunteer for special missions when you reach the front line ... Naturally,' he concluded, with a deprecating

35

movement of one elegant hand, 'we shall expect rather more from you than from your fellow-soldiers. This is only natural. This is only right and proper. You have a past to atone for, and you——'

'Sir!'

A big, burly chap, who, as rumour had it, had been a successful pimp in Berlin before the war, shot up his hand and interrupted the Captain in his full flow of eloquence.

'Sir!'

The Captain allowed himself only a faint wrinkling of his alabaster brow by way of showing his displeasure.

'Yes, my man? What is it?'

The jolly pimp sprang to his feet. He must have known as well as anyone that the chances of survival in 999 battalion were pretty remote. He had nothing to lose by making a nuisance of himself and annoying the Captain.

'Sir, can I ask a question?' he said.

'Of course you can,' said the Captain, smoothing out the wrinkles from his brow. 'Ask whatever you like. Just try not to take all day about it.'

The man's question was really very simple. He wanted to know what would happen if a criminal such as himself had his head blown off while he was fighting for the Führer and proving himself a good and loyal citizen of the Fatherland. Would it atone for his past misdemeanours? Would he then be deemed worthy of re-entering the Army as a fully-accredited soldier?

He asked his question in a tone of the most earnest sincerity. A genuine seeker after knowledge. Eager and willing to have his head blown off for the Führer and the Fatherland, so long as he could only be assured that it would reinstate him in the eyes of the Army.

No one dared to laugh, or even so much as smile. Hofmann's glittering eyes were everywhere at once, but he encountered only a most solemn silence. It seemed as if everybody was hanging in mid-air awaiting the captain's reply to this most burning of questions.

The Captain tapped his boots impatiently with his riding crop.

'My dear man, if one dies like a hero, then naturally one is treated like a hero ... Full provision is made for such a contingency. Article 226 of the Penal Code states quite clearly that anyone falling on the field of battle is granted an automatic pardon. You need have no fears on that score. I trust I have answered your question and set your mind at rest?'

'Oh yes, indeed, sir. You have indeed, sir. I just wanted to make quite sure that I knew what I was doing before I went and did it.' The man smiled, cheerfully. 'Didn't want to cook my goose, sir, without knowing whether I'd still be alive to eat it afterwards ... If you see what I mean, sir?'

Over in his corner, Hofmann had taken out his notebook and pencil and was scribbling rapidly. Tiny opened his mouth the merest crack and slid his words out sideways like a second-rate ventriloquist.

'Shouldn't care to be in your shoes, mate ... you've not only cooked your bleeding goose, you've gone and burnt it to a bleeding frazzle!'

The days that followed were tough and brutal, as was the normal pattern of Sennelager, and five more of our volunteers came to grief. One collapsed and died on a route march; one failed to move fast enough when a grenade went off by mistake; and three others panicked at their first encounter with a tank during a training period and were promptly run down and churned to mincemeat to serve as an example to others.

Shortly afterwards, there were several abortive attempts at desertion. Every single man who tried it was recaptured within the first six hours and brought back to Sennelager to be handed over to Lieutenant-Colonel Schramm, the camp executioner.

Schramm was a butcher merely by force of circumstances. Neither by temperament nor by talent was he fitted for the task. He had lost a leg under a tank at Lemberg, which had effectually ended his active career as a soldier. And instead of promoting him to a full colonel and giving him a comfortable job behind an anonymous desk, the authorities, with their malicious wisdom, had seen fit to reward him for his services by posting him to Sennelager. The first execution carried out under his command had given him a shock from which he never fully recovered. By the third and fourth he felt that he was losing his reason. But he had a wife and three young children, and he knew what both their fate and his would be should he refuse to obey orders. So he took to the bottle and had been drinking steadily ever since. He drank before executions to steady his nerves and come to terms with his conscience; he drank during executions to give himself the courage to go through with it; and he drank after executions to forget what he had just done. Since executions ran at the rate of three batches per week, it may be surmised that the Lieutenant-Colonel was very rarely observed to be sober. He used to limp round the camp using his sabre as a walking stick, never saying a word to a soul. Frequently on execution days it happened that he was too drunk to move without support and had to be escorted there and back by the execution squad. No one would ever have dreamt of reporting him to the Camp Commander. Schramm was regarded with pitying contempt, and yet was a general favourite among all the men.

Whenever you saw him in the blurred grey light of early morning, limping across the courtyard with his flask of kummel in his hand, you could be sure that an execution had been arranged. He used always to snatch a few minutes' extra drinking time at a point mid-way between the ammunition stores and the officers' mess, where he was safely out of sight of von Gernstein and his prying binoculars. He would sit down on a low wall, rest his chin on the hilt of his sabre, and stare into space thinking God knows what uncomfortable thoughts before pushing his flask back into his pocket and hobbling on his way with his artificial leg creaking with every step. When he arrived at the camp prison he was inevitably offered a large glass of beer; which just as inevitably he accepted. Some time later he would appear with the firing squad and make for the courtyard where the executions took place.

Once an execution was over, he obliterated all traces of the victims from his memory. There was a story told in the camp, and we all believed it, of how the Adjutant had asked him one night in the officers' mess 'what sort of show the General had put up?'

'General?' said Schramm, looking bewildered. 'What general?'

'The one you shot this morning, old boy,' said the Adjutant. 'Major-General von Steinklotz.'

'Von Steinklotz?' said Schramm. 'I shot Major-General von Steinklotz?'

He plainly thought he must be suffering from drunken delusions. Amid roars of delighted laughter, he finished off his kummel, staggered out of the mess and fell flat on his face. He was taken home to his wife by a couple of sympathetic lance-corporals, who undressed him and put him to bed without his ever knowing a thing about it.

On two occasions at least he attempted suicide. The first time he hanged himself from the rafters of the attic in his home, but his wife discovered him and cut him down. The second time he took an overdose of drugs, but was flushed out with a stomach pump and sent back on duty. Now and again, in his more lucid moments, he would sit down in the officers' mess and play the piano. He was an excellent pianist, but rarely sober enough to concentrate for more than a few minutes at a time.

Colonel von Gernstein had also lost a leg on active service. He lost two, as a matter of fact, but it was difficult to notice. One thought at first that he was just a bit ungainly in his manner of walking. He had a stiff neck, as well, and was unable to turn his head without also turning the rest of his body. His spine was supported in a steel jacket. His mouth was a thin mauve line, lipless and puckered. He'd left half his face behind at Smolensk, in a battle between German Tigers and Russian T34s. Von Gernstein had been the only survivor to crawl out of the hatch of a burning tank. But he had paid dearly for the privilege. His right eye was fixed for ever in a sightless glassy stare, and one of his hands was a withered talon. And yet it was impossible to feel sympathy for the man. His character repelled you, and after five years of war we had seen far too many obscenities inflicted on the human body to be easily moved to pity.

According to his batman, von Gernstein used to sit up till four o'clock in the morning playing poker with Death and the Devil. He swore that one night he caught a glimpse of them, Death was dressed all in black from head to foot with the cross of the Hohenzollerns round his neck and the Devil in the uniform of an SS Obergruppenführer. A fanciful tale, but some of the more credulous among us actually believed it to be the truth. Many were the rumours of von Gernstein communing with the Devil, von Gernstein holding black masses, von Gernstein resurrecting the dead ... It was certain, however, that there was some mystery about the man. The light burned in his quarters throughout the night, and always at his private door were parked two big black Mercedes, which arrived every night, punctually at midnight and left again at dawn.

Porta and I one bold, fine day, stoned half out of our senses, risked our lives taking a look inside the Colonel's quarters. For once even Porta was deprived of speech. It was like coming across Aladdin's cave in the middle of the Sahara Desert. There were thick pile carpets and Persian rugs all over the floor; Old Master paintings hanging nonchalantly on the walls; rich velvet curtains at the windows and a glittering chandelier winking at us from the middle of the ceiling ... It scarcely seemed possible that such splendours could exist within the squalor of Sennelager.

One night, I remember, I was on guard duty with Gregor Martin and Tiny. We were standing near the garages and we were watching the thousand flickering lights of the chandelier in the Colonel's apartment. Quite suddenly, Gregor yelped like a startled dog and dropped his rifle. I jumped backwards with a muffled squawk of terror, and Tiny turned tail and went galloping off with a shout into the night. For there, in profile at the window, there before our staring eyes, was the dread figure of Satan himself ...

We stood transfixed, Gregor and I. Even when the figure slid out of sight we were unable to take our eyes off the window. Gregor sagged at the knees and clawed about the ground for his rifle, his head tilted back at an angle and his gaze rigid. Tiny, back at the guardhouse, had obviously made his point with some force, for it was only a matter of seconds before Sergeant Linge appeared on the scene demanding to know what all the panic was about. Gregor straightened his sagging knees and extended a tremulous hand towards the window. He opened his mouth and made a croaking sound like a toad with a fishbone stuck in its throat.

'It was the Devil——'

'The Devil——'

'In uniform——'

'Uniform——'

'*Uniform?*' Linge looked from one to the other of us. 'What the hell kind of uniform?'

'SS,' moaned Gregor.

'Obergruppenführer,' I added, feeling it was about time that I made some kind of original contribution to the proceedings.

Linge looked exasperated.

'For Chrissakes,' he said. 'All SS Obergruppenführers look like the Devil. Tell me something new!'

'This one had horns,' said Gregor, on a note of sudden and desperate inspiration. 'Bloody great filthy horns ... two of 'em, sticking out of his forehead ... And what's more,' he added, with a touch of defiance, 'he was drinking smoke.'

'Drinking *smoke*?' said Linge.

'Sulphur,' I said. 'Sulphur and brimstone, that's what it was.'

By this time, the area around the garages was swarming with soldiers coming to our support. Linge clicked his tongue impatiently against his teeth.

'Hogwash,' he said, sharply. 'Balls and bloody hogwash.

41

I never heard such a load of flaming nonsense in all my flaming——'

'Look!' said Gregor. 'There it is again!'

The figure passed across the window and disappeared. Gregor turned and ran, and I wouldn't swear to it, but I rather think Linge followed him. At all events, when I came to my senses I found I was alone. The whole area was silent. Still as the grave, and twice as sinister. Only the pinpoints of light still flickered and winked in von Gernstein's apartment, and somewhere on the other side of the windows stalked Satan himself in devilish profile ...

Twice on my panic-stricken dash across the open courtyard my helmet tumbled off my head and went clattering on to the flagstones, and twice I had to crawl trembling on hands and knees in search of it before I eventually reached the shelter of the guardroom and flung myself, gibbering, through the door. Linge was there, with a face like a bowlful of tripe. He was muttering to himself in a sort of manic frenzy, and he clawed at me as I ran past him.

'Mum's the word!' he said. 'Don't tell a soul! You haven't been near the place all night! Remember that: you haven't been near the place!'

'Oh sure,' I said, sourly. 'Next thing I know, you'll be telling me there wasn't any Devil——'

'Fuck the Devil! You haven't been near the place!'

In a sudden frenzy, Linge kicked out at a tin helmet lying on the floor. It sailed up into the air and flew gracefully out the window, which happened to have been closed at the time. There was a shower of broken glass, a dull thud and a yell of angry pain.

'Someone's copped it,' I said.

Tiny crossed the room and peered out through the broken window, with its one jagged pain of glass sticking up like a broken tooth. He turned with morbid satisfaction towards Linge.

'Lieutenant Dorn,' he said, simply. 'He stopped it in the chest.'

The Lieutenant burst into the guardhouse as if a dozen T34s were snapping at his heels. He stared round, wildly.

'Who threw that helmet? Answer my question! *Who threw that helmet?*'

Sergeant Linge performed a sideways shuffle round the perimeter of the guardhouse and gave a nervous guilty grin.

'What the devil are you sniggering at?' barked the Lieutenant. 'Are you out of your senses? Are you a homicidal maniac? Do you realise you could face the firing squad for assaulting an officer?'

'Sir, I didn't throw it at you, sir,' said Linge, with extreme and unctuous earnestness. 'It slipped out of my fingers, sir. I happened to be standing near the window at the time, and it slipped out of my fingers. It was gone before I could stop it. I put out my hand to catch it, but it went before I had a chance.'

'Oh, for God's sake, Sergeant, stop babbling like a bloody cretin!' The Lieutenant took an impatient step forward, and it seemed suddenly to strike him that the guardroom was curiously overcrowded for that time of night. 'What's going on here. What are all these men doing in here?' He looked suspiciously round the circle of anxious faces, and instantly put his finger on the weakest link in the chain: Private Ness, who was universally acknowledged as a certified moron. Dorn strode up to him, snapping his fingers at him as if he were a dog. 'Come along, man! Out with it! Don't stand there dribbling!'

Private Ness gave him a look of vacant despair. Across the far side of the room, behind the Lieutenant's back, Sergeant Linge was busy informing him in hideous dumb show that his throat would be slit open if he dared say a word. Ness's lower lip began slowly to fall apart from its moorings.

'Well?' snapped the Lieutenant. 'Do you intend to answer my question or do you want to face the firing squad along with Sergeant Linge?'

Ness sprang quivering to attention. His eyes swivelled piteously from the Lieutenant to the Sergeant. His big baggy cheeks were shaking with fright.

'They seen the Devil,' he said. 'They seen the Devil, sir.'

Well, that was it, of course. As soon as Ness had opened his great gaggy mouth, the rest of the bunch were only too anxious to pipe up and start filling in the details. Give Linge his due. He had sense enough to know that it was a matter best kept to ourselves. He and I and Tiny stood in tight-lipped disgust as the cretins poured out their own varied and garbled versions of the tale. Gregor had wisely disappeared, God knows where. Ness was by now babbling louder than any of them, and the Lieutenant was thrashing about with his hands and trying to shout over the hubbub.

'For God's sake, shut up! Shut up, I say! I want a proper military report, not a bloody horror story!'

He got his proper military report: at precisely 0105 hours the Devil had been seen to walk in the Colonel's rooms. Every man present had witnessed it, and several were prepared to swear to the existence of horns, brimstone, forked tail, etc. One man in his zeal even added the embellishment of cloven hoofs, but this was angrily dismissed on the grounds that it could not have been possible to see them unless he was walking on his hands with his feet in the air.

Lieutenant Dorn perched himself gingerly on the edge of the table and sat for a while without speaking. I could under-stand his predicament. He himself could scarcely have been in ignorance of the rumours that ran round the camp; and even if he might not believe in horror stories, it was nevertheless pretty obvious that there was something untoward going on. No smoke without fire and so forth, and who was it who came a-visiting every night on the stroke of twelve in two big black Mercedes limousines? On the other hand, we could all picture the Colonel's wrath when a report came in that the night guard had been discovered gathered together in the guardhouse bab-bling about the Devil. And we all knew who would be in com-mand of the very next company to be despatched to the front: the officer who was responsible for making the report. Lieu-tenant Dorn . . .

I glanced sympathetically at him, and he raised a palsied,

44

grey face in my direction. It was his duty to report the incident, no doubt about it. I was only glad that I was in my own shabby, ill-fitting boots and not his.

'All right,' he said, at last. He rose heavily to his feet. 'Let's get matters straight. Who was it who first claimed to have seen this mythical creature in the Colonel's rooms?'

'Corporal Creutzfeldt, sir, and Private Hassel,' said Sergeant Linge, as quick as they come.

He would pay dearly for that accident with the helmet, and I daresay he was only too eager to drag someone else down into the mire while he was about it.

The Lieutenant walked across to Tiny and stood thoughtfully regarding him for a moment.

'Corporal Creutzfeldt,' he said. 'Did you by any chance have anything to drink before going on duty tonight?'

'Certainly, sir.' Tiny assumed an expression of imbecilic wisdom and counted up on his fingers. 'Four bocks and a couple of glasses of kummel.'

'A couple, Corporal Creutzfeldt?'

'Well—two or three. Four or five ... Say a round half dozen,' said Tiny, obligingly.

'In other words, Corporal, you were drunk?'

'No more than usual,' said Tiny, stoutly.

'Am I to infer from that remark that you are habitually drunk, when you go on duty, Corporal Creutzfeldt?'

Tiny paused gravely to consider the matter.

'Well, yes,' he said, at last. 'But not so's you'd notice it.'

'Just as I thought,' said the Lieutenant. 'Delirium tremens. You've been having visions, Corporal. If it's not pink elephants it's devils with cloven hoofs ... A mere figment of an overheated imagination. You saw the Colonel walk past his window—you saw him drinking a cup of steaming coffee—you saw him wearing his Uhlan helmet—you naturally mistook it for a pair of satanic horns. Is that not so, Corporal Creutzfeldt?'

'Yeah, I reckon that would be it,' said Tiny, cheerfully. 'I reckon you're probably right, sir. I reckon that was the way it must have happened.'

The Lieutenant turned, satisfied, to me.

'And you, Hassel,' he said, kindly. 'I need scarcely ask if you also have imbibed alcoholic beverages during the course of the evening?'

'No, sir,' I said. 'I'd rather you didn't.'

The Lieutenant smiled a tight little smile.

'Who is in command of your Company? Lieutenant Löwe, is it not?' An eager chorus assured him that it was. 'Well, well,' said the Lieutenant. 'I think on this occasion we shall leave him to sleep in peace. But if any more of this drunken carousing comes to my notice, I shall, you understand, be forced to take a far more serious view of it. You realise what the outcome would be should I choose to file a report of the night's proceedings? We should all of us, my friends, find ourselves in a very sorry situation ... I advise you for the future to keep your eyes turned away from the Colonel's windows. What the Colonel chooses to do at any time of the day or night is after all no concern of yours. He is at liberty to entertain whoever he wishes in the privacy of his own quarters, and he certainly won't thank you for spying on him.' He walked to the door, and then remembered. 'As for you,' he said to Sergeant Linge, 'next time you happen to be standing by a closed window with a tin hat in your hand, just check to make sure there's not an officer walking across the courtyard. I assure you you won't get away so lightly a second time.'

That should by rights have been the end of the affair, but you can't stop people talking and by the end of the following day the news was all over the camp. Creutzfeldt and Hassel had seen Colonel von Gernstein with the Devil. Creutzfeldt and Hassel and Sergeant Linge stood by and watched as Colonel von Gernstein and the Devil had played at cards together. Private Ness was ready to swear that every night on the stroke of twelve Colonel von Gernstein turned into a vampire ...

Twenty-four hours later, cloven hoofprints had been discovered beneath the Colonel's window. There was a constant pilgrimage of men from every part of the camp, and some of the more scientifically minded took measurements and even attempted to make a plaster cast. Some fool suggested it might have been a wild boar from the forest, but this, of course, was patently ridiculous: no German boar with any sense of self-preservation would ever risk its life in the courtyards of Senne-lager. For most men, this was proof incontrovertible that the Colonel's nocturnal visitors were no better than they ought to be, and now a tale was told which had never been told before. It was said to have originated from the Quartermaster of the Second Company, but soon it could be heard all over the camp a dozen times a day. It appeared that the Adjutant before the present one, rolling back to camp at four o'clock one morning from the nearest brothel, doubtless three parts drunk and in no fit state to withstand any sort of shock to the nervous system, had chanced upon the Colonel and his loathsome companions as he passed through the main gate. The Adjutant had been discovered next morning, lying on the ground with four broken ribs and teethmarks all over his body. He was raving mad and never again regained full command of his senses. He was eventually transferred to the Army psychiatric hospital at Giessen, where it was said he used to walk the wards with a broom over his shoulders telling everyone he met that he was the figure of death with his scythe. He hung himself one day in the officers' lavatory.

Meanwhile, back at Sennelager, the rumours ran through the camp like a horde of locusts, devouring everyone in their path. One of the best stories to emerge came from Lance-Corporal Glent, who went breezing into the Colonel's apart-ments one morning, on some errand or other. Believing the Colonel to be elsewhere, he suddenly discovered him sitting at a table playing poker with his two dread companions. The visitors, according to Glent, instantly muffled themselves up in their cloaks and jammed their hats down over their eyes, but not before he had had a chance to catch sight of their faces. Ghastly, he said they were. Like something out of hell. Like skulls covered in parchment, with black holes where the nose and the mouth should have been, flaming red eyes and no ears. And the whole room reeked of sulphur and brimstone ...

The next day, Glent put in for a transfer. It was curtly refused, but he was taken off the Colonel's staff and sent to work in Armaments, where I suppose they reckoned he would have less chance of meeting death and the devil round every corner.

More than ever before, men went in terror of meeting the Colonel. The creaking and grinding of his artificial limbs in the distance was sufficient to clear an area for half a mile around. One day, he came unexpectedly upon Sergeant Hofmann. No one stopped long enough to witness the scene. We scurried off like rats from a sinking ship, so no one ever knew for certain what took place, but for over a week Hofmann was kept in the infirmary with a fever so high, you could have boiled an egg in his mouth. He came back like one returned from the grave, and I swear he didn't say a word to a soul for the first twenty-four hours.

But if the Colonel did commune with the Devil, it was perhaps not so very remarkable in a place like Sennelager. You got all sorts there. From pimps and prostitutes to high-ranking generals. One general we had was von Hanneken, who in the days of his glory had been Commander-in-Chief of German Forces in Denmark. His downfall had been nothing more dramatic than petty greed. He'd overplayed his hand on the black market and someone had shopped him. Even a general was not immune. From living off the fat of the land in occupied Denmark, he had fallen to the very bottom of the dung heap in Sennelager. Porta had a most particular interest in the man. He was perfectly convinced that he had stashed away a small fortune in black market goods, and he was determined to force the secret out of him before he was sent into action and had his brains blown out.

'Well?' demanded Tiny, unfailingly each morning. 'Has he talked yet?'

'Not yet,' said Porta. 'I'm working on him.'

Working on him! He looked after him like a mother. He

supplied him with cigarettes and extra rations, he kept him out of trouble, he dogged his every footstep. Until one day, hearing rumours that our stay in Sennelager was coming to an end, he flew into a panic and had a change of tactics. He enlisted the help of Wolf, Hofmann's time-honoured enemy, and one of Porta's particular mates, and together they spirited the General away for what they termed 'a special exercise period'. We never knew what happened, but next day Wolf and Porta drank themselves ecstatic in the canteen and rolled off arm in arm to the nearest brothel. From that moment on, Porta had no more interest in the General, who was left on his own to sink or swim as he would.

As for the rest of us, we contented ourselves with gloating over the downfall of the former Gestapo man, Lutz. Lutz was Tiny's pigeon. He had in the past caused Tiny a loss of his corporal's stripes and three months' hard labour in the penitentiary at Besançon, and Tiny was now joyously hellbent on redressing the balance. As far as we were concerned, you could kick a Gestapo man all over the camp like a football, the harder the better. We waited avidly each day for a progress report. Tiny's favourite sport was taking Lutz out to be exercised. Tiny would sit on top of the car park roof chanting out his commands, while big fat Lutz, weighed down with every conceivable sort of armament, would puff to and fro, and round about in circles, and would inevitably end up by falling into a ditch full of thick black mud which happened, conveniently, to be there. On the point of collapse, he would then be marched back to the barracks at the double, with Tiny triumphant behind him, prodding him with the point of a bayonet and proudly exhibiting him to all who stood watching. As a final touch, Lutz was forced to sing a little song, the words of which began: 'A soldier's life is a grand life ...'

No one interfered. Lutz was in Tiny's section and he was Tiny's responsibility. It was up to Tiny to turn him into a good soldier. He tried on two occasions to kill himself, and the second time he was marched off to do four days' solitary. Upon reflection, it must have seemed like a glimpse of paradise after Tiny's rough handling.

When the training period was over, all those who had survived were now deemed worthy of going to the front line to be
slaughtered by enemy guns, or blown to pieces by enemy
mines. Sennelager had been but a rehearsal for the even
bloodier real thing. Some of the poor fools must have wondered why they had ever volunteered.

'A nation in which the average family has four children can afford to go to war once in every twenty years: this will allow for the deaths of two of the children, while still leaving the other two to perpetuate the race.'

Himmler. Speech to the officers of the School of Politics at Braunschweig, 9th January 1937.

OBERGRUPPENFÜHRER BERGER snatched up the telephone the minute it started to ring. He grabbed the receiver towards him and bellowed into the mouthpiece.

'Dirlewanger? Is that you?'

At the other end of the line, Dirlewanger pulled a face at his reflection in the window.

'I was told,' he said, 'that you wanted a word with me.'

He spoke cautiously; carefully neutral, determinedly non-committal, like a man reaching out a toe to test the temperature of the water. Had it indeed been a toe, it would have been instantly withdrawn: the temperature was well below zero.

'Wanted a word with you!' roared Berger. 'I should think I did want a word with you! What the devil are you playing at out there? What's going on?'

'What the devil do you think is going on?' Dirlewanger leaped instantly and aggressively to his own defence. 'What do you expect to be going on? I can't make an omelette without eggs, I'm not a bloody miracle worker! God damn it, Berger, this is no picnic out here! I need more men, and I need them fast.'

'Who doesn't?' said Berger. 'You think we're holding troops in cold storage just for the fun of hearing you bleat? Get your facts straight, man! We've cleared every prison and every detention centre in the whole of Germany. What more can we do? You want us to open up the concentration camps and send those men out to you?'

'I don't give a damn what you send me,' snapped Dirlewanger. 'You can open up the loony bins and send the nuts out here for all I care. I don't give a damn what they are, so long as I'm not lumbered with a bunch of screaming pansies. That's the one thing I do draw the line at. Jews and queens get right on my tits. But for the rest, send me anything you damn well like—*so long as you send me something*!'

There was a slight pause.

'Very well,' said Berger stiffly. 'You'll get your men. They might not be pretty, but you'll get them.'

The following morning, the camps, the prisons, the asylums were all combed in search of usable material. Anything did, so long as it was not a Jew or a known homosexual. Even a homicidal maniac could be turned to good use, provided he was trainable. And if anyone could train him, it would be Dirlewanger. Dirlewanger had served his apprenticeship under that master butcher of the SS, Standartenführer Theodor Eicke of the Death's Head Brigade. He prided himself—and not without good reason—that there was no man he could not break ...

DESERTERS

FROM Sennelager, we were sent to an area of stinking marshland, full of rising damp and mosquitoes, a few miles out of Matoryta. The battalion was up to strength, but only the First Company had been supplied with tanks. The other eleven were reduced to the level of infantry, and we had to wade ignominiously through the slopping waters of the marshes on foot. Tiny kept the faithful Lutz trudging at his heels carrying all his gear for him, while he strode in lordly fashion a few paces ahead, and the rest of us looked on with jealous hatred.

A new divisional commander had been appointed and turned up complete with monocle and champagne-blacked boots to take a look at us. Much to his disgust, Wolf had to arrange for two lorries to transport all the General's gear. Heaven only knows what the man thought he was going to do with two lorry-loads of stuff in that God-forsaken part of the world.

'The bastard's even brought a flaming grand piano with him!' said Wolf.

The General's inspection took place at mid-day. He was driven out from the village in a Kubel and was met by Colonel Hinka, the regimental Commander-in-Chief. We all stood to attention in the middle of a bog, and then trotted off to show our paces, marching like mad through the marshes, and ending up looking like columns of mud-covered statues. As we stood there, the mud dried on us and began to crack apart at the edges. But von Weltheim didn't appear to notice, or perhaps he thought that was the natural condition of the proletariat masses. He strutted up and down a few times, peering at us through his monocle. Then affably informed us that we were a credit to the German Army, that he was proud, yes, proud, that the Fatherland was still able to produce such a fine body of gallant men, and that when the final glorious victory came, our country would have cause to honour us. I was so astounded that my mouth dropped open and a chunk of hardened mud fell off my chin.

'Sod that for a laugh,' muttered Porta, at my side. 'No bloody heroics for me, mate.'

It was a sure sign that we were losing the war. To be lauded as the saviours of our nation, instead of being bawled out for being a bunch of lazy, cretinous, criminal-minded layabouts, which we undoubtedly were—or would be, given half a chance. It was enough to make you fold up in the middle, but we managed for once to exercise a bit of self-control and hear the man out in decent solemnity. He was, after all, a divisional commander.

'Only one more effort,' he said, earnestly. 'Only one more

53

effort, that is all we ask of you gallant lads ... One final burst of glory and the Russians will be routed and put to flight! We have lulled the enemy into a state of complacency. Yes, complacency! They think they have gained the upper hand, because we have chosen to employ—ah—strategical—ah—tactics. Tactics, yes. Strategical tactics. That is what we have employed, and by such means have we bluffed them! But before Christmas, before Christmas I promise you, our hour will have come!'

A faint-hearted cheer went up from the ranks, whereupon the General, evidently very much excited by such a display of loyalty, turned to Hinka and promptly ordered that we be given double rations that night. The faint-hearted cheer instantly increased in volume until it was a massive roar of approval. Hinka gave a sickly, green smile and inclined his head. I thought for one moment that he was going to disgrace us all by vomiting.

'Whatever you say, sir,' he muttered.

Von Weltheim removed his monocle and peered about him with a prominent myopic eye.

'This is good, Colonel Hinka. This is very good. I am proud of your regiment. When one thinks that these men, who, out of sheer love of their Fatherland and devotion to their Führer, have descended from their tanks and volunteered as foot soldiers, it makes one proud to be a German. Proud, I say! Proud!' He screwed back his monocle, apparently much moved. 'God bless them, Colonel Hinka! With such stout fellows as these, victory cannot help but be ours.'

It was obvious even to the least intelligent—as, for example, Tiny—that in all his long and distinguished military career, the General had very little experience of life at the front. Barely seconds after he had taken his departure, men were laying bets on the probable length of time he would manage to stick it out. It was the popular opinion that the first attack would see the General and his grand piano receding into the distance at twice the speed of light.

That same evening, we were dished out with our double

rations as promised. And, in addition, were given a fair tonnage of beer with which to wash them down. For a few blissful hours the pestilential marshes were forgotten, and the war effort was suspended while we shamelessly caroused and drank ourselves insensible. A couple of girls had stumbled in upon us, having taken the wrong turning out of Brest-Litovsk when fleeing from the advancing Russians. They were telephonists attached to the Luftwaffe, and should by rights have been shunted back to them immediately, but Sergeant Hofmann took command, and decided they would provide good entertainment for the NCOs. The girls, I have to admit, seemed by no means averse to the idea. The last I saw of them, Hofmann had them both flat out on a table top with their skirts pulled up. One of them, according to a wide-eyed Private Ness, was wearing no knickers. From what I could gather, it would seem to have been a somewhat traumatic experience for him. At all events, it was his main topic of conversation for weeks to come.

Later that night, when the Luftwaffe girls, with or without any knickers, and most of the NCO's too, had fallen into a drunken stupor, a select gathering of sergeants were left together to enjoy the last few bottles of beer. They were all, needless to say, unsteady on their feet and befogged in their brains, and as is the way with sergeants, they very soon began to grow disputatious and belligerent with one another. The conversation—such as it was—turned at last to Communism. And in order to settle a shouting match, which threatened before very long to lead to physical violence, Oberwachtmeister Danz conceived the brilliant notion of calling in little Lenzing to set them straight on the subject. Lenzing had come to us in the latest batch of volunteers. He looked like an undersized sixteen-year-old, although he was in fact approaching his twenty-first birthday. He had been a student once upon a time, in a past that must now have seemed to him to be lost way back in the mists of pre-history. He had been arrested on account of his Communist sympathies, of which he had made no secret.

He was asleep when the two drunken emissaries despatched by Danz called to collect him. They hauled him straight out of his blankets and down into the vomit-ridden, smoke-filled den where the sergeants were disporting themselves. They set him shivering on a table and gathered about him like a crowd at an execution. Danz bade him give them a lecture on the ideals of Communism—'simple enough so that even a bunch of bone-headed Nazis like us can understand them'—and there the poor fellow was, caught between hell and high water with death leering in his face whichever way he turned. If he held forth a second time about Communism, he was virtually sign-ing his own execution order; if, on the other hand, he refused to comply, Danz would almost certainly polish him off there and then. He really had no choice in the matter. He shrugged his bottleneck shoulders and began jerking out the first string of claptrap clichés that came to mind.

'Communism is the struggle of the proletariat against inter-national capitalism. It is the fight against imperialism. It is the rising of the working classes against their oppressors——'

For ten minutes they listened to him in a respectful drunken silence, and then Danz gave a loud cheer and smashed the last beer bottle against the wall. He dragged Lenzing down from the table and clapped him on the shoulder.

'That's not bad, my little red comrade! Not bad at all!'

Proudly he paraded his protégé about the room, showing him off like an exhibit in a fairground. See, this is the man who dared stand up and preach Communist propaganda to the soldiers of the Führer . . .

It was of course inevitable that before very long some quarrelsome ape like Hofmann or Sergeant-Major Kleiner—Kleiner it was, from all reports—should take it into his head to become obstreperous and break up the party. To begin with, he started arguing with Lenzing; and being far too drunk to speak clearly, he very soon got the worst of it. From there it was but a short step to denouncing Lenzing as a traitor, and a Communist dog, and a friend of the Jews; and from there an even shorter step towards a general howl for blood. Danz, by this time, appeared to have taken Lenzing under his wing, for when someone bawled across the room that all Communist sympathisers were lily-livered cowards, Danz was instantly up in arms in his new friend's defence. It was thereupon proposed to put his courage to the test by standing him up against a wall and playing William Tell with him, taking pot-shots at a beer bottle perched precariously on top of his head. This idea seemed to have satisfied Danz, for at that point he faded out of the picture—in all probability lying on the floor unconscious. It was Kleiner who appointed himself chief marksman.

'Just try to keep still, Communist puppydog, unless you fancy having your brains blown out ... I don't very often miss the mark, but even if I do, there's no cause for alarm. You'll be dead before you even know you've been hit.'

He pulled out his revolver and took aim with a hairy porcine paw which wavered perceptibly from side to side. It was then that Hofmann, of all people, began to lose his nerve. We were, he no doubt reasoned, at the front now, not at Sennelager, and awkward questions might well be asked if a man was found dead next morning with a bullet through his forehead.

'You reckon?' jeered Kleiner, in high good humour at the prospect of murdering someone. 'I'd like to see the court martial as would tear a man off a strip for shooting a lousy Communist. More likely give you a medal for it.'

He held the revolver before him and squeezed the trigger. The bullet ricocheted off the wall and went screaming out through the window. Half the assembled company at once dived under tables and chairs, while the other half, either more drunk or more full of patriotic fervour, urged Kleiner to 'have another go at the bastard'. Kleiner scarcely needed any encouragement. He seemed puzzled that he should have missed the target first time round, though whether the target was by now a beer bottle or a man's head was anybody's guess.

'For Chrissakes!' gasped Hofmann, holding a chair in front of him by way of protection from stray bullets. 'For Chris*sakes*, you'll have the whole place buzzing round our ears!'

Kleiner ignored him. He staggered back against the wall and again took aim. Someone bet him three bottles of vodka that he'd miss. Someone else offered a month's pay that he wouldn't. The revolver in Kleiner's sweating hand waved slowly from side to side. Hofmann, from behind his chair, began to babble tearfully about repercussions if anything should happen to Lenzing.

'Go and stuff yourself,' said Kleiner, quite amiably for him. 'When I want your advice I'll ask for it. Meanwhile, piss off out of it, and leave us alone. There's three bottles of vodka at stake here.'

Not, of course, to mention a man's life. Kleiner closed one eye and squeezed the trigger a second time. The bullet tore into the wall only centimetres away from Lenzing's head.

'He moved!' screamed Kleiner. 'The stupid cowardly bastard went and moved!'

By this time, Lenzing was trembling all over from head to foot, and Kleiner himself looked as if all his bones had turned to jelly. His knees caved in and he kept wavering from side to side. He took a third shot, with his hand dancing about like a snake in a high wind. The beer bottle bounced off Lenzing's head and crashed to the floor, but the shouts of jubilation were silenced by an acid voice which spoke from the doorway.

'Would someone be kind enough to tell me what the hell is going on in here?'

Slowly, Kleiner turned his head. From all over the room, men crawled out of their shelters and staggered to their feet. Lieutenant Löwe stood with his helmet pushed down over his eyes, his thumbs stuck in his belt, coldly regarding them all. He jerked his head at Lenzing.

'Get back to your quarters. I'll deal with you later.' He waited until the terrified boy had left the room, then kicked the door closed behind him. 'Sergeant-Major Kleiner,' he said. 'You have obviously been hiding your light under a bushel. I had no idea you had such a passion for firearms. We shall have to make better use of your talents ... As from this moment you are transferred to the anti-tank section. I shall expect great things of you.' His lip curled distastefully. He let his eyes travel slowly over the rest of the assembled company. 'You realise,' he said, 'there is one reason and one reason only that I am not hauling the whole miserable puke-making lot of you up before a court martial and having you packed straight off to Torgau? We're in the fifth year of the war, and we're on the verge of disaster, and by God I'd rather keep you out here to get your heads blown off by Russian artillery than send you back to the comparative luxury of a military prison. I may as well tell you here and now that I don't give a damn if every man jack of you ends up with your guts hanging down between your legs and both your arms blown off. It's not going to be any use coming whining to me about it. As far as I'm concerned, you stay out here and you fight until you drop. And when you drop, you die, because believe you me there's not going to be anyone hanging around long enough to stop and pick you up again.'

He turned abruptly and left the room, slamming the door behind him. There was a shocked silence. Suddenly, no one was drunk any more. Perhaps at that moment, for the first time, they were realising what it meant to lose a war. Perhaps they knew, then, that Löwe had not spoken in vain, and that they were all under sentence of death.

Kleiner collapsed heavily into a chair and lay there, sweating, with his legs sprawled out before him, his arms dangling down to the floor. His revolver slipped out of his grasp and he let it lie where it had fallen. Grimly, Hofmann picked it up and thrust it at him.

'Best hang on to that,' he said. 'Might come in handy one day for shooting yourself with ...'

The following morning we took up a position alongside the 587th Infantry Regiment, relieving the 500th, which was a disciplinary regiment composed not of criminals but almost entirely of disgraced officers. All the WUs,* no matter to which regiment they belonged, had to wear a red badge on their backs. Thus, they were easily distinguished.

* Wehrmacht unwürdig—those unworthy of service in the Army.

We found the front line at that point almost uncannily quiet. The first of the Russians' trenches was over on the far side of the marshes, and the no-man's-land between them and us lay silent and deserted. The day we arrived was a Thursday. According to those who had been in the area some time, this was the day when the vodka rations were dished out to the Russian troops; one and a half litres per man, generally consumed in less than an hour. We were informed that we could look forward to an eventful night.

Here, in the very midst of the marshland, the mosquitoes swarmed and buzzed like one of the plagues of Egypt. They were worse by far than the ever-present lice which we carried around. We had been issued with mosquito nets, but the brutes found their way inside and set about guzzling blood to their hearts' content. Porta claimed to have found a remedy, but in our view it was every bit as bad as the presence of the mosquitoes. He covered himself in foul-smelling grease scooped out of a truck which had been blown up and left to bury itself in the marshes, and from that moment on he was shunned not only by the pestilential insects but by everyone else as well. We were waiting with interest to see if he repelled the Russians as well.

Dotted all round us in the trenches were the prominent red badges of the WUs. Cannon fodder pure and simple. They had been promised free pardons if they distinguished themselves in battle, but we knew and they knew, that this was merely a myth for the credulous. They were lost men. They were there to swell the numbers. They were there to die. They huddled together in groups, full of resentment and misery, waiting only to be herded out into the middle of a minefield, or kicked out of the trenches to meet the first blast of the Russian guns. No one took any notice of them save to curse or kick them. Like loathsome prisoners of war, they were avoided and treated with contempt. When the fighting began, they would be of no use to themselves nor to anyone else. They had nothing left to live for and might just as well die.

Shortly after 2000 hours the fun started. For some time we

had listened to them shouting and laughing over on the far side of the marshes, bracing ourselves for an attack. But mortar grenades are no easier to live with simply because you've been expecting them. They were aimed with uncomfortable accuracy, and a couple of WUs were blown to shreds before Tiny (who was always one of the first to jump into action), had a chance to retaliate with his machine-gun. After that it was phosphorus bombs which caused wholesale panic when they exploded directly in front of the unfortunate WUs, who ran about screaming in all directions like sheep with a wolf in their midst.

The firing went on spasmodically throughout the night. We had a short burst of peace during the morning, and then in the afternoon the snipers started playing havoc with us. They were Siberians, perched like great black crows in the treetops. I swear they must have been handpicked for the job, because they never wasted a shot. If you showed your head over the edge of the trench for even a hundredth of a second, you'd get a bullet straight between the eyes. They were devils in disguise, those Siberians. Even the Russians themselves feared them. They killed for the sheer animal joy of killing, counting their toll day by day, saving up the corpses for a medal as other people save sixpences for their grandmother's birthday present. Still, I suppose we could scarcely complain. We had almost their exact counterpart in the Tyroleans, who showed the same zeal and accuracy in splattering people's brains about.

It was the little Legionnaire who scored our first definite hit in reply. I saw him shoulder his rifle, take careful aim, fire, and from one of the topmost branches of an oak tree a body came hurtling to the ground. We had barely finished congratulating him when Porta followed suit and a second Siberian came skydiving out of nowhere and plummeted down into the marshes. For a brief moment the sun appeared from behind the clouds, and a stray metal object in the bushes glinted in a shaft of light. Barcelona grabbed Porta's arm and pointed.

'There he is ... over there in the reeds with bits of grass

stuck on his head, stupid git——'

Porta, in his excitement, snatched the field-glasses away from Barcelona and pushed him to one side to take a closer look. An explosive bullet thudded into the ground where he had been standing. Porta wasted no time. The field-glasses were abandoned. He stood up and fired three shots in quick succession, and out of the reeds, a body reared up. The top half of its head had been blown off. It threw its arms into the air, took a step forward into the mud and collapsed. In a few moments it was sucked out of sight, down into the depths of the heaving marshes. Only a few, obscene brown bubbles in the mud were left to mark its downward passage. The area was becoming one vast burial ground. One day, perhaps, when all the fighting was over, the bog would release its numerous victims and all the empty skulls would be thrown back to the surface to float in silence on the sea of mud. That would be a sight worth seeing. That would be a fine memorial to five years' butchery.

While Porta was still gloating over his triumph, a well-aimed shell obliterated the entire 1st section of the Seventh Company. All that was left was one empty coat-sleeve drifting in the air. When the dust had settled, we discovered a few fragments of bone and pieces of twisted metal. The WUs were thrown into such a state of panic that we were given orders to shoot if need be.

Parson Fischer was cowering in a dugout with an ex-postman from Leipzig. The postman had been caught stealing registered packets (an offence which carried the death sentence), but the man must have had friends in high places for he escaped with his life and ten years' imprisonment. He had been lured like a fool into 999 battalion with promises that if he behaved himself he would be reinstated in his old position at Leipzig. There are some men who will believe anything, even Nazi propaganda. It had taken only a short time at Sennelager to dispel the illusion, but by then, of course, it was too late to back out.

'Eh, parson!' he said, digging the trembling Fischer in his

62

skin-and-bone ribs. 'How about if we made a run for it?'

He jerked his head in the direction of no-man's-land. Fischer hesitated. He stared out across the marshy wastes towards the Russian front line.

'The way I see it,' said the postman, 'it can't be any worse on that side of the fence than it is on this.' Fischer turned a pair of filmy blue eyes on him. They seemed in some way to be questioning the assertion. The postman grabbed hold of his arm. 'Look at it this way,' he said. 'They'll kill us for sure if we stay on here——'

Even as he spoke, the firing came to a sudden halt. A thick curtain of silence fell over the marshes. And then slowly, one by one, a whole new range of little sounds came creeping in towards us. We heard the crackling and spitting of fire as a nearby village went up in flames. We heard the distant lowing of terrified cattle. We heard the groans of the wounded, and the calls of the dying for their wives and their mothers.

And suddenly a new sound. The sound of men's voices raised in song. It was the old German tune of 'Alte Kameraden'—and it was coming to us from somewhere behind the Russian lines ...

'See what I mean?' whispered the postman, excitedly. 'See what I mean?'

The music faded away. We heard the sizzling of hidden microphones, and then a whole network of loudspeakers burst into life.

'The Red Army salutes number 999 battalion—and in particular all political prisoners who have been forced against their will to fight for a corrupt régime. We urge you to use your best endeavours to bring Hitler's infernal war machine to a halt! We are your comrades, and you shall have all the support we can give you ... Listen to us, German soldiers! Hear what we have to say to you! This morning you were told that your rations had been cut to half because saboteurs had blown up the railway line. That is a lie! That is a Nazi lie! Your supply lines are still open. We know, because we are out there, waiting to cut you off whenever we feel like it. But for the moment we are staying our hands. We have seen the trains come in. We have seen the food unloaded—enough for everyone, and some to spare. So where has it gone, you ask? Look to the viper in your bosom, German soldiers! Ask your Sergeant-Major Bode of the Eighth Company what he has done with your rations ... Ask him where he has hidden the two hundred cartons of cigarettes and the twenty-three bottles of vodka! And if he refuses to talk, look for yourselves behind the truck which is numbered WH6 651.557. Look underneath the petrol tank, and see what you will find there. And if you should have any difficulty, get the Polish woman, the whore Wanda Stutnitz, to take you there and show you ... To-morrow evening, your General Freiherr von Weltheim is throwing a party at Matoryta. Laskowska Street, Matoryta. Remember the address, German soldiers! All the drinks and all the cigarettes are being supplied by Quartermaster-Sergeant Lumbe. They have been stolen by him from the Fourth Tank Regiment ...'

The voice stopped, and the speakers blared forth once again with the menacing strains of martial music. No one spoke. No one moved. We just stood still and stared, glassy-eyed and vacant, like a herd of bovine creatures waiting for the butcher's axe. The music crackled into silence and the harsh, guttural voice of a German-speaking Russian returned with more propaganda.

'Comrades! German comrades! Hear what I have to say! Throw down your arms and liberate yourselves! Throw off the yoke of imperialism and come to join your brother workers! The Free Army of the Socialist Peoples is waiting to welcome you. Marshal Rokossovsky offers you an honourable place among his troops. Here you will be treated as one of our own Russian soldiers. Your Nazi officers call us a sub-species—low, mindless creatures of the bogs and the marshes. We laugh in their faces! Who is it, I ask you, who is it who has won victory after victory ever since the débâcle of Stalingrad? You of 999 battalion who have been forced against your will to take up arms to defend your overlords—it is you to whom I address myself. Throw off your shackles and join us in our fight for freedom! Have they promised you rehabilitation? And have you trusted them? Have you put your faith in them? Have you believed them in their lying promises? Comrades, do not let yourselves be deceived! You will never see Germany again. None of you. Your death warrants have already been signed. You have been sent out here to die for them. You have been sent out here for us to kill ... But we do not want to kill you! Come to us now, while there is still time, so that we may avoid spilling the blood of our brothers! We can offer you the hope of a new life. We can offer you a war of revenge against the Nazi criminals who are condemning you to die for them ... We shall fight and we shall be victorious! We shall not stop until we reach Berlin! Come and join us in our struggle. We shall not let you starve, nor go to your deaths in a dishonourable fight of worker set against worker ... This evening we shall be waiting for you to come to us. Between 1900 and 2100 hours. We shall give you covering fire and protect you on the crossing. Take heart and have courage! Rise against your persecutors and put them to flight!'

The voice shouted itself to a raucous halt. In their dugout, the postman and the parson sat together shivering. The postman was the first to break the silence.

'You heard him,' he whispered. 'You heard what he said. It's only the same as it was earlier. It stands to reason, doesn't it? There's only one sensible thing to do, and that's get the hell out while there's still a chance ... How about it, padre? You coming with me?'

Slowly, Fischer shook his head.

'I can't,' he said. 'I wish you luck, but I cannot desert my people. They have need of me and I must stay with them.'

The postman stared at him.

'Are you off your saintly rocker? You must be raving bloody potty! What's the point of staying here to succour that load of perishing shits? You want to be a martyr, do you? Is that what you want? You want to be a bloody martyr like that Jehovah's flaming Witness?'

'Christ died on the cross,' murmured Fischer, a trifle obscurely. 'I will meet whatever fate the Lord has in store for me. I will not turn my back on what I consider to be my duty.'

'Duty!' said the other, scornfully. 'Well, it may be your idea of duty to stay here like a sitting duck and get your holy head blown off, but it certainly ain't mine! I'm going to make a break for it while the offer still holds good.'

Fischer turned a pair of mild blue eyes upon him.

'If I were you,' he said, gently, 'I shouldn't place too much reliance on the Russians keeping their word. They also have their concentration camps and their political prisoners. I fancy they will use you little better than the Nazis.'

The postman shrugged a shoulder.

'That's a risk I have to take, old man. It may not be much of a chance, I grant you that, but at least it's better than nothing ... I hope you won't shoot me in the back as I make the crossing?'

'I would never shoot any man,' said Fischer, gravely. 'May God go with you.'

In all the other shellholes and dugouts, the WUs were mumbling and muttering among themselves as they considered the implications of the Russian offer.

'You heard what they said? You heard what they just said?' Paul Weiss, ex-banker, ex-swindler, ex-con man, turned agitatedly to his companion. 'Why don't we give it a go? Eh? Why don't we give it a go? I'd as soon die fighting for the Reds as for the Nazis. Sod the Party and the lousy flaming Fatherland! What have they ever done for the likes of you and me? There's certainly never been any freedom in Germany. Not in my lifetime, there hasn't. Every move you make, there are Gestapo snapping round your heels like a pack of starving dogs. Why not make a break for it and see what the world looks like from the other side of the fence for a change?'

Shortly before 1900 hours it began to rain; a tremulous grey drizzle quickly covered the area in a watery haze. Almost at once, the Russian barrage began. The artillery fire, which until

66

then had been spasmodic, gradually gathered in intensity. Shells began ripping up the earth in front of the trenches, and a shower of napalm bombs set the ground alight behind us. This was no doubt the Russians' subtle way of encouraging any would-be deserters, by demonstrating just what would be in store for them if they chose to stay behind and fight for Hitler.

Promptly at 1900 hours, the firing stopped. Only one large shell broke the sudden silence as it exploded. The noise came from behind us, somewhere near the village where Hofmann was still amusing himself with his two female telephonists from the Luftwaffe.

'Let's hope it got the bastard,' muttered Tiny, with all his accustomed goodwill towards his superiors.

From their forward position, Paul Weiss and his companion peered through the creeping mist towards the enemy lines, which appeared to be deserted. We knew we were being spied on from all directions, but there were no signs of activity anywhere.

'OK, this is it,' hissed Weiss. 'Let's get a move on before the crowd arrives. It only wants a few more of 'em to get the same idea into their heads, and this place is going to be packed out like a pleasure park on a Sunday afternoon ... Come on, let's shift!'

His companion hesitated. Before they could move, a couple of WUs from a neighbouring shellhole crawled across to join them. Weiss clicked his tongue impatiently.

'Well? Are you coming or aren't you?'

Under the dubious eyes of his companions, he took a leap forward into no-man's-land. He landed in a crater, fell flat on his stomach and was gone from sight. Seconds later, Sergeant Repke arrived. He looked at the three remaining men and frowned.

'What's going on round here?' He put his field-glasses to his eyes and peered suspiciously into the mist. 'There were four of you a moment ago. Where's the fourth one gone?'

The three men exchanged fearful glances.

'He hasn't gone anywhere, Sergeant——'

'We've been together all the time——'

'Just the three of us——'

'Together——'

Repke coldly ignored them. Finding nothing in the gathering gloom of the mist, he shouldered his M.PI and strode off, without a backward glance, to inspect a nest of machine-gunners. The three men wasted no more time. Repke would be back again for sure, and they had no intention of hanging about to be questioned further on the subject of Weiss and his disappearance. Jettisoning their arms, they dashed helter-skelter into the rain towards the north.

The artillery of both sides had now started up again. The earth shook beneath the pounding of the heavy guns, and shells exploded right and left. We waited, immobile.

'Let 'em have their fun,' said the Old Man, dryly. 'They'll wear themselves out before very long.'

The drizzling mist had turned to a steady downpour. A wind blew up, and within seconds we were soaked to the skin. The distant hills occupied by the Russians gradually faded to a dark blue haze as night began to fall. It was a grand evening for deserters.

Staff Sergeant Wolte was standing with Bugler and Treiber, a couple of WUs. He was staring fixedly towards the Russian lines. Bugler looked at Treiber, and they both looked at Wolte and nodded at each other.

'Sergeant,' said Bugler, in a suitably humble tone of voice, 'excuse me troubling you like this, but do you happen to know if we're likely to get anything to eat today? It's not that I'm bothered on my own account, of course. It's just that my belly's rumbling so loud I reckon they can hear it half a mile off.'

Sergeant Wolte slowly turned to regard the pair. He pushed his helmet to the back of his head.

'Well now,' he said, 'why ask me? Why not nip across and ask the Russians? They seem to know more about it than we do. You heard what they said, didn't you? Over there you can have all the food you want. Why not go across and get it?'

Treiber nervously fell back a step, his mouth sagging slightly. It seemed almost as if Wolte was giving them an open invitation to go and join the enemy, though that would have been impossible. Wolte was a good Nazi. He believed in the Party and the Führer. Wolte would never contemplate desertion.

Bugler swallowed a few times before replying.

'You'd shoot us,' he said, thickly. 'You'd shoot us down the minute we moved.'

'You think so?' Wolte let his eyes rove back again towards the Russian front lines. 'Who knows what I might or might not do? I might even join you. The more that turn up, the more inclined they'll be to give us a decent welcome ...' He suddenly stretched out an arm and pointed. 'Look,' he said. 'Look over there. Four more of your companions waiting for the off ... Suppose we were to join forces with them? If things went against us and it looked as if we weren't going to make it, we could arrest the four of them and bring them back here with us. Who could possibly dispute the fact that we had gone out in pursuit of them?'

Bugler looked uncomfortable.

'Yeah, that's all very well,' he said. 'That's all very well, but somehow I don't reckon we'd get much of a welcome from the Reds if we turned up with a Nazi in tow. They're not fools, are they? They're not bleeding stupid. Even if you tore all that crap off your chest, all them badges and things, they'd still know you wasn't one of us.'

'You think I haven't already considered that? You think I haven't already made provision?' Wolte smiled; a tight little smirk of self-congratulation. 'I have taken very good care to supply myself with two sets of papers: one for everyday use, and one for emergencies ...'

There was a grudging pause.

'So. All right.' Bugler hunched a shoulder. 'So you've got false papers and they're not going to find out you're a Nazi. So perhaps it might be worth giving it a try. But there again, perhaps it might not. I mean, how do we know they were speaking the truth? How do we know they're going to keep their word?'

'We don't,' said Wolte. 'It's as simple as that. You never do know, with the Russians. One minute they're slapping you on the back and toasting you in vodka, the next they're sticking the muzzle of a Nagan into your mouth. It's a chance you have to take.'

'Well, in that case,' said Bugler, 'I'm not sure that I want to take it.'

'I shouldn't worry too much about it.' Wolte tapped a finger against the small canvas satchel which was slung over his shoulder. 'I've got one or two little goodies in here which I fancy Ivan will be only too pleased to get his hands on. With this lot in his possession, he can wipe out the entire German front line at a blow. I reckon that should be enough to earn his gratitude.'

'Yeah, but——'

'But what?' Wolte gave a short crack of laughter. 'If it's me you're scared of, you might bear in mind that I've said enough already to get myself hanged. Surely that's sufficient proof of sincerity.' He paused. 'Incidentally,' he said, 'one word of warning before we set off. No funny stories about Sennelager. It really wouldn't be worth your while. Because if you shop me, just remember that I can always shop you in return. The Russians don't care for the criminal classes any more than the Nazis do. If they ever got to hear of your past records, it would be straight down the lead mines for you two. So no telling tales out of school. All right?'

Bugler hesitated.

'I guess so,' he said, resentfully.

Wolte turned to his companion.

'And you?'

'I'm game,' said Treiber.

'Good. In that case——' Wolte held out a hand. 'Let me have your papers.'

There was a momentary flicker of doubt, and then, with

obvious misgivings, they passed them over. Wolte selected a couple of blank pages and on them he scrawled the letters 'PU'.* From his canvas satchel he took a rubber stamp on which was the Colonel's signature. He carefully printed it below the handwritten letters; and then for good measure added the word 'Buchenwald'. He handed back the papers, and a broad smile of relief spread over Bugler's face as he examined the Sergeant's handiwork.

'Fine,' he said. 'That's fine. Buchenwald, eh? That makes me feel a whole lot safer.'

Wolte stowed away his rubber stamp.

'Let's get cracking,' he said. 'It's now or never.'

The journey across no-man's-land was surprisingly swift and simple. Our men put their heads down and ran like stags. Almost before they knew it they had reached the first of the Russian trenches. They tumbled into them with their hands held high, and a crowd of others soon followed. It seemed that the whole wide stretch of land between the two armies was suddenly filled with violent activity. Russian propaganda had done its job well.

Tiny was watching the whole show through a pair of field-glasses. He kept up a running commentary for our benefit.

'I've never seen anything like it. They're milling about all over the bleeding place ... And fuck me!' he added, in excitement. 'There goes another of 'em! And another! There must be half the bleeding Army out there! Seems they can't get away fast enough——'

At one point Porta made a move to fire, but the Old Man held him back.

'Let them go,' he said. 'Let the poor sods go. Let them run, if that's what they want. They'll soon discover their mistake.'

Out of the arms of Berlin and into the clutches of Moscow. I wondered how many of them had the least idea of what it was they were running to.

A major of the Pioneer Corps suddenly came galloping up to us, his face aglow with fanatical fury.

* Politically undesirable.

'What the devil are you doing?' he screamed at Löwe. 'Why aren't you firing at them? Sweet Christ almighty, the rats are deserting!'

Before Löwe could even open his mouth to reply, the Major had hurled himself behind a machine-gun and was yelling 'Fire! Fire!' at the top of his frenetic, strangulating voice. From somewhere out in no-man's-land a chorus of agonised voices started up, and the sounds of our firing brought Colonel Hinka on to the scene. He almost tripped headlong over the manic major behind his rattling machine-gun.

'Who is that?' he said irritably. 'What is he doing down there?' He turned impatiently to his ordnance officer. 'Who is this man? Why have I not been told about him?'

The ordnance officer peered down cautiously at the Major. 'I really don't know, sir,' he said. 'I really couldn't say who he is.'

'Then take a look at his papers and find out!' snapped the Colonel.

The Major sullenly left his post at the machine-gun, and even more sullenly handed over his papers. The sight of Löwe's cool smile and the sound of Porta's inane snickering doubtless did nothing to help the situation. The ordnance officer glanced briefly through the papers. He compared one photograph with another, scrutinised a couple of signatures and a dubious-looking stamp. He frowned, and turned to the Colonel.

'Something fishy about all this, sir. I can't quite put my finger on it, but I'd like to have these papers looked at more closely.'

'I beg your pardon?' said the Major, outraged. 'Are you daring to suggest that those papers are false?'

'And what if they are?' said the Colonel, crisply. 'He is doing no more than his duty. What is one supposed to think when one discovers a complete stranger has suddenly marched in from God knows where and calmly assumed command of one's company without so much as a "by your leave"? It strikes me as being a trifle bizarre, to say the very least. I could have you shot on the spot if I felt so inclined.'

The Major lost a little of his hectic flush. He wiped the back of his hand nervously across his mouth. Porta, as always quite incapable of holding his tongue, now bounded exuberantly forward to offer the Colonel his valuable advice.

'Best to take no chances, sir! That's what they told us in Ulm, sir. Shoot first and ask the questions afterwards, that's what they always said. That was counter-espionage, that was. I took a course in it.'

'So what the devil is that supposed to do? Make you some kind of an expert?' snarled the Major. 'Next thing I know you'll be trying to tell me I'm a Russian spy in German uniform!'

Porta drew himself up to full height and bared his teeth.

'It was the Reichsführer himself who said it was better by far to kill five innocent people than to let one guilty man go free.'

'Oh, for God's sake!' snapped the Major. 'Can no one stop this cretin and his endless bibble-babble?'

The Colonel, who had been studying the man's papers, now thrust them back at him.

'Take these and return to your battalion,' he said, coldly. 'I shall be looking further into this matter at a more propitious moment. You have exceeded your authority and I shall expect a full explanation of your behaviour. Now go.'

The Major disappeared even faster than he had come. The Colonel picked up his binoculars and thoughtfully studied the frenzied, fleeing shadows that still came and went in no-man's-land.

'Very well,' he said. 'Carry on firing.'

Tiny shrugged a shoulder.

'Mad as a bloody hatter,' he muttered. 'Wasting good ammunition on that load of creeps. Leave 'em to the Reds, I would. They'll polish 'em off soon enough.'

Mechanically, without any enthusiasm for the task, we opened fire. Tiny loaded and reloaded like an automaton, whispering his usual sweet-nothings to each shell as he rammed it home. Tiny always addressed every single one of them as if it were an old and valued friend. He was by far the best loader we had. He was fast and accurate and apparently tireless. He could carry on for hours at a time without flagging. He might not have been too sure about two plus two equalling four, but he certainly knew how to handle a mortar.

'Three-fifty metres,' said the Old Man.

'Prime, load, fire,' chanted Tiny, as one reciting a litany. 'Off you go, my sweetheart ...'

Human remains were spouting into the air, but now the Russians had opened up with covering fire for the would-be comrades who were hurrying to join them. Grenades began bursting around us, uncomfortably close, and Porta swore and jammed his hat further down on his head.

'Bloody Russians,' he said. 'Bloody Russian swine. You know they use women to fire those things? Must have biceps the size of bleeding footballs, that's all I can say.'

An hour later, the barrage from both sides had petered to a standstill. Only a few of the deserters had successfully managed to leap out of the Nazi frying pan and into the Communist fire. A few had been recaptured and put under arrest. Many more lay mangled and dying in the churned-up mud of no-man's-land. Meanwhile, there was hysterical activity all the way along the line, with telephones ringing non-stop and messengers dashing to and fro with their usual self-important fervour. Both Security and the Secret Police had been informed of the débâcle, and we settled back gloomily to await their arrival.

A lieutenant-colonel of the Gefepo was sitting in a corner with his head in his hands. His uniform was still new and shiny, but his face looked furrowed and aged before its time. Not only had twelve of his NCOs deserted with the WU contingent, but now they informed him that one of his captains also had defected. The lieutenant-colonel had pleaded with Hinka to report the captain as killed in action, but Hinka was stern and adamant.

'You can have a word yourself with Security,' he said,

74

which of course was the very last thing that any man in his right senses would want to do.

A little before midnight, the Russians opened fire on the divisional HQ. Their range and direction were uncannily accurate. The ammunition dumps went up one after another. Tanks under camouflage were picked out with calm precision. It seemed obvious that someone on the staff must have succeeded in deserting and supplying the other side with much valuable information.

With the slow coming of a grey dawn, we awoke to a witch hunt of those WUs who either through choice or necessity were still with us. It was partly a form of reprisal; partly a desire to find a scapegoat, to demonstrate loyalty to the Führer and hatred of his enemies by striking down a few defenceless men. I saw Parson Fischer attacked in the middle of a prayer by an infuriated Sergeant Linge, who slashed him across the face with the rim of his helmet. I saw Oberwachtmeister Danz come running up to join in the fun. I saw him slam the butt end of his revolver into the Parson's jaw and grind his face down into the mud with the heel of his boot. And then I saw the pair of them go rollicking away in search of new victims. Parson Fischer staggered to his feet with blood pouring out of his broken mouth and down his chin. It could have been worse. At least he was still alive. The lieutenant-colonel whose captain had deserted him had been found earlier on with his brains blown out.

Later in the morning we were relieved by an infantry regiment. The ragged remnants of 999 battalion were rounded up and marched off to a nearby village, where they were eyed with much astonishment and misgivings by the troops already in occupation.

'Prisoners,' said one man knowledgeably to his neighbour. 'That's what they'll be. Prisoners.'

'Spies,' said another.

It never occurred to them that these half-naked skeletons could possibly be their own countrymen; that this wretched collection of skin and bones had been sent from Germany to die. The Führer in his almighty wisdom and bountiful good-ness would never allow such a thing.

The battalion was kept on the move through the village, and out of sight of the gaping soldiers, on for another six miles. They were brought to a halt at last, and were treated to a warm reception by a body of guards from Warsaw Security, with the forbidding insignia of the death's head on their helmets. They were lined up and assaulted in the usual friendly fashion of the Security people. Anyone even slightly out of line received either a blow on the head or a bullet through the back of the neck from a P38. Those who fell to the ground were casually kicked unconscious and left to the mercy of the prowling dogs. There was a great deal of yelling and screaming and confusion, dogs barking, boots stamping, men shouting orders. All this was quite normal procedure.

After a bit, when the battalion had been suitably pruned and was apparently thought to be presentable, it was handed over to a major and two of Dirlewanger's special companies. The Major instantly commanded the shivering dregs of 999 to take off their rags and to line up facing the wall with their hands behind their heads. Anyone who dared to move, he informed them, would be shot. It appeared from the subsequent reduc-tion in numbers that a great many of them had so dared.

The Major continued calmly talking as the murderers of Dirlewanger continued with their task of selective weeding and hoeing. For almost an hour he talked. He described in glowing detail the various punishments they could look for-ward to if any of them departed from the rules and regulations by so much as a hair's breadth. He cautioned them most emphatically against attempting to follow their erstwhile com-panions across the lines to the Russian trenches: the families of every man, wives, children, mothers and fathers, had been rounded up and were being held as hostages. Finally, he an-nounced that those who were still alive might now put on their clothes preparatory to being transported to the 27th Tank Regiment. There they would find plenty of opportunities to die like heroes.

By now, probably even the prospect of standing knee-deep in mud with Russian mortars whistling through the air had begun to seem like a fairly pleasant way of passing the time. The survivors climbed back thankfully into whatever bits and pieces of clothing they could find, and were suitably impressed to discover that a fleet of lorries was waiting to convey them to their new destination. Unfortunately for them, however, the 27th Tank Regiment was still a long, long way ahead; and some were not destined to reach it. A secret tribunal had been held, and it had been somewhat arbitrarily decided that one man in three should be condemned to death without trial. It was to this that they were now being driven.

The lorries drew up at the appointed place and disgorged their sorry load. With bayonet and rifle butt the men were driven through an archway of soldiers armed with rods of iron towards the slaughterhouse. Some of them never even reached the slaughterhouse. It is truly amazing what mortal blows can be dealt by a thin sliver of iron in the hands of an expert. Of course, when a man is in the army, he kills by whatever method is demanded of him. One pretty soon became expert in most types of murder.

Those who had successfully run the gauntlet were herded down into the damp darkness of the cellars of a ruined building. The ground beneath was quickly ploughed into a glutinous mud. Water dripped from the ceiling. Sewer rats, made bold from hunger, scurried about, gnawing at the men's legs. There was scarcely sufficient room to house so many bodies. The guards had to use their whips before the doors could be closed and bolted.

All day and all night the men were left to starve and suffocate. It was each man for himself, there was no place left for sentiment. The weakest were pushed under. Shortly after midnight the doors were opened and half a dozen names were called. The chosen few clawed and tramped their way to the exit. It must have seemed to them like a reprieve. The doors were forced shut behind them, and those inside heard the sudden burst of machine-gun fire.

And then there was silence, and they knew what it meant when a man's name was called ...

A strange collection of criminals this depleted band of brothers were. Some had been caught listening to foreign radio stations; some had dared to doubt out loud the ultimate victory; some had spoken their minds in a public place. Others had robbed, swindled, and murdered. Still others had been inconveniently committed to an ideal of non-violence. And now, one and all, they were waiting for death in a rat-ridden cellar.

Ten minutes passed. Once again the doors were thrown open, and another six men were called to face the machine-gun fire. By dawn, it was considerably more comfortable down in the mud of the cellar. There was plenty of room to move and plenty of air to breathe. Men even began feeling human, talking once again, and speculating as to whose turn it would be next time the door opened. One person put forward a theory that it was only those criminals wearing a blue or a red stripe who were being taken away. Instantly all those wearing green stripes heaved sighs of relief.

'Yeah, I get the idea,' said a murderer from Leipzig. 'I get the drift. It's only the politicians and the traitors they're polishing off. And I reckon that's as it should be. Why should Adolf go on feeding and clothing them that wants to betray him. Get rid of 'em, I say, and let the rest of us have our fair share.'

The green stripes began to grow quite complacent as time passed and still none of them had been called out. Prison mentality reasserted itself. They began stealing all they could lay hands on from the weak and the dead. One turned on Parson Fischer, who was still hanging limply on to life, and slapped him across his already bruised and bleeding face.

'Why aren't you praying, you lousy priest? Why don't you get Him up There to come down and give us a hand?'

There was a sour laugh from the far side of the stinking cellar.

'Him up There! Fat lot of good He'd be against the SS...'

Late in the afternoon, the doors opened for the last time and an SS captain addressed them from the threshold.

'All right, listen to me, you load of swine! By rights you should all be dead by now. If I had my way, I'd take you outside and get rid of the whole damn lot of you. It's the Reichsführer himself who's decided to give you another chance to prove yourselves worthy of being allowed to go on living. I hope you're feeling fit and strong, because you're going to go on a long march to a spot where you won't be tempted to run away and join the enemy. You'll know where you're going when you've got there, and not before. You'll be marching without boots. The Bulgarian Army marches without boots, so why shouldn't you? Those of you who do arrive safely will be supplied with whatever you need. If anyone falls behind on the way, he'll be shot. And if there's anyone who feels he's not fit enough to march without boots, let him come forward and say so now.'

There was a tremulous silence, and then a man slowly advanced from the shadows of the cellar. The Captain watched him approach.

'Well? What's the matter with you?'

The man limped forward. His right foot was bloody and broken. It told its own tale.

'My, my, that doesn't look too healthy,' said the Captain. 'You should have had that seen to a long time ago.'

He called up an orderly and motioned him towards the man. The Dirlewanger Brigade had no doctors. All operations were carried out by the unskilled and fumbling hands of the orderlies, without the benefit of anaesthetics. They reckoned this toughened a man up.

'So what do you think?' murmured the Captain. 'Will he be able to march?'

The orderly dug a probing finger into the raw flesh of the damaged foot. The man gave a scream of pain, and the orderly stood up, grinning.

'I'm afraid not, sir. He's quite unfit.'

The Captain pulled a sympathetic face.

'It seems a shame,' he said, 'to have a casualty even before we begin. However, if the man can't march, he can't march, so let there be an end to it.'

A guard came in to the cellar. The unfortunate invalid was pushed to his knees and his head thrust forward. A shot rang out. That particular problem was solved.

'So,' said the Captain. 'Is there anyone else who feels himself unfit to march?'

It appeared from the silence that everyone was in blooming health. But when the wavering column did finally set out on its journey, it left a long trail of blood behind it.

The survivors were delivered up to the 27th Tank Regiment shortly after midnight. They were thrown into a hovel to sleep, and the next morning were fitted out with arms and uniforms. Now they were all ready to die for their country.

That same evening we set off again for the front.

*'He who takes oath on the Swastika must henceforth
renounce all other loyalties.'*

> Himmler. Speech to Jugoslav Volunteers at
> Zagreb, 3rd August 1941.

Two thousand Poles had been herded together in a barracks a
few miles beyond the forests which border Warsaw to the
north. The surrounding villages had been stripped of men and
women; only small children remained.

'Are there any among you who understand German?' demanded Haupsturmführer Sohr of the terrified crowd.

He tipped his grey cap, with its sinister death's head on the
peak, down over his forehead to shield his eyes from the glare
of mid-afternoon sun. An old Polish man slowly shuffled his
way towards him.

'I speak some words, sir. I can perhaps be of help to you.'

'Good. Tell your people to form themselves into three rows.
Tell them to link hands, and when I give the order to march,
tell them to go towards the woods, leaving at least ten yards
between each row.'

'And what must I tell them to do when they are in the
woods, sir?'

'Tell them to—pick strawberries. The fruit is excellent at
this time of year.'

Faithfully, unquestioningly, the old man translated this
strange order. The worried faces of the people gradually relaxed. They formed up obediently into their three rows, link-
ing hands and laughing as they did so. Strange people, these
Nazis! Rounding up two thousand men and women only to go
and pick strawberries in a wood! None of them knew, because
no one had seen fit to tell them, that the wood had been laid
with mines by Polish resistance workers.

The first column set off, hand in hand and still smiling
slightly with relief. The few laggards, the few who felt instinctively mistrustful, were urged forward by SS men armed with
rifles. The SS men kept pace with the column. They them-

81

selves had as yet no knowledge of the mines. They only knew that a few days ago they had been condemned to death and that they had now, suddenly and unaccountably, been offered free pardons. It was not up to them to reason why.

The old man was in the centre of the first column. He was clutching the hands of his two sons, one on either side of him. He trod with care, expecting that at any moment the ground would open up under his feet. He knew the Germans. He knew that he was marching to his death. He stiffened himself as they reached the edge of the wood, and suddenly, as if instinctively, the whole column came to a standstill. The SS guards ran up and down behind them, firing their guns into the air and kicking people forward. Reluctantly, the mass shuffled onwards.

They had barely gone two paces into the trees when the whole area blew up in their faces. The old man's sons were torn from his grasp. Broken bodies were shot high into the air. People screamed and sobbed, and ran in panic through this inferno. There were more explosions, more shrieks. Pandemonium. The second row of victims were driven forward to their death. A young woman with a long splinter of wood embedded in her hip had been thrown clear. She dragged herself forward, along the dusty blood-spattered ground, moaning in pain and begging for mercy. But mercy was not the order of the day. She was tossed back into the terror that raged among the trees.

The third column found themselves caught between a minefield on one side and a row of SS rifles on the other. Some ran towards the guns and were riddled with bullets. Some fled into the woods and were blown apart as they scrambled and stumbled over the writhing bodies of their companions.

Haupsturmführer Sohr tipped his cap to the back of his head as he stood surveying the carnage. He smiled as he watched the woods burning.

'Two thousand human detonators,' he murmured. 'The most efficient mine-detecting squad it has ever been my pleasure to command ...'

THE MAJOR FROM THE PIONEER CORPS

THE Regiment was back in the middle of the marshes. The marshes of Tomarka, this time. Actually one patch of bog is really very much like another. The same sticky dampness, the same endless swarms of mosquitoes.

We had got used to it by now, and during quiet periods even managed to find compensations for being there. Once you'd settled in, and the native wildlife had survived the shock invasion, you came to realise that in fact the place was a fascinating nature reserve. There were swallows and frogs in abundance. One day a couple of storks flew down to investigate the heavy machine-gun, and since then made a habit of fishing for frogs directly underneath it. Their nest was high up in the trees near to our front lines. After the first few days they seemed to grow accustomed to the constant clatter of machine-gun fire and the bursting of shells. It was remarkable how quickly the animal life came to terms with the disruption caused by men and machinery. They took it in their strides as a new pattern of daily life. There was a family of hares which came visiting every morning, begging for scraps of food. We used to throw them bits of cabbage, which they'd gobble up despite the activity going on. Then they'd lope off towards the Russian lines, where, doubtless, they were given a second meal.

By the end of our stay, we'd collected quite a menagerie. As well as the storks and the hares, there was a family of foxes which used to come scavenging each evening at sunset. One of the cubs we'd christened Toscha. He was a magnificent creature, pure white from head to foot. Tiny made the mistake one day of trying to capture him. He received a nasty bite in the leg from the infuriated animal, and from then on he had to content himself with watching from a distance. Behind the communications post was a badgers' nest. We used to open cans of condensed milk and leave them at the entrance to tempt them out into the open. Such were the small amusements of the marshes.

As for the Russians, we saw far less of them than we saw of the animals, but we knew where they were, all right. Every night, without fail, between 1900 and 2100 hours, we used to open up with the mortars. And every night, as soon as we stopped, they would send us their reply. It was really quite a gentlemanly and predictable procedure. There was no need for anyone to get himself killed if he took due precaution. It was only the raw idiots of 999 who ran into trouble. They insisted on wearing their steel helmets, only because they had been issued with them. Gleaming and glistening as they did in the humid atmosphere of the swamps, they presented the enemy with a target that was too easy to miss.

Porta and I were standing guard together one night, near the advance machine-gun post. We found the heavy silence quite oppressive, and were not perhaps as grateful as we should have been to the unknown bird that serenaded us from time to time from the middle of the marshes. It had a curiously raucous voice, harsh and gravelly. It persistently sang two notes followed by an off-key trill which began to grate on the nerves after a while.

'Bleeding bird,' I said. 'Like a bleeding donkey with hiccups.'

Tiny and Gregor turned up at last to relieve us, but we stayed on with them to keep them company. We were due back on guard in a couple of hours and it scarcely seemed worth our while to go away and come back again. Porta produced his dice and a strip of green baize and we settled down to a game. They were beautiful dice. Ivory, with the figures embossed in gold. They had been picked up by Porta from the Casino at Nice. We spread the cloth over an ammunition box, and between each throw either Tiny or Gregor would take a stroll up to the parapet and casually glance over to see what the Russians were doing. As usual, they were doing nothing at all.

Playing cards, in all probability. The bird in the marshes continued to bray, otherwise the night was silent.

Time passed slowly. We were all alert for the slightest sound, and even the beautiful ivory dice failed to hold our attention. Gregor kept tearing at his fingernails and spitting out the pieces. Every time the marsh bird opened its beak and trilled, he gave an agitated jerk and said, 'For Christ's SAKE!' After a bit, even Porta lost interest in the game. He started prowling about in the darkness, pacing up and down by the machine-gun. It was asking for trouble, but no trouble came. Finally, in exasperation, he danced about in the shadows playing his flute, and the marsh was suddenly alive with the sound of birdsong. We listened, entranced. Perhaps the Russians listened too, but they made no attempt to fire.

And then, quite suddenly, Tiny put a finger to his lips and waved an admonitory hand at Porta. I could hear nothing myself except the bemused twittering of the birds, but Tiny had an animal instinct for the approach of danger and all three of us fell respectfully silent as he sat listening. At last we heard it : the drone of aeroplanes in the distance. Porta put his flute back to his lips.

'Stukas,' he said, contemptuously.

Tiny frowned.

'You reckon?'

Before Porta could reply, the night sky was abruptly torn apart with a blinding flash of light. It was as bright as day, and we were standing exposed in the middle of it.

'Stukas my arse!' screamed Gregor, and he dived for cover beneath the parapet of the trench, with the rest of us falling pell-mell on top of him.

Somewhere behind us, the anti-aircraft batteries opened up. The drone of aeroplanes increased to a pulsating roar of engines. We saw them going overhead, wave upon wave of them. So much for Porta and his Stukas : they were Russian bombers.

No more the silence of the night. No more the braying donkey bird with his off-key trill that had so annoyed us. The marshes came alive with a hail of bombs, they were turned into a furnace, into a burning sea of flames.

'Get the hell out of it!' screamed Porta; and we got.

The air was filled with flying fragments. The entire third section, thirty-two men strong, were killed by one direct hit. Everywhere men were running and shouting. Bunkers and trenches, command posts, ammunition dumps and petrol stores, were all being torn apart by enemy bombs. No sooner had one wave of aircraft passed overhead than another appeared only seconds behind. There was no let up, no breathing space. You could only run from cover to cover in a vain attempt to get somewhere. Exactly where, God only knew. The whole of the front line was being ripped to shreds. The confusion was total. We discovered afterwards that the strength of the entire Fourth Wing of the Soviet Air Force had been directed against us. Seven hundred bombers had attacked that night. Whichever way you looked, you could see nothing but destruction. Dead men lying in heaps; mad men hopping about like jack rabbits; wounded men screaming; frightened men cowering; officers shouting orders that were never carried out because there was scarcely anyone left to listen.

After the seven hundred bombers, the heavy artillery came to complete the ruin. We could only crouch in the few trenches that remained and hope to weather the storm. Bomb damage had caused full-scale collapse, and the water from the marshes had begun to force its way in. The stench of sulphur was overpowering. Our bodies doubled up standing in the ooze and the mud and we coughed until our very guts seemed to rise into our gullets.

When the barrage finally ceased, we crawled out like ghosts from another world and grimly took stock of the little we had left. The trees were twisted and charred into grotesque shapes. Near by was a Panther tank, neatly sliced in two. All five occupants were dead. One man had been sliced in half along with the tank. A squad of terrified WUs were being driven along by a sergeant, in search of dead officers who, after all, had to be given decent burials.

86

They allowed us only a short respite before they came at us again. A thick yellow mist was sent rolling across the swamps towards us, and God help the fools who had discarded their gas masks. The yellow mist contained a chemical substance which ate its way right down into your lungs, and no man could survive without some form of protection. Sergeant Linge attempted it, and his sufferings were so hideous to watch that in the end we had to put him out of his misery. From that day on, men never let their gas masks out of their sights.

Behind the swirling banks of poison, we could hear unmistakable sounds of enemy activity, which we were at a loss to identify. I would have said troop movement, except that the Engineers had long since blown the only bridge that spanned the marshes, and there was no other way across. Finally, the advance observation post sent back the information that the noises we could hear were tanks assembling.

'Tanks?' said Löwe, incredulously. 'What the hell do they imagine they're going to do with tanks? They'll never be able to get them across.'

Half an hour later the fog had dispersed, and there indeed were the tanks, nosing their way forward from the enemy positions on the far side of the marsh. The great cannons were set ready to fire, and already the first hail of grenades was coming over.

Slowly, as we watched with disbelieving eyes, the tanks descended towards us; and in their wake, the tight-knit ranks of infantry. Over on our own side, the remaining WUs, by now thoroughly demoralised, were whimpering with unconcealed terror. For most of them it was their first sight of tanks in action, and the great green creatures looked like primeval monsters about to lower themselves into the slime. A section of flame-throwers was moved up to support us, and an anti-tank battery was hastily installed at two hundred yards. However, it was demolished by one of the advancing T34s, before it could open fire.

'They're crazy!' yelled Löwe, and it was a cry of sheer despair. 'They're raving bloody crazy, they'll never be able to make it!'

The first of the monsters dipped its nose downwards and plunged headfirst into the squelching swamp. Great clumps of mud flew up on either side, and to our astonishment the tank straightened out and began a determined path towards us. It looked like a well-laden vessel wallowing in a heavy sea. It rolled and it floundered, the water lapping at its tracks, and still it kept on coming.

'How the devil——?' Barcelona turned in stupefaction to face us. 'The bridge has been blown! There's no way across!'

The Legionnaire hunched a thin shoulder.

'Obviously,' he said, 'they've gone and built another one.'

They must have had it already prepared: a floating bridge, which they had thrown across the marshes during the general pandemonium of the air bombardment. Through the glasses you could make out the shining strands of wire with which they had secured it round the trunks of trees. It must have cost the lives of many of their men, but the Russians along with the Nazis had never rated human life very high on the general scale of values. Humanity, after all, was by far the cheapest form of raw material.

As the cavalcade proceeded, a great many more lives were lost. Several of the tanks found themselves sliding off the floating causeway. They balanced for a moment on the extreme edge of disaster, and then plunged to their doom into the bubbling brown waters. All over the marshes the green frogs were leaping, croaking their protest against this invasion of their privacy. There was a reek of oil which the wind carried across to us in the wake of the yellow poison mist.

Löwe had seen enough. He waved the anti-tank section forward, and they moved up at the double, followed by a straggle of panting WUs carrying boxes of grenades.

The advance positions were eliminated by the leading T34 in classical fashion before they could fire more than a few pitiful shots: the heavy tank simply churned the men to pieces, reducing them to a raw red pulp and then continuing serenely on its way with scraps of human flesh and bone still clinging to its tracks. It was, however, destroyed before it could do any further damage, and an exultant cheer went up. Two more tanks were wiped out in quick succession, but all the time the monsters were lumbering across the marshes, hauling themselves like hippopotamuses out of the rank, brown mud.

I felt myself shivering involuntarily, and Porta jabbed an elbow hard into my ribs.

'What are you shaking for? You got the galloping palsy or something?'

The Engineers had by now arrived with a supply of T mines, which they dumped at our sides. The tanks were barely twenty yards away. We could feel their breath hot upon us, and the soft earth heaved beneath our feet. Löwe yelled at us to prepare for action. Each man had his own target, but then there were still the oncoming waves of infantry to be reckoned with. He snatched up a mine and crouched, ready to spring. You had to admire the man. Whatever might be your opinion of officers in general, Lieutenant Löwe was always there, always with you in the thick of the fighting. He had a cold-blooded courage that commanded respect. For my own part, I pressed myself trembling against the earth and made no attempt to play the hero. Sooner or later I would be forced out of the illusory safety of my hiding place, and pushed into the open to battle with fifty tons of enemy iron and steel. Until that moment came I preferred to make myself as small as possible. I had no false notions of my own bravery.

The colossi bore down upon us. Grenades from their cannons passed over our heads, falling in the hills and creating havoc among the reserve troops. From the far side of the marshes the enemy artillery had found its mark and the shells exploded all round as we lay in our shallow holes in the earth. The familiar débris of human remains soon began to litter the ground. Material from the swamps was thrown up. Plant life, animal life were splattered all over.

Near by, Barcelona suddenly caught my attention and pointed with a frenzied hand towards the Russian lines. Cautiously I raised my head. Whole columns of green-clad infantry were emerging from the trenches and walking on the water! I was so taken aback that danger of being blown to pieces was momentarily forgotten, and I sat bolt upright to get a better look. Upon closer inspection, they were not so much walking as skating, with snowshoes strapped to their feet. And behind them came a line of motorised sledges, equipped with machine-guns. In all my time as a soldier, I had never seen anything to equal it.

'What cretin was it who told us the Russians didn't know how to fight?' I demanded, collapsing again into my shallow fold of earth.

'Adolf,' said Barcelona, bitterly. 'That's who it was. Little Uncle Adolf, who doesn't know any bleeding better because he's never been out here to have a bleeding butcher's.'

Lieutenant Löwe was speaking rapidly into the field telephone.

'They're attacking in force—there's at least a division of them. I shan't be able to hold the position very much longer. I request reinforcements. I——'

The telephone began to crackle rather querulously. I saw Löwe's fingers tighten on the handset.

'I tell you, I can't possibly hold this position unless you send me some reinforcements. I need support, for God's sake! They're throwing everything they've got at us—I'm not a bloody miracle worker! What the hell are we expected to do? Sit back and be slaughtered? That's not going to stop the advance. It's probably not even going to delay it. I need men! I need more men, and I need them immediately!'

The telephone crackled again, louder and more aggressive than before. I heard the sound of exploding sibilants. Löwe drew his eyebrows sharply together and pursed his lips.

'Very well,' he said, stiffly. 'If those are my orders.'

He slammed the set to the ground, and Porta turned and winked in my direction.

'Fancy yourself with a row of medals on your chest? Looks like this is going to be your big chance at last ... death or

90

glory, here we come!'

Löwe stood a moment, his blue eyes narrowed, staring out at the advancing tanks. They had been forced to a temporary halt, to give the infantry a chance to catch up with them. It's no fun in a tank when you're supposed to be accompanying foot soldiers. Löwe gave a small, hard smile.

'Second section, stand by! Prepare for action!'

Only two years earlier, it had been considered heroism verging on madness for men to launch an attack against tanks. A deed of outstanding valour meriting a decoration. Since then it had become a commonplace. None the less suicidal, but all in a day's work.

Löwe and the Old Man were the first to spring into action. Each was clutching a T mine. The Old Man flung his under the belly of one tank, Löwe deposited his down the turret of another. There were two simultaneous explosions. Both men flung themselves to one side. Löwe landed in a shellhole, where Kleiner was hunched up with his arms round his legs and his knees drawn up to his chin. His face was grey and leathery with fear, and it was plain he had no intention of partaking in any form of action. Löwe stared round until his gaze fell upon an abandoned bazooka, whose operators were lying dead near by. He jerked Kleiner in the ribs to gain his attention.

'Nip across,' he said, 'and bring that bazooka over here.'

Kleiner took no notice. Somewhat impatiently, Löwe repeated the order, but the man only began to snivel. Löwe regarded him with a mixture of bewilderment and disgust. It was at this point that Tiny slithered down to join them, jumping into the shellhole in a spray of black mud. He took in the situation at a glance, and his methods of dealing with it were cruder and probably more effective than any that Löwe could permit himself to employ.

'Go and get that flaming bazooka!' he shouted.

He picked up the shivering Kleiner by the scruff of his neck and booted him bodily into the open. He then sprang out after him and sent a fist crashing into his face. It was a blow that

would have rendered most men unconscious, but surprisingly it
served to bring Kleiner to his senses. He crawled across to the
bazooka, snatched it up and scuttled back with it to the Lieutenant. A T34 was wreaking havoc only about twenty yards
off. Very calmly, Löwe raised the bazooka to his shoulder.
The grenade hurtled on its way towards the target. The tank
had caught sight of us and its machine-guns were instantly
trained on the Lieutenant, who had just time to duck back into
his shellhole before the bullets started flying.

We waited. There was a loud explosion, and a red tongue of
fire leapt skywards from the turret of the tank. At my side,
Tiny gave me a dig with the toe of his boot.

'Off you go, kid!'

Somehow, without knowing it, I had acquired a couple of
mines and was grasping one in each hand. The Old Man gave
me an encouraging nod and a pat on the shoulder. It seemed I
had no alternative but to get out there and play at being a
hero. I scrambled over the top and stared wildly round. Right
in front of me loomed the bulk of a T34. God knows where it
had come from. Above my head was its long cannon, pointing
like a bony finger into the distance. Without allowing myself
time for thought, I thrust one of my mines directly under the
turret, jerked myself to one side and rolled over, nose to tail,
into the mud.

The blast of the explosion tossed me into the air and
brought me down again about thirty yards away. Another tank
was almost on top of me. Terrified, I hurled my remaining
mine towards it, twisted out of its path and covered my head
with my hands. Nothing happened: I had forgotten to prime
it. The tank moved on, and I had to sit there and watch,
helpless, as it wiped out the last of our anti-tank guns. I had
only my automatic rifle and a handful of grenades, and you
don't attack a T34 with that.

I took refuge for a moment in a shell hole full of muddy
water. Oil slicks floated on the surface, and a mutilated body
lay near by in a pool of dark red blood. The air all round was
filled with black smoke and the fumes of cordite, which made

you cough until you vomited. Suddenly, out of nowhere, I saw Tiny surging into the midst of the tanks. He hurled himself towards the nearest one, sprang on to the turret and hammered like a maniac on the hatch. A leather-helmeted head appeared. Tiny instantly shoved it back down, stuffed a grenade after it, slammed down the hatch and dived to the ground. There was a muffled explosion and the huge tank came shuddering to a halt. I saw Tiny pick himself up and go tearing off with a couple of T mines in his hands. His face was streaked with oil and blood and he curled up his lips with animal pleasure, showing a row of sharp white teeth, as he thrust the first of his mines under the tracks of an oncoming tank. He was blown backwards by the blast, and the second mine flew out of his hand and rolled away from him. Tiny went hurtling into a ditch. One of the T34s had obviously caught sight of him, for it immediately altered course and began making straight for him. As I watched from my muddy shellhole, the tank caught up the stray mine in its tracks, and in the resulting explosion the vehicle was crushed and shattered like an eggshell. The sides caved in and the hatch blew open. Only one man was thrown clear. He landed in the ditch with Tiny, and the two of them stood for a moment gaping at each other.

Tiny was the first to recover. He thrust his M.PI into the man's ribs and pushed him on to his knees. I daresay the Russian thought his last moment had arrived. They took no prisoners in the Red Army, and there was no reason why the Germans should behave any differently. He raised his arms nervously above his head, and from my shellhole I could here his anxious babbling assurances that he was no Communist, he was no Stalinite, he only fought because they made him fight, he had no quarrel with the Germans, he loved the Germans, the Germans were his friends, the Germans were his——

'All right, all right, knock it off,' growled Tiny. 'It's the same for all of us, mate. You're not a Communist, I'm not a Nazi, I love Russians, you love Krauts—so why don't we just get together and be friends?' Deftly, he dipped a hand into the man's pocket and wrenched his revolver away from him. He gestured with it towards the bed of the trench. 'Down you go. Let's have a gander and make sure you're quite safe.'

The man obediently sank to his knees, and Tiny patted him all over from head to foot with an expert hand. A trench knife was flung out in disgust. A Nagan was retained as a prize worth having. Tiny tapped the man amiably on the shoulder.

'OK. That'll do. Up you get.'

They stood for a few moments side by side in the ditch, listening to the sounds of battle raging above them. The Russian seemed slightly puzzled by Tiny's attitude. A T34 passed by, so close that it almost touched them, and both men instinctively ducked down under cover. By the time they reappeared, several minutes later, they seemed on the most companionable of terms. The Russian was grinning and gesticulating, and Tiny had abandoned his threatening gestures with the M.PI. The Russian suddenly opened his haversack and brought out a chunk of bread and meat and a flask, and they stood together in the ditch, laughing and munching and exchanging pleasantries. My mouth began to water as I crouched in my stinking mudhole and watched them. I considered for a moment crawling over to join them, but there was too much activity in the strip of land which divided us and I remained where I was and staved off the pangs of hunger by eating a few fingernails.

Tiny and his new pal polished off the last of the food and drink and began showing each other photographs. The Russian's were probably of his girl-friend or his mother. Tiny's were without any doubt obscene.

Tired at last of crouching in the mud, I began cautiously to heave myself into the open. Grenades were flying in all directions, and our own artillery had found their range and were keeping up a concentrated barrage. I saw a tank crew leap like human torches from their burning vehicle and throw themselves screaming to the ground. Near by lay a Russian colonel with both his legs blown off. He was calling repeatedly and in vain for stretcher-bearers, and as I watched one of his own tanks drove right over the top of him and minced him into a pot pourri of torn flesh and broken bones. The same tank was making straight for the ditch where Tiny and the Russian were taking cover. I yelled at them to get out, and Tiny snatched up his M.PI and was up and over the top in one swift action, right in the path of the lumbering tank. The Russian stayed where he was, white-faced and obviously terrified. Tiny shouted at him to shift, but he only shook his head and crouched cowering at the foot of the ditch. I guessed it was the first time he had ever encountered tanks from ground level, so to speak. He was making the elementary mistake of imagining himself to be safer in a ditch than out in the open. Tiny, evidently reluctant to abandon him, held out a hand for him to grasp, but it was too late. The approaching tank was almost on him, and he flung himself to one side as it passed by with only inches to spare. The Russian suddenly perceived his danger: the tank was going right over the ditch, and he would be caught beneath it. Too late, he hurled himself at the parapet and tried to claw his way out. He had lost his leather helmet, and his fair hair was streaming in the wind, his eyes open wide with terror, his arms extended towards the oncoming monster. His comrades probably never even saw him. And even if they did, I doubt if they could then have avoided him. They drove straight over the top, crushing him beneath their tracks, and went on their way sublimely ignorant. Their goal was a German anti-tank gun somewhere behind the enemy lines. They had been told to wipe it out at all costs, and they could not afford to waste time delicately picking their way through the dead and disorientated that strewed their path.

Tiny rose to his feet and stood in the midst of the flying débris shaking his fist and swearing at the departing tank. I yelled at him across the fifty or so yards which divided us. He turned and came towards me. I could see he was in a dangerous mood, uncaring of his own safety and ready to let fly at anything that moved. As he strode, defiant, with the shells bursting before and behind, he brought down his boot on the outstretched arm of a German captain, who was lying on the ground with a hole the size of a grapefruit in his belly. He clawed feebly at Tiny's legs, and Tiny, taking him for a Russian, turned in a fury and emptied his magazine straight into the man's head. Too late, he realised what he had done. He stood for a moment, his jaw hanging slack, then fatalistically shrugged his shoulders and continued on his way towards me. The man would probably have died in any case, and God help him if the Russians had laid hands on him. And anyhow, this was war. There could be no room for regrets.

Tiny landed by my side in the shell hole and sent a shower of stinking black mud all over me.

'What's happened to your boot?' he said.

I looked down at my feet, and for the first time I saw that my right boot was hanging in shreds. It must have been torn off my foot by the blast of the first explosion. I hadn't noticed it before, but now that it had been brought to my attention I felt a great wave of self-pity sweep over me. I suddenly realised exactly how much I was suffering. Cold, wet, hungry, with an injured right foot and no boot to cover it——

'It's bleeding,' I said, and my voice was shrill with horror. 'Look at it, it's bleeding! My foot's bleeding——' I ripped off the remnants of boot and gingerly picked out the pieces of sock that were embedded in my flesh. 'I can't go about like this,' I said. 'How can I be expected to go about barefooted over this sort of country? How can I be expected to——'

Tiny thrust his face pugnaciously close to mine.

'Shut up bleeding moaning!' he snarled. 'Just fucking shut up or I'll fucking belt you one!'

I sat whimpering to myself in the mud and cradling my injured foot in my hands. Tiny gave me a look of mingled hatred and disgust. He suddenly leapt out of the shell hole and cantered away, and I thought he was deserting me, but within seconds he had returned.

'Here,' he said. 'Try those on for size.' He thrust a pair of boots at me. Boots such as I had never seen before. Pale lemon leather, soft and supple and almost brand new. I gazed at them in wonderment and awe. 'I got 'em off a dead Russian officer,' said Tiny, carelessly. 'I reckon they'll do you all right.'

I discarded my own one remaining boot, all beat up and

battered as it was, and slipped my feet into the new pair. A smile of infantile delight spread itself over my face. I turned up my toes in ecstasy. It was like wearing a couple of swansdown muffs on your feet. Amazing to think that only a few years ago, back in the palmy days of the beginning of it all, we had been fighting an army of rags and tatters; and now it was we who were in rags, it was our uniform which was in tatters, and in order to equip oneself with a decent pair of boots a German soldier must resort to pillaging from a dead Russian officer. The end of the war must surely be in sight.

There was a sudden resurgence of enemy tanks and infantry. Tiny and I sank lower in our shell hole and were forced to lie for minutes at a time holding our breath and our heads submerged beneath the filthy water.

It was late in the evening before we could make our way back to our own lines. The Russian attack had failed, but it had cost both sides dear. The ground was littered with dead and dying bodies, and already the lewd green marsh flies were bloating themselves on human flesh and blood. The flies and the rats were the only ones to multiply and prosper in times of war.

We sat watching them, unmoved by a sight we had seen too often before. Porta handed round a great stone flagon full of rather repulsive-looking liquid. Barcelona was the first to sample it, and he instantly fell back, gasping, with his fingers tearing desperately at his throat. We observed him with interest, wondering if he would recover. Porta himself had already imbibed freely of the concoction, but it was well known that Porta had a stomach of cast-iron and a digestive system that could attack and demolish even prussic acid or cyanide as if they were slices of bread and butter.

'Sod that for a laugh!' gasped Barcelona, with the tears streaming down his cheeks. 'What the bloody hell is it? Someone's lousy stinking piss?'

Porta smiled, evilly.

'Spuds,' he said. 'Rotting spuds. That's all.'

He raised the flagon to his lips and took a long draught.

Barcelona tore open his collar and began to massage his throat.

'More like rotting corpses,' he said, sourly.

'That,' agreed Porta, wiping a contented hand across his mouth, 'is more than likely ... Anyone else want a swig?'

During the night, reinforcements arrived. They were an SS rifle brigade, and the flash on their collars was the Union Jack. We studied them with undisguised curiosity, and when we heard them speaking English among themselves we could scarcely believe our ears. British soldiers in the SS? Had Churchill and Hitler come to terms at last? Had we formed a new alliance? To present, perhaps, a united front against the Russians?

'You must be bleeding joking!' A British Oberscharführer with a mass of flaming red hair turned and spat contemptuously. 'Those stupid sods in London still think they can work hand in glove with the Communists and get away with it. They still think everything in the garden's bright red and rosy.' He spat again. 'They'll find out, when it's too late.'

We listened in silent wonderment to his accent. A real live Englishman in SS uniform ...

'You got any objections?' he said, coldly.

'None whatsoever,' the Legionnaire assured him. 'It's all one to us whether you're blood brother to the King of England or a yellow-arsed git from Outer Mongolia. We were merely interested,' he said, 'to know what brought you here.'

The man scowled.

'We're volunteers. We're all volunteers.'

He plainly had no wish to talk about it, but a little Unterscharführer at his side spoke up readily enough.

'They went round the camps recruiting people. I was in Stalag VIII. I was captured after Dunkirk.'

'And you volunteered for this lot?' I said, incredulously.

'Well——' The man shrugged. 'I reckoned the way things were going, I might just as well. It seemed better than sitting on my arse doing sweet bugger all for the rest of the war.'

He looked at us, defiantly, and the Legionnaire shook his head, more in pity than reproof.

'What about afterwards?' he said.

The man hesitated.

'Afterwards?'

'That's right,' said the Legionnaire. 'Afterwards ... When the war comes to an end. When one lot of shooting stops and the next lot starts up ... When they're raking in the war criminals and the traitors, and the collaborators and the black-marketeers ... What happens then?'

The man licked his lips. The rest of his companions looked nervously in the other direction. Only the red-haired Ober-scharführer seemed to have the answer.

'Nothing happens,' he said, curtly. 'They'll still need all the fighting men they can get. Only it won't be Nazis they're having a go at, it'll be the Communists ... A year or two in the nick's the worst that can happen to us. After that I reckon we'll be going at it hammer and tongs with the Reds and they won't be able to let us out fast enough.'

The Old Man raised an eyebrow.

'There speaks an optimist,' he murmured. 'Suppose it's the Russians that lay hands on you first?'

'Well? So what if it is? So what if we tell them that the Jerries forced us into fighting for them? Who's to know otherwise?'

The Old Man smiled rather sadly. It was almost incredible that after five years of war anyone could still be so naïve.

'You'll find out,' he said. 'You'll find out ...'

With the approach of dawn we picked up our arms and took leave of the British volunteers, returning once again to our positions in the trenches. The Old Man cocked an ear in the direction of the Russian lines and turned down the corners of his mouth.

'There's going to be trouble,' he said. 'They're up to no good over there.'

We stood listening to the sounds of activity in the Russian trenches, and we knew the Old Man was right. He could always sense when a storm was brewing. It was something he felt in his bones, and we accepted his word without question.

'Won't be for a while yet,' he said. 'Let's get the cards out and have a game or two.'

Porta produced a pack, and we settled down to the inevitable pontoon. Lenzing, the Communist, was with us. He had managed to survive the various hells through which he had been dragged since Sennelager, and he had toughened up considerably in the process. He wasn't yet a soldier, but at least he was a man. There could no longer by any mistaking him for a boy of sixteen. He was now the loader on Porta's machinegun.

'So,' said the Old Man, as he handed round a packet of cigarettes, 'you were a medical student, were you?'

Lenzing inclined his head in silent acknowledgment. Porta leaned towards him, interested as always to learn the exact details.

'Ever get around to cutting people open and messing about inside 'em?' he asked.

Lenzing smiled slightly.

'No, I never got that far. They arrested me before I'd finished the course.'

'More fool you,' said Gregor, shortly. 'That's the trouble with you student types. Always bloody shooting your mouth off about something or other. Where's the point of it? Eh? Where's the point of it? Why can't you just shut up and get on with the job like the rest of us?'

Lenzing hunched an indifferent shoulder.

'You're probably right,' he said.

'Never speak unless you're spoke to,' said Porta, who was a fine one to talk. 'That's my advice, mush.'

'Yeah, but there's more to it than that,' said Tiny, earnestly. 'There's a damn sight more to it than that. You want to keep your head on your shoulders, you got to learn how to play the game. It ain't just a question of saying yessir and no sir all the time. It's more a question of not letting on you've got anything up here. Know what I mean?' He tapped a finger to the side of his head. 'Whatever you do,' he said, 'don't let 'em suspect that you got anything more than a load of old sawdust in there.

100

Take me, for example.' He picked up his two cards and slowly added the pip value on his fingers. 'Take me,' he said. 'How do you reckon I've got away with it all this time?'

'I've really no idea,' said Lenzing.

'No?' said Tiny. 'Well, look, I'll tell you. I play dumb, see? Make like I'm an idiot ... Like I don't know what's going on. Right?'

'Right,' said Lenzing, very solemnly.

Tiny bought a third card from the dealer and did another simple addition on his fingers. He smiled complacently at Lenzing.

'You know what?' he said. 'A trick cyclist once told one of my officers I was only one step removed from a moron. Meaning,' he said, 'that I was dead stupid. Meaning I didn't have no brain ... Well, a student type like you, studying to be a doctor and all, chances are you wouldn't be too happy if they told you you was a moron. Chances are you'd get your knickers in a twist. Try and show 'em different. Go round shooting your mouth off. Get yourself into trouble ... Now me,' said Tiny, blandly, 'I just played right up to 'em. And I been playing up to 'em ever since. You ask anyone what knows me. They'll all say the same. And the result is,' said Tiny, laying down a winning hand, 'no one never troubles me. I say what I like and I do what I like and no one takes no notice on account of I'm supposed to be stupid.'

'All very well,' said Porta. 'But it's not so easy for some of us. Some of us don't have your great natural advantage.'

'What's that, then?' said Tiny, looking interested.

'Having a dirty great space where your brain's supposed to be,' said Porta.

The next day, the rain started again. It came down in ropes and there was no escaping it. Arms began to rust, leathers began to grow stiff, boots began to rub and pinch. Even one's skin began to wrinkle and look waterlogged. To make matters worse, orders came through that we were to change positions. Cursing and swearing, we collected up our gear and went squelching off in the heavy mud, single file behind Lieutenant

101

Löwe. Leather straps as hard as iron cut into our shoulders. Bare feet in leaking boots began to grow sore and blister. At the head of the column, Löwe was wearing a fur-lined jacket which had been removed from the body of a dead Russian major. It still had the enemy dressings on it. No one seemed to care about such minor details any more.

Tiny was carrying the machine-gun tripod across his shoulders and was marching through the clinging mud with easy strides. Behind him, Helmuth was struggling with four boxes of ammunition. He was cursing everything indiscriminately as he walked. The rain, the mud, the Russians; Himmler, Hitler, Goering, Goebbels; the bloody British, the bloody Yanks; the rain, the mud, the Russians; Himmler, Hitler——

'What's the date?' demanded Heide, suddenly.

There was a momentary pause of surprise in Helmuth's catalogue of hatred; and then he started up again:

'Bloody Russians. Stupid bloody bastards. Stupid bloody sodding bastards. Stupid bloody——'

'I said what's the date?' screamed Heide.

'Second of September,' said Helmuth. 'Bastard bloody Russians. Bastard bloody Yanks. Bastard bloody——'

'Why?' I said, cutting straight across him. 'What the hell difference does it make if it's the second of September or the second of any other flaming month?'

'It makes a great deal of difference,' said Heide, coldly. 'It's a pity you don't take a bit more notice of what the Führer has to say.'

Helmuth stopped abruptly in the middle of his droning.

'Why? What does he have to say?'

'Only that in three months' time,' Heide informed us, 'the war will be over. The Führer promised that all troops would be back home by Christmas.'

There were loud shouts of derision from all sides.

'If that turns out to be true,' jeered Porta, 'then my prick's a bloater!'

A gloomy silence gradually descended upon us as the march continued and the rain went on falling. Even Helmuth ran out of epithets. Even Porta faded into speechlessness. My new yellow boots were caked with mud and all my clothing was sticking to me. The ground shook periodically beneath our feet as shells exploded in the distance. No one seemed to know where we were going or why we were going there. It was the general opinion that we were marching purely for the sake of marching, because they could find no better way of employing us.

We reached a patch of bogland and waded knee-deep through the muddy waters. It was difficult, once your feet were down, to pick them up again. Men heaved and grunted and lifted their legs on high, while the marshes sucked and gurgled and clung with all their might. I daresay we looked more like a troop of performing elephants than a regiment of soldiers on the march.

From time to time, when Löwe himself was mercifully too exhausted to go on, we sat on our packs on the wet ground and stared blankly into the rain with our minds as vacant as our faces. It was possible to reach a stage where thought itself was too much effort. For much of the time I marched with my eyes closed. It was a tip the Legionnaire had given me. You plodded forward automatically, step after step like a pack-horse, following the man in front. If he stopped, you stopped. If he walked into a minefield, you walked into a minefield. It was a chance you had to take. If you didn't occasionally snatch a quick forty winks on the march, you might well find yourself going without sleep for days on end.

Lieutenant Stegel, half-way down the column, was staggering like a drunkard, slipping and stumbling and swaying to and fro. He had been running a high temperature for the past four days, but they had refused to let him report sick. He hadn't been out at the front long enough to be allowed the luxury of a hospital bed. In any case, they didn't believe in his fever. It must have been obvious to even the most prejudiced observer that Stegel was in genuine distress, but he would need to lie down and die before he could hope to convince the authorities.

I suddenly heard a crash, and opening my eyes I saw that the suffering lieutenant had pitched forward into the mud, losing his helmet and his rifle. A sergeant ran to pick him up. He was hauled to his feet, mumbling and incoherent, but even with a man supporting him on either side, and relieved of the weight of his pack, it seemed doubtful that he could go on very much longer.

The Old Man was marching in uncomplaining silence alongside the Legionnaire at the head of the second section. Despite the rain, the Legionnaire had his inevitable cigarette stuck between his lips.

Suddenly, from somewhere overhead, we heard the busy drone of engines. We craned our necks and peered up into the sky, but the rain obliterated everything, there was only a grey mist and some unseen terror lurking behind it. The drone of the engines increased to a rumble, to a deafening roar, and now above the mist we could see black phantom shapes on the move.

'Storm clouds?' murmured Fischer, in his vague parsonical fashion.

'Storm clouds my anus!' shrieked Heide, and he dived for the nearest ditch.

Tiny gave Parson Fischer a shove that sent the old fellow flying. Barcelona and I followed Heide into the ditch. Seconds later the earth began to split apart as the first bombs fell. I heard Löwe shouting to everyone to take cover. I saw the ground ripped open by a long tongue of flame which ploughed a gaping furrow before it. I pressed my face hard into the damp earth with my hands over my ears to muffle the sound of the explosions. The bombs were aimed at a village half a mile away. The village was completely obliterated, and the road on which we had been marching now no more than a jagged mound of rubble.

Löwe rose cautiously to his feet and waved his hand at us to follow him. We set off again, in line behind him, picking our way over the chunks of tarmac, side-stepping the craters. The dead and the injured we left where they had fallen.

'There's a war on,' said the Legionnaire, shrugging his shoulders. He lit another cigarette and glued it to his lip. 'That's the way it goes,' he said.

The Russians had a system whereby at the end of every action they sent out a shoal of postcards with the single word 'Missing' printed on them. No soldier from the Russian Army was ever reported dead or captured. Only missing. There was, after all, a war on. It didn't do to undermine morale.

Night at last covered us with a protective black shield and we began to feel slightly safer. The rain went on falling. Lieutenant Löwe brought the straggling column to a halt, and stiff and footsore as we were we began to dig ourselves in at the edge of a forest. Fortunately the earth was soft and peaty and gave us no trouble. As we dug, Gregor began to lecture Lenzing yet again on the value of keeping your mouth shut at all times and never believing a word that anyone in authority ever said to you. The subject seemed to obsess him.

'All this crap,' he said, contemptuously throwing a load of earth over his shoulder. 'All this crap they give you about Russia being the ideal state. Communism and all the rest of it. Workers unite and let's all be jolly comrades together and so forth. It's all a load of bloody wank. It's all one bloody great fantasy.' He paused in his digging and pressed a hand into the small of his back. 'You reckon you'd be any better off in Russia than in Germany? Forget it, mate! Forget everything they ever told you. Nazi, Communist, Fascist, what the hell? They're all the bloody same when you get down to it.'

'Do I take it,' said Lenzing, cautiously, 'that even though you're not a Communist you don't care for the present régime in Germany?'

'I don't care for any bloody régime,' said Gregor, banging his spade hard into the earth. 'All I ask is to be left alone to get on with my work. At the moment there happens to be a flaming war on, so I reckon we've all got to pull our fingers out and do our best to get it finished with as soon as possible. I don't give a sod which side wins just so long as I can get back to civvy street and pick up the threads where I left off. That's all I ask.'

'What did you do,' said Lenzing, 'before the war started?'

'Me?' said Gregor. 'I drove a van, didn't I? Worked for a removal firm. Didn't do so bad, neither. The tips some of them rich bastards used to give us, just for humping a few bits and pieces of furniture about—bloody ridiculous it was!'

'You should worry,' said Lenzing.

'I should worry,' agreed Gregor.

There was a pause.

'Did it never bother you,' said Lenzing, after a bit, 'that you should have to do that sort of work? Humping furniture about for people who could afford to sit back and give you filthy great tips for doing it?'

'Why should it?' said Gregor. 'If they want to chuck their money around, who am I to complain?'

'But you don't think it's wrong,' persisted Lenzing, 'that some people should have that sort of money to burn while others are homeless and starving?'

Gregor hunched a shoulder.

'That's the way it goes, ain't it? That's the way of the world, mate. Some have it, some don't.'

'And it doesn't strike you as being unjust? You wouldn't rather see a system in which wealth was more evenly distributed?'

'Sod that for a laugh,' said Gregor. 'Who wants a world where we're all bleeding equal? It's every man for himself, that's what I say.'

Lenzing slowly shook his head. Gregor was one of those who had been brainwashed even before birth, and there was obviously little point in attempting to convert him. Gregor was just opening his mouth to make some provocative remark on the subject of socialism and sour grapes when the Old Man came running up and put an end to the discussion.

'You're wanted back there.' He gave Gregor a push. 'Look sharp, there's a bit of a panic on.'

'When isn't there?' Gregor threw down his spade in disgust and set off with the Old Man. 'What is it this time?'

'Reconnaissance behind enemy lines—and don't start whining to me about it, it wasn't my idea!'

They jumped down into a bunker, where Porta was stretched out full length on a camp bed. Gregor's eyes opened wide with accusation.

'Where'd you get that from?'

'Found it,' said Porta, simply.

Really, the man was something of a genius in his own way. The sort of person who would accidentally stumble over a crate of champagne in the middle of the Arizona Desert. The sort of person who found stray camp beds lying about in the middle of nowhere.

The Old Man pushed his feet out of the way and sat down rather wearily beside him.

'Right. This is it. Porta, Tiny, the Legionnaire, Gregor and Sven will all come with me. As soon as we've——'

'Fuck my bleeding uncle!' Porta sat bolt upright on his bed. 'Anyone'd think we were the only flaming soldiers fighting this flaming war!'

He aimed a furious kick at someone's tin helmet, and now the rest of us joined in in an aggrieved chorus.

'Yeah, why us? It's always bleeding well us!'

'Why can't some other buggers go for a change?'

'Why can't they get someone else to do their dirty work for them?'

The Old Man held up a hand and silenced us.

'Moaning and bloody groaning isn't going to make it any easier,' he said. 'Orders are orders and you know it as well as I do. Where's Tiny?'

'Gone back home,' snarled Porta. 'He said the war didn't amuse him no more. He took the first train back to Berlin and he told me to tell you goodbye for him.'

The Old Man frowned. He jerked his head irritably at me.

'Sven, go and find him—and don't be all bloody night about it!'

I ran Tiny to earth playing dice with three privates from the Fourth Company. At some point during the game they had obviously come to blows: one of the men had a black eye and another was nursing a badly bruised hand. Tiny himself reacted most unfavourably to the news I brought him. He stamped back with me to the bunker, shouting all the way, in total defiance of the order for silence.

'Look here,' he roared, as soon as he came face to face with the Old Man, 'I can't go traipsing about behind enemy lines at this time of night! I'm not well. I'm a sick man, you don't seem to realise. I've got a backache. My legs are all wobbly. My head feels like sawdust. My bones is aching. I think I've got the flu.'

'I don't care if you've got a dose of the galloping clap,' snapped the Old Man. 'I don't care what you've flaming well got. You've been given your orders and you're bloody well going to carry them out even if you have to crawl along on your hands and knees to do it!' He turned to the rest of us. 'Now, then. Shut up talking and just pay attention. These are the passwords: wooden legs and a pair of felt boots.'

'Wooden legs and a pair of felt *boots*?' I said.

The Old Man glared at me.

'That's what I said, isn't it? What's the matter with you? Going deaf or something?'

He picked up a box of grenades and began to dish them out. Gloomily, we stuffed them into our pockets and prepared to set off on our unwelcome mission.

'I don't want to hear another word from any of you!' hissed the Old Man.

Silently, resentfully, single file and sullen, we slipped out behind him into the darkness. There was a low, clinging mist which swirled about our feet and gave us all the cover we needed. We crouched, listening, in the wet grass, straining our eyes until they gradually became adjusted to the dark. From somewhere ahead we could hear muffled sounds, and we knew that the enemy lines could not be far away. The Old Man turned and whispered to us.

'We're going to move forward. Keep as low as you can and don't fire unless I tell you to.'

108

We set off again, through the mist and the gloom, with the tall grass brushing against us. From near by came the sudden alarming chink of metal on metal. Scarcely enough to frighten a bird, but more than enough to scare the living daylights out of six wary soldiers creeping through the darkness. The Old Man dropped to his knees in the grass, and the rest of us followed suit. For a long time we stayed as we were without moving or speaking, and then the Old Man whispered to the Legionnaire and the message was passed back down the line: there was an enemy machine-gun post dug in by a pylon, only a few yards to our right. Beyond that, undoubtedly, lay the first of the Russian trenches. After several moments of silence, the Old Man rose cautiously to his feet and beckoned us on.

'What the hell's he playing at?' hissed Gregor, furiously. 'We've found out where the bloody Russians are. What more does he want?'

'Fuck knows,' I said.

Disconsolate, we trailed onwards in the Old Man's wake. Even the Legionnaire, indifferent as he always was to personal danger or discomfort, began to question the wisdom of going any further.

'Be reasonable,' he urged. 'I heard what the orders were just as well as you did. We've done what we were sent to do. There's no point in pushing our luck.'

'That,' said the Old Man, grimly, 'is for me to decide. So long as I'm in command round here, we do what I say. All right?'

The Legionnaire shrugged a shoulder.

'OK, OK. No need to get shirty. I only thought——'

'Well, don't,' advised the Old Man. 'Keep it till we get back. There'll be plenty of time then to lodge a complaint.'

The pylon, with its sheltering nest of machine-gunners, was now behind us. We edged our way out of the long grass and entered the wood, where the twigs crackled and snapped underfoot like a breakfast cereal and the low-hanging branches of trees dragged bony fingers across our faces. Once more, our sodden uniforms were sticking to our bodies. Once more, our bare feet were being rubbed raw in their waterlogged boots. Shivering and trembling, we pushed on through the undergrowth. For all we knew, the whole wood might be alive with Russians, but when once the Old Man had taken an idea into his head there was no shifting it, and we could only tramp along behind him and pray that he would find himself satisfied before we had gone very much further.

Quite suddenly, he came to a stop. The rest of us piled up behind him. Silently, he motioned us into the shadow of the trees, and for one marvellous moment I thought we were going to turn back, but no such luck. We had stumbled upon the Russian front line, and the next step must be to go across and see what lay beyond.

'The old boy's losing his bleeding marbles,' hissed Gregor, in my ear.

Beyond the parapet, we could hear the low murmur of voices, the rattle of arms, men's footsteps. A twig cracked beneath Porta's feet. It went off like a gunshot in the dark night, and automatically we braced ourselves for trouble. A head appeared briefly over the parapet. We heard voices speaking rapidly in Russian. The Old Man jerked his head.

'Let's go.'

He dropped to his hands and knees, and to our horror began to crawl straight for the Russian trenches. Even the Legionnaire seemed a trifle taken aback. He hesitated a moment, and we then saw that the Old Man was making for a break in the lines, at a point where it was just possible, given an unlikely amount of luck, that we should be able to pass unseen. The Legionnaire spread out his hands in a gesture of resignation. He set off in the wake of the Old Man and we had no option but to follow him.

Our luck, amazingly, held. Even when a hare came darting out of the undergrowth, running straight through Gregor's legs and bringing him crashing to the ground, no one came to investigate. We crossed safely through the front line, and I was just beginning to breathe a little more easily when Tiny, walking at my side, unleashed one of the biggest, the boldest and the brassiest farts of all time. The Old Man turned on him in a cold fury.

'You do that again and I'll——'

Without waiting for him to finish his threat, Tiny promptly did it again. It cracked through the night like a cannon ball. Instinctively, we threw ourselves to the ground and rolled out of sight among the undergrowth. Even Tiny himself seemed somewhat appalled.

We picked ourselves up at last and cautiously moved forward, but before we had gone more than a few yards the Old Man again brought us to a halt. Somewhere in front was the sound of voices. We slid silently forward to investigate. We had come upon one solitary machine-gun, guarded by a couple of drunken Russian soldiers sharing a bottle of vodka, and we stood a while, listening as they talked. One was decidedly more drunk than the other. He was embracing the machine-gun with both arms, and in between gulps of vodka kept breaking into loud snatches of song about the Volga. His companion seemed understandably nervous. He glanced over his shoulder several times at the lurking trees and the tangled underbrush, and every now and again he said, 'Hush, hush!' and pushed the vodka bottle into the man's mouth to shut him up. Finally, when the bottle was empty, he flew into a panic and threatened to knock his head off if he didn't keep quiet. With drunken dignity, the man shouldered his rifle and staggered to his feet.

'I shall take a turn,' he said.

He clambered over the parapet and came singing and swaying in our direction. Angrily, his companion hurled the empty vodka bottle after him. It narrowly missed Gregor and landed with a thud at Porta's feet. The Old Man tapped Tiny on the shoulder and nodded at him. Tiny nodded back. He slipped away in the darkness to deal with the drunken prowler. The Legionnaire pulled his knife out of his boot and disappeared in the direction of the machine-gun.

Minutes later, we were camouflaging a couple of corpses beneath a pile of damp leaves. One had been strangled with a thin strand of wire; the other had a knife in his ribs. We

111

stripped them of their weapons and pushed them out of sight. It would be some time before their companions discovered they had gone, and their first thought, in all probability, would be that they had deserted. Our first thought, without any shadow of a doubt, was to return to our own lines post haste. Gregor even turned to go without waiting for the Old Man to give the order, and got bawled out for his pains.

'We return when I say,' said the Old Man, coldly, 'and not before.'

'Not ever, the rate you're going,' muttered Porta, mutinously.

The Old Man ignored him. It always was best to ignore Porta. He was a law unto himself, but an excellent soldier for all that, and the Old Man was not the first to discover that it was worth putting up with his continual insolence and lack of discipline for the sake of having him at your side in a crisis.

We moved on, deeper into the woods. It was the Old Man's avowed intent to discover what lay on the far side, but by now we were beginning to view the whole expedition with a distinctly cynical eye. I had visions of him marching us all the way to Moscow just to take a look at the Kremlin.

At last the trees began to thin out and we knew that we must be approaching open country. We reached the edge of the wood, and there, spread before us like a patchwork quilt, was what appeared to be the entire Russian Army. A constant stream of men and vehicles were coming and going. It was not what I personally should have called a heart-warming spectacle, but it seemed to give the Old Man something of a thrill.

'Good, good,' he murmured, rubbing a hand reflectively over his chin. 'That's fine ... We can be getting back now.'

All of us except the Legionnaire and the Old Man himself at once turned tail and ran. Tiny and Porta went galloping off into the wood with Gregor and me only a few yards behind. We caught up with them unexpectedly when they were tempted to pause in their headlong flight in order to investigate three dead bodies in a shellhole. Three dead officers, two Russian and one German. Tiny and Porta exchanged glances.

'Can't be bad,' said Porta.

Together they jumped into the shellhole and began greedily to ransack the bodies in search of money and mementoes. Porta went through the pockets while Tiny yanked open the mouth to look for gold fillings. They had stripped them almost bare by the time the Old Man and the Legionnaire appeared on the scene. The Legionnaire looked on dispassionately, but the Old Man, as usual, went almost berserk.

'Get out of there this instant! Leave those bodies alone! I've told you before, I won't stand for this sort of thing, it's disgusting, you're like a pair of wild animals! God damn it, you're worse than wild animals!'

'All right, all right,' said Porta, amiably. 'Keep your wig on. You'll give yourself a rupture, carrying on like that.'

'What's all the fuss about?' demanded Tiny, for all the world as if the Old Man were not there. 'Sure as eggs is eggs, if we didn't nick the stuff someone else would.'

With a howl of rage, the Old Man sprang into the shellhole beside them. As he did so, the night sky above us was suddenly illuminated by a flare, and instinctively we all dived for cover.

'They're on to us,' said the Legionnaire, grimly. 'Now we shall have some fun.'

Somewhere, a machine-gun started up. A shower of rockets tore up into the heavens and transformed night into day.

'Scatter!'

We needed no second bidding. We took to our heels and raced hell for leather through the woods, crashing through the undergrowth, squelching across the boggy ground, tearing ourselves to shreds on thorns and brambles. We met up at last in an abandoned machine-gun post. Only Gregor was missing.

'Where the hell is he?' asked the Old Man, irritably. 'Where the devil has he got to? Did anyone see him?'

No one had.

'I'll go and take a look,' said Porta.

The Old Man at once shot out a hand.

'I forbid you to move from here! That's an order!'

'Get stuffed!' snarled Porta, shaking him off.

He disappeared into the trees, back the way we had come. We could hear him shouting as he ran.

'Gregor? Where the bloody hell are you, you bloody fool?'

Instantly, the clamour of the Russian guns started up again. Tracer bullets and flares flew overhead. The Old Man hesitated just a moment, then swore softly under his breath and sprang out into the open in pursuit of Porta. The rest of us immediately followed. We had been through too much together during the long course of the war to leave Gregor to the mercies of the Russians.

Menacing shapes appeared in the darkness. Porta scattered a handful of grenades and went on running. The rest of us surged after him. We discovered Gregor crouched all by himself in a foxhole, and we hauled him out indignantly.

'What the bloody hell do you think you're playing?' demanded the Old Man. 'Sitting down there twiddling your thumbs as snug as a bug in a blasted rug while we go chasing round in circles looking for you with nine million screaming Russians on our tail——'

'It wasn't my fault,' said Gregor, sullenly. 'I had the whole pack of them after me. I can't be expected to take on the entire Red Army single-handed, can I?'

'It would have served you bloody well right,' snapped the Old Man, 'if we'd left you there to rot!'

The rest of the journey was accomplished without incident. On the way back, Tiny informed us that according to Heide, who always knew everything there was to know and a great deal more besides, we were shortly to be sent to Warsaw.

'There's a hundred thousand British paratroops there, that's what Heide said ... one hundred thousand British paras, and the whole town swarming with Polish soldiers ... we'll be there by the New Year, that's what Heide said.'

'Oh yeah!' jeered Porta. 'I thought we was all going to be back in Germany in time for Christmas?'

It took us the better part of an hour to reach the comparative safety of our own lines. The Old Man went off to make his report, while the rest of us collapsed on to our mattresses to snatch what sleep we could. In the event, we couldn't snatch any at all. Barely had we closed our eyes than the Old Man reappeared and shook us awake again.

'I'm sorry, lads. They're not through with us even yet.' He spread out his hands in an apologetic gesture. 'The Pioneers are going to try to break the enemy lines and we're being sent along to back them up.'

Porta's camp bed almost collapsed with the shock. For a moment, we were all too flabbergasted to speak.

The Old Man smiled rather wearily.

'I'm well aware that I'm not doing too well in the popularity stakes just at the moment, but I'm afraid it can't be helped.' He hunched a shoulder. 'There is, after all, a war on——'

'Get away!' said Porta, with heavy sarcasm. 'Who told you that?'

Gregor sat up and stared round piteously with sleep-crumpled eyes.

'Why send us?' he complained. 'Why send anyone at all? Why can't they clear the bloody place up with napalm?'

'Because we're running low on ammunition,' said the Old Man, shortly. 'I'm sorry, but that's the way it is. There's nothing I can do about it. It's no use looking at me like that, I didn't start the flaming war ...'

Sullenly, we filed one by one out of the trench and fell in behind Lieutenant Löwe. We were carrying only essential assault kit. When you worked with the Pioneers, you worked fast: you didn't clutter yourself up with any unnecessary gear. It seemed that on this occasion we were not even to be given the usual support of tanks. The war was growing grim indeed.

We found the Pioneers, five companies of them, constituting one battalion, all ready for the off and variously strung about with hand grenades, stick grenades, small arms, and a few napalm bombs of Russian origin. One company was armed with flame-throwers. They had a bad reputation, these Pioneers. We found them a strange, silent, uncommunicative bunch, and were only too willing to believe all the stories of

115

their gratuitous cruelty both towards the enemy and one another. They ignored us completely from the moment we arrived, and when Porta asked if anyone had a cigarette to spare it was an officer who handed one over, holding out a packet without a word, without even glancing in his direction.

'What's the matter with 'em?' demanded Gregor, irritably. He turned on a dour-faced corporal who was picking at his teeth with a horny fingernail. 'What's the matter with you? Lost your bleeding tongues, have you?'

A fair enough question, one would have thought, but for some reason the corporal chose to take exception to it. Within seconds, he and Gregor were at each other's throats, and from then on it was only a matter of time before everyone else was joining in. Tiny was just on the point of choking the life out of some terrified private when an angry voice called us to order, and we turned reluctantly to see who it was that was spoiling the fun.

It was our old friend the Major, who had had the contretemps with Colonel Hinka. He stood with his legs apart, his hands on his hips, looking us over with a cold, reflective eye as if we were a load of specimens for the research lab. Behind him, his face expressionless, stood Lieutenant Löwe.

'If I were you,' said the Major, drily, 'I should reserve all your strength for murdering the enemy rather than one another. I can assure you that this is going to be no Sunday school outing.' His eye roved round and suddenly lighted on Porta. 'My friend the talkative corporal!' he murmured. 'Step forward and let me take a look at you. We must get better acquainted, you and I ...'

Porta pushed his way belligerently to the front. The Major stared for a moment at the yellow top hat which Porta would insist on wearing wherever we went. He had had it since the beginning of the war, and officers who were wise learnt to live with it.

'Take that abomination off your head!' snapped the Major. 'What the devil do you think this is? A fancy-dress ball?'

'I'm afraid I wouldn't know, sir.' Porta removed his top hat and held it respectfully before him like an undertaker. 'I've never been to one, sir.'

'Don't be impertinent, Corporal! How long have you been in the Army?'

'Too long, sir. Far too bloody long.'

The Major's eyebrows snapped together.

'Be more precise, Corporal!'

'Yes, sir.' Porta stiffened his legs and clicked his heels. 'Permission to consult my military papers, sir?'

The Major made an impatient noise in the back of his throat. I saw Lieutenant Löwe hastily convert a broad grin into a smothered yawn.

'Are you a bloody cretin, Corporal?'

'Yes, sir.' Porta bowed his head, apologetically. 'I was once examined by an army head-shrinker in Potsdam, sir. He gave it as his considered opinion that I was congenitally feeble-minded. He said in his opinion I was incurable. He said I oughtn't to be let loose with other men. He said I——'

'Oh, for God's sake, Corporal, shut up!'

The Major gave up the unequal struggle. He turned on his heel and stalked away, followed by Lieutenant Löwe, who was struggling again with a yawn. Porta smiled, thoughtfully. He replaced his top hat and winked at Lenzing, who had been watching him with a certain reluctant admiration.

'That's the way to do it,' he said. 'Drive 'em stark staring raving bloody bonkers if you keep on long enough ...'

The order for action came through and the Pioneers tightened their belts and prepared to move. The Major, busy sending men to almost certain death, sat in security in a dugout and chewed on a big cigar. The Russian artillery sounded strong and healthy compared with the feeble and spasmodic bursts of fire from our own depleted guns.

We watched as the first of the five companies were sent into the field to be butchered. They were commanded by a lieutenant who had the grey, sunken eye of a nonagenarian set in the smooth face of a young boy.

We watched as they emerged from the trenches and went

running straight into the mouths of the enemy guns.

'Bloody suicide,' said Barcelona, standing at my elbow.

'Bloody murder,' I said, thinking of the Major in his dugout smoking his big fat cigar.

They were blown to pieces before they had advanced more than a couple of hundred yards. Only one small group, headed by a sergeant, succeeded in reaching the objective. Coldly and calmly, with apparent indifference to the hail of gunfire all round them, they tossed their grenades into the enemy lines and ran for cover.

When the dust had settled, there was no sign of the sergeant and his men. Only a wide sweep of devastated land, and here and there a headless body, a human trunk with no arms and legs, a pile of twisted metal, a heap of charred flesh. It was not enough for the Major. He called up the second company, commanded by a Lieutenant Kelz, and sent them off in the wake of the first. They traced the same path, running through the same smoke and the same bullets, running through hell to be killed by the Russians, trampling underfoot the scattered limbs of their dead companions. A handful survived. Barely a handful. A few scattered men forced a small breach in the enemy lines and went down fighting.

The Major chewed his big fat cigar to ribbons and frenziedly called upon the next company. Their commanding officer was young and new and keen. Fresh out of the school at Gross Born and eager and willing to die for a lost cause. He raised his arm above his head and went galloping off into the arena, yelling at his men to follow him. Like well-trained performing animals, they did so.

The first salvo caught the young officer in the stomach. The second sliced off both his feet at the ankles. He went on running on the two bloodied stumps for several yards, still waving his arms and screaming encouragement. No doubt as he died he had visions of the Holy Iron Cross ...

The attack was repulsed. The flame-throwers were thrown into the action, but before they had reached half-way a rolling sea of phosphorus came belching forth to meet them from the

118

Russian lines. They ran in circles with their clothes on fire, they lay writhing like snakes on the ground and the flesh fell off their bones and stripped them clean and white. Only six men returned from the inferno. One was the lieutenant who had led them.

'I'm sorry, sir.' He stood downcast before the Major, his face blackened with smoke, his uniform charred, his hair and his eyebrows singed. 'I'm sorry, sir, but it's just not possible to get across——'

'Not possible? Not possible? What the devil do you mean, not possible?' The Major snatched the ruins of his cigar from his mouth and crushed them underfoot. 'By God, I'll have you shot for this! Cowardice in the face of the enemy! You're a disgrace to the German Army!'

'I'm sorry, sir. We did our best——'

'Best? You call that your best? It's a bloody disgrace!'

'In that case, sir, permit me——'

A shot rang out, and the Lieutenant crumpled up at the Major's feet. His revolver fell from his hand and went clattering across the ground. The Major made a noise of exasperation. He glared round at the few remaining officers and his glance fell on the youngest of them.

'Dietel! Lieutenant Dietel!'

'Sir?'

'Get out there and show those bloody Russians that the German Army is still a force to be reckoned with! Show me, for God's sake, that I still have at least one officer who can be relied upon to carry out an order!'

Dietel was not of the stuff from which reckless fools are made. He had no wish to throw away his life on a hopeless mission. But an order was an order even when it was a death warrant, and he had no choice but to obey. He walked tight-lipped to the door. The Major clapped a benevolent fatherly hand upon his shoulder.

'Show them what we're made of, my boy! No need to be scared of the scum!'

Lieutenant Dietel and his men set out on their last journey,

119

covered by our machine-gun fire. Before they had gone even a quarter of the way, they were in trouble. The Major instantly condemned Dietel as a fool and a coward, who would be shot on the spot if he dared come back alive. He turned savagely on yet another officer.

'All right, Plein, it's up to you! Get out there and clear up the mess that those snivelling swine have made of things!'

Lieutenant Plein hesitated just one second, and then quite suddenly he plunged forward into the chaos, roaring at his men to keep up with him. Through the smoke and the flames we saw him striding onward. Shells exploded at his feet, bullets whistled past his head, and still he was there, in the midst of it all, fighting like a demon, screaming at a heap of corpses to get up and walk, shooting at a sergeant who tried to run away, advancing ever nearer to the Russian front line.

The enemy flame-throwers were wiped out. We saw Lieutenant Dietel blown to pieces. We saw Lieutenant Plein and a group of men reach the first of the trenches and engage in savage hand-to-hand fighting. The Siberians were like robots, trained to kill or be killed. They fought with a cold determination, unemotional, impassive, indifferent to either life or death. Plein and his men were having their last fling. They seemed intoxicated with the heady joy of slaughter. Corpses began to pile up, one on another, German and Russian indiscriminately. Men with their throats slit, men with their bellies ripped open, men with their heads hanging by a thread from their shoulders.

When the killing was done and the small band had been obliterated, the Siberians calmly wiped their knives clean of blood and took up their positions over again. Only one man survived to regain the German lines, and he dropped dead at the Major's feet even as he opened his mouth to make his report.

'Fools!' screamed the Major. 'Fools and cowards! Nothing but incompetent fools and cowards!'

He stormed away to the field telephone, and we heard him yelling and hectoring down the line, complaining that his battalion was made up of fools and cowards and that he would need far better artillery support than he had been getting up until now if he were ever to stand any chance of achieving a breakthrough. He haggled like an old woman in an eastern market-place over the number of mortars he would need before he would consent to launch another attack.

'Ten? Did you say ten? Don't be so bloody ludicrous, man! What kind of support do you call that? It wouldn't hurt a flea ... Make it twenty and I might consider it ... I said make it twenty and I might consider it ... Well, all right, fifteen then. If that's the best you can do. Make it fifteen, and God help you if you let us down!'

He threw away the receiver and rounded up the shreds of his battalion for his final onslaught. The first of the grenades started to go over, and the familiar débris of men and armaments began spouting into the air on the far side of the battlefield. The Major stood counting, with one arm raised. As he reached fifteen, he abruptly dropped his arm and leaped forward into the fray. He slipped and fell, scrambled to his feet, waved an arm over his head and ran on with the remnants of his Pioneers streaming after him.

This time, the attack succeeded. The Russians fell back under the onslaught. Hand grenades were tossed into communications trenches and bunkers. Explosives were thrust into the gaping mouths of cannons. Sub-machine-guns chattered and barked, men decapitated one another with spades and shovels and ran one another through with bayonets. The Major was discovered with a fresh cigar in his mouth, lying on his back by the side of a Russian officer. Both were dead. They were but two among a thousand who had died that day.

Before we could consolidate the hard-won position, a new attack was launched by the Siberians. Hordes of them descended on us from nowhere, little slant-eyed men, thickset and broad-shouldered, with short legs and long arms, shouting in raucous voices in praise of Stalin. We fought them in the trenches and out of the trenches, slipping and squelching in the blood and guts of the dead, but the Siberians were stolid and

121

immovable and slowly but surely they pushed us back the way we had come.

All about me men were stumbling, falling, sobbing as they ran. A grenade rolled towards me and I narrowly escaped treading on it. I jumped sideways like a startled horse, snatched it up and hurled it into the midst of a pack of oncoming Siberians. The blast threw me sideways and I landed in a crater, directly on top of a fresh-killed body, lying nose to tail in a pool of its own blood with its head hanging limp and its belly ripped open and spilling out its contents over my feet. I gave a shrill scream of horror and scrambled out again. I began running in mindless panic, but it seemed that the Siberians were all round us, they were firing from all directions at once and I could see no road to safety. And then suddenly I caught sight of Porta, moving backwards and firing from the hip as he went, and I stumbled across towards him, in and out of shell holes, sliding and slipping in pools of blood and oil, in my haste to be at his side. I felt calmer the moment I was with him. Porta was one of the untouchables. Porta was indestructible. Impossible to imagine an enemy bullet ever finding its mark in that tough, scrawny body. So long as I was sheltered behind him, I would be all right.

We continued our headlong flight, retreating to God knows where. At one point we came across Parson Fischer, wandering in the wilderness with a gaping hole in the side of his chest through which his lung could be seen. One of his fellow-WUs came crawling across the rubble towards him.

'Don't worry, old man, we'll get you back safely. We'll see you're all right. We won't let you die ...'

It seemed somehow to be desperately important to this man that Parson Fischer should not die. Perhaps in a way he had become a talisman. A symbol of hope. If he could survive, then so, surely, could the rest of them. As long as Fischer lived, it meant that God had not entirely abandoned them.

A stretcher-bearer came running up, but upon seeing that Fischer was a WU he instantly turned and went off in search of someone more worthy of his help. Morphine was scarce, and

122

it could not be wasted on the likes of Parson Fischer.

'Let me die,' said the old man. 'Leave me here and let me die. I am not important.'

His companion hauled the Parson's arm over his shoulder and began painfully to drag him towards the illusory safety of a shell hole.

'You're not going to die. I'm not going to let you die. I'm going to get you back, I'm going to get you into hospital, I'm going to see that they give you proper treatment if it's the last thing I ever do . . . Don't moan like that, old man! For God's sake, don't moan! I'm doing my best, what more can I do?'

They fell together into the shell hole. Parson Fischer lay with his head in his companion's lap, his blood staining the ground. Somewhere near by a shell exploded. Behind them in the forest a machine-gun started up.

'So how's it going, old man? Say something to me. Say something to me! Say anything you like, but talk to me, for God's sake! Don't leave me here on my own!'

The Parson's face was grey and sunken. His lips were growing blue. Another shell exploded, a little nearer than the last.

'It won't be long now, old man. Is the pain any better?'

Perhaps it was. Perhaps the pain was better. Parson Fischer was silent now. His eyes were closed and his mouth was hanging open. The blood seemed not to be pumping out so fast as it had been.

'Why don't you pray, old man? Why don't you pray for us, eh? It can't do any harm . . .'

It couldn't do any harm. It might even have done some good. But the time for prayer had come and gone. Parson Fischer was dead at last.

'The best political weapon is the weapon of terror.
Cruelty commands respect. Men may hate us if they
will. We do not ask for their love; only for their fear ...'

Himmler. An address to SS officers at Kharkov.
19th April 1943.

NICOLAS KAMINSKY was a former schoolteacher from
Briansk, in the Ukraine. His mother was Polish, his father
German, and he was fiercely loyal to the Nazi cause. During
the winter of 1941/2 he set out with a handful of like-minded
fanatics to wage war against the partisans. He was thirty-five
years old, and his cruelty became a byword. He was self taught
in the art of killing slowly by degrees and was reputed to have
invented more tortures than the Chinese had.

Himmler heard of him through Obergruppenführer Berger,
and instantly began to take an interest in him. He had him
brought to Berlin, where he developed a considerable respect
for the man's ability to inflict pain upon his fellow-human
beings. From that moment on, the Ukranians achieved almost
equal status with Germans in the eyes of the Reichsführer.

Kaminsky's career was meteoric. Despite the initial handi-
cap of not belonging to one of the superior Germanic races, he
nevertheless became an SS Brigadenführer and divisional general in the Waffen SS in little under three months. His powers
were such that not even the highest-ranking officers in the
Army dared speak out against him.

Towards the end of 1942, General Kaminsky conceived the
idea of making a German republic of the province of Lokot,
which was at that time overrun with partisans and guerrilla
fighters. His brigade consisted of six thousand men, mostly
deserters from the Russian Army. It was composed of eight
infantry battalions, one tank battalion, two sections of artillery, one section of Cossacks and a company of pioneers. In
less than two years, Kaminsky and his six thousand had con-
founded their critics by sweeping the province of Lokot clear
of all troublemakers and annexing it to Germany.

In the spring of 1943, Himmler had the Brigade transferred to the region of Lemberg, in Poland, and there Kaminsky surpassed himself, spreading death and destruction wherever he went. His name became synonymous with hatred and with terror; but 'we do not ask for their love; only for their fear ...'

DOWN THE SIDE OF THE MOUNTAIN

'SERGEANT BEIER! Sergeant Beier!'

We were playing a peaceable game of pontoon when we heard the call. Porta raised an eyebrow at the Old Man, and the Old Man continued calmly to smoke his stinking pipe and study his hand.

'I'll buy another,' he said. Tiny gave him a card. A slow smile of satisfaction spread itself over the Old Man's face. 'I can't bust,' he said, and he laid down his hand on the ammunition box that served as our table.

Tiny scowled and threw a fifth card towards him.

'Sergeant Beier!' The call came again. 'Has anyone round here seen Sergeant Beier?'

I closed up my cards and made as if to throw them away.

'I think someone's shouting for you,' I said. I had a vague sort of hope that we might be able to chuck the hand in. I had been dealt an ace, and it had gone to my head. I had staked the whole of my next year's pay on a ten or a court card turning up to go with it, and had ended up with a handful of rubbish. 'Some chap from an anti-tank section,' I said, twisting my head round to see.

He noticed me looking at him and came up at once.

'Sergeant Beier?' he said. His eyes rested a moment on each

one of us in turn and settled at last on the Old Man. 'Are you Sergeant Beier?' he demanded. 'I've been looking for you for the past thirty minutes! Where the hell have you been?'

'Right here all the time,' murmured the Old Man. 'What's the panic?'

'You're to get your section together and come with me. Lieutenant-Colonel Schmeltz is already on the way with an assault group, and you're supposed to be joining them. They're over on the far side of the river. I'll show you the way.'

'Go and get knotted,' said Porta, without taking his eyes off the cards. 'We've got better things to do ... twist me one, and make it small——'

Tiny obligingly turned up a six. The Old Man stared wistfully at his five-card trick, torn between the call of duty and the lure of a large sum of money. I was in the same position myself, but in my case the choice was somewhat easier to make. I flung down my cards, snatched up my rifle and hastily jumped to my feet, accidentally overturning the ammunition box as I did so. Tiny looked at me sourly.

'Some of us are mighty eager to go off and get themselves killed,' he said.

'Not at all,' I retorted. I crammed my cap on my head and pulled my belt a notch tighter. 'I just don't like the thought of keeping a lieutenant-colonel waiting.'

'Friend of yours?' sneered Tiny, who knew perfectly well that I had been sitting there with a handful of rubbish and praying for deliverance.

Porta's old mate Wolf turned up to watch us go.

'My compliments to Old Nick,' he said. 'Looks like you'll be meeting up with him before I will ...'

I had an uncomfortable feeling that we probably should. For all my expressed anxiety not to keep Lieutenant-Colonel Schmeltz waiting for us, there was something about this particular mission that I instinctively disliked.

Our guide hustled us across the bridge in a hail of shellfire. On the other side of the river the ground rose quite steeply, and before we had gone very far we found ourselves in single file struggling up a narrow slope which seemed almost vertical.

'Talk about the bleeding Devil,' grumbled Tiny, as we puffed and panted and slipped all over the place. 'More likely to meet Saint bleeding Peter the way we're going.'

Our guide turned his head to look at him.

'You could well be right,' he said. 'You could very well be right.'

The Old Man paused for a moment to get his breath.

'What exactly is this?' he demanded.

'What is it?' The guide also paused. He planted his hands on his hips and smiled derisively. 'Well may you ask! It's a bloody suicide mission, that's what it is. If you take my advice you'll cut loose and get the hell out of it just as soon as you can, and before the Reds come down and cut you off.' He jerked his thumb back towards the bridge. 'How much longer do you think that's going to be there?'

The Old Man stood frowning.

'How about you?' he said.

'Me?' The man laughed. 'I'm shoving off again the minute I've got you safely up there, don't you worry! I'm not staying to see the bloodbath!'

We reached the top at last and reported to the Lieutenant-Colonel, who looked like something left over from the Flood. His veined hands trembled and his eyes were sad and baggy. Doubtless war was not what it used to be in the days of his youth.

The captain of the regiment we were relieving gratefully handed over to the Colonel.

'This path here,' he said, pointing to the narrow slope up which we had just toiled, 'is the only route the Russians can use to mount an attack. There's no other way up or down. As you can see, it can easily be held by a couple of machine-guns. We don't usually get into any trouble at night, it's a bit risky, but during the day——' He paused, and shrugged. 'Well, any-how, you should be able to hold it a few hours longer. That's all that's necessary. Just a few hours, that's what the General said ... Just hang on until you see the signal to pull out, and then run like bloody hell. We'll send up three flares. Three green flares. The minute you see them, give the order for retreat and get back to the bridge at the double before it's blown up. There's no other way across the river, so you don't want to run the risk of getting yourselves cut off.'

We took up our positions as indicated to us by our guide. High up in the rocks where we now were, there were naturally made parapets and loopholes. The captain and his men pulled out. All round us were boxes of ammunition, baskets of mortar grenades, piles of mines and hand grenades.

Tiny jumped about in the midst of them like an excited child, liberally helping himself to a little of everything.

'So this is where they've been hiding it!' He snatched up a fistful of grenades and began juggling them. 'I haven't seen nothing like this since 1937!'

'God knows what it's all doing up here,' said Barcelona, who had been silent and disgruntled ever since we arrived. 'Fat lot of chance we'll ever have to use any of it.' He waved a hand down the hillside. 'We're nothing but sitting ducks, perched up here on this lump of bleeding rock. A blind man with a pea-shooter could hardly miss us.'

'Why don't you give your arse a chance and shut up bleeding moaning?' said Porta. 'At least we're out of those piss-awful sodding trenches.'

'I'd sooner be sitting in a trench than stuck up here for target practice,' retorted Barcelona.

Porta ignored him. He settled himself comfortably within a circle of rocks, took out his square of green baize and spread it over the ground.

'Anyone fancy a game?' he said.

The Legionnaire and the Old Man joined him. I picked up a cow-bell which was lying about and experimentally shook it. The noise it made sent everyone diving for cover with their hands pressed against their ears. I have to admit, I was a bit disconcerted myself.

'You do that once more,' panted Barcelona, as the last clanging echoes died away in the mountains, 'and you'll get my boot right up your flaming arse!'

Gingerly, I laid the bell on a patch of grass.

'How did I know it was going to make such a bloody awful racket?' I said. 'I'm not a perishing cow, am I?'

I sat and brooded while the rest of them resumed their interrupted game of pontoon. From time to time the Colonel came doddering round to take a look at us. Despite all the years behind him, it seemed that this was the first time he had ever been nobbled for the front line, and it was plain he was scared to death.

Tiny was still dragging round his appointed slave, the ex-Gestapo, Adam Lutz. By now, the man was but a pale shadow of his former fat self, but by some miracle he had survived without so much as a scratch.

'I reckon this is going to be your big chance,' Tiny kindly informed him. 'When they sound the retreat and the rest of us start pulling out, I'm going to leave you here to cover the pass and shoot as many Russians as you can. All right? Just stay put and fire like buggery until you run out of ammo. They'll give you a medal for that.'

Lutz nervously licked his lips. Porta gave him an evil grin.

'Don't you worry, mate. You'll go down in the annals of history, you will. You'll make this Regiment famous. There'll come a time when they'll all be reading about you in their picture books ... "ex-Gestapo Adam Lutz, who threw himself fearlessly into the midst of the oncoming horde. Although his left leg was blown off at the crutch by a Russian shell, he picked it up and waved it round his head like a club ... He succeeded in slaying six hundred Siberian soldiers before he received his mortal blow, but tucking his head under his arm he fought on bravely for as long as his heart continued to pump ..." Jesus God,' said Porta, wiping the tears from his eyes, 'ain't that moving? To think that the Fatherland can still produce such heroes!'

'Talking of heroes,' said Gregor, 'I wonder what's happened to old man Weltheim?'

'Weltheim?'

We looked at him, blankly. Who was Weltheim?

'The name does ring a slight, far-off bell,' admitted the Legionnaire.

It was not until Gregor jogged our memories that we realised who he was talking about: Walter Baron von Weltheim, our divisional commander, who had briefly inspected us in the mud and marshes of Matoryta, and had then gone on his way with his grand piano and his two lorry-loads of personal effects and never been seen or heard of since. The Legionnaire hunched a shoulder.

'He'll be safe and sound in some gold-plated bunker, no doubt. Sozzling gin and working out how he can give the order for yet another strategic retreat and still manage to make it sound like a victory.'

'He's probably already given it,' said Barcelona, gloomily. 'The entire ruddy Army's probably pissed off out of it by now. We're the poor stupid sods left behind as a farewell gesture. Stuck up here on a lump of bleeding rock miles away from nowhere waiting to be slaughtered.'

'Anyone as miserable as you are,' said Tiny, 'deserves to be bleeding slaughtered. Why don't you stay behind with Lutz and earn yourself a medal?'

The Colonel was still restlessly pacing to and fro, waiting for the signal of the three green flares which never came, but shortly after midnight the horizon suddenly burst into flames and the rocky ground rumbled and shook beneath our feet as the Russians opened up with their heavy artillery.

'What the devil is going on?' cried Schmeltz, snatching up his field glasses. 'Who the devil is firing at whom?'

'It's the Russians, sir.' The Old Man, calm and sure of himself as always, took his stand at the Colonel's side. 'They're moving up to attack while the troops are pulling out. They'd be mad not to. It's the chance of a lifetime.'

He stared dispassionately across at the smoke-filled horizon. The Colonel dropped his field-glasses.

'What should we do?' he said. 'They were going to give a signal. They were going to fire rockets for us. We were to stay

130

here until we saw the flares——' He passed a hand across his brow. 'What do you suggest we do, Sergeant? You probably have more—ah—experience of this sort of—ah—terrain than I have. You have been in the area far longer. Tell me what you think we should do.'

'Fuck the flares and get the hell out,' muttered Porta.

The Old Man raised a warning eyebrow. He turned to the trembling Colonel.

'I think we probably ought to go down and see what's happening, sir. See if the bridge is still there. I can't see we're doing any good staying up here, and I really don't——'

The sound of an explosion suddenly ripped through the night, cutting off the rest of the Old Man's sentence. Everyone rushed to the parapet to look over. Geysers of flame were spouting into the air all the way along the skyline.

'The bastards!' screamed Barcelona. 'The bloody bastards! They've blown the bloody bridge!'

I looked at the Colonel's face. It was grey and scaly, and his lower lip was twitching.

'I reckon that's it,' said the Old Man. 'I reckon we've left it too late, sir.'

'Nonsense!' The Colonel drew himself up very straight. 'Nonsense, Sergeant! They would never blow the bridge without first giving us the signal.' He gestured nervously with a paper-thin hand. 'Take these three men with you and go down there and see what's happened. I shall follow on with the rest of the Company.'

'Very well, sir.' The Old Man turned towards us. 'Sven, Tiny, Porta——' He slung his rifle over his shoulder and jerked his head in the direction of the river. 'Let's go.'

'Us *again*?' I said.

'Fuck that for a laugh,' muttered Porta.

The Old Man turned on him, furious.

'Will you kindly keep your bloody mouth shut and just do what you're told?'

Porta mutinously slapped his yellow top hat on to his head and set off in the Old Man's wake, using his rifle as a walking stick. Tiny slipped and fell going down the steep slope of the rocks, and his machine-gun went clattering ahead of him, making a noise like a thunder peal. Tiny's shouted oaths went ringing after it.

'For Christ's sake!' said the Old Man, irritably.

Barcelona leaned over the parapet and called down to us.

'Why don't you just pick up a loudspeaker and tell 'em you're coming?'

The rest of the Company caught us up before we had gone very far. It seemed they had decided among themselves that they had waited long enough, and accordingly they shouldered arms and set off, leaving the Colonel to follow them or not as he would. It was obvious that the man was quite unfit for command.

'Knicker-brained old goat,' muttered Porta. 'He should have been preserved in pickle many years ago.'

The night was warm and heavy, and we sweated as we descended the same narrow path up which we had come only a few hours earlier. The mosquitoes were abroad in their multitudes, rising from the marshes which lay below. We could smell the familiar sweet, rotten stench of the bogs, and we knew that somewhere down there was the enemy.

From way ahead of the rest of us, Tiny suddenly fired two warning shots, and we guessed he must have caught wind of the Russians. The Colonel shouted a vague, hysterical order, but men had already followed what had become instinct and were leaping to the side of the path, taking up their positions, setting up machine-guns and mortars.

I saw Lutz crouched behind a boulder. He was shaking so violently I could hear his teeth chattering.

'Look at him,' jeered Barcelona, who had regained all his usual good humour now that the time for action was upon us. 'Like a bloody rice pudding!'

Gregor crawled up to the man and stuck his revolver threateningly into his ribs.

'Just remember,' he said. 'One false move and you're for the high jump, mate ... we don't go too much for the Gestapo round here.'

A whole series of shots resounded from further down the path, and then the Old Man suddenly appeared. He looked round for the Colonel, located him in a ditch, and calmly went up to make his report.

'Russians all over the place, sir. We don't stand a chance in hell of breaking through. We've managed to wipe out one small section, but the whole area's lousy with 'em ... I reckon the best thing we can do is sit tight and wait to see which way they jump.'

Before the Colonel could reply, the sky over our heads was suddenly illuminated with a bright light. Full of joy, the Colonel started to his feet.

'The signal——'

'No, sir.' The Old Man held him back with a restraining hand. He pulled him down again just in time to avoid another flare which burst over our heads. 'It's the enemy, sir, trying to locate us.'

Not a single man moved. We stayed where we were, hidden among the rocks, while the flares hovered overhead for what seemed an eternity. Gregor kept his revolver pressed hard into Lutz's ribs. The Old Man respectfully hung on to the Colonel in the safety of the ditch. The slightest movement could have betrayed our presence.

The last flare went shooting high into the night. It rose in an arc above us, showering us with its light, and slowly, very slowly, fell away across the river and burnt itself out.

'Right, sir.' The Old Man helped the Colonel out of the ditch and began to stuff tobacco into the bowl of his pipe. 'I think perhaps we ought to prepare for action, sir——'

Most of us were already occupied. Heide and the Legionnaire were laying T mines down the length of the narrow path. Porta was busy preparing Molotov cocktails. Gregor and Barcelona were camouflaging the mortar beneath branches of trees. It was stationed well back from the road and was pointed in the direction from which the Russians must come. Tiny was sitting on a rock happily attaching hand grenades to sticks of explosive. As weapons they were verging on the suicidal, but they made a good loud bang and that was enough for Tiny. He seemed cheerfully unconcerned at the prospect of having his head blown off or his arms wrenched out of their sockets. No one else would go anywhere near him.

The Colonel bustled busily from group to group issuing a series of contradictory orders, all of which were discreetly cancelled or corrected by the Old Man going round after him. He reached Tiny, who was perched on his rock playing with his box of hand grenades. He turned in horror to the Old Man.

'Sergeant, does this corporal of yours know what he's doing? Is the man feeble-minded? Is he aware that he is about to blow himself up?'

'That's all right, sir.' The Old Man edged the Colonel nervously away from Tiny and his lethal toys. 'It's just his idea of fun.'

'Fun?' said the Colonel. 'Is the fellow a cretin?'

The Old Man was spared the trouble of replying. From somewhere below us a machine-gun opened up, and we could hear pieces of broken rock cascading down the hillside.

'That's it,' said the Old Man, calmly. 'They're on their way.'

Heide suddenly came scrambling up the slope. He put a finger to his lips and pointed silently down the path towards a clump of bushes. We all squinted at them in the semi-darkness. The Old Man raised an eyebrow.

'Well? What are we supposed to be looking at? Just a handful of lousy bushes——'

'A handful of lousy bushes that weren't there half an hour ago,' said Heide.

The Old Man looked again.

'Are you sure?'

'Bloody positive. That area was nothing but rocks.'

The Colonel clicked his tongue impatiently.

'Stuff and nonsense!' he said. 'What is the matter with your men, Sergeant? Are they all sub-normal?'

The Old Man frowned.

'Sergeant Heide is one of the best soldiers in the entire Regiment, sir.'

It was quite true. The man may have been a louse and a bastard and a Nazi into the bargain, but call him what you like there was no denying his skill as a soldier. (Despite his fanatical belief in the Party, he was to end up, twenty years after the end of the war, as a lieutenant-colonel in the Russian Army. Not bad for a child of the Berlin slums!)

The Colonel stared haughtily at Heide.

'Are you trying to tell us that a whole plantation of trees has suddenly sprung up out of nowhere?'

'Bushes, sir,' said Heide. 'They're bushes.'

'Bushes or trees, Sergeant! What difference does it make? Have you ever heard of a bush that grows at the rate of five feet an hour?'

'No, sir, I haven't,' said Heide. 'I'd be a great deal happier if I had.'

The Old Man suddenly drew in his breath. All eyes were instantly trained on the mysterious shrubbery below. As we watched, a couple of the bushes uprooted themselves and walked. They shuffled forward a few yards and then settled down again. Another pair followed them, and then another and another. Lutz gave a frightened yelp, and Gregor closed a hand over his mouth. Tiny picked up one of his home-made weapons. The Colonel stood gaping.

'When I give the signal——' said the Old Man.

He held up a hand. We all watched him like hawks. His arm fell, and one hundred and thirty-six hand grenades were sent hurtling through the air. The walking bushes shrieked in agony. Dark shapes were seen bounding off among the rocks. The noise of the explosions died away, and the dust settled on a chaos of torn flesh and severed limbs. The Legionnaire went off to examine the remains.

'Mongols,' he said, on his return. 'Ugly-looking bastards. Still, we seem to have scared them off all right.'

'Don't worry, they'll be back,' said the Old Man, grimly.

We settled down again, nervously awaiting the next at-

135

tempt. The Colonel seemed unable to keep still and persisted in marching up and down tearing at his fingernails. Porta was trying to play dice in the dark, right hand against left, and Barcelona sunk back into his former mood of disgruntlement.

'One Mark a day,' he was saying. 'One Mark a bleeding day. Join the Army and have your brains blown out, and that's all you get for it ... and me with another twenty years to go! Jesus God Almighty, I must have been mad. I must have been off my rocker. I must have——'

He stopped abruptly as Tiny suddenly made a dive for the machine-gun and began firing frantically into the gloom. The Old Man sent up a flare. By its light, we could see what Tiny's sharp ears had heard. Bundles of grass moving slowly up the hillside ...

They were barely thirty yards away, and as Tiny opened up with the MG they abandoned their attempts at camouflage and came running towards us up the path. They were Mongols, all right. I could see their slanted eyes and their broad, flat cheekbones. Strange soldiers of the Russian Army who could scarcely speak a word of Russian.

'Fire at will!' shouted the Old Man.

The Colonel was screaming his usual stream of inanities, but fortunately they were drowned out by the noise of rifle fire. Sergeant Koblin and Corporal Lutz, working without steel gloves, were shoving one grenade after another into the mortar and never seemed to notice their burnt and blistering hands. Heide had snatched up a flame-thrower and was firing in short, accurate bursts into the midst of the oncoming Mongols. The grass was scorched and the path running with blood, but as fast as one man fell, another came leaping up to take his place.

A line of Russian infantry now appeared behind the Mongols, and we picked them off like flies. There is nothing more deadly than attacking on an open slope. They had no form of cover, no protection of any kind, and yet still they kept on coming, wave upon wave of them into the slaughter. I wondered why the enemy should be trying so hard to eliminate us,

136

one solitary company, abandoned and forgotten in the general flight of the German Army.

'Fire low!' called the Old Man. 'Sighting three hundred.'

It was a massacre. In such conditions, it could scarcely have been anything else. Not even the sheer weight of numbers could compensate for our superior position, at the top of the narrow track. When danger point was reached, we simply activated the mines which had been so carefully laid by Heide and the Legionnaire. The resulting blast made us stagger. Great cracks appeared in the path, and a landslide of rocks and rubble tore down the hillside, carrying half the enemy along with it. The other half either fled or were left behind to die. We hurled ourselves after them down the slope, with Tiny in the lead, firing at anything that moved and shouting and hallooing like a maniac.

An enemy officer, with the red star gleaming on his fur cap, suddenly stepped out from behind some rocks and raised both arms over his head. He was holding an S mine in each hand, but before he could throw them, a shot rang out and his face shattered in fragments like broken glass. Porta laughed sardonically and lowered his rifle. Eyeless and faceless as he was, the man still tried to drag himself over the ground towards us. Tiny gave an exultant shriek and plunged the point of his bayonet into him, pinning him to the ground. It seemed that all the world had gone mad. We were killing in a frenzy, killing for the sake of killing, wallowing like animals in a bath of blood.

Slowly, the hillside fell silent. The enemy had departed, and there was nothing left to kill. Only the dead and the injured to dispose of. We could hear the moans of dying men as we trailed back to our rocky plateau, and Heide picked up a can of petrol, unscrewed the cap, and tossed it down the slope towards them.

'What are you doing?' screamed the Colonel, who had so far taken no part in any of the night's activities. 'What the devil do you think you're doing? Lighting a funeral pyre?'

Heide bowed his head.

'It seemed the easiest way, sir.'

'The easiest way? What do you mean, the easiest way?'

'To clear the place up, sir.'

'Clear the place up?' The Colonel was almost beside himself with indignation. 'There are wounded men out there, Sergeant!'

Almost imperceptibly, Heide hunched a shoulder.

'I hear them,' he said.

'I forbid you to kill any of those men!' snapped the Colonel. 'For God's sake, if we must fight a war let us at least try to keep it clean!'

'Just as you wish, sir,' said Heide, with arrogant indifference.

It was just as well the Colonel did not see Tiny and Porta slipping off together into the darkness, their pliers in one hand, wash-leather bags in the other, to go pillaging for gold teeth and fillings. The Old Man had tried too often in the past to put an end to their sordid post-battle forays. Now he just shrugged his shoulders and let them go.

'There'll come a time,' he said, 'when their greed will cost them dear.'

Not this time, however. They returned with quite a little goldmine, bitterly complaining that it was always the enemy who possessed the most profitable mouths, never the Germans.

'On one Mark a day,' said Barcelona, sourly, 'it's scarcely surprising, is it?'

The Colonel came flouncing up again. He was trying to organise a burial party. We stared at him, blankly. We were liable to come under attack again at any moment. Did he really expect us to go back down the hillside and start digging holes in the rock?

'Sergeant, what is the matter with your men?' The Colonel turned angrily to the Old Man. 'Have they all come from a lunatic asylum? Have you no control over them? Have you no——'

Tiny suddenly held up a hand and made an impatient gesture for silence. The Colonel stared at him with eyes like dartboards. Could it be that this cretin of a corporal was actually daring to interrupt a lieutenant-colonel in the middle of a sentence?

'Sergeant,' he said, in a menacing tone, 'if there is very much more of this impertinence, I shall be forced to——'

'Belt up, can't you?' said Tiny. 'I can hear tanks.'

'Tanks?' shrieked the Colonel. He rushed to the parapet and leaned over. 'Did you say tanks?'

We all stood listening. As usual, Tiny was proved correct. It was not long before the rest of us could also hear the grinding of tank tracks, and could feel the hillside faintly shaking beneath us with their approaching bulk. The Colonel pressed the back of his hand to his mouth.

'We're done for,' he said. 'If they're sending tanks against us, we're done for.'

'We probably were in any case,' said the Old Man, prosaically. 'Tanks or no tanks, we never stood much of a chance.' He stuck his empty pipe into his mouth and sucked on it a while. 'I'm buggered,' he said, 'if I can understand why they're taking so much trouble with us. What could they possibly want with this miserable lump of rock?'

'Has it occurred to you,' said the Legionnaire, coolly, 'that they may be out for blood because they think we're SS? In which case'—he ran a finger across his throat—'God help the lot of us.'

There was a pause.

'Why?' said Lenzing.

We all turned to look at him.

'*Why?*' said Gregor, as if he could hardly believe his ears.

'Why God help us?' said Lenzing.

The Legionnaire placed a paternal arm about his shoulders.

'Because, my dear child, if we fall into their hands they will butcher us by very slow and painful degrees, that's why ... They certainly won't take any prisoners. They won't even be merciful enough to put a bullet through the back of your head. They'll string you up and torture you until you're on the very point of death, and that's how they'll keep you for just as long

139

as they feel like titillating themselves . . .'

The Colonel edged back from the parapet.

'What the devil are we to do?' he demanded, a trifle fret-fully.

The Old Man chewed thoughtfully on the stem of his pipe. 'We can't fight 'em,' he said. 'A handful of men can't com-pete with an army of tanks, that's for sure. And I certainly don't advise surrender, unless you have a fancy to be strung up by the knackers and left to rot——' The Colonel swallowed uneasily, and the Old Man took his pipe from his mouth and stood frowning at it. 'Try it and see, if you don't believe me, sir. Those little slant-eyed bastards, they're not like ordinary human beings. They don't just kill, they pull you to pieces bit by bit and laugh while they're doing it. I've seen the results of some of their handiwork. It's not a very pretty sight.'

'So what are you advising?' said the Colonel. 'Mass sui-cide?'

'I'm advising that we pull out,' said the Old Man. 'Stay and fight as long as the ammo lasts, and then pull out.'

'And which way do you suggest we go?' asked the Colonel, with heavy sarcasm. 'Straight back down the hill into the arms of the Russians?'

'I had thought,' murmured the Old Man, 'of finding some other way . . .'

'There is no other way! You know that as well as I do. If there were any other way, we should doubtless have taken it long ago. Do try to talk sense, Sergeant! We obviously can't go down by the same route we came up, and since that's the only route there is, it seems to me to be quite senseless to talk of pulling out.'

'Excuse me, sir, but there is one other route.'

The Old Man pointed with the stem of his pipe towards the far side of the parapet, directly opposite the path by which we had come, and up which the Russian tanks were now advan-cing. The Colonel let his mouth sag open.

'But that's madness! That's lunacy! It's almost a sheer drop! We might just as well try flying to the moon and have

140

done with it!'

'Well, of course, if that's the way you feel, sir——'

'Eh, Old Man!'

Tiny suddenly appeared reeling and staggering across the rocks. He was clasping a bottle to his chest, and he was uncertain on his feet. He collapsed with one arm affectionately round the Old Man's shoulders, and there he hung, reeling and hiccupping and attempting to push the bottle into the Old Man's mouth. The Colonel regarded him with horror and contempt.

'Sergeant Beier, is this man drunk?'

'I believe he is, sir.'

The Colonel leaned forward to investigate. He received the full blast of an intoxicated belch, and took a hasty step backwards.

'This is disgusting, Sergeant Beier! This is a disgrace! Your men are like pigs! They are worse than pigs! They are lower than the beasts of the field! They are not fit to be in the German Army!'

'One Mark a day,' said Tiny, suddenly remembering Barcelona and his grievance. 'One lousy sodding Mark a day.' He raised the bottle to his lips and drank deeply. 'It just ain't worth it,' he said. 'There ain't nobody could afford gold teeth on one Mark a day.'

The Colonel made a noise of suppressed displeasure somewhere in the back of his throat.

'I shall report this man,' he said. 'If we ever manage to get out of this mess alive, I shall make it my business to do so.'

He turned sharply on his heels and strode off towards the far edge of the parapet to study the sheer drop which was to be our escape route. Kuls, one of our stretcher-bearers, nervously approached the Old Man.

'You're mad,' he said, hoarsely. 'You're a raving nutter. We'll never get down that mountainside in one piece. If I had my way, we'd show the white flag right here and now before they get to us——'

'Fortunately,' snapped the Old Man, 'you're not very likely

141

to get your own way!'

'You'll regret this,' said Kuls.

'You'd regret it yourself,' retorted the Old Man, 'if you tried negotiating with that load of homicidal maniacs down there. Don't be such a fool, man! They'd tear you to pieces in no time.'

He walked across to the Colonel and stood gravely at his side.

'Well, sir? Can I ask what decision you've come to?'

The Colonel shrugged. He knew, and all the rest of us knew, that the decision had already been made for him. If the Old Man said we went over the side, then we went over the side. It was as simple as that.

'We shall hold the position as long as we can.' The Colonel turned away from the parapet and stood pulling at his chin agitatedly. 'As long as we can, Sergeant. Mark that. As long as we can. There must be no disgrace attached to our withdrawal.'

'Naturally not, sir.'

The Old Man respectfully lowered his head. A flare was sent up, and by its light we could see a long line of T34s making their way up the hillside towards us. Fully-grown pine trees were snapped like twigs and cast disdainfully aside. Vast boulders and chunks of rock were dislodged and sent crashing down into the valley. Each tank was smothered in infantrymen, hanging on by toes and fingernails, great clusters of them draped over the rear hatches like bunches of human grapes.

The sight of the enemy seemed suddenly to have sobered Tiny. He was no longer reeling and hiccuping. I saw him, quite steady on his feet, making his way down the path towards the oncoming tanks, with T mines and grenades slung over his shoulder.

Lenzing was following the Old Man like a puppydog and appeared loth to let him out of his sight.

'You reckon we're going to get out of this alive?' he said, with a show of careless bravado which deceived no one.

'Could be,' said the Old Man, calmly sucking on his empty

142

pipe. 'Could well be ... Just keep your head and try not to
panic. When we've dealt with the first few tanks, remember,
there'll still be the infantry to reckon with. Try to keep them
at bay as long as you can. And no ideology, eh? Those murdering bastards down there are no more your blood brothers than
Himmler is mine. So shoot to kill, and just remember that it's
either you or them, and that's all there is to it ... Pass me that
box of grenades, there's a good lad.'

'I'm scared,' said Lenzing.

The Old Man smiled.

'Who isn't?' he said. 'Fear's nothing to be ashamed of. Just
don't let it get the better of you, that's all.'

The first of the tanks were coming within striking distance,
their long cannons trained upon us. The leader skidded several
times on the narrow path and seemed on the point of crashing
down into the abyss below, but the tracks held and it managed
each time on the very brink of disaster to right itself.

We stood in our stronghold waiting for them. The Old Man
had put his pipe in his pocket and was chewing thoughtfully
on a wad of tobacco. Little Lenzing was still at his heels,
clenching his fists and frowning fearsomely with the effort of
keeping his nerves under control. The very sight of him made
me feel almost sick with fear myself.

In a crevice in the rocks Porta was busy opening a tin of
meat with 'Produce of the USA' written on the label. Porta
always stuffed himself silly before a battle. He claimed it was
a nervous reaction. According to all the best medical advice, a
man should never go into battle on a full stomach. It appears
it's not too healthy if you get your guts ripped open, there's a
danger of peritonitis setting in. But Porta declared he'd sooner
face a quick death with a good meal in his belly than a slow
death half starved. I watched him now as he dug out chunks of
bright pink meat with the point of his bayonet and washed
them down with a bottle of sake, which he had taken from a
dead Mongolian. He finished the first tin and instantly prised
his way into another. I couldn't make out what it was, but
from the way he was shovelling it in he seemed to be enjoying

it. It made me want to heave just watching him.

The leading tank crawled slowly onwards. Suddenly, from nowhere, Tiny appeared. He darted forward, clapped a magnetic mine under the belly of the tank and dived back headfirst into his hiding-place. The explosion was almost instantaneous, and even as the dust and the débris was settling the second T34 came ploughing its way through—men and metal churned up together in its tracks. A shower of grenades rained down upon it, and it was the clinging groups of infantrymen who were hit. They slithered and slipped off the sides of the tank in time to receive the third of the monsters which ground them up beneath it before they had a chance to disentangle themselves from the blood and bones of those who had gone before. I heard Lenzing catch his breath, and I looked across at him. Sentiment would avail him nothing. Let him keep all his pity for himself: he was likely to need it before very long.

The Legionnaire went tearing down the path towards the leading tank. He hurled a petrol bomb at the turret and threw himself to one side, rolling behind a pile of Russian corpses for protection from the blast. A long blue flame leapt skywards from the crippled vehicle. The hatch burst open and a man appeared, but before he could jump clear he was blown to pieces along with his companions who were trapped inside.

A shell from the third tank suddenly burst somewhere behind us. I spun round to see what damage had been done, and found a gaping hole in the earth where a second earlier Sergeant Litwa and his men had been. The entire group had been wiped out. Within the crater was a tangled mess of human remains, unidentifiable obscenities that made your guts rise up into your mouth even as you looked.

I turned back hastily to my post. I saw Tiny reappear, clasping a couple of mines in his right hand. He sprang on to the tank and hammered on the hatch with the butt of his revolver. The hatch opened cautiously and a face peered out. Tiny instantly rammed it down again. He thrust the mines after it, slammed the hatch shut and threw himself over the back of the vehicle, all in one quick, practised movement.

The Old Man waved his arm over his head and shouted at us to follow him. We streamed after him, down the hillside, with bayonets and flame-throwers. The Russian infantry were in a state of confusion, but they were backed up from below by heavy mortar fire. I saw Sergeant Blaske running forward, plunging over the body of a wounded Mongol. He tripped and fell, and before he could scramble to his feet the man had tugged the pin out of a grenade and blown them both sky-high.

Down in the valley the ground was shaking with the thunder of artillery fire. There must have been heavy fighting along the river. I wondered if the bridge had been blown or whether it was still standing, but either way it was a purely academic question, since we had no earthly means of reaching it.

The mortars were now beginning to find their length, and we were forced to retreat to the plateau. Porta came running past me, followed closely by Tiny. He waved a hand and yelled to me.

'What are you hanging around for? Let's get the hell out of it!'

'What about the wounded?' panted Kuls, who had decorated himself with a Red Cross armband in the hope that the enemy would thereby treat him with respect.

'Fuck the wounded!' shouted Porta, over his shoulder.

The Colonel said nothing. He could hardly have missed hearing Porta's words, but he must have known as well as anyone that it was quite impossible to take wounded men over the parapet with us. We had neither the time nor the necessary equipment to lower them by ropes and stretchers. There were no footholds in the smooth face of the rock, and it was going to be a question of launching oneself over the top and trusting to luck that we would reach the bottom without too many broken bones.

Heide was still fighting his own rearguard action over on the far side of the parapet, running amok with a flame-thrower. The Colonel was creating havoc among the rest of us by firing off a succession of flares, with which he seemed suddenly to be obsessed. He was evidently under the impression that he was lighting our way down the sheer slope of the mountainside. But with the constant swinging to and fro from brightness to blackness we were thoroughly confused and dithered about on the edge like a pack of mentally deficient sheep. The night itself was not so dark that we could not pick out the general shape of things, but the flares were too dazzling, they blinded rather than illuminated. The Colonel strode up to the Old Man in a state of self-righteous fury.

'What the devil is the matter with your men, Sergeant? Do they want me to carry them down there on my back? If they don't make a move pretty quickly, I shan't have any more flares left . . .'

Heide came running towards us.

'Time to go!' he said, and without more ado he flung himself over the edge and disappeared.

In a shower of dust and stones, the rest of us followed. I found myself instinctively curling into a ball with my hands over my head, bumping and bouncing from one outcrop of rock to the next, never knowing when I might be hurled into space. Some slid down on their backsides and tore themselves to shreds. Others attempted to snatch at trees and bushes as they hurtled past and had arms almost wrenched from their sockets. I heard Porta screaming with manic glee as he zoomed downwards like a human bobsleigh. I heard a bloodcurdling yell of terror as someone else was thrown clear into the void, disappearing to God knows where. I found myself gathering momentum, scarcely aware any longer whether I was still in contact with the hillside or whether I was falling into the gaping chasm below. And then my headlong flight down the mountainside was brought to a sudden and shattering halt by a pine tree. I went crashing into it when I was doing what must have been about fifty miles per hour. My helmet flew off and went racing on down the mountain all by itself, bouncing from rock to rock, while I hung gasping to the trunk of the tree and wondered how many bones I had broken. Blood was pouring from my nose and my mouth. I felt sick and giddy and almost paralysed with terror. From somewhere below me came a shout.

'Get a move on up there! I'm not going to wait all day for you!'

It was Porta. Still alive and in one piece, perched on a slab of rock and beckoning impatiently to me.

'Come on down! You can't spend the rest of the war sitting half-way up a mountain!'

I wrapped both arms round the trunk of my pine tree and crouched there, shivering with fright, snivelling like a baby and dripping blood all over myself.

'Oh, for God's sake!' snapped Porta.

He clambered up towards me, and still I held on tight to my tree and whimpered self-pityingly.

'You're going down this perishing mountain if I have to throw you down!' snarled Porta.

He pushed his bottle of sake into my mouth and forced me to drink. And then, when I was half choking and almost purple in the face, he tore my arms away from my protective pine tree and set off again down the steep slope, dragging me behind him. It was easier now, there were patches of coarse grass and a few stubby bushes growing out of the rock, there were footholds and handholds and a man could at least control the speed and the direction of his descent. But my nerve had been broken and I shouted and fought the whole way down to the valley, where I was met by Tiny and slapped soundly across the face until I managed to pull myself together.

'I should bloody well think so,' he said. 'Bloody awful racket.'

We collected ourselves up at the foot of the accursed mountain. We were a sorry-looking lot. Tattered and torn, with an assortment of bruised and broken limbs, uniforms ripped from top to bottom, faces covered in blood and dust and half our equipment wrenched away in our landslide descent. From far above us, from the other side of the plateau which we had just vacated, came the steady pounding of artillery. The enemy had obviously not yet discovered we had fled, and we had a

147

few moments' breathing space.

I threw myself to the ground, my heart still hammering against my ribs. Slowly I became aware of the racking pains in my body. The whole of my right side was bruised and battered. My head was cut open, my lips were hanging in shreds, my nose was swollen to twice its normal size. But it could, of course, have been far worse. I could have broken my back, or shattered a leg so I'd have to be shot like a horse. There was no way of taking the badly injured along with us. A man either kept up or he fell behind, and that was the end of it. We were in no condition to carry passengers.

There was a sudden lull in the firing, and the Old Man hauled himself to his feet.

'Let's go,' he said, abruptly.

We strung out behind him in a long, limping line. The Colonel was still with us, marching grimly, head down, by the side of the Old Man. We left the valley and passed through the bottom of a narrow gorge, where we found ourselves up to the waists in a glutinous bog. Several of those who lost their footing floundered deep in the mud and were never seen again. There was no time to stop and organise rescue parties. It was each man for himself. You struggled on as best you could and had no energy left for anything other than your own survival.

We left the bog and cut across the middle of a cornfield. To one side of us lay a burning village. To the other side lay the river, and the Russian artillery. The Old Man pressed relentlessly on. I staggered and stumbled and would have fallen but for Gregor who gave me a hearty kick.

'Pick your feet up, you stupid clumsy sod!'

I wiped the sweat from my forehead and the blood came cascading down my face, dripping into my eyes and half blinding me. The straps of my pack were cutting into my shoulders, rubbing them almost raw. I could hear my own breath coming and going in great gasping sobs, and the black night suddenly turned vivid scarlet before me. I stumbled again, and this time Gregor's infuriated kick had no effect. I lay where I had fallen, with my head on the cool earth. Let them go on without me. I wanted no more part in it. Let the Russians capture me and do with me what they would. I was beyond caring.

'Shoot that man!' screamed the Colonel, galloping past me on his way to round up the stragglers. 'The advance must continue!'

'Advance?' sneered Porta. 'I thought it was a strategic withdrawal?'

The combined efforts of Gregor and the Legionnaire hauled me to my feet. Tiny forced open my mouth and poured half a bottle of singularly repellent liquid down my throat. It was so utterly vile that I vomited it all up on the spot and at once felt a great deal better. God only knows what it was. I never had the courage to inquire.

Another half mile and we were on the edge of a forest. We dragged ourselves thankfully into the welcoming shelter of the great trees and hacked our way through the undergrowth into the comparative safety of an encircling thicket. There at last, as the dawn rose, we were able to find peace. You could hide an entire army in a Polish forest, and we were but one depleted company. The Russians would never find us there, unless by some most unhappy accident.

We stretched out on the ground, and the earth was as soft and as welcoming as a feather bed, and the sheer luxury of being able to relax was almost enough to convince a man that life was after all still worth living.

*'We shall not flinch from the shedding of blood, be it
foreign blood or be it German blood, should the nation
so demand it of us.'*

> Himmler. Article in the *Völkischer Beobachter*,
> 17th January 1940.

PELAGAJA SACHAROVNA, captain of the NKVD and liaison
officer for the Polish partisans of Lublin, had endured seven-
teen hours of torture at the hands of the SS. Not until they
held her naked body over an open furnace did they manage
to break her resistance—and even then she passed out before
she could tell them anything.

They brought her round by douching her with icy water.
The burns on her back were deep and searing, and a judici-
ously placed finger was enough to make her scream in agony.
She had been a beautiful woman before her torturers had been
let loose upon her. Dirlewanger himself had slept with her on
several occasions. Now there was nothing left of her former
glory; nothing but the ugly wreckage of humanity, degraded
beyond the limits of what is endurable. A body flayed raw and
burnt to the bone, and a creature that moaned and called out
for death.

When at last she had told them all that she knew, they put
her out of her misery with a bullet through the back of the
neck.

THE POLE

WE had been in the forest for thirty-six hours, and it was
raining again. It had started shortly after we arrived, and it
showed no signs of letting up. It dripped off the trees and ran

in torrents down the rutted paths of the forest. The ground was soft and spongy, it squelched as we walked on it, and then men at the back of the column found themselves having to splash through muddy water ankle deep.

We stopped for a rest in an area of dismal brown marshland, and Porta took off his boots and wrung the water from them. Heide, to the astonishment of those who did not know him, took out a cleaning kit from his pack and began solemnly to scrub and polish himself. He removed his boots and scraped them free of mud. He examined the soles and discovered that three of the thirty-three regulation studs were missing. But naturally, being Heide, he carried a spare tin of studs with him wherever he went. Having fixed up his footgear, he next turned his attention to his uniform. He sponged dry blood off the sleeve of his jacket with a piece of rag dipped in a pool of rainwater. He brushed the mud off his trousers. He counted all the buttons he could find, and then solemnly pulled out a rag and began polishing them. Even the Colonel sat watching him in unconcealed fascination.

'Any minute now,' said Porta, 'and he'll start checking his pubic hairs to make sure they're all present and correct.'

Heide laid down his brushes and his cloths. He buttoned up his tunic and he smoothed back his hair and he turned, very slowly, to contemplate Porta. He let his gaze run up the length of the mangy body, from the bare black feet with their horny nails, to the unshaven face and the matted hair that was caked with mud. He didn't say anything. He just gave a cold, superior smile and began to reassemble all his cleaning kit.

The Colonel leaned across excitedly to the Old Man.

'Tell me, sergeant,' he whispered, 'is there something wrong with that soldier?'

'Wrong?' said the Old Man.

'Up here,' said the Colonel, and he tapped significantly at his forehead with one bony finger. 'Something loose in the top storey, eh?'

The Old Man allowed himself a faint smile.

'Not really, sir. He's just what you might call a Living

151

Rule, as it were.'

'A living rule, Sergeant?'

'Like in convents, sir——'

'Ah! Aha! Yes, indeed, yes.' The Colonel slowly sat back, never once taking his gaze off Heide. 'Frightening,' he said. 'Positively frightening.'

Private Abt, who had been a schoolteacher before joining the Army to do his not very useful bit for the Fatherland, had been hit by a bullet in the thigh. It had passed right through and left two clean, neat holes, but the way he was carrying on you'd have thought he'd had his whole leg amputated. He lay moaning on the ground calling out for morphine, while men far worse off than he sat silently in pain because they knew there was nothing to be done for them. We had no morphine, and hadn't had any for some time. Private Abt was very well aware of the situation, but still he went on whining and groaning and driving us all mad.

I wondered how many of his pupils he had beaten into submission in the good old days before the war, when any child who flinched from pain was accused of cowardice, when boys were taught that suffering would make men of them, when tears were punished by ten regulation strokes of the cane. I wondered how many of Abt's former pupils were now coming to manhood on the battlefields of Europe, while Abt lay on the wet ground and slobbered and snivelled with a bullet hole in his leg. It was easy enough to rear and train cannon fodder for the Führer, but not nearly so easy when you yourself were being fed into the mouths of the Russian guns.

Tiny, who had been sitting next to Abt, suddenly walked across to the Colonel and stood to attention before him. The Colonel looked up, mildly amazed.

'Yes, Corporal? What is it?' It was some time since anyone had taken any notice of the Colonel. He seemed both surprised and gratified. 'Speak out, man! I shan't bite you!'

'Well, sir,' said Tiny, 'it's not for myself, you understand, but for him over there——'

He gestured towards Private Abt, who was still histrionically clutching at his leg and writhing on the ground.

'Yes, yes?' said the Colonel, eagerly. 'What is wrong with him?'

'Well, he reckons as he's dying, sir, and he keeps on nagging at me to come and ask you if you don't think it'd be a good idea if we—er——' Tiny glanced across towards Abt, who anxiously nodded his head and made unmistakable gestures of encouragement. Tiny shrugged a contemptuous shoulder. 'Well, all right, then,' he said, turning back to the Colonel. 'He reckons as we ought to surrender, sir. Give ourselves up, like. Call it a day and go over to the other side ... on account of he thinks he's dying, sir. He says he's made a study of the Reds and they're not nearly as bad as what everyone says they are. He says they're civilised people same as us and they——'

'Oh, he does, does he?' The Old Man leapt to his feet and strode angrily across to Private Abt. 'Snivelling little rat! Haven't you been in the Army long enough to know by now that if you've any suggestions to make you make them to me, you don't go bothering senior officers!'

He picked the man up by the collar and shook him, while the Colonel watched with wide eyes and said nothing. I had never seen the Old Man lose his temper like that before. I think perhaps he didn't place too much importance on the Colonel's strength of mind. It only needed some yellow-bellied punk like Private Abt to go putting ideas into his head and before we knew it we might all be handed over to the tender mercies of the civilised Russians. The Colonel meant well, but he was old and he was frightened, and he should have been pensioned off some time before the First World War.

The Old Man flung Abt away from him, slinging him towards Tiny, who received him with wide open arms.

'All right, Corporal Creuzfeldt, he's all yours. From now on, he's under your command. He does whatever you say, and if you catch him trying to escape, shoot the bastard in the back.'

'You bet!' said Tiny, enthusiastically.

We set off again, single file behind the Colonel and the Old

Man, skirting the edge of the marshes. Thanks to his persistent whining, Private Abt was now far worse off than he had been before: Tiny had loaded him up with half his own gear plus the machine-gun tripod into the bargain, and the man was bent double beneath his burden. Lutz, finding himself temporarily forgotten, had slunk off to the tail end of the column, as far away from Tiny as he could possibly get, and was keeping very silent.

Half-way down the column, Porta and Heide were exchanging obscenities and threatening to punch each other's heads in. Heide had accused Porta of deliberately pushing him into the bog in order to mess up his newly polished boots. It was more than likely true. Porta certainly wasn't bothering to deny it. He was merely jeering and sneering and generally goading Heide into one of his states of manic wrath, and they were on the point of flying at each other's throats when the Old Man held up a hand and brought the column to a sudden halt.

'What is it, what is it?' demanded the Colonel. 'Why have we stopped? What have you heard? Where is it coming from? What are we——'

'For God's sake, shut up!' said the Old Man, tersely and without ceremony. It at least startled the Colonel into a temporary silence. The Old Man beckoned Tiny to the head of the column, and the two of them stood listening.

'Sounds like dogs,' said Tiny, after a while. 'I reckon they must be out looking for us.'

'With dogs?' said the Colonel. 'What utter rubbish! Stuff and nonsense!'

He was, as usual, ignored. The Old Man began giving orders.

'The rest of you had better stay put. I'll take my section up ahead and find out what's going on.'

'Us *again*?' said Gregor.

We crept silently forward through the forest. I could hear now for myself the occasional whimpering and whining of dogs, and as the trees began to thin out we could see that we were approaching a small village. The Old Man waved us to

154

another halt, and we crouched in the undergrowth while he surveyed the scene through field-glasses. I could make out four large trucks with American markings, and a group of men wearing the green uniform of the NKVD, the dreaded equivalent of the German SS. At the head of the group, tugging at their chains and obviously eager to be off, were half a dozen dogs, fierce-looking creatures rather similar to Alsatians but larger and heavier. Probably some Siberian breed, judging from the thickness of their coats.

'Well, they're obviously not just out for a Sunday afternoon stroll,' observed the Old Man, drily. 'I reckon it must be us they're after.'

'If they'd offer us a good square meal and a bed for the night,' muttered Gregor, 'we'd be theirs for the asking, without all this stupid fuss and bother.'

Private Abt limped up, eagerly.

'Why don't we try it, now that we're here?' he said. 'If we gave ourselves up voluntarily, as an act of good——'

He was cut short by a savage blow on the head from Tiny.

'Any more of that and I'll throw you to the dogs myself! Get that machine-gun set up and be quick about it.'

'OK.' The Old Man turned and motioned to us to take up our positions. 'Porta, your group stays here with me. Gregor, you take your men and spread out on the left. The rest of you, be ready to fire the minute I give the signal.'

We crouched among the trees, waiting for the unsuspecting Russians to come within range. The dogs were whining and straining to go, having evidently picked up our scent.

Porta was eating again. He had opened his last tin and was greedily licking his lips.

'Bully beef,' he said, as he saw me looking at it. 'You want some?'

'Not right now,' I said. 'I don't much care for the smell of it just at this moment.'

Porta buried his nose in the tin and inhaled ecstatically. It smelt to me like a million city dustbins. No wonder the dogs were so anxious to be off. Half the animals in Poland were probably twitching their nostrils and turning their heads into the wind.

Private Abt was sitting on the damp grass complaining again about his leg. The bullet holes had now turned blue at the edges and his thigh had swollen up like a sausage, but by now we had reached the stage where we didn't care if his entire leg dropped off. It would, in a way, have been a relief. At least he'd have had nothing left to moan about.

'You know what you want for that, don't you?' said Barcelona, solemnly.

'No, what?' Abt looked up at him with a gleam of hope in his piggy schoolmaster eyes. 'What do I want?'

'Sheep piss,' said Barcelona. 'Old country remedy. Works wonders. Find yourself a castrated ram and get it to piss all over you ... Cure it in no time.'

He strolled nonchalantly away, with a happy smile playing on his lips, and Abt struggled wildly to his feet.

'Bastard!' he yelled. 'Bloody bastards, the whole goddamned lot of you!'

'All right, all right,' growled Tiny, pushing him down again. 'Keep it for the Russians. Don't waste it on us.'

Away to my left, Gregor was in the middle of telling Lenzing some long and garbled story of how he had once moved a grand piano from the fifth floor of a house down a spiral staircase without getting so much as a scratch on it. Somehow a brothel and a naked Swedish whore with breasts like pumpkins came into the story as well, but for the life of me I couldn't make out quite how, and neither, from the look on his face, could Lenzing. In fact, I'm not at all sure that Lenzing was even listening. He was staring through the trees in the direction of the approaching enemy, and perhaps he was wondering how many of his blood brothers he would be able to kill before they killed him.

Heide, stern and silent, had brought out one of his cleaning rags and was obsessively polishing his machine-gun. It already shone like a beacon and probably advertised our presence to every Russian soldier in Poland, but Heide never could leave well enough alone.

The Legionnaire was watching the approach of the men and dogs, and indicating their distance to the machine-gunners. They were advancing with bayonets fixed, the dogs still tugging on their chains, heads down and noses to the ground. At the head marched an officer, his nagajka in his hand.

'Five hundred yards,' said the Legionnaire.

The Old Man shouldered his rifle and slipped back the safety catch.

'Range two hundred.'

Barcelona turned towards me.

'You ready?'

I nodded, and indicated the pile of grenades which were laid out before me.

'OK. After the second salvo.'

'Three hundred yards,' said the Legionnaire.

Private Abt gave a low moan, and was clouted over the head by Tiny. Porta reluctantly jettisoned his empty corned beef tin, and then picked up his rifle. The dogs were really going mad by this time, and the handlers bent down to set them loose.

'Two hundred and fifty,' droned the Legionnaire. 'Two twenty-five ... two hundred———'

'Fire!'

The four MGs crashed in unison. The officer with the nagajka was riddled from head to foot with bullets. Tiny laughed, exultantly.

'It's like a game of darts!' he said.

'With a human dartboard,' muttered Lenzing.

The Russians hesitated. Some of them tried to turn back, but they were caught between two fires and they had no choice but to go on. Before them lay the German guns and behind them the Russian. One of their own officers had opened up with an automatic rifle and was firing warning shots over their heads. The dogs needed no such encouragement. They came bounding towards us, snarling and showing all their teeth, and Private Abt gave a terrified scream and turned to run. Fortunately for himself, he tripped over a tree trunk and was kicked back into line by the Legionnaire while Tiny was occupied with his machine-gun, otherwise it would have been a bullet in the back and farewell Private Abt.

A second salvo was fired, and all but one of the dogs fell. The one remaining was a great black brute which hurled itself in a frenzy upon the Old Man, teeth bared and mouth flecked with saliva. The Old Man calmly took aim and shot it as it came towards him. He never was one to panic. I don't think I ever saw him lose his head in any situation. The dog sprang sideways, howling in agony, and the Legionnaire dispassionately took out his revolver and put a bullet through its brain.

There was scarcely any need for my grenades. The battle was over almost before it had begun, and the Old Man gave the signal for us to pull out.

'If war were always as much fun as that,' declared Tiny, very happy with himself, 'it wouldn't be half bad.'

'Strange sort of fun,' muttered Lenzing, gloomily. 'What happens when it's all over, that's what I'd like to know?'

'When what's all over?'

'The war—the fun—the fighting——'

'Well, when it's all over, it's all over, ain't it?'

'As simple as that?' said Lenzing.

'I rather fancy not,' murmured the Legionnaire. 'Ten to one, when they've got rid of Adolf, they'll start off all over again trying to get rid of each other.'

'And then where shall we be?' demanded Lenzing.

The Legionnaire smiled.

'Well, we know where you'll be, don't we? Out on the barricades waving your little red flag and crying death to the Yankee capitalists!'

'I don't know,' said Lenzing. He sighed. 'I don't know ... I sometimes think I've seen enough to last me the rest of my life.'

Shortly before sunset, we recovered the Colonel and the rest of the Company. The Colonel was so relieved to see us that he almost burst into tears of joy. I wondered what would have happened if we hadn't come back. I wondered who would have taken charge, and whether they would have given themselves up to the enemy.

'Sergeant, I've been thinking,' said the Colonel. He clapped a hand on the Old Man's shoulder. 'I've been thinking,' he said, 'and I'm damned if I can see how we're going to get down to that river.'

There was a pause. The Old Man waited respectfully to hear what the result of all this thinking might be, but it appeared, in the end, that there wasn't one.

'I see,' said the Old Man.

'Well, there you have it,' said the Colonel. 'There you have it, in a nutshell. That is my opinion.'

'So—ah—what do you suggest we should do, sir?'

'Ah, well, now—as to that——' The Colonel tipped back his helmet and mopped at his furrowed brow with a ragged handkerchief. 'That, of course, is a matter of some concern, is it not?'

'It is indeed, sir,' agreed the Old Man, gravely.

There was another pause. The Colonel looked grey and ancient. He looked like a half-buried corpse. I felt almost sorry for him.

'You know what?' said Barcelona, suddenly. 'I just had an idea.'

We turned, hopefully, to look at him. Barcelona didn't very often have ideas, but when he did they were sometimes worth listening to.

'Well, look,' he said. 'Here are we—and here's the river—and here're the Russians. Right?'

'Right,' said the Colonel, with a fine grasp of the situation. 'We are surrounded.'

'So what do we do?' said Barcelona. 'We attack a Russian section—we obliterate them—we take their uniforms. We make our way down to the river. We see if the bridge is still standing. If it is, we go across. No one stops us. They think we're Russians. If it isn't——' He jerked a thumb over his shoulder. 'Porta here can speak the lingo. He can ask around, find out if there's any other way across, find out what's happening. And if all else fails, we can build our own bridge. Orders from up top. Simple. Who's going to argue with us?'

'Hey!' shouted Tiny. 'That's not such a bad idea!' He turned excitedly to the rest of us. 'Imagine that,' he said. 'Put on Russian uniforms and we could march all the way to Berlin in 'em!'

'Except that if I'm going to be the one to do the talking,' said Porta, who always was the one to do the talking in any situation in which he found himself, 'then I insist on being a colonel.'

'Be what you like,' said Barcelona, 'just so long as you get us across that river.'

The Colonel by this time was looking pretty worried. As well he might: Porta and Barcelona were quite capable of attempting to put the plan into practice. The Colonel cleared his throat.

'We'd better be pushing on,' he said, nervously. Doubtless he had visions of being arrested in Russian uniform and shot as a spy, though it could scarcely have been any worse than being arrested in German uniform and shot as an enemy combatant. 'You know, Sergeant,' he said, in a low confidential voice to the Old Man, 'some of these chaps of yours are enough to make one's blood run cold ...'

We plunged back into the forest, deeper into the towering trees and the matted undergrowth. The rain had stopped and steam was rising from the marshy ground. The mosquitoes were everywhere, they followed us in a great buzzing cloud and were enough to drive a man mad. Tiny suddenly paused in the act of swiping them away from his face and held up a warning hand.

'Russians,' he said.

We froze. None of us could make out anything other than the normal forest sounds, but he was a vainglorious fool who argued with Tiny on such matters.

'Let's make a dash for it,' hissed Kuls, who was now wearing two Red Cross armbands on both sleeves, just to make quite sure that no one could mistake his occupation.

'Don't be a damn fool!'

The Old Man held him back. We stood listening, and Tiny silently pointed a finger. We inclined our heads in the direction he indicated, and slowly I began to make out a series of sounds which had nothing to do with the rustling of leaves. They were the sounds of rifles clicking, the sounds of men's voices, the sounds of heavy boots in the undergrowth ...

'In there!'

The Old Man made a dash for the side of the path, where vast mounds of leaves had piled up. He tore away the top layer with his hands, then used his bayonet to dig his way through the soft, moist earth beneath. He was very soon buried up to the neck, and the rest of us were burrowing after him like oversized moles.

'Are you sure this is altogether wise?' panted the Colonel.

Wise or not, it was too late now to do anything else. We curled up nose to tail in our peaty nests, with the leaves thick above us and the earth closing in all round. The Russians were very close. I heard the safety catch click on a rifle. I could feel the heavy footsteps as they passed by. I could hear the voices as they talked.

'Njet germanski! Job rwojamadj Piotr.'

Under the earth, I felt that I was suffocating. I had left myself a small passage for air, but now I became obsessed with the idea that the hole had closed up, that I was slowly poisoning myself with my own exhalations. The sweat began to pour down my back and my chest. I was bent double like an embryo in the womb, my knees tucked up to my chin, my arms wrapped round my legs. Panic swamped over me, my lungs were bursting, I could bear it no longer, I had to get out ... I sank my teeth hard into the butt of my revolver, pressed as it was against my mouth. Bright lights darted like multi-coloured fish before my eyes. I could feel something crawling over my face and up my nose and any moment now I was going to sneeze ...

Overhead, the Russians were crashing about in the undergrowth and shouting and laughing at one another.

'Job twojemadj!'

They were striding along the path, prying and poking our bed of leaves. I was suffering from hideous cramp in both arms, but there was no room to move even so much as a finger. Somewhere outside, a shot was fired. I thought for a minute we had been discovered, and my mind was filled with waves of terror as I imagined the tortures they would inflict upon us if they caught us like this, buried beneath the earth and unable to defend ourselves. A living death. Would it not be wiser to break free and run for it, now, while one still had the chance? Better to die in the sweet, fresh air than to slowly suffocate in an underground coffin.

'Ruski veks Stoi!'

How many more of them? How long before they gave up the search and left us in peace? My bladder was bursting, it was sending hot, shooting pains up through my body. Slowly and guiltily I let the burning urine dribble down between my legs, and the relief it gave me was so intense that it momentarily blotted out all my other problems.

Up above us, but moving further away, there were more cries, more shots. They must be firing on anything that moved; crows, mice, even mosquitoes.

I took a deep breath of stale air and felt my pulse beating in desperate protest. I knew, now, how an apple must feel when it was put into a hay box. I remembered at school putting apples into hay boxes. If you left them there long enough, they started to cook, and that was what I was doing. Surely anyone outside must be able to see the steam rising ...

'Hey, that's funny,' said Porta. 'Where's Sven?'

'I'm down here,' I said. 'I'm down here!'

I struggled desperately to move my head and clear a passage through the leaves, but I seemed to be paralysed from the neck down. I tried shouting for help, but my voice was drowned and they didn't hear it.

'He must be somewhere about,' said Tiny, and he brought one of his hefty great boots crashing down on top of my head.

They hauled me out and shook me, punched me in the chest and slapped me in the face. Kuls ran about with his Red Cross armbands telling the others what to do several seconds after they'd already done it. Very soon I began to feel almost normal and even became aware of the warm damp patch in my trousers.

'I thought you was a goner,' Tiny amiably informed me.

We marched on our way, through the never-ending forest. We had long since exhausted all our rations, and our bellies were beginning to scream aloud with hunger pains. Porta, in particular, found the deprivation hard to bear. He began making up menus in his head and reciting them out loud to the rest of us. At last the Old Man could bear it no longer and curtly told him to shut up, whereupon Porta retired in a magnificent sulk and didn't say a word to a soul for almost ten minutes.

At nightfall a halt was called. We settled down under the trees and through sheer exhaustion fell asleep at once. Private Abt was to take the first watch. He was almost sick with fear. Every shadow, every blade of grass made him jump. His thigh was throbbing, and he was convinced by now that his wound was gangrenous. Cautiously, from one of his pockets, he pulled out a small square of paper which he had been keeping secret for many days. It was a piece of blatant enemy propaganda, dropped by an aeroplane to be picked up by a gullible fool such as Private Abt. He turned his back on his sleeping comrades and by the light of the stars read the paper yet again.

'SAFE CONDUCT,' it said. 'This permit guarantees safe passage to any member of the German forces who wishes to transfer his allegiance to the Russian Army. (Signed) M. S. Malinin, Divisional General. K. K. Rokossovski, C-in-C, Russian Forces in Poland.'

Abt folded the paper and replaced it carefully in his pocket. He opened his ammunition pouch and took out a morsel of dry bread, upon which he thoughtfully chewed for several minutes. At last he made up his mind. He sidled away into the trees, and there he took to his heels and began to run as if all the devils in hell were after him. His gangrenous leg was forgotten. He tossed his revolver and half a dozen hand grenades into the bushes. He tore off his belt and his ammunition pouches, and discarded his helmet and his rifle. Head down, he pelted through the wood towards the village occupied by Russian troops.

'Don't shoot! Don't shoot! I've come to join you! I have a safe conduct from your generals!'

Two Siberians stood watching as he staggered up to them through the long, tough grasses of the marshland. He was waving a filthy grey handkerchief over his head as a sign of good intent, and anyone could see that he was unarmed. It must have been obvious, even without all his screaming and shouting, that he was a German deserter.

The Siberians raised their sub-machine-guns and prepared to fire.

'Don't shoot!' screamed Private Abt. 'I'm not a Nazi!'

He stood before them, waving his flag of truce in one hand and his safe conduct in the other. Coldly and deliberately, the Siberians blasted him out of existence. He still screamed for mercy as he fell.

The wind caught the handkerchief and tossed it high up into the trees. The safe conduct scuttered along the ground and was lost in the undergrowth.

It was Barcelona who discovered that our would-be deserter had finally left us.

'Why the pissing hell didn't we shoot the bastard while we still had a chance?' grumbled Porta.

It was small solace that by now, if he had succeeded in reaching the enemy, he would almost certainly be dead. The alarm had been raised, the Russians would be out looking for us, and we could ill afford to take any chances.

We pushed on as fast as we could during the rest of the night and the following morning, hacking our way through the dense undergrowth, tearing ourselves to ribbons on thorns and twigs, sliding down muddy slopes, wading waste deep through evil-smelling bogs. Towards mid-day, we came to a clearing with a broad, winding path running across it. The path was full of soldiers on the march. They were Russian soldiers, going west.

Silently, we withdrew into the shelter of the trees. If we didn't cross that particular path, it would mean a detour of several miles and the strong possibility of losing our way in the vastness of the forest. There was nothing to do but stay hidden in the bushes, to wait until darkness and hope that by then the troop movements would have ceased.

Dusk came, and there was no let up. The traffic was as heavy as ever. We waited another hour. By now it was dark, and it looked as if the entire Russian Army was on the march and likely to be so throughout the night.

'Fuck hanging about like this,' muttered Porta. 'We'll be here till bleeding Doomsday at this rate. My belly ain't going to stand the strain much longer.'

'So what exactly,' said the Old Man, in frigid tones, 'do you intend to do about it?'

Porta stared out thoughtfully at the road. He gazed up at the night sky, which was starless and cloud-covered. He looked back again at the road, and before anyone could stop him he was up and off, shooting across from one side to the other almost under the wheels of a truck. We waited for the panic and the shooting to begin, but the convoy continued peaceably on its way.

'How about it?' said the Legionnaire. 'Is it worth a try?'

The Old Man hunched a shoulder.

'Where one can go, I suppose the rest can follow . . .'

In half an hour, we were all safely across. I, in my panic and haste, caught my foot in a rut and fell straight into the path of an oncoming T34. I managed to twist out of the way only seconds before disaster overtook me, and I lay cowering in the ditch while the vehicle lumbered past and showered me with mud from head to foot.

We pressed on, deep into the dark forest, thankful to be on the move again after spending the last few hours hunched up in the bushes. We marched through the night, and towards dawn we began to make out the sounds of the river, lapping against its banks somewhere below us. We were approaching the edge of the wood, moving single file along a narrow path. Tiny and Porta were in the lead. They were laughing and tossing casual remarks over their shoulders as if they were out for a Sunday afternoon hike and thousands of miles away from danger. I was never quite sure whether those two had nerves of steel or simply lacked any imagination. But for all their apparent insouciance, they remained very much on the alert. We suddenly saw Tiny drop to his knees and gesture behind him to Porta to do likewise. The Old Man held up a warning hand. The column came to a halt. Slowly and silently, we edged our way forward on our bellies, inch by painful inch over the rocky ground.

Before us stretched fertile green farmlands, rolling down to the banks of the river. The bridge had been blown, and the twisted remains pointed upwards like warning fingers from the deep water. Nearby were the ruins of a building, charred and still smoking slightly. It had probably been a guardpost for the bridge. Directly beneath us lay a farmhouse. The Old Man studied it a moment through his field-glasses.

'Russian cavalry,' he said. 'Cossacks, by the look of them.'

Almost before he had finished speaking, a man stepped out of the trees a few yards further on and began walking down the path away from us. He never so much as glanced in our direction, and was obviously quite unaware of our presence. Tiny sprang after him, swift and sure and silent. He clamped an arm round the man's neck and pressed his revolver hard into his ribs.

'One squeak and you've had it!'

The man was far too frightened to make any sort of noise. His mouth fell open and his eyes froze in a glassy state of terror. I thought for a moment he had had a seizure. He was unarmed and was evidently a non-combatant.

'All right, let him go.' The Old Man gestured to Tiny, who reluctantly relaxed his grip on his victim's neck. 'Who are you? What are you doing here?'

'Me comrade,' said the fellow, very earnestly. 'Me friend.

166

No Communist. Friend ... Panjemajo?*'

'Oh, sure we panjemajo!' sneered Porta. 'You no Communist. You friend ... sure, we know all about that, mate!' He turned and spat contemptuously on the path. 'A likely bloody tale!'

'But please, sir, is true—is true what I say——'

'Oh yeah?' said Porta. 'You know something? It really amazes me the number of Russians you come across these days who swear blind they aren't Communists. It really does amaze me ... One minute they're shouting their heads off in praise of bleeding Stalin, the next they're telling you, me no Communist, me friend ...'

The man moved eagerly forward, waving his hands in the air like an excited rabbit.

'Me no Russian, me no Russian! Polka! Polka! Me Polka! Ladislas Mnasko.'

'Come again?' said Tiny.

'Ladislas Mnasko.' The man pointed a finger into his chest and beamed at us. He gestured over his shoulder towards the farm. 'Is my house. Down there. My house.'

'Your house?' The Old Man raised an eyebrow. 'Full of Russian soldiers?'

'They take it from me, Pan Sergeant. My wife and child, they still down there. My sister also. My father'—he pointed again, this time across the valley to the smouldering ruins of the guardhouse—'my father, they kill. He look after bridge. They shoot him, burn down house.'

There was a pause. We looked from the man to the farm to the ruined bridge. His story seemed plausible enough, on the face of it.

'And you?' said the Old Man. 'What about you?'

'I home from war. I see Russians. I run. I not know what to do——'

'Kill the bastard!' screamed Kuls, suddenly bursting forward. 'Kill him and be done with it! Never trust a bleeding Polak, you know that as well as I do. It's all a pack of filthy

* You understand?

167

lies! It's just a trick to get us down there! Cut his throat and send him back to them!'

'That will be quite enough of that sort of talk,' said the Colonel, coldly. 'Kindly remember that I am in charge round here.'

Kuls looked at him mutinously. Porta held out his flask to the trembling Pole, who accepted it with a nervous twitch of the lips by way of thanks.

'Tell me,' said the Old Man, 'now that the bridge has gone, is there any other way of getting across the river? Could you manage to take us across?'

The man nodded.

'Tak jest,* Pan Sergeant. Only——' He jerked his head in the direction of the farm and extended his hands in a helpless gesture. 'The Russians, Pan Sergeant——'

'Don't worry about the Russians,' said the Old Man, curtly. 'They're our business. We'll see to the Russians for you. You concentrate on thinking how you're going to get us over that river.'

As we cautiously approached the occupied farmhouse, we could see the Russians making merry in the yard outside. They had built an enormous fire and were spit-roasting the carcass of a cow, and they were drinking and shouting as they danced round the flames. One man lost his footing and fell headfirst into the burning outer embers of the fire. It was hard to tell whether his companions were too drunk to notice or simply too callous to care, but either way they made no move to pull him back to safety.

'If only they don't let it burn!' muttered Porta.

He was referring to the beef, rather than the man. He had been carefully following the cooking process through a pair of binoculars as we made our way down the path, and he was growing increasingly anxious lest the meat should be overdone by the time we arrived.

'Sod the meat,' said Tiny. 'It's the booze I'm interested in.' He turned impatiently to the Old Man. 'Let's get a move on,

* Yes.

168

can't we? That's your actual genuine Russian vodka they've got down there.'

'All right, don't panic,' said the Old Man, amiably. 'We're on our way.' He called us to a halt. 'Barcelona, you and Gregor stay here and keep us covered. Tiny, you and'— he hesitated—'you and Kuls go ahead with Ladislas. The rest of us will follow. And remember—no grenades. There are three civilians somewhere down there. I want them brought out alive.' He nodded at the anxious Pole. 'OK. Off you go.'

Tiny set off towards the farm. Ladislas followed. The Old Man looked expectantly at Kuls.

'Well? Did you hear what I said?'

Kuls tossed his head.

'I heard! And if you imagine I'm going to put my neck in a noose just to rescue a couple of lousy stinking Polish whores and one snivelling brat, you've got another think coming!'

The Old Man frowned.

'Are you refusing to obey an order?'

Kuls dropped his defiant stare. He shuffled a toe in the dust.

'We don't need that half-witted Polak to show us how to cross a bleeding river ... Why don't we put a bullet through his brain and leave him here to rot?'

'Because the Colonel is in command round here, and the Colonel has decided otherwise!'

We all turned to look at the Colonel, who scraped his throat in a severe, military fashion and squared his shoulders.

'Precisely so,' he said. 'Consider yourself under arrest.' He beckoned to Gregor. 'Keep an eye on him.'

'Yes, sir!' said Gregor, with a somewhat malevolent relish.

Kuls scowled.

'You haven't heard the last of this,' he said, impartially to both the Old Man and the Colonel. 'You can't get away with this sort of thing. I've got a brother in the RSHA.* They know how to deal with people like you. Risking the lives of German soldiers for the sake of one lying, cheating Pole. You'll be

* Security Service of the Reich.

169

sorry.'

Gregor prodded him hard in the kidneys with the butt of his rifle.

'One more bleep out of you, Kuls,' he said, 'and your brother in the RSHA has seen the last of you ...'

On the outskirts of the farm were a couple of sentries. They were very obviously drunk. One was vomiting copiously into a hedge, the other was trying to dance, squatting on his heels and flinging his legs about in a series of unco-ordinated movements. Tiny and the Legionnaire moved stealthily towards them. Their deaths were swift and silent, and drunk as they were they probably didn't even know they had died.

Tiny picked up a vodka bottle and raised it eagerly to his lips: it was empty. He threw it away in disgust and aimed an angry kick at the nearest corpse.

'Greedy bastard!'

He consoled himself by plundering for gold, and managed to yank out three teeth before Porta came galloping up and set to work on the second of the dead sentries. Tiny tipped the contents of his wash leather bag into the palm of his hand and gloated a moment over his collection of trophies. The Old Man shook his head.

'One of these days,' he said, 'that little lot's going to cost you your life. And I, for one, shan't shed a tear.'

'What's eating him?' demanded Porta, busy with his pliers.

Tiny shrugged.

'Search me. I reckon he's just got his knickers in a twist again.'

Porta shook his head philosophically and continued with his grisly task. He was well accustomed by now to the Old Man's peculiarities of conscience. It was best to ignore him when he had one of his sanctimonious fits. The way he and Tiny saw it, they weren't getting much else out of the war. Only one Mark a day and the chance of a bullet through the belly, why not help themselves to a few gold teeth when the opportunity arose?

'A man's got to have something to fall back on,' said Porta, wisely. 'The war ain't going to go on for ever. You got to look ahead a bit in this life.'

We moved up closer towards the farm. The yard was full of carousing Cossacks. They had formed an enormous circle and were dancing round the fire with their arms round one another's shoulders. As they danced, they shouted and sang, and every now and again one of their number would break away from the rest and go leaping across the flames to the sound of thunderous applause.

From the stables came the whinnying and stamping of horses. One or two men were sitting quietly in groups, drinking and smoking, but as far as we could see they had posted no more sentries. We set up a machine-gun directly opposite the house, and Porta shook his head, regretfully. These rough, merrymaking Cossacks were men after his own heart, and in any other circumstance than this accursed war, he would have gone running forward to join them. As it was, he had to prepare for butchery in order to please his masters and save his own skin.

'Seems a shame,' he said, 'to break up the party like this ...'

'Never mind the party!' snapped Heide, the fanatical. 'Let's get on and do the job we were sent here for! Just remember that these men are Communists and the lackeys of international Jewry!'

'Lackeys my arse,' said Porta. 'Who strung you that load of codswallop?'

We stood in silence, watching the antics of the leaping Cossacks. From somewhere in the woods behind us a dog fox barked and an owl began to hoot. Darkness was closing in, but the flames of the fire lit up the night for half a mile around. Slowly but surely, the Russians drank themselves to a full stop. One by one they began to stagger into the farmhouse. A few remained outside, snoring on the ground where they had fallen. At last the place was silent and still. The Old Man turned towards us.

'Ready?' he whispered.

We crept forward, crouching low in the long grass. The farm was in darkness, not a light shone in any of the windows. The horses in the stables had caught wind of us and were rearing and whinnying, stamping on the floor and kicking at the doors in an effort to be free. They were good military beasts, and they sensed instinctively that we represented danger. But their masters lay in a drunken stupor and did not respond to their calls of alarm. The warm, sweet smell of hay and horse mingled with the acrid stench of stale vomit and spilt vodka. The smoke from the dying fire drifted towards us, bringing with it the fragrant delights of roast meat, and Porta ripped off a chunk with his bayonet as we passed. The flesh fell easily from the bones. Porta crammed a piece into his mouth, and the juice dribbled down his chin and on to his collar. His eyes clouded over in sheer ecstasy, and as if in a trance he reached out his hand for more.

'Oh no, you don't!' said the Legionnaire, smartly. He prodded him towards the farmhouse with the nozzle of the flame-thrower he was carrying. 'You can come back for the rest of it when we've cleaned this place up.'

At the foot of the steps leading into the building were half a dozen Cossacks, lying one on top of another in an indiscriminate heap of arms and legs.

'Pissed as newts,' said Gregor.

Barcelona prodded one of them, experimentally, as he went past. The man smiled in his sleep. He reached out his hands and clutched amorously at Barcelona's leg.

'Nevaesta,*' he muttered.

'Charmed, I'm sure,' said Barcelona, shaking himself free.

'Kill the bastard,' urged Kuls.

From the top of the steps, the Old Man waved a hand for silence.

'Shut up and follow me!'

Cautiously, he pushed open the heavy wooden door. The hinges were in need of oil and squeaked loud enough to wake the dead. But the Russians went on snoring. The Old Man

* Sweetheart.

172

tiptoed into the hallway, with Ladislas scuttling crablike at his heels. Bodies lay all over the place, sprawled in chairs, stretched out on the floor, hanging over the banisters. There was a litter of empty bottles, and pools of urine and vomit. Ladislas drew his lips together into a thin line. He no longer looked quite so much like a rabbit. He looked like a man who was prepared for the worst and bent on avenging himself. He caught the Old Man by the arm and pointed up towards the bedrooms on the next floor. The Old Man nodded.

We stepped forward over the bodies and made our way down the hall. At the bend in the stairs were two enormous Cossack sergeants. They were seated side by side on the same step, wedged together by the width of their shoulders and sleeping with their heads drooping forward on to their chests. They had machine-guns in their laps. We took no chances. Tiny strangled them both with his bare hands.

We continued on our way. From somewhere down in the hall, Kuls was heard to mutter something about his brother in the RSHA, but a warning clip round the ear from Gregor soon shut him up.

As I carefully skirted the two dead sergeants, there was a sudden noise and a vodka bottle came hurtling towards me, followed at full speed by Tiny, who had trodden on it in the semi-darkness and missed his footing. They both crashed on to the stone floor. One of the sleeping Russians opened his eyes and sat up in a panic, but Heide slit his throat before he had time to take in what was happening. Tiny leaped roaring to his feet. He caught sight of his own vast bulk looming at him from a full-length looking-glass, and in the gloom he mistook it for one of the enemy. With a shout of fury, he raised his rifle and fired a couple of shots. Then he gave a grunt of satisfaction as his own image dissolved in a shower of broken glass.

'For Christ's sake!' hissed the Old Man, from the top of the stairs. 'What the devil's going on down there?'

'It's only Tiny tilting at windmills,' I said.

Tiny pushed past me and went galloping back up again, his face streaming with blood and embedded with slivers of broken glass.

'I killed the bastard,' he said.

Lenzing caught my eye. He gave a bray of nervous laughter and clapped a hand to his mouth.

'What bastard?' demanded Porta.

'Bastard who jumped me,' said Tiny.

There was a pause.

'Smashed his face in,' he said.

Lenzing laughed so much he almost fell over the banister. I was happy to see him enjoying himself for once.

We reached the landing, and Ladislas pushed past the Old Man and made a dive for one of the doors. The Old Man held him back. We stood outside, listening. It sounded like a swarm of bees had been let loose in there.

'OK. Open it up——'

The Old Man nodded, and gently the Legionnaire turned the handle. A quivering mound of flesh was lying naked on a bed. It was snoring, rhythmically in a long, low drone which echoed about the room. From its discarded clothes, we could see that it was a major. It was completely bald and somewhat resembled Taras Bulba.

At the foot of the bed, crumpled up and unconscious, lay a young girl. Ladislas stood staring at her, white-faced and trembling.

'Your wife?' said the Old Man, softly.

He shook his head.

'Your sister?'

Slowly, Ladislas nodded and turned to face the wall. The Legionnaire pulled out his P38 and held it to the Major's temple, but Tiny suddenly stepped forward and pushed him out of the way.

'Let me,' he said. 'I like killing Russians.'

He liked killing them best with his bare hands. It was quick and clean and it made no noise. A slight choke, and the major was no more.

'Here's another of 'em,' said Gregor, dispassionately.

He indicated an outflung hand which was projecting from

beneath the bed. Tiny at once seized hold of it. A captain appeared, naked apart from his tunic and socks. He was cradling a vodka bottle in one arm, and he was smiling and crooning to himself as he slept. He was still smiling as Tiny snapped his neck.

The girl, meanwhile, was slowly coming back to consciousness. She opened her eyes and stared round in horror at the sight of a room full of soldiers. I daresay we weren't a very pretty sight; unwashed, unshaven, covered in mud, stinking of sweat, with our uniforms in shreds. I'm not really surprised that she screamed when Tiny approached her with a proprietary leer on his big ugly face and his great basketlike hands stretched out before him. I can't say I altogether blame her for sinking her teeth into Porta's arm when he sat down on the bed beside her and smiled suggestively at her. I reckon I would have done exactly the same if Tiny or Porta had come anywhere near me when I was lying half naked on a bed.

'Leave her be!' said the Old Man, sharply.

Tiny and Porta swung round to face him.

'What's up with you, Granddad?'

'I said leave her be!' snapped the Old Man.

He picked up the Major's discarded tunic and handed it to the girl. Silently, she wrapped it round herself.

'OK, let's go.'

The Old Man led her across to Ladislas, who all this time had stood by the wall with his hands over his face, as if even after all these long and painful years of war, he could not bring himself to acknowledge the truth of man's brutality.

'We must look for your wife,' said the Old Man, gently. 'Take us over the rest of the house.'

Down in the cellars we found them, his wife and his young son. Surrounded by a crowd of drunken Cossacks sleeping off their debauch, in the blood of their victims. The woman had been raped and slashed open with a knife. The child had been spitted on a bayonet. There was no need to look twice to see that they were dead.

We stood in silence. Lenzing turned away with a hand to his

mouth. The Old Man stretched out an arm towards Ladislas. The Legionnaire took the girl and led her outside. Even Porta was at a loss for words.

And then, quite suddenly, Ladislas, gentle, frightened, rabbity Ladislas, gave a howl of agony and hurled himself at the nearest Cossack. He had choked the life out of three of them before Tiny came to his senses and leapt forward to join in the slaughter. Within minutes the butchery was complete. There was no one left to kill.

We made our way up the cellar steps and out into the farmyard. There was no more reason for exploring the house. Porta and Tiny, never ones to suffer from over-sensitivity, at once set off to round up the remains of the food and drink while they still had a chance. Kuls was heard to be muttering again about his brother. From behind the stables came a sound of water as if poured from a jug. The Legionnaire and I crept up to investigate and found a semi-conscious Cossack emptying his bladder into a rain-butt. The Legionnaire turned to me and winked. Silently, he drew his knife from the side of his boot. I left him to it.

Someone had been round the farmyard slashing throats. The carcass of the cow had been stripped bare. The fire was still smouldering gently, the embers glowing crimson in the darkness. Tiny and Porta had disappeared, and we ran them to earth in one of the outbuildings. There they were, seated astride a barrel of home-made wine and singing patriotic songs in loud and raucous voices. In the space of ten minutes they had managed to drink themselves almost senseless.

Barcelona came running up with the news that he had discovered three Russian trucks loaded with petrol drums parked under the trees. The Colonel then appeared, from heaven knows where, stinking of vodka and slightly unsteady on his feet. He had about the same intelligence as Barcelona.

'Sergeant, what are we waiting for?' he said, in a voice that was thick and slurred. 'There are three perfectly good trucks beneath the trees. Why do we not make use of them?'

We surged back again into the open air and followed Barcelona and the Colonel across the yard. Before we left, we liberally sprinkled the entire place with petrol—house, out-buildings and stables. We opened the doors for the horses, and after a moment or two of surprise they threw up their heads and thundered away into the security of the forest.

'All bleeding well for them,' said Gregor, jealously. 'The war's over as far as they're concerned.'

'Quite right, too,' said the Colonel. 'Dumb animals have no place in the bloody affairs of men.' He suddenly hooked an arm about Gregor's neck and leaned confidentially towards him. 'You know what?' he said. 'Before all this began, I had a stable full of the most magnificent beasties. Wonderful creatures. Most beautiful animals you've ever seen … You know what happened?'

'No. What?' said Gregor.

'They took them away,' said the Colonel. 'Took them away for horse meat. Shocking business. Shocking.'

'Fucking awful,' said Gregor, sympathetically.

The Old Man was doing his best to round everyone up and make preparations for departure. Half the company was stoned senseless, and the other half was still foraging in the farmhouse for smoked hams and cheeses to carry on the journey. There wasn't a man among us who didn't have a couple of bottles of wine or vodka pushed into his pockets. There was a general reluctance to leave, and it wasn't until Ladislas went berserk and tossed a lighted match into the courtyard that the Old Man was able to impose at least some semblance of order. Men came running from all directions as the petrol leapt into a thousand roaring tongues of flame. Unfortunately, the trucks had not yet been moved, and they were among the first things to disappear in the ensuing conflagration.

We backed away into the trees and stood watching as the fire caught hold of the farmhouse. I thought of all those coma-tose Cossacks inside, and I wondered how it must be to slip from life to death without ever being aware of it.

'Not such a bad way to go,' said Barcelona, at my side. 'A drunken funeral pyre … Not at all a bad way to go!'

'I want the youth of Germany to be bold; to be brave; to be violent and remorseless ...'

Himmler. Letter to SS Hauptsturmführer Professor Dr Bruno Schultz, 19th August 1938.

ONE hour after the Warsaw uprising, the Reichsführer Heinrich Himmler was informed of what had taken place. At first he was not able to believe it. It was impossible, after all, that these sewer rats, these Poles, these miserable Jews, should set themselves against the might of the German Army and hope to get away with it. Not even a Pole—or a Jew—could be so criminally insane. It was nothing more than suicide. Had they run mad?

Evidently they had. When the news at last sank in, the Reichsführer was seen to have fallen prey to great and disturbing agitation of mind. He paced about his room, up and down, corner to corner, taking his spectacles on and off his nose and repeatedly wiping a hand across his glistening brow.

'Very well,' he said. 'Very well, then ... We shall show them how we deal with animals which have the impertinence to show their teeth to their master!' He turned to face his subordinates, who were humbly standing in the centre of the large room awaiting their instructions. 'For this we shall wipe Warsaw clean off the map. Every man, woman and child shall be destroyed ... every living creature. Every building shall be razed to the ground, and every paving stone shall be torn up!'

He stalked to the window, and there he stood, rocking on the balls of his feet, breathing heavily through flared nostrils, hands twitching convulsively behind his back.

'In addition,' he said, turning back into the room, 'every Pole in every prison camp shall be liquidated. Do I make myself clear?'

'Yes, Reichsführer.' Obergruppenführer Berger bowed his head. 'Perfectly clear.'

'All those who were born in Warsaw or who have relations living in Warsaw shall be shot this very night. I shall person-

178

ally make a check that this has been done. I shall expect a full list of the dead to be delivered to me within twenty-four hours.'

'Very good, Reichsführer.'

Himmler pinched his nostrils together and drew a long, thin breath. He looked back again to the window, staring out at the rain as it fell on the cold, grey city.

'As for Gauleiter Fischer,' he said, 'he shall be hanged for not having prevented the uprising ...'

It was General Erich von demn Bach-Zalewski of the Waffen SS who had been given the task of crushing the Warsaw uprising. Neither he nor the Reichsführer ever seriously imagined that a relatively small group of Polish partisans could give them very much trouble. There were twelve thousand German troops stationed in the district, plus the ten thousand SS of the Kaminski Brigade. Under the circumstances it was difficult to imagine how Gauleiter Fischer could have allowed the situation to get so out of hand.

It was doubtful if at that stage either Himmler or Bach-Zalewski fully realised the strength of the revolt. They were not left in ignorance for long, however. The Poles, under the leadership of General Bor-Komorovski, an ex-officer of the Austrian Army, promptly moved in to occupy the Wola district and the entire central area of the town, wiping out both the Gestapo HQ and the command post of the German garrison. They next took over control of the power station and the central telephone exchange. By the third day, the Germans were in retreat and the victorious Poles had taken possession of the several arms depots and ammunition dumps in the town.

Himmler was forced to withdraw three SS divisions and six divisions of the Wehrmacht from the Russian front—mercifully quiet at that period—and send them out to repair the damage. At the beginning of September, the German troops in Warsaw were issued with the latest weapons, and three squadrons of Stukas were sent over to bomb the city.

Himmler had played his ace, and still there were small groups of partisans who refused to give in. He had only his joker left, now. He played it, and from then until the final surrender a total of five thousand Polish prisoners were murdered every day ...

THE WAY OVER THE RIVER

THROUGHOUT the rest of the night and the whole of the next day, we followed Ladislas and his sister through the forest towards the point where we should be able to cross the river. We travelled slowly, with frequent halts to allow enemy patrols to pass by. Kuls was constantly complaining that we were being led into a trap and would be sorry when it was all too late. It did cross my own mind that we seemed to be taking a somewhat roundabout route, but we had no reason for mistrusting our guide, and the Old Man appeared to be quite happy to follow him.

Towards midnight on the second day we reached the towering cliffs which overhung the river. There was a sheer drop into the gorge far below, where the waters roared and crashed and threw up an angry, white-flecked spray high into the air. I could see rocks sticking up like rows of needle-sharp teeth, and I moved hastily away from the crumbling edge of the cliff and scrambled back to join the others.

'So what are we supposed to do?' said Kuls, sourly. 'Flap our wings and fly?'

The Old Man jerked his thumb upstream.

'According to the Pole, there's a bridge half a mile further on, but it's too risky to attempt the crossing at night. We'll kip down for a few hours and give it a go in the morning.'

'Bridge!' said Kuls. 'A likely bloody story!'

I rather thought so myself. I could certainly see no signs of any bridge, and if there was one it was bound to be heavily guarded. However, our guide obviously knew the district. He led the way to an opening in the rocks, a crevice which widened into a fair-sized cavern, and there we installed ourselves for the night. We set up the machine-gun at the mouth of the crevice, camouflaging it with creepers and branches. We felt we were in comparative safety. The rocky cavern was like a luxury suite after the misery of the mud and the marshes. It was dry and it was warm, and for the first time in days we had an adequate supply of food and drink. Even sleep was possible for those who had cultivated the happy knack of closing their ears to all external sounds. The Legionnaire curled into a ball and never moved a muscle all night long. For my own part I was unable to blot out the continuous drunken bickering of Heide and Porta, interspersed with the inane guffaws of Tiny and the general roaring and belching. I passed the hours until dawn in an irritable stupor somewhere between waking and sleeping, and I was thankful when the first light streaked across the sky and the Old Man called us to our feet.

We dismantled the machine-gun and set off behind the Pole and his sister along the cliff tops. The sky was grey, gold-tipped on the horizon with the waking of the sun, and a large black crow slowly beat its way across the river on undulating wing. I had an uncomfortable feeling that our own passage was not likely to be quite so free and easy.

'There,' said Ladislas; and he stood pointing upstream, to a point where a giant pine had come crashing down and now lay stretched across the chasm, its torn roots on one side and its branches on the other. 'There is the way we must go.'

Even the Old Man betrayed a moment of doubt.

'Is it safe?' he said.

'Safe?' said Ladislas. He shrugged a careless shoulder. 'Who can tell if it is safe or not? Maybe it fall—maybe we fall. Maybe it break. Maybe the wind blow. Maybe the Russians come.' He spread out his hands. 'Who cares?' he said.

Not, apparently, Ladislas, or his sister. They walked on

181

together, hand in hand, towards the fallen pine. After all they had been through, they probably felt they had nothing left to live for. So let them commit suicide if that was what they wanted; the rest of us were not so keen.

'What did I tell you?' said Kuls, savagely. 'What did I bloody tell you?'

We hung back and watched as Ladislas first and then his sister took off their boots and stepped barefoot on to the improvised bridge.

'Ever been across this way before?' asked Barcelona, casually.

'Never,' said Ladislas.

'Why should we?' added his sister. 'Always before there is a bridge to walk on.'

Slowly and carefully, one foot after another, they shuffled out into space. Ladislas had his hands on his hips to give him better balance. The girl had her arms stretched out at shoulder level. Both held their heads high and stared straight across at the opposite bank. They moved like sleepwalkers in slow motion. As they passed the half-way mark the trunk began to tremble. The girl caught her breath, and stood poised for a moment on one foot. Ladislas braced himself firmly, legs apart, and held out a hand towards her. The girl tilted slightly backwards. Ladislas bent forward from the waist. It seemed impossible they could maintain their equilibrium, but inch by inch they straightened up, the girl managed to regain her footing and they continued calmly on their way along the swaying trunk. About six feet before it reached the far bank it narrowed considerably. It was scarcely the width of a man's shoe. We could see it sagging beneath the weight of the two people. It must have been a temptation for Ladislas to take a flying leap on to the bank, but had he done so the girl would almost certainly have been flung into the air by the springboard reaction of the slender tree trunk. He pursued his course grimly to the end, and when at last he reached the opposite side, he turned and held out a hand. The girl snatched at it, and together they clambered to safety.

'Where one can go,' said the Old Man, with a faint smile at the Legionnaire, 'the rest can surely follow ... Who's next?'

There was silence. Not even Porta opened his mouth. Ladislas and his sister stood on the opposite bank and waved and shouted to us, but all I could see was the swaying tree trunk and all I could hear was the angry rushing of the waters far below. The Old Man made an impatient noise in the back of his throat.

'Well, come on!' he said. 'We can't hang about all day. There's only one way to go, and that's across the river ... And there's only one way to cross the river, and that's the way we're going.'

'Like hell!' snarled Kuls. He drew his lips back over his teeth, showing his gums like an angry dog. 'I'm staying right here, and no one's going to budge me!'

The Old Man took a step towards him. Kuls backed away. He pointed his rifle at the Old Man.

'You come another step and I'll kill you! I'll kill you, so help me God.'

The Old Man took another step. With one hand he slapped Kuls hard across the face. With the other he snatched his rifle away from him. Coldly and contemptuously, he slung it over the edge of the cliff.

'And that's exactly where you'll end up yourself if I have any more trouble with you,' he said, grimly. He turned back to the rest of us. 'So who's next for the high wire?'

'Not me,' I said.

It made me dizzy just looking at the thing. For once I was in full sympathy with Kuls. Wild horses weren't going to drag me across that tree trunk.

'Do I have to drive you all at gun point?' demanded the Old Man.

There was a general muttering, and an uneasy shuffling of feet, and then Tiny suddenly gave a great roar of anger and plunged forward. He ripped off his boots and slung them round his neck. He pulled out his one remaining bottle of

183

raspberry wine and emptied it down his throat. The bottle flew over the edge of the cliff in the wake of Kuls's rifle, and for one moment I thought that Tiny was going to follow it. He charged forward, head down, like a tank out of control, and he was half-way across to the opposite bank when he lost his balance and slipped. Someone screamed. The tree trunk was twanging up and down like a rubber band, and Tiny was hanging on with both hands, suspended in space with his legs dangling. All the blood in my body turned to water, and I was chewing on my bottom lip as if it were a piece of particularly tough rump steak. However much I wanted to turn my eyes the other way, I found myself compelled to watch.

'He'll never make it,' said Barcelona. His fingers closed over my arm and bit deep into the flesh. 'He'll never make it——'

Tiny swung himself up and hooked his legs round the tree trunk. Slowly and carefully, hanging upside down like a koala bear, he inched his way along. Hand over hand, foot over foot. He reached the last couple of yards. There was an ominous creaking sound. Ladislas and the girl grabbed hold of the branches, as if their combined weight would be any sort of counterbalance to Tiny's vast bulk.

'Christ almighty,' said Gregor, his face like a stale mushroom drained of all colour. 'Sweet Christ almighty . . .'

Tiny had reached the edge of the trunk. He stretched out a hand and caught hold of a stunted tree growing from the side of the cliff. With one foot he felt round for a ledge or a crevice, and at last he found one and was able to haul himself somewhat ponderously to safety. From his pocket he pulled out the filthy bloodstained rag which had once been his handkerchief and mopped his brow with it.

'Come on over!' he yelled. 'There's nothing to it!'

'Next one,' said the Old Man, curtly.

The way he said it, you'd have thought we were queueing up for the dentist. He looked anxiously over his shoulder in the direction from which we had come. Somewhere deep in the forest we could hear gunshots. It could mean only one thing: the NKVD were on our trail.

'Get a move on for God's sake!'

The Old Man snatched at the person nearest to him and gave him a shove towards the edge of the cliff. Had it been me, I would have taken to my heels and galloped off to seek help and comfort from the advancing Russians rather than follow Tiny and his display of acrobatics across the yawning chasm. As it was Barcelona, he merely swore terribly and sat down to take his boots off.

Half-way across the trunk, he suddenly stopped. Until that point he had been moving forward with all the assurance of a circus tight-rope walker, using his rifle as a balancing rod. He never once stumbled or slipped. What happened to upset him, I never knew. Perhaps he made the mistake of looking down at the torrent below. Or perhaps, because it was at that same half-way mark that Tiny had come to grief it was purely psychological. But whatever it was, Barcelona was at a full stop and neither the Old Man's threats, nor Tiny's cries of encouragement, could persuade him to go on.

'So now what do we do?' said Gregor, and I thought I detected a faint note of relief in his voice. As if to say, well, that was that, we might as well call it a day and go home. No one could be expected to cross to the other side with Barcelona cluttering up the middle of the gangplank ... 'What happens now?' he said.

The Legionnaire pursed his lips together.

'Someone has to go and shift the stupid cunt,' he said, savagely.

He slung his boots round his neck and set off to the rescue. Small and lithe, and sure-footed as any cat, he never looked as if he were in the least danger. But he had the terrified Barcelona to cope with, and Barcelona was by now beginning to lose control. His rifle fell from his hands and went spinning into the abyss. Barcelona swayed and would have fallen straight after it had the Legionnaire not reached him in time and clamped a firm hand on his shoulder. For a moment they crouched there together, frozen like statues, perilously perched on the extreme edge of nowhere. And then slowly, very slowly,

Barcelona began to crawl forward.

The combined weight of the two men was about as much as the trunk could stand. When Tiny suddenly bounded out from the far side with the intention of extending a helping hand, there was a protesting groan and the whole thing began to sag.

'Get back!' yelled the Old Man. 'Back, for God's sake!'

Tiny fortunately realised the danger just in time to avert a triple catastrophe. He edged his way back to the cliff top and contented himself with plucking Barcelona to safety the minute he came within reach. The Legionnaire finished the journey without difficulty and stood calmly smoking a cigarette while he waited for the rest of us. The Old Man turned to Porta and jerked his head.

'Off you go.'

'What, me?' said Porta.

'Yes, you,' said the Old Man.

There was a pause.

'Do I have to?' said Porta.

'I think it would be advisable. I shouldn't like to have to make an example of you.'

'No,' said Porta. 'No, I can see that. I can see you wouldn't like to have to make an example of me ...' He pulled a wry face and slung his rifle over his shoulder. 'OK, then. Here goes.'

'What about your boots?' objected the Old Man. 'You'll never get across there with your boots on.'

'Fuck the boots,' said Porta, cheerfully. He turned and blew us a kiss. 'God bless you, my children!'

Porta, of course, no more than Tiny had, could make the crossing in a conventional manner. Porta chose to sit astride and play ride-a-cock horse all the way over. Half-way across he felt the need of a little refreshment, so he pulled a flask from his pocket and had a drink. It must have been something a great deal stronger than raspberry wine, because from then on he sang lustily at the top of his voice and only interrupted himself from time to time to crack an imaginary whip against his meagre backside and shout, 'Giddyap, there!' before going on his way at a pace which appalled me.

'Sergeant, what is wrong with that man?' said the Colonel. 'Is he simple-minded?'

Gregor was the next to go. He was sweating profusely and was obviously scared to death, but Gregor was not one for histrionics. He seated himself astride the trunk as Porta had done, and he dragged himself very slowly and carefully, from one side to the other, where he was dragged to safety by several willing pairs of hands. He passed out the moment he got there, but it had been an impressive display nevertheless.

'You see?' said the Old Man. 'It's all perfectly simple.'

Heide was already half-way across. He had his boots tied neatly round his neck and he was marching with head held high and shoulders well back as if he were on the parade ground. He made it look absurdly easy.

Others were not quite so lucky. Lutz had to be driven across at gun-point, and never reached the other side. Two others followed him into the abyss. We heard their screams echoing as they fell.

And now there were only four of us left. The Colonel, the Old Man, Kuls and myself. My turn had come, I could put it off no longer, and the Old Man was prodding me forward towards the edge of the chasm.

'No,' I said. 'No! I'm not going over, I'd rather stay here and wait for the Russians, I'd rather stay here and die!'

'Don't be silly,' said the Old Man, calmly. He bent down and undid my boots for me. 'Off with them, and be quick about it.'

'I'm not going!' I said. 'You go! You and the Colonel! I'll stay here with Kuls and cover you!'

The Colonel, who until this point had kept in the background, now suddenly became exceedingly agitated and began running to and fro waving his revolver in the air and threatening to shoot me if I refused to obey orders.

'I'm not stopping you,' I said.

The Colonel gave a wild cry.

'For God's sake, Sergeant! If you haven't got that man across to the other side by the time I've counted ten, I'll shoot the pair of you!'

The Old Man laid a paternal hand on my shoulder.

'All right, now listen to me, Sven. You're going to do exactly what I tell you. You're going to take your boots off, you're going to step on to that bridge, and you're going to walk across just like all the rest of them have done. I'm going to be right behind you, so there's no need to panic. If you start feeling bad, just let me know and we'll stop and have a rest. There's absolutely nothing to be scared of. If that tree were lying flat on the ground you'd run along it without even thinking. All you've got to remember is, don't look down. Keep your eyes straight ahead and you can't go wrong.'

Under his calming influence, I plucked up sufficient courage to tie my boots round my neck, sling my rifle over my shoulder, and take my first few hesitant steps out into the void. I tried pretending I was a child again, doing a balancing act on a fallen log, or walking along the top of a brick wall. There was nothing to worry about. The Old Man was quite right. If the ground were only a couple of feet beneath me, I would have no difficulty at all in keeping my balance. I could walk straight across without even thinking about it ...

I kept my eyes fixed firmly on my comrades, who were waiting for me on the far side. If they could do it, then so could I. There was absolutely nothing to be scared of.

A gust of wind suddenly came through the chasm. Down at ground level it might have been no more than a gentle zephyr; up there, in the middle of nowhere, it felt like a hurricane. I found myself wavering. I glanced down at my feet on the tree trunk, and I saw the river and the rocks below me. I saw myself crashing down to meet them. I wanted to scream and shout, I wanted to clutch at something to save myself from falling, but there was nothing to clutch. There was nothing but empty space between me and death, and I stayed where I was, trembling violently from head to foot.

'Keep going,' said the Old Man. He put out a hand and took

a firm hold of my belt. 'Keep going,' he said. 'Don't look down. Whatever you do, don't look down.'

We reached the last couple of yards where the trunk narrowed and the least movement made it rock and sway. The Old Man took his hand away from my belt and gently propelled me forward. I knew he was indicating that I should finish the journey alone, under my own steam, while he hung back and waited his turn. I knew the last six feet were suspect. I knew it might not take our combined weight, and I knew that I was putting us both at risk. But for all that I was quite unable to continue without the comfort of his guiding hand. They were yelling at me from the bank, the Colonel was shouting furiously from the far side, the Old Man was pushing me from behind, and still I could not move. I crouched down very low, clutching the trunk with both hands, all my limbs petrified with panic. The Old Man crouched down near me.

'Come on now, Sven, pull yourself together. You can't give up at this stage. We've only a few more feet to go. What are you scared of? You've seen all the others do it.'

Yes, I'd seen all the others do it, and I'd seen Tiny hanging upside down and I'd seen three men fall to their death, and any minute now I was likely to join them, because I couldn't hold on very much longer ...

'Sven, for crying out loud!'

The Old Man was growing excited, and no wonder. Who wouldn't be, perched up in space with a two hundred foot drop below you and a gibbering idiot only a yard away from you who was likely to go mad at any moment and drag you down with him into the void ...

'I can't move,' I said. 'It's no use, I can't move.'

Scurrying up and down the tree trunk were hundreds of ants. An entire nation of ants. They were swarming along the highways and byways of the various cracks and crevices, some of them taking short cuts over my hands. I watched them toiling up the hillocks of my thumbs and skating down again the other side. I stared as they fought their way through the jungle of fine hairs, and I knew that were I to take my eyes off them for even a second, I should go plummeting down on to the rocks below ...

'All right, then, stay there! Bloody well stay there and rot!'

The Old Man had lost patience at last. He clambered over the top of me and scrambled the last few feet to safety. I heard Porta calling to me from the bank, but I had lost all power of movement. I could no longer even raise my head to look at them. And then the branches suddenly sagged under the weight of a new and heavier body than that of the Old Man. A couple of brawny arms reached out towards me, they plucked me off my perch and they held me a moment, suspended in space.

'All right,' said Tiny. 'I've got the bastard. Haul him in.'

Hands reached out from all sides and pulled us in like a couple of stranded fish. The very moment I was safely landed, the storm broke. No more friendly smiles and shouts of encouragement. Now it was oaths and curses and angry buffetings from all sides. Only Barcelona, who had had to be rescued himself, gave me a sympathetic and slightly shamefaced grin.

Suddenly, from the other side of the chasm, came the sound of a shot. Me and my miserable failings were abruptly forgotten as we watched a macabre drama being played out on the far bank. The Colonel had ordered Kuls across the makeshift bridge, and Kuls, in a vicious panic which I could well understand, had pulled out his revolver and taken a pot-shot at his tormentor. The Colonel fired back, but missed, whereupon both men instantly ducked behind the rocks and began a Wild West shoot-up, with bullets flying in all directions. Tiny put two fingers in his mouth and sent a loud, jeering whistle echoing round the canyon. Porta began to stamp his feet up and down and cheer. A bullet caught Kuls in the shoulder and sent him spinning to the ground. He scrambled to his feet and tried to run, but lost his footing on the loose scree and went slipping and sliding down the slope, straight over the edge of the cliff and down towards destruction in the foaming waters far below. Morbidly I stood watching as he fell. When his body hit the sharp edge of a rock it burst open at the seams like a sawdust puppet, and its contents spilled out.

The Colonel stood sponging his brow with a handkerchief. He put his revolver back into his holster and very slowly sat down to remove his boots. He knotted them together and hung them round his neck. Then he took out his revolver again and carefully checked the number of bullets it contained. For one who had been so eager, he now seemed oddly reluctant to set foot on the swaying tree trunk. Tiny and Porta began a series of catcalls, and the Old Man shouted anxiously:

'Better get a move on, sir!'

The Colonel cleared his throat.

'Very well, Sergeant,' he called. 'I'm coming.'

Gingerly, he set foot on the tree trunk. He had scarcely taken more than half a dozen wobbling steps forward when a series of gunshots rang out. The Colonel instantly abandoned his upright position and slipped down astride the trunk, pulling himself along in a series of nervous twitches and jerks. From the forest, a horde of Russian troops now burst forth. The Legionnaire swore and threw himself down behind his machine-gun. A hail of bullets and grenades was soon flying back and forth across the gorge, with the unfortunate Colonel caught in the middle of it all. To our astonishment and disbelief, some of the Russians, goaded as usual by their officers, now also began attempting to make the crossing.

'Poor fools,' said Gregor. 'Poor bloody fools.'

They were amazingly surefooted, and seemed quite unperturbed by the bouncing and swaying of the trunk, though they must have known they were walking to almost certain death. We would hold our fire so long as the Colonel was there, but the minute he reached safety we would not hesitate to pick them off, one by one, as they arrived on our side of the bank.

The Colonel never did reach safety. He was hit in the head by a Russian bullet and was probably dead long before he reached the jagged-toothed water two hundred feet below.

'Right,' said the Old Man, in brisk tones which indicated that at least one problem was solved. 'Get that bridge blown and let's pull out of here.'

While the rest of us engaged the enemy and Barcelona gave them cover, Tiny and Porta roped together several T mines and attached them in a cluster to the end of the trunk. Seconds later, there was a shattering explosion, which not only blew up the pine tree and its foolhardy line of approaching Russians, but also tore away great chunks of the cliff, starting a landslide of rocks and boulders. That was the end of the enemy's attempt to come over and join us.

We set off again. Another weary, footslogging march that went on for hours, through all the usual hazards and discomforts of the rain-sodden countryside. Leather belts and shoulder straps cut through the frayed remains of jackets and shirts and bit deep into bare flesh. Feet without socks were rubbed raw in rotting boots. We had no food or drink left and no idea when or where, or even if, we should meet up with our retreating army. Twice we were forced to dive for cover, flat on our bellies in stinking roadside ditches, as squadrons of Russian Jabos dived out of the clouds towards us.

Towards dusk, a feeling of despair began to creep over me. It nagged at me like an aching tooth, it throbbed and it pounded and it hammered in my head. Where were we marching and what were we marching there for? What were we going to do when we finally got there?

What, indeed, were we going to do? The answer was simple: we weren't going to do anything. There was nothing left to do. There was nowhere left to go. We weren't actually marching anywhere at all. We were running from the Russians, but we couldn't go on running indefinitely. The war was over, we all knew that. Germany had been defeated, Adolf Hitler had had his day, and the tattered remnants of the glorious German Army were being chased half-way across Europe and driven into a corner.

It was all so very pointless. Why spend your life aimlessly marching from one place to another when you might just as easily stay still and be slaughtered in comparative comfort on the spot?

'Sod this for a laugh!' I said.

I threw my machine-gun away and flung myself down at the side of the road, where I sprawled at my ease and watched the feet go by. Poor fools. There they went, with their endless march, march, march, down the eternal road to nowhere. Poor stupid fools.

A hand suddenly took hold of my hair and jerked me painfully to my feet. Another hand thrust my gun at me. From behind, a boot caught me a hefty clout in the backside. I turned indignantly and saw Porta giving me one of his evil leers.

'What are you bellyaching about?' he demanded. 'Christ had his cross to carry, you've got your machine-gun. Seems fair enough to me.'

Before I could think of any fitting retort, we heard a shout from further along the road.

'Halt! Wer da?'*

Whoever it was, he didn't wait for a reply. A shot rang out, and Barcelona, who happened to be up at the front, was thrown to the ground with half his left arm and shoulder blown off. We had evidently caught up with our retreating army.

'Which fool did that?' roared the Old Man.

A child of perhaps sixteen years of age, wearing SS uniform, appeared nervously from behind a tree. He was dangling a sub-machine-gun from his hand as if it were a child's toy.

'Are you raving bloody mad?' shouted the Old Man.

The boy hung his head.

'I thought you were the Russians,' he muttered.

'Russians!' said Gregor, indignantly. 'Do we look like bloody Russians?'

He knelt beside Barcelona and tore open the rags of his uniform. His arm was smashed and bloody, but the bullet had missed the bone. He could count himself fortunate, indeed : by the time he was fit once more for active service, the war would almost certainly be over. I wouldn't have minded a shattered arm myself.

* Halt! Who goes there?

193

An Oberscharführer appeared, followed by a group of young SS infantrymen. They looked more like schoolchildren than soldiers.

'What's going on?' demanded the Oberscharführer. 'Who are you? Where have you come from?'

'Over the hills and far away!' snapped the Old Man. 'We've been having a tea party with the Russians, and we've run away with all the best silver stuffed up our arses ... What the devil does it matter where we've come from?' he said, testily. 'Are you people in the habit of shooting up your own side?'

The Oberscharführer hunched an apologetic shoulder.

'What can you do?' he said, and he indicated his flock of smooth-faced cherubim. 'They only got here yesterday. They're taking them straight out of the cradle and expecting us to fight a war with them. It's hopeless. They don't know one end of a gun from the other.'

'Well, you hang around here very much longer,' said the Old Man, grimly, 'and they'll soon have the opportunity of finding out. The Reds are on their way, and it's my bet they're going to catch up with us any minute now.'

'The Russians? On their way here?'

'That's what I said,' said the Old Man.

The Oberscharführer mopped gingerly at his face with a pad of material. He had no flesh at all on one cheek, and his left eye was puckered up like a piece of smocking.

'Have they got tanks?' he said.

'Well, they're certainly not pushing through the forest in wheelbarrows, I can tell you that!'

A Hauptsturmführer now arrived on the scene, strolling leisurely as if he were doing the rounds of his estate. He heard the Old Man's report and frowned, querulously.

'Why did your company not pull out along with the rest of the division?'

'We never had any orders to pull out,' said the Old Man, shortly. 'We were told to wait for the signal; and the signal never came.'

The Hauptsturmführer immediately took a note of all the details, including the name of the divisional commander, General von Weltheim and his grand piano, who had been responsible for the débâcle. Tiny and Porta made no attempt to conceal their glee. The prospect of a full-blown general for once being held responsible for his own criminal negligence was sweet indeed.

Barcelona was shipped safely aboard an ambulance which was leaving for Warsaw, but it scarcely looked like it would be a very pleasant journey. The ambulance was full to overflowing, and he had to share a stretcher with a man who was quite plainly going to die long before he arrived. An hour later, the rest of us pulled out and subsequently fell in at the tail end of a long line of trucks and ambulances heading for Warsaw. The procession was accompanied by a straggle of Polish refugees, clutching their belongings in pillowcases or pushing them on rickety handcarts.

We had not been going long before the inevitable squadron of Jabos roared out of the clouds and came diving down towards us. The truck we were in reared up and plunged off the road, overturning in the ditch. We scrambled out before it could catch fire and tore hell for leather into the meadow which bordered the road, dropping down behind a hedge for cover. There was the sound of explosions as the Jabos scored direct hits on some of the vehicles in the convoy. Over the brow of the hill, away across the other side of the fields, a KW2 surged into view, accompanied by several T34s. As we watched, the tanks ploughed right through the middle of a knot of infantrymen and calmly continued on their way. A section of pioneers came running up to us. With quite astonishing rapidity they distributed bazookas all round, and promptly shot away out of sight across the road. The Old Man scuttled sideways like a crab on his short bandy legs and tapped Gregor and me on the shoulder.

'OK, Sven. You take the leading T34. Gregor, you take the second. I'll leave Porta to look after the KW, and Tiny can have whatever's left over. Nobody to shoot until——'

His words were cut short by the sudden and premature firing of a bazooka further along the line. The grenade went hurtling straight towards the leading tank, ricocheted harmlessly off the turret and flew fizzing into the air like a firework display. The Old Man swung round, his face pursed up with fury.

'Who the bloody hell did that?'

Whoever it was, he had successfully taken away all element of surprise. The tanks were now aware of our presence. They hesitated just a fraction of a second, as if to draw breath, then turned in formation and came towards us, cannons firing. A small fleet of ambulances and stretcher-bearers were wiped out *en route*. The ambulances were reduced to burning wrecks. The wounded lay scattered in the mud. Some were caught up in the tank tracks and churned to mincemeat. I saw one of the stretcher-bearers sitting on his own stretcher and staring with blank incomprehension at his legs, which had been sliced off at the thigh and were lying on the ground in front of him. A major from an infantry regiment was running about like a headless chicken with great geysers of blood pumping out of his neck. A sergeant stooped to pick up his severed hand, but was blown to pieces by Russian artillery before he could reach it.

The leading T34 was coming nearer, and I took a firm hold on my bazooka. The KW2, all eighty tons of it, reared up slightly each time it fired its cannon. The nose had been painted to look like the open mouth of a killer shark, with all the teeth carefully depicted in a luminous gold. A couple of grenades which some fool had fired too early bounced harmlessly off its belly. It was useless attempting to fire at more than fifty feet; the grenades were unable to pierce the heavy steel plating.

I fixed my eye to the sights. Still a good thirty yards away. Much too far. I forced myself to keep calm and patient. There was always a temptation, when other people were losing their heads, to join in and start going berserk along with them. The

Old Man had his hand held up in readiness for the signal to fire.

A couple of men were caught by the leading T34 and tossed limbless into the air. I caught a brief glimpse of an officer as he took a casual glance out of the open turret, but he disappeared before I had a chance to pick up my rifle.

It was said, these days, that the Russians were using female radio operators in their tank crews. I looked steadily at the approaching T34, the one that was my own particular target, and I wondered if I was going to kill some poor woman. Not that I really cared. There was no room for sentiment when you had sixty tons of tank lumbering towards you. But if there was a woman inside, I did hope it wouldn't turn out to be Tania. Tania had once saved my life, and I didn't want to kill her.

Tania had saved many men's lives. She was a young surgeon, a captain in the Red Army, who had worked as a prisoner of war in our divisional hospital at Kharkov. We were short of doctors, and it was Tania who performed most of the emergency operations. It was Tania who had so patiently dug all the shrapnel out of me when a shell blew up under my feet and almost killed me. She had disappeared one night during the Russian advance on the town. She had gone round the wards shaking hands with every patient and wishing him luck, and then she had slipped away in the darkness and presumably rejoined her own side. I often wondered what had become of her. The Russians would not easily forgive her for having tended the German wounded. She could well be in that T34 at this very moment, stripped of her rank and sent to the front to be killed——

'Fire!'

The field before us disappeared beneath a rolling sea of flame. I caught the leading tank on the upper half of the turret, which was where I had aimed—just in case there was a girl like Tania somewhere inside. It would give her a bit more chance of getting out alive. The officer whom I had previously seen was blown out by the explosion. He was lifted high up in the air, sitting astride a great blue tongue of fire. As the flames

197

roared upwards they opened out into a vast black umbrella which covered the entire sky. Three of the tanks had been put out of action, but the fourth was still intact. Tiny stared at it, indignantly. He seemed scarcely able to believe that he, of all people, could have failed to hit the target. He aimed a savage kick at the bazooka, as if that alone were to blame, snatched up a magnetic mine and went racing with it towards the tank. Nothing happened: the mine was a dud.

A sergeant from the Pioneer Corps seized upon a discarded bazooka and raised it to his shoulder. He fired, and the weapon exploded in his face. A tongue of flame about twenty yards long shot out backwards and wrapped itself round him, and he hurled himself, screaming, into the ditch. There was nothing anyone could do to help him. Withing seconds he looked more like a side of underdone roast beef than a human being. Raw flesh falling off the bones and an appalling stench of burnt meat. And, incredibly, the creature was still alive. It rose up in its ditch and extended its twisted claws towards us. From eyes which could no longer see in a face which was no longer there, it seemed to be begging us to take pity on it. I recoiled in disgust and bumped into Gregor, who was standing directly behind me. He nudged me forward again with his elbow.

'Do something,' he said. 'Do something.'

I pulled out my revolver and slipped back the safety catch, then moved hesitantly forward to the thing in the ditch. Before I could take aim, it had snatched at the weapon with its bare-boned fingers and turned it towards the black hole where a mouth had once been. A shot rang out, and I stood watching in silent horror as the last charred remains of flesh slipped away from the skeleton and what was left of the creature sank back into the ditch to die.

The T34 moved implacably onwards. We abandoned our positions and fled, but even as we left the shelter of the hedge a squadron of fighter planes came swooping down upon us. They skimmed low across the fields, strafing everything within sight, and were followed almost immediately by Jabos dis-gorging napalm bombs.

The whole world seemed to be on fire. The fields were burning, the roads were burning, even the topmost branches of the very tallest trees were alight. Men, women and children, soldiers and civilians, milled in panic in the centre of the inferno. Those on the edges stood more chance, provided they were young enough and fit enough to outstrip the encroaching flames. The very young and the very old, the sick and the wounded, were left behind for the funeral pyre. I saw a peasant woman drag herself along the ground with her belly ripped open and all her insides trailing after her. I saw a mother crouched over a small child who had had both its arms blown off. I saw men writhing in agony with all their clothes on fire.

The Jabos came roaring overhead a second time, and a lance-corporal who was a perfect stranger to me suddenly snatched my bazooka away and turned it up into the sky.

'Don't be a fool!' I yelled. 'You won't do any good with that!'

'You wanna bet?' he said.

I probably would have done, had there only been time. I had never seen anyone bring down an aeroplane with a bazooka. But the Jabos had become over-confident. They were darting and diving like swallows in search of flies, and one made the mistake of coming just a little bit too close to my friend with the bazooka. We shouted together in evil triumph as it went crashing into the trees and smashed itself to pieces.

'Very clever,' said the Old Man. 'Now perhaps you'll be satisfied.'

We looked at him, reproachfully.

'We just got a Jabo,' I said.

'That's as may be!' he snapped. 'Meanwhile, it may have escaped your attention that while you've been fooling about taking pot shots at enemy aircraft, there's been a full-scale retreat going on!'

He prodded us both forward, and suddenly infected by the general confusion, we took to our heels and joined in the flight. For three hours we continued along the road, with its dismal scattered wreckage of abandoned humanity and burnt-out vehicles. The dead and the dying were left for the Russians to mop up. There was no time to be spared for men who were clearly beyond help. The wounded, if they were lucky enough to draw attention to themselves, were picked up and bundled pell-mell into trucks and ambulances. There were no more bandages, no more ointments, no more morphine. They should have considered themselves fortunate that they had not been left lying on the road.

Suddenly, out of nowhere, appeared a company of T34s, with hordes of Siberian infantrymen clinging to them like flies on a flypaper. At once the column broke up and dived for cover, but some were not quite quick enough. The tanks churned straight through the middle of us and wiped out almost an entire company at one blow. I myself was caught in the neck by a stray bullet and instantly went galloping off in search of a free place in one of the ambulances. I was streaming with blood and I knew perfectly well that the bullet was lodged against my vertebrae and that at any moment I should be attacked by total paralysis. The Orderly who attended me was a coarse, brutal fellow with evidently no medical knowledge whatsoever.

'Bullet?' he said. 'I can't see no bleeding bullet. All you've got, mate, is a slight scratch.'

'A slight scratch?' I said. 'Are you raving mad? I've got a bullet stuck in my neck, and if you don't get me to a hospital pretty damn quick you'll have a corpse on your hands!'

He shrugged his shoulders. He obviously couldn't have cared less.

'Hospital!' he said. 'That's a good one!'

'Look here,' I demanded, 'are you or are you not going to do something about this wound?'

'Not,' he said; and he winked at me. 'Next time, sonny, try getting your head blown off. You stand more chance that way.' He turned to the next customer, who was sitting smugly on the ground with a couple of raw stumps where his feet had been. 'No doubt about this one,' said the orderly, cheerfully. He

200

selected a red form from a pile by his side and grinned at me. 'That's the way to do it,' he said.

'But I can't get my helmet on!' I said. 'I can't move my head!'

'A German soldier shouldn't want to move his head.' He picked up a rubber stamp and thumped it on the form. 'Where else do you need to look but straight ahead?'

It was obviously no use arguing with the fellow. I slid my eyes away to the pile of forms. One red form and a rubber stamp, that was all it required ... Slowly, I stretched out a hand.

'Oh, no, you don't!' The orderly had turned, quick as a flash, and caught me in the act. 'Go and get yourself decently torn to shreds, and then perhaps I might think about it. Until then, get the hell out of here and stop pestering me. There are sick men waiting to be seen to.'

A couple of sergeants picked me up and frogmarched me outside. They threw me to the ground and beckoned to a nearby military policeman.

'Hey, you! Just keep an eye on this skyving bastard. Make sure he doesn't try any more funny business.'

Furious, I scrambled to my feet and found myself facing straight into the barrel of an automatic rifle.

'Funny business, eh? You been trying it on, have you?'

'Trying it on!' I said, indignantly. 'I've got a bullet pressing on my spinal chord and the swine refuses to send me to hospital!'

'That's hard luck,' he said. 'That's real hard luck ... I suppose you was trying to nick one of them little red passports to a free holiday?'

I raised my eyes from the barrel of the rifle and saw that the man was a corporal. I relaxed slightly. You stood a fair chance with a corporal. You could sometimes even talk to them like human beings.

'I reckon a man's entitled to it,' I said. 'After five years of war.'

There was a pause. He could shoot me for that, I thought. It all depended upon whether he was a Prussian or a Porta. Slowly he lowered the rifle.

'I guess you're right,' he said. 'Trouble is, mate, everyone's got the same idea. You're the fourteenth what's tried it on in the last hour ... I'd try it on myself if I thought I'd get away with it. But not a hope. Not a hope in hell.'

'Bastards,' I said. I felt cautiously at the hole in my throat. I was glad to note that it was still bleeding. 'I suppose I'd better try to rejoin my company,' I said. 'Though I doubt if I'll ever make it. I'll probably get gangrene long before I get there.'

The corporal slung his rifle over his shoulder and we set off together.

'You'll be lucky,' he said. 'You'll be lucky if you're alive long enough to get gangrene. Between here and Warsaw the whole place is crawling with MPs. You know what for? To shoot deserters.'

'I'm not a deserter,' I said.

'Everyone's a deserter, these days. They catch you strolling about the countryside all by yourself, they'll shoot you soon as look at you. That's the way it goes. Shoot on sight, that's what we been told. Seems like half the bleeding Army's running in the wrong direction. Still——' He closed one eye and pulled a cunning face. 'Don't you worry, mate. You'll be all right with me. I'll see you through it.'

We walked the road together, swinging along quite cheerfully. No enemy aircraft came to disturb us. For nearly half an hour we were by ourselves, following in the wake of the retreating army, picking our way through the trail of carnage and desolation. I forgot about the bullet pressing on my spine, and for a while we played at kicking a stone in and out among the corpses and the wrecked vehicles, laughing like children on their way home from school. At one point we were interrupted by a convoy of trucks. An impatient sergeant in a large Krupp stinking of petrol fumes, leaned out of the cabin and yelled at us to get off the road. But at the sight of a military policeman he instantly withdrew his head and sent the vehicle careering onwards in a cloud of dust.

'Deserters,' said my companion; and he shrugged a careless shoulder. 'They'll never make it, poor fools. There's a road block somewhere ahead. They don't stand a chance.'

We sat down under a hedge to rest our legs, and the corporal pulled out three packets of Camels and insisted on giving them to me.

'You take them,' he said. 'I can get plenty more ...'

There was no reason to break our necks to arrive anywhere. We sat smoking and chatting together for almost an hour, until a column of SS tanks appeared and covered us in a spray of mud and oil from the churned-up road.

'Bastards,' said the corporal. 'They'll get what's coming to them when they reach the roadblock ...'

Another thirty minutes and we ourselves had reached it. The road was swarming with MPs, and a tight-lipped captain came towards us. Thanks to the intervention of the corporal, I was allowed to pass safely through this ante-chamber of death and go on my way unmolested. I could see that many others had not been so fortunate.

I reached the far side and turned to wave goodbye to my erstwhile companion. He had taken up his position behind the barricade, and suddenly he was no longer the man with whom I had smoked and talked and played at football, he was a military machine primed to kill. I raised my hand in a farewell gesture. His eyes flickered very slightly in recognition, but he did not return my salute.

I continued my journey alone, under skies that were grey and menacing.

'We live all our lives in close proximity with death. Let us therefore turn that fact to our advantage. Let us learn how to make full use of it ... If the future of the German race is to be assured, there must be room for expansion: Europe must be wiped clear of the inferior nations ...'

Himmler. Talk given to SS Generals at Weimar
on 12th December 1943.

'IT is a stain on the honour of the German Army that a single Pole should still be left alive in Warsaw!' Himmler turned in cold fury upon Obergruppenführer Berger. 'Why have you not carried out my orders? Did I not tell you to destroy them down to the last man, woman and child? So! Why has it not been done?'

Berger wiped his perspiring forehead with a hand that trembled.

'Reichsführer, we have done all that we can. The losses have been appalling. The uprising in Warsaw has already cost us the lives of two thousand German soldiers——'

'Don't talk to me of losses! I am not interested in your tales of woe. Results are the only things that matter. You think the Fatherland should sit down and weep for every soldier killed in battle? On the contrary! It should be proud that it has sons who are willing to lay down their lives for their country!'

'Yes, indeed, Reichsführer, but——'

'But me no buts!' Himmler made a fist and brought it crashing down on to a table. 'I gave you an order, and I expect that order to be carried out. Raze Warsaw to the ground! Wipe it off the face of the map! It has no place in the German Reich. It has forfeited all claim to such an honour! Do I make myself quite clear? Because if not,' said Himmler, with a glacial smile, 'it can always be arranged to have you transferred to the Russian front. There is no room in the SS for those who are scared to spill a little blood. Blood, my dear Berger, is the currency of war. And it is from rivers of blood that strong nations are born ... Remember that, and act accordingly.'

The Reichsführer swept from the room. Berger put away his handkerchief and crossed rapidly to the telephone.

'Dirlewanger? This is Berger speaking. Why the devil haven't you carried out my orders? I thought I instructed you to raze Warsaw to the ground? Why the devil is it still standing?'

There was a guarded pause.

'Well?' snapped Berger.

'My dear fellow,' said Dirlewanger, 'I assure you we have done the best we can. Perhaps you are not aware that we have suffered ninety per cent losses trying to exterminate this place?'

'I am not interested in your losses! If you think the task is beyond your capabilities, just say so and I can easily arrange to have you transferred to the Russian front. Otherwise I give you forty-eight hours in which to complete the job. By the end of that time I shall expect the name of Warsaw to have disappeared once and for all from the face of the map ...'

AT THE SIGN OF THE WELCOMING GOAT

WARSAW. Gregor and Porta were reclining on the wreckage of a burnt-out JS* tank. They were passing a bottle of vodka between them. Porta had his feet propped nonchalantly on the charred remains of a Russian major, and Gregor was using the upturned hand of a dead man as an elbow rest.

'It's a known fact,' said Porta. 'Churchill's got a list of

* JS—Joseph Stalin.

every Nazi in the country. He's sworn they're all going to be hanged.'

'He can skin 'em alive and tear their guts out as far as I'm concerned,' said Gregor, vindictively. 'Serve 'em bloody well right.' He took hold of the vodka bottle and squinted at it thoughtfully. 'What I can't understand,' he said, 'is why Adolf had to go and pick on England in the first place.'

'He couldn't stand Churchill,' explained Porta. 'It's a known fact.'

Gregor downed another quarter of a pint of neat vodka.

'God will punish the English,' he said, righteously. 'That's what the Kaiser said.'

'Adolf thinks he is God,' said Porta.

He leaned back with his hands behind his head. He crossed his legs one over the other and one of the Major's feet dropped off. Gregor stared dispassionately at it as it rolled into the gutter.

'Know what?' he said.

'What?' said Porta, with his eyes closed.

'I reckon I'll be bleeding glad when it's all over,' said Gregor.

Porta shrugged.

'Who won't? Might get a bit of peace and quiet at last.'

Gregor picked up a spent shell and flung it moodily at the blackened remains of the foot lying in the gutter.

'Maybe now we've had the arse kicked out of us all the way round Europe and back, they won't be quite so keen on picking quarrels no more.'

'You wanna bet?' said Porta, cynically. 'It's them up top who picks all the quarrels. It's easy, ain't it? They pick the quarrels and we do all the dirty work for 'em. They don't hardly know there's a war going on, they don't.'

Gregor selected another shell.

'It's all a bleeding con trick,' he said.

'You're right it is,' agreed Porta. 'Whole of life's a bleeding con trick, ain't it?'

Over on the Praga side of the town they were fighting a

battle for the Kommandantur in the Place Adolf Hitler, where Armija Krajowa and his partisans had installed themselves. They had slaughtered all the personnel and were now themselves being subjected to a fierce barrage by German troops, who had been trying unsuccessfully to dislodge them for the past couple of hours. The Poles were returning the fire with captured German guns, and as we listened the battle began to increase in intensity. Shells started to fall uncomfortably close, and Porta sat up and swore as a flying splinter embedded itself in his cheek.

'This place is getting to be unhealthy,' he complained. He snatched the precious bottle of vodka from Gregor, swung himself off the wreckage of the tank and set off down the street. 'Let's go,' he said.

We had barely taken half a dozen steps across the square when a hail of machine-gun fire sent us diving for the nearest doorway. We crowded inside, trampling our way through the usual scattering of corpses.

A couple of young girls went running past, their skirts flying high in the air. Tiny, risking his life, poked his head out of the doorway and whistled at them. This instantly provoked another stream of bullets from the far side of the square.

'Damn you, get back!' snapped the Old Man.

We retired hastily behind our stockade of human sandbags.

'For crying out loud,' said Porta, as half the ceiling collapsed on top of us and covered everything in grey powder. He clutched anxiously at his vodka bottle. 'We can't stay here all day. There's nothing to eat.'

The Old Man glared at him.

'We'll stay here until I say we go!'

There was a fresh burst of machine-gun fire. Porta's vodka bottle was shattered. He gave a yell of rage, but it was drowned out by an agonised scream from a corporal of the Pioneer Corps who had attached himself to us earlier in the day. I turned in time to see a jet of thick purple blood spurting from his mouth, and then he fell forward on to the barricade of corpses.

'This is no longer a joke,' snarled Porta, hurling his broken bottle into the street.

'It's coming from that house over there,' I said, pointing.

Porta turned furiously on me.

'If you can see where it's coming from, why don't you go and do something about it instead of standing there like a fart in a bleeding trance?'

'I was only trying to be helpful,' I said.

'Helpful, my arse! You're worse than bloody useless!'

'So what do you want me to do?' I said, frigidly. 'Go across and ask them to stop?'

Before Porta and I could make matters even worse by cold-bloodedly attempting to murder each other, Tiny had suddenly snatched a couple of hand grenades from his pouch and gone bounding over the barricade and across the street. He dived for cover behind an overturned car, and as he did so a grenade was thrown from one of the windows of the house and landed directly in front of him. Tiny promptly scooped it up and sent it flying back again. There was the sound of an explosion, and the entire front of the house was torn away. Three men scrambled unhurt out of the rubble and attempted to make a run for it, but the Legionnaire eliminated all three with one burst from his sub-machine-gun.

'Let's get the hell out of here,' said Gregor.

We fled from the house and round the corner of the square into a narrow street which was filled with smoke and the stench of burning flesh. The men of the SD had blown up the central prison and all the prisoners. Warsaw must be wiped off the face of the map. Every man, every woman and every child must be exterminated ...

Porta was complaining about his belly. It was almost two hours since he had last eaten, and even the Old Man agreed that he could scarcely be expected to go any further without stopping off somewhere for a refill. There was only one place to stop off in Warsaw, and that was at the Sign of the Welcoming Goat. It was a bistro which had been discovered by Porta within an hour of his arrival in the town. It was small, filthy, noisy and overcrowded and it stank of sweat and unwashed feet, but Porta had come to some sort of an arrangement with Piotr, the vast red-bearded Ukranian to whom it belonged, and he made sure we had the best of whatever was going.

We seated ourselves at an unscrubbed table which was covered with the mouldering remnants of yesterday's meals. Piotr came to take our order.

'I think we'll try the duck today,' said Porta.

A military policeman at the next table swung his head round sharply, his eyes bright with suspicion. He need never have worried. The duck was only a crow, boiled until it tasted like an old dish cloth. It was served with cutlet of dog, and followed by a particularly foul-smelling fish preserve. Each delicacy was washed down with a strong red wine. This was part of Porta's financial arrangement with Piotr. How he ever came to make such an arrangement, we never found out. We always maintained a discreet silence on the subject. It never did to inquire too closely into Porta's commercial affairs, particularly when you yourself were reaping the benefit. On any reckoning, boiled crow and cutlet of dog were preferable to a slice of sewer rat or a leg of mouse.

Not far away from us was an Army padre. He studied us a while, but seemed more interested in an officer who was slumped in a corner by the stove drinking beer. His eyes returned again and again to this man, and in the end he rose and walked across to him.

'Excuse me, Captain——' He pulled up a chair. 'Do you mind if I join you?'

The officer looked up from his beer glass. His head and one eye were swathed in layers of bloodstained bandages. Half his face had been badly burnt, the skin was red and puckered and the features were all distorted. His uniform was tattered and torn, covered in mud and blood and oil. The hand holding the beer glass was shaking. The padre sat down with a gentle pious smile.

'I wonder,' he said, 'if you would let me help you?'

'Help me?' The Captain threw the last of his beer down his

throat and called across to Sofja, behind the bar, for a refill. 'How the devil can you help me?' he demanded. 'Unless, of course, you have a regiment to offer me?'

'I did not mean that sort of help, my son——'

'No?' said the Captain. He twisted his lips into a parody of a smile. 'A new face, then? How about a new face? I mislaid the old one somewhere. Rather careless of me. That's why they won't issue me with another one, you understand. A man is given only one face in his lifetime. It's up to him to make sure he looks after it. Don't you agree?' He raised his beer mug. 'Your health, Father. May your beauty never desert you.'

The padre shook his head gravely.

'Beauty is not external,' he said. 'The Lord does not look upon a man's outward appearance. He does not judge a man by the quality of his flesh, but by the quality of his soul.'

'Spare me the sick-making sentiment, for God's sake!' The Captain banged down his glass on the table. He wiped a hand across his mouth and rose somewhat unsteadily to his feet. 'Go and prate elsewhere! You offend me with your pious gibble gabble. Go out there and get half your head blown away, and then come back and tell me what it feels like. I might be a bit more willing to listen to you.'

He staggered out of the bar, and the door swung shut behind him. The padre remained silent a moment, then he, too, rose to his feet. He made a brief sign of blessing to everyone in the room.

'God be with you,' he murmured, and followed the Captain out into the street.

'Daft old goat,' said Porta.

He reached across the table for the bottle of vodka, but before he could pick it up there was the sound of an explosion and all the lights went out. The door was blown off its hinges and was carried across the room by the blast. Tables and chairs were overturned, windows shattered and men thrown to the floor.

We lay for a moment where we had fallen. Flakes of plaster

rained down upon us from the ceiling, and the floorboards quaked beneath us. Slowly, the smoke and the dust began to clear. We crawled cautiously to our feet and looked about us at the damage. Piotr rose up ghost-like from behind the bar, his head and shoulders covered in plaster. Through one of the gaping windows we could see across the street to the Radio Building. Polish partisans had set up a mortar on the roof, and half a dozen German soldiers were engaged in a mountaineering expedition up the side of the building. They went hand over hand up a length of rope which had been attached to the railings on one of the balconies.

While Piotr and the Old Man struggled to put the door back on its hinges, the rest of us began setting up the chairs and tables, trying to figure out the cost of broken glasses and bottles. Tiny stepped outside to have a closer look at the progress of the mountaineers and returned with the information that the rope had been cut and that there were half a dozen bodies lying on the pavement.

'What about the padre?' asked the Old Man. 'He must have walked right slap into the middle of it.'

Piotr clapped a hand dramatically to his forehead.

'I should have warned him! Fifteen hundred hours, every day, regular as clockwork, it's always the same, boom!' He thumped a fist on to the nearest table, which promptly collapsed. 'I should have warned him.'

'Well, where is he?' said the Old Man. He turned to Tiny. 'Did you see him?'

Tiny shrugged a shoulder.

'I didn't stop to look. There's too much going on out there for my liking.'

'That's the end of it,' said Piotr. 'They've finished for the day. They won't start up again. Not unless the Army comes along and starts interfering with them.'

We clattered down the stairs in search of the padre and found what was left of his body lying in a pool of blood only a few yards away. I remembered the Captain, with his ruined face and his bloodstained bandages.

211

'Your health, Father. May your beauty never desert you ...'

But the Lord does not judge a man by the quality of his flesh, but by the quality of his soul——

'Just as well,' I muttered, as I stared down at the mangled remains.

'Just as well what?' demanded the Old Man, bending over the body and searching for the identity disc and personal papers.

'Just as well,' I said, 'that the Lord's not too fussy about appearances.'

The Old Man frowned.

'That's not funny!' he snapped.

'It wasn't meant to be,' I said.

A Kubel suddenly drew up with a loud screech of brakes. A major stepped out, followed by a little rat-faced corporal.

'What is that?' he said, pointing his cane at the remnants of the padre scattered about the road.

The corporal approached cautiously.

'It's a body, sir.' He bent down to make a closer inspection. 'A chaplain, sir, I think.'

The Major looked pained.

'A chaplain?' he said. 'Dear God, is nothing sacred any more?'

He strolled nonchalantly across the road and poked about with the tip of his cane. The head and trunk of the body rolled over to face him. There was a long pause. The Major raised his eyes, unseeing, in the direction of the Vistula. I saw his adam's apple move. He cleared his throat and tucked his cane back under his arm.

'Corporal,' he said. 'Stay behind and make sure this man receives a decent burial. We can't leave a parson lying about in the middle of the road like this. It's not seemly.' He climbed back into the Kubel and seated himself behind the wheel. 'I leave it in your hands, Corporal. See to it that my orders are carried out.'

'Yes, sir.'

The corporal saluted smartly and the Kubel shot off up the road. The minute it was out of sight he dropped his hand and sent a coarse, two-fingered gesture winging after it.

'Decent burial, my flaming arse! He'll get exactly the same as anyone else, no more and no less!' He turned and spat into the gutter. 'Two-faced old git! What's a bleeding parson?'

Tiny stepped forward and waved the man out of the way.

'Off you go, mate,' he said. 'I'll give him his decent burial. You can piss off out of it.'

He collected up the mangled remains of the unfortunate padre and dragged him down to the river. There was a loud splash, and then silence. Seconds later, Tiny returned with a pair of boots in one hand and a crucifix in the other.

'Where did you get those from?' said the Old Man, suspiciously.

'These?' said Tiny. 'I found 'em, didn't I? Found 'em down by the river ...'

We began to make our way back to rejoin the Company, but by now the Poles were attacking in force from the direction of the Momoro Bridge and we were unable to get through. We were forced to hole up for a while in the ground floor of an abandoned house, with shells exploding all about us. The tower of a nearby church received a direct hit and went thundering to the ground. It was only with the greatest difficulty that the Old Man was able to keep Tiny from running out to examine it, to see if the cross were made of gold. A couple of shells demolished the building next door and brought the ceiling down on our heads. The top floor was in flames and in danger of collapsing. We were finally driven out by the smoke. The streets were on fire all round us. Heavy artillery was pounding the whole area, and buildings were caving in on every side with a roar of falling masonry.

We caught up at last with the rest of the Company, which was in a state of considerable confusion. It was in the process of being reformed under the command of Lieutenant Löwe, who had one hand heavily bandaged and whose face had been splashed on one side with burning petrol.

It was noon on the following day before we were pulled out of the battle area and allowed a few hours' respite. Men's thoughts turned instantly to food, and Tiny, Porta and I were the unfortunates selected by the second section to go in search of it. The field kitchens were some distance away, and in order to reach them we had to retrace our steps through areas that were under constant bombardment.

We managed to collect the mess tins and plunged back with them into the chaos of bursting shells and flying bullets. A sheet of flame suddenly reared up in front of us and we fell back, choking. Turning down one of the side roads, we heard a shell land on the roof of a nearby building and we had to hurl ourselves to the ground to escape the falling rubble. We turned the corner and were instantly met with a hail of machine-gun bullets. Only a few yards further on, a rooftop sniper with an automatic rifle began taking pot shots at us.

'For God's sake!' roared Tiny, almost beside himself with rage. 'Knock it off, can't you?'

To our amazement, the firing immediately ceased. I gazed upon Tiny with a new respect.

'You must try that again some time ... I wonder if it would work with T34s?'

There were three field kitchens set up in the Place de la Vistule. Three field kitchens and three queues each half a mile long. We tagged on at the end of one, and settled down, disgruntled, to await our turn.

'What's on the menu today?' yelled Porta. 'Stewed sock and dumpling?'

The cook looked sourly down the line at him. He and Porta were old enemies.

'You'll find out when you get here,' he said.

Someone turned round and volunteered the information that it was bouillabaisse. A derisive cheer went up. Bouillabaisse was a polite term used to describe a mess of rotting fish bones floating in a pool of greasy, grey liquid. Still, it was better than Porta's stewed sock and dumpling, otherwise known as ragoût of beef. Even the smell of putrefying fish could make a man lick his lips after almost twenty-four hours without food.

We moved tantalisingly slowly towards the head of the queue. Porta began to tell us about a real bouillabaisse he had once eaten in France. He described it in mouth-watering detail, dwelling morbidly upon each mouthful, until you could smell it and taste it. I closed my eyes and I felt it slowly slipping down my throat, towards my grateful belly. Even such a rare treat as Piotr's roast crow and cutlet of dog could not altogether satisfy the constant craving.

The sound of an explosion brought me sharply to my senses. I opened my eyes and found the place full of smoke. All round me, men were milling in panic with their empty mess tins.

'The bloody food's gone up!' shouted Porta.

A stray shell had landed in the centre of the square. Porta's enemy, the cook, had been dismembered. But never mind him —it was the bouillabaisse that mattered. We stared down at our feet in unbelieving horror. Across the square ran a stream of greasy grey liquid, carrying its cargo of festering fish bones down to the gutter ...

'Intellectual methods of education hold no interest for me. What is essential is that we should push youth to the very limits of his endurance, and even beyond, so that in those who survive we shall have a race of men and women who have learnt to rise above pain and to conquer the fear of death ...'

> Himmler. In a letter to Professor K. A. Eckhardt dated 14th May 1938.

IT was the élite Kedyv Regiment who were still fighting in the ruins of the ghetto. General Bor-Komorovski had given the order that the ghetto must at all costs be held, for it was the only area in the centre of the town where General Sosabowski* and his paratroops could make a landing.

The Regiment fought on, but it was a battle which had already been lost. It would not be General Sosabowski and his paratroops who came to liberate the city, but Polish communists from Moscow. Bor-Komorovski and his army had already been condemned to death; not only by Himmler in Berlin, but equally by Stalin in the Kremlin. The German with his full-scale slaughter was paving the way for the Russian, and Stalin could afford to sit back and smile. He was in no hurry. Let the Reichsführer complete his task of destruction. Then it would be time to move in.

In despair, when the paratroops failed to arrive, Bor-Komorovski despatched one of his colonels to Moscow to speak to the Russian Marshal Rokossovski. For an hour and a half the Colonel pleaded the cause of the Polish partisans. He described their plight in heart-rending detail, while the Russian listened in unyielding silence.

'All we ask is that you should let us have the support of our own two divisions. Release them and let them come to us! It's not as if we're asking you to send us any of your own troops ... For God's sake, won't anyone lift a finger to help us?'

No one would. Not the British, nor the Russians. The mission was a failure.

* Fighting with the British Army.

The Colonel disappeared on his way back to Warsaw. No one ever knew what became of him. Bor-Komorovski waited in vain for the two divisions he had requested; but like Sosabowski and his British paratroops, they never came.

THE BROTHEL

IT was Tiny and Porta who led the stampede up the staircase to The Kaiser's Night Cap. The noise of their boots on the uncarpeted steps thundered through the darkness like a herd of wild bullocks on the run.

Awaiting us on the landing was Madame Zosia Klusinksi, proprietress of one of the most elegant brothels to be found anywhere between the Volga and the Rhine. She stood with arms folded close over vast, swelling bosoms, and the expression on her face was frankly forbidding.

Tiny pounded up the last few steps and staggered into the wall. A vase of flowers standing on a cabinet was flung over the banisters and went crashing down to the ground floor. It sounded like a bomb going off. Gregor at once flung himself to the ground and put his hands over his head. We were all drunk, but Gregor was drunker than any of us.

Madame gave us a look that was plainly intended to put us off.

'I should be grateful,' she said, 'if you gentlemen would endeavour to make less noise.'

Heide put a finger to his lips. Gregor attempted to haul himself up by the banisters, but they broke under his weight and a large piece of wood followed the vase down to the ground floor.

'Sh!' said Heide, turning mottled red with rage.

'Arsehole!' shouted Gregor.

He climbed up the stairs on all fours and dragged himself to his feet by means of the cabinet. The cabinet toppled over and fell, and Gregor clutched out wildly at the first thing that came to hand. It happened, unfortunately, to be one of Madame's voluminous breasts.

'Where's the whores?' said Gregor, thickly.

Madame gave him an adroit jab in the ribs with a sharply turned elbow. Gregor tottered backwards into Tiny.

'Where's the whores?' he demanded. 'I've come here for the whores. Who's this ugly old bitch? She's not one of 'em, is she?' He pulled himself upright and snatched at the ticket which Porta was holding. 'See here,' he said, thrusting it under Madame's nose, 'I paid twelve hundred pissing zlotys to get into this dump, and now you're trying to withhold the goods ... I demand my rights! I demand to see the whores!'

Madame calmly fitted a Russian cigarette into a long holder.

'All in good time, gentlemen. All in good time.' She led the way into a large room crowded with expensive knick-knacks. 'This is a very high-class establishment, you understand. We cater only to people of taste and discretion.'

'Bring on the whores!' bellowed Gregor.

Madame sighed. She walked across to a bureau and pulled out two large albums, which she laid before us on a table.

'Perhaps you would care to look through and make your choice?' she suggested. 'Though naturally, you understand, I cannot guarantee that all the young ladies are available just at present.'

'Balls!' said Porta, sweeping both albums to the ground.

Madame turned her frosty eye upon him.

'I beg your pardon?' she said.

'I said balls!' shouted Porta. 'Gregor's quite right! Bring on the whores and let fucking commence!' He caught Madame round the waist and slapped her hard on the bottom. 'If your arse were as big as your tits,' he told her, 'I'd almost be tempted to have a bash at you ...'

Heide, almost as drunk as Gregor, had found a bright red parrot in a cage and was poking at it through the bars. The bird jumped away, slashing him viciously with a claw.

'Damn you!' screamed Heide.

'And damn you too!' screeched the parrot in reply. 'Damn your eyes, go to hell and burn alive!'

Heide picked up the cage and rattled it.

'Bloody parrot! Bloody Yid! Look at its beak, it's a bloody Yid!'

He hurled the cage across the room. It landed in my arms, and I stood holding it, trying to decide whether we were playing a game of some sort or whether it was a grenade which was going to blow up in my face.

'Fuck off!' said the parrot.

I set the cage on the floor. Gregor was trying to light some candles which stood on the table in a silver holder. It was his third attempt, having twice before set fire to his hair—having to be rescued by Tiny wielding a soda syphon.

'This is disgraceful,' said Madame. She thrust Porta to one side and like a battleship surged majestically to the window. 'I shall call the police,' she said. 'I shall call the police and have you arrested.'

She struggled a moment with the catch of the window, and when it did not immediately yield, Tiny gallantly decided to lend a hand. He hurled the soda syphon across the room. It tore through the window creating a show of splinters, leaving a jagged frill of broken glass behind it.

'There,' said Tiny. 'Now you can put your head out.'

Heide, who had by now been reduced to floor level by his total incapacity to remain upright, came crawling across to the parrot. It seemed to fascinate him. He studied it a while, then solemnly outlined the shape of its beak with his fingers. He felt his own nose and he compared the two shapes.

'It's a Jew,' he said. 'There's a filthy Jew loose in here. I'm going to kill it.'

He tore open the door of the cage and attempted to get both

hands round the parrot's neck and throttle it. The parrot stretched out a claw and scored a bright red line all the way down Heide's face.

'Ten to one on the parrot!' yelled Gregor, growing excited.

I bent down for the empty cage, and with a vague intention of being helpful attempted to cram Heide inside it. Before I knew it, he had me on the floor with him and was trying to tear my throat out with his teeth.

'Ten to one on the parrot!' shouted Gregor, chasing the bird about the room.

The door suddenly burst open. The parrot scuttled out screaming obscenities at the top of its voice. Just then a bullet embedded itself in the ceiling. Uule Heikkinen and half a dozen of his Finnish guerrilla fighters had arrived.

'OK, Grandma! Where are you hiding them?' A second bullet zipped across the room and landed in the opposite wall. Everyone instantly dived for cover. 'We want the goods, you whoremongering old bitch! We've been away fighting Russians while you've been sitting here on your great fat slobbering arse raking in the shekels ... I reckon we deserve a little fun now we're back in civilisation, don't you?'

Madame rose up from her hiding-place. She was quivering all over like a big pink jelly, but I think it was more from rage than fear.

'Get out of here!' she screeched, and her voice had lost its veneer of gentility, it was harsh and grating and could have belonged to any old slut from the nearest gutter. 'Get out of here, you load of filthy shit! I wouldn't let a single one of you anywhere near my girls! You're not fit to fuck a pig!'

Uule flung back his head and laughed appreciatively. Porta lifted one leg high in the air and farted.

'Do you mind?' said Tiny. 'This is a very high-class establishment.'

'Run by a very high-class lady,' added Gregor, and he put his hand over his mouth and made a sound that outrivalled even Porta's effort at vulgarity.

The very high-class lady aimed a vicious kick at his crutch.

Gregor caught her round the neck and held her hard against him. He had a knife in his hand and he was pressing the sharp edge against the rolling fat of her belly.

'Well? Which is it to be, you old cow? You or the girls?' He leered down into her face. 'You're an ugly old biddy, but I guess we could always put a bag over your head.' He turned her round to face the rest of us. 'What do you reckon?' he said. 'Who wants first poke?'

Heide, still lying on the floor, deposited a neat pile of vomit in the parrot's cage.

'Two at a time,' he said. He sat up and wiped his mouth on his sleeve. 'One up the back and one up the front. We can draw lots for who has what.'

'Let's see what it's like up there first,' said Tiny; and he stepped forward and rammed his hand between Madame's ample legs. 'Like a horse's collar,' he announced. 'I don't mind having a bash at it.'

Madame broke away from Gregor. She snatched up an SS knife which was lying on the mantelshelf.

'Over my dead body!' she said.

Uule leapt eagerly forward, his revolver twitching in his hand.

'That's easily arranged!'

A shot rang out. Madame gave a scream and fell backwards. She lay on the floor in a great heap of palpitating flesh, and Heide crawled forward to examine her. He sat back on his heels and looked up wonderingly at the rest of us.

'You know something?' he said. 'I never screwed a stiff before.'

'Me neither,' I said.

Gregor kicked out at the quivering mound.

'So aren't you the lucky one?' he jeered. 'It's all yours, mate! And welcome.'

Heide thrust an experimental hand up Madame's skirt. There was a shriek of outrage, and the corpse sat up and punched Heide full in the face with a clenched fist.

'You keep your hands off me, you filthy Nazi!'

Heide fell back with a bloody nose. Madame was on her feet in an instant. She showed surprising agility for one so heavily encumbered by rolls of fat. She snatched up a potted cactus and made straight for Uule. Before he could defend himself, she had brought it down on top of his head. Uule crumpled slowly to the floor, and Madame stared wildly around in search of another weapon.

'Oh no, you don't, old woman!'

One of the Finns, a massive fellow even larger than Tiny, stepped forward and grabbed her by the folds of flesh round her neck. He put both his hands to her throat and began to squeeze. Madame turned slowly from blush pink to purple. Her eyes began to bulge. Her body grew limp.

'OK,' said Porta. 'That'll do. Let her go. I reckon she might be feeling a bit more co-operative by now.'

He was quite right. Madame had looked death in the face twice in quick succession, and she knew now that we meant business.

We set her on her feet and slapped her about a bit and rammed half a bottle of brandy down her throat. She eventually tottered off quite meekly to fetch the girls. They had been well worth waiting for. These were none of your ordinary, workaday whores. They were something special, the crème de la crème, whores par excellence. Madame's capacious bosoms swelled with pride as she presented them to us. She was playing the role of general now, strutting and prancing while her troops lined up for inspection. She advanced them in line, one by one, and the parrot came waddling in with them, shrieking its usual blasphemies. Madame thrust it into its cage and threw the tablecloth over it, hushing it to silence.

'Well, gentlemen,' she said.

She looked at us rather sternly. Her gaze rested a moment on Heide, with his bloody nose, moved across to Uule, still sprawled on the floor with half a cactus on his head, moved on to Tiny and Porta and Gregor. The scum of the lower ranks. A slight shudder rippled through her body. The place already resembled a battlefield. It was like entertaining a herd of swine fresh out of the pigsty ...

'Well, gentlemen,' she said again. 'I hope we shall have no more trouble?'

She only got away with the remark because everyone's attention was riveted on the girls. Heide and Uule staggered to their feet. There was a moment of stunned silence, and then Tiny gave a loud whoop of glee and galloped forward. He seized the nearest girl round the waist and thrust a hand beneath her skirts. The girl gave a small shriek of outrage and delight. Madame flew at Tiny like an incensed tigress. She began beating at him with both fists, kicking at his legs and shouting obscenities even the parrot could not have dreamed up. Tiny recoiled like a dog shaking water from its coat. Madame hurled herself at the window. She thrust her head through the jagged hole in the glass and began screaming at the top of her voice for the police. Uule gave a great guffaw. He crossed the room and hauled Madame back inside.

'I like a woman with a bit of spirit,' he said, and he laughed as she struggled against him. The more she scratched and bit and swore, the more Uule enjoyed himself. 'Mitri, mitri!' he said. 'Do your worst, you venomous old bitch! I'm not letting you go till I've finished with you!'

The girls stood flapping and clucking like a row of broody hens. One of them caught my eye and giggled. The parrot under its tablecloth began screaming for air.

'This is something!' said Gregor, bounding forward.

Tiny had thrown his prize across the top of the grand piano and was knocking her like a man who's been tied down in a strait-jacket for the past six months. The girl gave no signs whatsoever of disliking such treatment.

Madame sunk her teeth into Uule's neck and was hanging on grimly like a bulldog. Heide was wiping his nose clean on the tablecloth, preparatory to going into action. The girl who was giggling took a fresh look at Madame and went off into paroxysms. I was just about to go across and claim her as my own personal property when heavy footsteps resounded in the

223

passage outside. A couple of military police appeared in the doorway.

'What's going on in here? Who was it shouted out the window at us?'

The orgiastic scene froze to a standstill. Madame removed her teeth from Uule's throat. Heide stood gaping, with the tablecloth wrapped about him like a toga. The parrot, uncovered, seemed too surprised to speak. The giggling girl clapped a hand to her mouth. Only Tiny, unperturbed, continued with his activities.

One of the MPs stepped forward into the room.

'Someone called the police,' he said, doggedly. 'I want to know who it was.'

'It wasn't anyone,' said Madame. She glided like an overweight sylph across the carpet. 'I'm afraid you must be mistaken, Officer. This is a private room in a private house. I and some of my friends are having a party. I resent this unwarranted intrusion.'

The man narrowed his eyes. His hand went at once to his holster, but before he could draw his revolver, Uule had advanced upon him.

'You heard what the lady said. This is a private party and she resents your intrusion ... Now get out!'

I thought for a moment there was going to be trouble, but in the end they thought the better of it. They looked at Uule, with his broad chest covered in ribbons and medals. They looked at his six Finnish partisans grouped menacingly behind him, and they wisely contented themselves with a few threatening gestures and a warning that we should think twice in future before trifling with the police. They then went clattering back down the stairs and we heard the front door slam behind them. Madame turned towards us and flung out her arms in an expansive gesture.

'Make yourselves comfortable, gentlemen. The establishment is at your disposal.' She took Uule by the hand, smiling coquettishly. 'Come,' she said. 'I will show you the way.'

The bedrooms on the next floor were like self-contained

palaces. We raced from one to another, shouting and laughing and dragging the girls with us on our tour of inspection. The Potsdam room had a marble floor and a bed which floated on a lake of water. Gregor tried it out, but complained of feeling seasick and soon transferred next door to the Turkish room, which was hung with deep scarlet draperies and smelt sweetly of incense. Porta ended up in the Room of the Seven Gardens, where every wall contained a maze of split-level aquaria with brightly coloured fish darting in and out from one pool to another.

At the far end of the passage, in a place fitted out like a vast marquee, we found a couple of SD officers and their whores. We chased them all the way down the stairs and sent them naked into the street, only consenting to drop them their uniforms out of the window. This was, of course, after we had been through their pockets, and divided their money and other possessions among us.

One of their abandoned whores, after having surveyed each of us in turn, came up to me and wound herself sinuously about my neck.

'Why did you treat those men like that?' she said, reproachfully.

I shrugged a careless shoulder.

'Because they were officers—because they belonged to the SD—because we didn't like the look of them—because we were drunk——' I pulled her along the passage and back into the marquee room. 'Take your choice,' I said.

She smiled seductively at me.

'By all means,' she murmured.

She spoke German with a strong Russian accent. She seemed more intelligent than the rest, and I was pretty sure she was a spy. Undoubtedly she had picked me out as being the youngest and greenest and the most likely to talk, but for the moment I couldn't have cared less. And for the first half hour, in any case, we neither of us had very much opportunity for speech. There were far more important matters to attend to ...

It was only afterwards, when temporarily exhausted we lay side by side in the middle of the vast circular bed, smoking cigarettes and drinking vodka, that she remembered her mission. She propped herself on one elbow and smiled down at me, her long hair falling over her shoulders and tickling my throat.

'It's funny,' she said, 'but it seems to me that we've met before somewhere ... Don't you have that feeling?'

'No,' I said. 'I can't say that I do. Perhaps I haven't read my script properly?'

'Your script?'

I hunched a shoulder.

'I don't seem to know my lines too well.'

'Oh ...' She smiled again and ran a hand along my thigh. 'I feel so sure we have met. Where have you been lately? Where were you before Poland?'

'Where wasn't I?' I said. 'Practically everywhere save the South Pole.'

'Russia?'

'Yes,' I said. 'I've been to Russia.'

'You like it there?'

'Lovely,' I said. 'The trenches were some of the nicest I've ever known. I can thoroughly recommend it.'

She grinned at that, and took a sip of vodka in an effort to cover it up.

'Where do you live?'

'Live? I don't live anywhere. I live with the Army. You could hardly call that living.'

'But where were you born?'

I stubbed out my cigarette and felt round for another.

'I wasn't born,' I said. 'I was invented. Put together bit by bit like Frankenstein's monster. I'm not a man, I'm a machine.'

'Some machine!' she said. She lit two cigarettes and put one into my mouth for me. 'Are you with a tank regiment?'

'A tank regiment?' I said, horrified. 'We don't have tank regiments in the Salvation Army!'

We stayed together all night on the big circular bed under

226

its snow-white canopy. At dawn we woke up and bathed in a scented bath. The carnage of war seemed very far away and long ago. The shrieks of men in agony no longer pierced my eardrums, and the blood of the dying seemed not so red as once it had been.

'I should like to stay in this room for ever,' I said.

The girl stepped, dripping from the bath. She stretched out on top of me on the bed, winding her arms round my neck and twisting her legs in mine.

'But don't you have to attack Warsaw?' she said.

'How should I know?' I murmured. 'I'm only a machine, remember? I don't make decisions. I have to wait until I'm programmed.'

She ran her tongue over her teeth and pressed herself against me.

'I'll programme you,' she said.

Five minutes later, an explosion shook the building. The canopy collapsed on top of us. The bed was flung across the room. We heard the roar of falling masonry and the staccato crackle of flames.

We fought our way out of the all-enveloping folds of the canopy. The girl raced for the door, which was hanging lopsided off its hinges. I snatched up my clothes from the side of the bath and bounded after her. As we reached the passage, the ceiling caved in. Great chunks of plaster came crashing down, followed by a wooden beam, which was on fire at both ends. The bedclothes caught fire almost at once, but we didn't stay behind to put the flames out. The passage was full of naked girls and half-dressed men. I saw Porta galloping along wearing nothing but his socks.

It was Madame herself, resplendent in a cherry satin negligée which successfully revealed all, who led the stampede down the stairs. The next floor was not too badly damaged, as the fire had not yet caught hold. We saved what we could from the wreckage, tossing armfuls of clothing out of the windows, and snatching the Persian rugs off the floor. Everyone carried as much as he was able to manage down the stairs to safety.

Tiny and Uule managed the grand piano between them. Porta went scavenging in the kitchen. I rescued the parrot. Madame stood outside on the pavement checking everything as it arrived, watching with hawklike eye lest anyone should attempt to run off with the silver.

'Mean old goat,' said Porta. 'Here——' He dug a hand into his pocket and pulled out a packet of new-minted roubles. 'A little parting gift. You might find 'em useful when the Russians arrive.' He winked at her. 'Just one thing,' he said. 'Make sure you rough 'em up a bit before you try using 'em. Looks better that way. Not quite so obvious ... Know what I mean?'

Madame eagerly snatched her bundle of illegal tender. Then she caught Porta into the folds of her cascading bosoms and cried over him like a mother.

'How sad that you have to leave us so soon! If you could only have stayed another night—what a time we should have had!'

'We didn't do so badly this time,' I muttered, with a wink at the parrot in its cage.

'I am an advocate of the very severest forms of punish-
ment. It is essential that strict discipline be maintained
in all our schools. Faults must be corrected, weaknesses
eliminated, and under my régime the youth of Ger-
many will rise and conquer the world . . .'

> Hitler. In a talk at the SS Officers' Training
> School. Tölz, 18th February 1937.

GENERAL ZYGMUNT BERLING was the Commander-in-Chief of
the two Polish divisions fighting with the Russian Army on the
eastern frontier of his unhappy country. After the failure of
the Colonel's mission to Rokossovski, General Zygmunt in his
turn approached the Marshal with the plea that he and his
men be allowed to cross over the Vistula and return into
Poland to help defeat the invading Germans. And he in his
turn received no for an answer.

'Niet,' said Rokossovski, in uncompromising tones.

He knocked the ash off his cigar and returned to his contemplation of a map of Europe hanging on the wall. General Berling hesitated a moment, then crossed impulsively to his side.

'Konstantin, for God's sake!' he said. 'We've known each
other a long time, you and I. You can surely grant me this one
favour? How would you feel if it were your country that was
at stake? Give me a free hand,' he urged. 'If things go wrong,
I'll accept full responsibility.'

Rokossovski picked up a pin and stuck it in the map.

'Niet,' he said, without even troubling to look round.

The General turned abruptly and left the room. He went
back to his two divisions and to the anxious inquiries of
Colonel Lisevka, his Chief of Staff.

'The answer,' said Berling, 'is niet.'

Colonel Lisevka frowned.

'And the reason?' he said.

'No reason,' said Berling. 'Just niet . . .'

At one o'clock that morning, the two Polish divisions
crossed over the Vistula and marched back into Poland. They

were accompanied by a Russian regiment composed of Ukranians from Kharkov, under the command of Colonel Rilski. All three men, Berling, Lisevka and Rilski, knew that if the attempt failed they would have signed their own death warrants. Nevertheless, they believed that what they were doing was right, and they went ahead and took the risk.

Luck was not with them. After two hours of fierce street fighting, the Polish partisans and Rilski's Ukranians had been decimated by Theodor Eicke and his SS division. Eicke's men were experts in the close combat of the streets. The Poles were used to rolling plains that stretched to the horizon and beyond. They never stood a chance. They died by the thousands on the west bank of the Vistula. They lay in the gutters, drowning in rivers of their own blood. Poland could not now hope to be free.

THE CEMETERY OF WOLA

WE had been fighting non-stop for three days, with spades and bayonets and even bare fists, in the streets surrounding the cemetery at Wola. Countless numbers of men had died for that cemetery. We had just snatched it back for perhaps the twentieth time from the partisans of Armija Krajowa, and now it was their turn to launch an attack and regain possession. It changed hands with a regularity that was becoming monotonous, and with every attack and counter-attack the corpses lay piled high in the streets. Yet another batch of graves had to be dug. But the cemetery was in a strategic position, dominating Praga, and no matter if every partisan and every German soldier gave up his life for it, the battle must be fought to the bitter, futile end.

A burnt-out chapel littered with the bodies of the dead served as our shelter. Gregor had been hit in the head by a bullet and was now wrapped up like a mummy in dirty blood-stained bandages. All of us had been injured in some degree or another, but Gregor had come very near to death. Another centimetre lower, and he would not now have been sprawled on the floor simply complaining of a headache.

A major from the General Staff appeared in the entrance of the chapel and began barking out a series of totally nonsensical orders. We stared at him with glazed eyes. The man was obviously a maniac, but he was also a major. Sullenly, resentfully, we hauled ourselves to our feet and followed him out into the inferno of the streets. Happily for us, before we had gone very far, he set eyes upon a group of SS sharpshooters of the Reich Division and decided they would serve his purpose better than a rabble of bleary-eyed and apathetic soldiers from a tank regiment. He marched them off with him towards the river, and we shot back like rabbits into the shelter of our ruined chapel with its rampart of corpses.

For a while they left us in peace and we took the opportunity to snatch a little sleep. It was the first respite we had had for seventy-two hours. We had not eaten for the past two days, and it was over a week since we had been able to remove our boots. Even Heide was beginning to stink.

At midnight we were dragged off to the Rue Wola, with instructions to set up the machine-gun in the basement of a bombed house and keep the road covered.

Shortly after dawn the first of a long column of civilians turned into the road. They were of both sexes, all ages, old men and children, invalids and pregnant women, cripples pushed in wheelchairs. Many had obviously been dragged straight from their beds, for they were shivering in their night clothes. Some had had time to pack suitcases or trunks, which they carried on their backs or dragged along behind them. Others had net bags and brown paper parcels containing what few precious possessions they had been able to snatch up as they rushed out of their homes.

'Where are they going?' I said. 'The road only leads to the cemetery.'

'Then that,' said the Old Man, dryly, 'is obviously where they are going.'

There was a pause. I looked again at the pitiful column of people. I saw one man being carried along on a makeshift stretcher. It seemed to me that he was dying.

'Why should they be going to the cemetery?' I said.

The Old Man shrugged.

'What do people usually go to cemeteries for?'

The group was being chivvied along by Dirlewanger's SS men. A police car turned in from a side road and took its place at the head of the convoy. I leaned out of the window to listen as the loudspeakers began to crackle.

'Attention! Attention everybody! For military reasons, this area is being cleared. You have five minutes in which to vacate your houses. I repeat, five minutes. We regret the necessity for this, but Communist Polish traitors leave us no alternative. This area is now a military zone and your lives will be endangered if you stay. SS Obergruppenführer von dem Bach Zalewski gives you his personal assurance that you will be well cared for until such time as you can be rehoused. You will be under the full protection of the German Army. You have permission to bring with you whatever personal possessions you are able to carry, but it is essential that the evacuation is completed within five minutes ... Attention, attention! For military reasons, this area is being cleared ...'

The car turned off down another side street, and the strident tones of the loudspeaker faded gradually into the distance. All up and down the Rue Wola, windows and doors were flying open and distraught citizens were pouring out to join the passing column. Dirlewanger's men shouted directions and offered reassurance and condolences. I saw one of them stoop to pick up a toy dropped by a small child. I saw another give a helping hand to an old woman. I saw a third smiling, and at that point I shivered and turned away. There was something very disturbing, something peculiarly sinister, in the sight of SS men behaving like normal human beings. I knew then that something must be very wrong.

The feet went on shuffling past. Hundred upon hundred of them, some in shoes, some in slippers, some in rags. Many of the children were barefoot. And now, lining the route, appeared the menacing grey shapes of Kaminski's SS. They stood like statues, unsmiling, unmoving. Just stood there and watched as the people marched by.

The police car returned, its loudspeaker still blaring.

'Attention, attention! This area is about to be shelled. I repeat, this area is about to be shelled. You have half a minute in which to get out. Anyone failing to do so will be regarded as an enemy of the German people and will be shot. This is your last warning ...'

The car moved on. A few hesitant householders came scuttling out of their doors and were pushed forward into the column. Kaminski's men now began to search the houses. Sick people were shot in their beds. An old fellow discovered hiding in an attic was tossed out of the window and was dashed to pieces on the pavement below. He landed on a small child, and she, also, was killed. The kid gloves were off, now. The SS were behaving true to form. The crowd began to grow increasingly uneasy. They had to be urged on by kicks and punches, and some even required the added encouragement of a revolver jammed into the small of the back.

The column wound slowly on its way. The hundreds of feet had turned into thousands. They were marched down the broad slope of the Rue Wola towards the cemetery, which had changed hands twice since we had pulled out and was now once more under German command. At present it was being held by Dirlewanger's Brigade, who had set up their HQ in the Chapel of St Nicholas. The altar was being used as a card table, and Dirlewanger, as usual, was drunk.

The leaders of the column had by now reached the Vistula and could go no further. They were brought to a halt and told to remain where they were, contemplating the graves. Kaminski arrived in an amphibious Volkswagen and looked them over with a scornful eye.

'Why are they still alive?' he said. 'They should be dead by now.'

'They will be,' promised Dirlewanger.

The two men stood facing each other in the riverside cemetery gardens. They were rivals in brutality, each was jealous of his own reputation.

'All this,' said Kaminski, waving a contemptuous hand, 'all this is a mere puff of wind compared to Minsk.'

'Minsk?' said Dirlewanger, as if he had never heard of the place.

'Complete liquidation,' said Kaminski. 'I cleaned up the entire area.'

'Only of partisans,' said Dirlewanger, smoothly. 'Only of partisans ... By the time I've finished with Warsaw, there won't be a single house left standing. It will be as if the place had never existed. The Reichsführer has given orders that every man, woman and child is to be exterminated.'

There was scarcely room to move, now, down by the river. The people were packed shoulder to shoulder, and more were arriving every second. A line of trucks, fitted out with machine-guns, was already in place and awaiting the order to fire.

'A pity,' murmured Kaminski, 'that something a little more elaborate could not have been arranged.'

Dirlewanger hunched a shoulder.

'It will do well enough,' he said, indifferently. 'We don't have time for refinements ...'

The last of the column was pushed into place and the exit gates were closed. Dirlewanger picked up a loudhailer, and an expectant silence fell over the crowd. Now perhaps they would be told what was to happen to them. Now perhaps they would be given some of that protection they had been promised.

'Attention, everybody! Attention!' said Dirlewanger; and he dropped his hand as the signal to open fire.

The machine-guns started up on one side; and Kaminski's men on the other. There could be no escape. Those who were not killed by the bullets were trampled underfoot. Invalids' chairs and children's prams rolled down the bank and into the river, where their occupants were drowned. A small group of men managed to seize control of one of the trucks, but they were blown up by grenades before they had gone more than a few yards.

Dirlewanger clapped a friendly hand on Kaminski's shoulder as they strolled back together to the Chapel of St Nicholas.

'Co-operation, my dear fellow. That's the way to do it. As you have just seen ... They co-operate with us, we co-operate with each other, and by Christmas, I promise you, the whole of Poland will have been cleared.'

When the machine-guns had completed their task, the field of victory was sprayed with petrol and a vast funeral pyre was lit. Many people were still alive and conscious as the flames engulfed them. Every now and again a burning spectre would rise up in a frenzy from a pile of bodies and crawl dementedly in circles until it finally collapsed. The obscene stench of charred flesh hung heavy over the town for many days to come.

The next morning, two brigades under General Michal Karaszewicz-Tokarewski recaptured the cemetery area and slaughtered an entire German battalion. By way of revenge Kaminski rounded up every Pole he could lay hands on, hung them by the feet and left them to a slow death. The Army lodged an official complaint with the Führer, indignantly protesting such barbaric treatment of civilians, but Hitler ignored them and gave Kaminski another medal to hang round his neck. Another medal for Kaminski, and another snub for the generals of the Wehrmacht. The SS exulted, and sadism reached a new level of horror. Men of the SS went out at nights to rape and murder in much the same way as others went out for a drink or a meal. Those who preferred to play the role of spectator could always go to watch a torture—there was nearly always one taking place. The latest fad was death by slow drowning. It could be made to last all night in the hands of a really skilled operator.

Tiny went off one morning on what he self-importantly called 'a special mission'. He returned half an hour later dragging one of Dirlewanger's Unterscharführer with him.

'I could have shot it on the spot,' he said, 'except I thought you'd all like to have a bash at it.'

'Where'd you get it from?' said Porta.

Tiny tapped the side of his nose.

'Mind it,' he said. 'Where I found it's my business.'

'So why bring him here?' said the Old Man. 'You know perfectly well we can't shoot him without cause.'

'Without cause?' echoed Tiny, indignantly. 'Ain't it enough he's SS?'

'Of course it isn't. Don't be so ridiculous. Either let him go or give me one valid reason why he deserves to be shot.'

Tiny stuck out his lower lip as a sign of disapproval.

'He was bleeding looting, wasn't he?'

'Looting?'

'Yeah. Helping himself out of a jeweller's shop——'

The Old Man sighed. He held out a hand.

'Show,' he said.

Grumbling, Tiny cleared out his pockets. He was carrying half a hundredweight of rings and watches with him. A jeer went up from those of us who were assembled.

'Well, it's proof, ain't it?' said Tiny.

Not even the Old Man needed much in the way of proof where a member of Dirlewanger's murder squad was concerned. Tiny eagerly drew out his knife.

'So what'll it be?' he said. 'Eyes or guts?'

'Castrate the bastard,' urged Gregor.

'Afterwards,' said Tiny. 'Eyes is more fun. I'll do them first.'

'Not while you're under my command, you won't!'

Two shots rang out and the Unterscharführer fell forward. The Old Man put his revolver back into its holster. He nodded grimly at Tiny.

'You're in the Army, remember? Not the SS.'

Out on patrol, investigating a row of deserted houses, we

discovered the remains of someone's dinner still lying on a table. Dry bread and a pan full of haricot beans. The bread was green and the beans were shrivelled and hard, but we sat down and made a meal of them. It was the first food we'd tasted for almost twenty-four hours.

Porta was regretfully licking up the last of the breadcrumbs when a young captain burst through the door announcing that he was going across the road to recapture the central power station. I felt very tempted to ask him what that could possibly have to do with us, but unfortunately I knew the answer only too well. When he said that he was going across the road, what he actually meant was that we were going across the road ...

With the help of a group of Pioneers, we managed to force our way into the ground floor of the building, but before we could make any further progress we came under fierce attack from the Polish Jena Regiment and had to retire in a hurry. The power station remained very firmly in the hands of the guerrillas.

For a couple of days there was something like peace in the town, and then the German net began slowly to close. Marshal Rokossovski's forces were unaccountably immobile at Magnuszewo, which gave the Germans the opportunity to withdraw much-needed troops from the Russian front to complete the encirclement of Warsaw. Our numbers were swelled by the arrival of seven tank divisions, nine infantry divisions, and a great many specialised units, including Pioneer Corps and Engineers. Two heavy cannons were set up, and at intervals of ten minutes throughout the day and night they sent their shells to pulverise the centre of the town. Slowly but inevitably the city was crumbling towards total destruction.

Against the full force of the German machine, the Polish Commander-in-Chief, General Taddeus Bor-Komorovski, had pitifully little to offer save a spirit of fanatical determination. His faithful band of partisans would fight to the end, but that end must now be very close. For arms, they were forced to rely upon whatever they could capture from the Germans or manufacture themselves. Their most effective weapons were the petrol bomb, flame-throwers fashioned from lengths of piping, and hand grenades made from old tin cans. For explosive material they plundered the many unexploded German shells which lay scattered about the streets. It was all very ingenious, it was all very deadly, but sooner or later the supply must run out.

Meanwhile, however, the Polish partisans were still capable of giving us a good run for our money. They recaptured the central telephone exchange in the Rue Zilna, and in order not to waste valuable ammunition they rid themselves of the German troops by throwing them out of top-storey windows. They had been in possession of the building barely twenty minutes when the Pioneers turned up and began hurling explosives from the shelter of armoured cars. The occupying Poles had little with which to oppose the attack, but they held on grimly until the exchange finally blew up in a shower of bricks. Not one of them survived the wreckage.

With the support of an assault battery we launched an attack on the police headquarters, but the partisans who held it fought like demons out of hell and even went so far as to come streaming after us as we beat a hasty and undignified retreat through the neighbouring streets.

One Polish unit was enough to put paid to five hundred aged German gendarmes still occupying a wing of the Ministry of the Interior. The Germans had been dragged out of their mothballs, in which they had been buried knee deep ever since 1918, and set down in the midst of a strange type of warfare which made no sense to them. The Poles swarmed all over the building, the fighting was conducted in the corridors, on the stairs, face to face across office desks, and the few surviving sections of gendarmerie fled in panic from the scene, while two SD companies under the command of a Russian colonel of the Kaminski Brigade marched forth to put the upstart Poles in their place. The partisans, gloriously drunk on German blood, caught them neatly in a trap. They let them into the building with virtually no resistance at all, then promptly came out of their hiding-places and surrounded them. And this time, as an added refinement, they set light to them before throwing them out of the windows. They then went roaring into the streets to mop up the last survivors of the five hundred gendarmes with hand grenades parachuted to them by the British.

The remnants of the five hundred had taken shelter in the Church of the Holy Spirit; not because they placed any importance upon the Poles' respecting their right of sanctuary, but simply because the church happened to be one of the few buildings in the area still standing.

Three German infantry regiments marching to their rescue crossed swords with Colonel Karol Ziemski Wachnowski, and his partisans and were anihilated. A group of suicidal Poles then burst into the church with explosives strapped to their backs, and the half dozen gendarmes who survived the holocaust were sprayed with petrol and sent running in flames through the streets.

SS Obergruppenführer von dem Bach Zalewski commanded a fresh attack. Behind the assault columns marched the sub-humanity of Dirlewanger's SS, but before they had even reached the great fountain in the Place Royale, the columns were brought to a panic-stricken halt by a bombardment of petrol bombs and hand grenades. The Poles were behaving like madmen, and the confusion was total. Dirlewanger's gangsters were among the first to turn and run.

Colonel Ziemski Wachnowski immediately sent his men tearing after them, and the demented Poles raced screaming through the narrow streets in pursuit of the fleeing army, trampling the injured underfoot.

Meanwhile Dirlewanger and Kaminski between them had succeeded in bringing their troops under some sort of control. Himmler had their death warrants already written out, awaiting his signature should Warsaw not be flattened within twenty-four hours. With such a threat hanging over their heads they turned their men round and sent them straight back again. This time the Army was sent along behind to back them up. Our orders were to shoot on sight anyone not wearing a

German uniform. Man, woman or child. Young or old. Himmler had condemned to death the entire Polish race, and we were to be their executioners.

We emerged into the Place Napoleon, and suddenly, above the tumult of shooting and shelling, we heard the sound of music. Music in such a place, at such a time as that? It was coming from a house over on the north side of the square. A Polish captain was playing the piano, apparently oblivious to the fighting going on all round him. The sound seemed to drive Kaminski berserk. He sent an entire battalion racing across the square to put an end to it, and screamed after them that he would promote the man who brought him the captain's head on the end of his bayonet.

The battalion had gone only a few yards when Colonel Wachnovski threw his Janislau Brigade into the attack. The Janislau Brigade was made up mainly of women and girls and young boys, but they were none the less dauntless. They fought like all the partisans, like lunatics intoxicated with the taste of blood ...

Behind us, the support troops started hurling smoke grenades, which belched forth great clouds of sickly green fog. Most of the Poles had no gas masks and they fell back in disorder. In fact it was not gas. It was a smoke used for camouflage purposes and was therefore accepted as a perfectly legitimate tool of war. Anyone unfortunate enough to be caught in it for as long as twenty minutes would certainly die an agonising death, but that, apparently, counted as fair game.

There was a momentary lull, while both sides fell back. Then the Poles, evidently having decided that they might just as well die one way as another, plunged onward through the swirling mists and came howling and screaming at us, with explosives strapped to their chests. Kaminski and Dirlewanger's SS were virtually anihilated by the first wave.

Those few who survived the slaughter turned and ran. Corpses lay piled in the gutters, and at every street corner flew the Polish flag with its proud white eagle.

Far away in Berlin, Himmler had retired to bed with a

fever. Even Hitler himself hesitated to trouble him with mere matters of state, for Dr Kirstein had pronounced the Reichsführer's life to be in grave danger. He had received a severe nervous shock upon hearing the news from Warsaw. The Poles had destroyed eight hundred Tigers and wiped out three divisions. The entire centre of the town was now in their hands. From his bed of agony, Himmler had just sufficient command over his faculties to sign the death warrant of Gauleiter Fischer, the traitor who had originally abandoned Warsaw to the enemy. The Gauleiter was dragged through the streets by a Tiger from Eicke's Third Tank Division and his head was sent to Himmler in a box. General Rainer Stahel, the commander of Warsaw, was also condemned to death, but was given a reprieve on condition that he recaptured the old quarters of the town. Unfortunately for him, he fell into the hands of the partisans before he could carry out the task.

At dawn we came under attack from a cavalry corps, who charged through the streets with their sabres like a horde of howling Cossacks. Hooves thundered over the cobblestones, creating showers of sparks as iron met flint. The horses were foam-flecked and the sabres red with dripping blood. Many were the men who were caught up in the stampede and trampled to death. Many were those who had their heads severed from their shoulders as they dived too late for cover.

I found myself running for my life with Porta by my side. Neck and neck we raced, with the sabres whistling past our ears and the breath of the horses hot and sweet in our nostrils. We reached the Place Pilsudski, heaped high with bodies. Porta tripped and fell, and I was unable to stop myself. I came down on top of him, knowing that this would surely be the end for both of us.

And then, suddenly, from the far side of the square, the machine-guns opened up. The advancing Poles were confronted by the SS Regiment 'Der Führer'. Men and horses were cut to ribbons. Those who could, turned and fled, but many more were left behind in the graveyard of the Place Pilsudski. A horse and its rider were brought down directly in front of the spot where Porta and I were crouched among the dead. They missed us only by inches, and we were able to take shelter behind them from the flying bullets.

The following day the sky above Warsaw was black with bombers. They were Wellingtons, belatedly sent over to aid the Poles in their hour of need. But of all the arms and all the rations they dropped over the town, scarcely one-tenth were picked up by Bor-Komorovski's beleaguered partisans. The rest were divided equally between the Germans and the Russians.

Joining forces with the 104th Grenadiers, we launched an attack on the Rue Pivna in an attempt to liberate the northern quarter of the town, which had now been in enemy hands for over a month. It was of strategic importance to the German Army, and we had been supplied with tanks, P64s, to make sure we did the job properly.

'Forward tanks!' ordered Colonel Hinka, across the radio.

The vehicles ground their way slowly down the slope of the Rue Pivna.

'Range four hundred yards,' said the Old Man. 'Load and prepare to fire.'

We were back at the old routine. It had been a long time since we had seen the inside of a tank, we had been too often on the receiving end these past few months. Now, at last, we were back where we belonged, on the inside looking out. It was as if we had never been anywhere else.

Tiny was loading and reloading with all his usual unfailing regularity. He even managed now and again to snatch a sip of vodka or a bite of sausage without interrupting the rhythm. It was a matter of complete indifference to Tiny what we were aiming at. The target could have been anything from a crowd of innocent bystanders to a nest of enemy machine-guns. He knew only that the machine must be kept in constant motion, and that it was his task to feed it with its supply of grenades.

A row of small terraced houses lay in our path. They crumpled up before us as if they were made of cardboard, but suddenly there was the sound of an explosion, the whole tank shuddered and tilted over and ended up resting on one track and shaking violently.

'Magnetic mine,' said Heide, tight-lipped. 'The right track's been buggered.'

There was a second's silence, then Porta swore and got to his feet. He jerked his head at Tiny.

'Repair squad outside. Let's go.'

Tiny settled himself comfortably on the floor and stuffed his mouth full of sausage.

'You just gotta be joking,' he said.

'You want to sit here and wait for them to blow us to bits?' demanded Porta, furious.

Tiny shrugged his shoulders.

'It's better than going outside and getting yourself nobbled,' he said.

Before Porta could reply, we were hit for a second time. A shell crashed into the outer casing and exploded in a ball of flame. It did no serious damage, except to our nerves. Our companion tanks had by now disappeared. We were being fired on from behind, and we had to rotate the turret by hand, for the electric circuit had been knocked out by the first shell. There was a third explosion, and this time the whole of the back axle was torn off. There could now be no possibility of sending out a repair squad. Even if they did survive the raging inferno of the roads, they could certainly not replace the back axle.

The Old Man reluctantly gave the order to abandon the vehicle. A stationary tank is a sitting duck. It could blow up at any moment, and it would have been suicide to hang around any longer.

Every hatch was flung open, and I saw a scramble of arms and legs as my companions disappeared. It was my job to stay behind and destroy what remained of the vehicle.

'See you in heaven,' said Porta, blowing me a kiss.

I watched him as he scrambled out. I waited until I saw the soles of his boots, and then I primed the self-destruct mechanism and dived after him towards the nearest hatch. It refused to open. It had fallen back and it was stuck fast. I was seized at once with panic. The tank was going to blow up, and I was still going to be inside it. I had only seconds left. I was never going to make it. I hammered in futile sobbing fury at the closed hatch. The blast of a grenade had battened it down, and it was jammed tight. It needed more strength than my puny blows to force it open, and more sense than my terror-flooded brain possessed to lead me to another exit.

Suddenly, I saw daylight. Two hands, vast like carpet bags reached down towards me. They hauled me up through the turret, and Tiny and I fell together over the side of the crippled tank.

'Bloody fool!' snarled Tiny. He boxed me soundly round the ears. 'Could have got us both bloody killed, buggering about like that!'

It was only the blast of the explosion which shut him up. We were blown across the road and hurled straight through the windows of a nearby house. Even Tiny was too shattered to do more than lie on the floor and gasp until one of the walls began slowly to sag towards us and we both went diving out again on to the pavement.

We tagged on behind a company of infantry and attacked the old Buhl Palace, once the home of royalty, now in the hands of the partisans. They did not give it up without a struggle. We fought from room to room, on the landings and the staircases, in the galleries and the gardens, until at last the place resembled a barracks—its beauty destroyed, its pride humiliated. The partisans retreated, and we were now in sole possession. The silence was oppressive after the ferocity of the combat. The royal palace was a desolate wreck, and it gave me no comfort to stretch my unwashed, aching body on a four-poster bed in a room that had once belonged to princes. Tiny wiped his boots clean on the damask coverlet, and Porta wrenched down the velvet curtains and slept curled up on them like a dog in its kennel. For a few hours we were the lords and masters of a war-torn palace. But with the coming of the dawn we were thrown back into the gutters where we belonged, put to flight by a detachment of Wachnowski's blood-thirsty guerrilla fighters. Our moment of glory had been very brief.

The entire town seemed suddenly to be swarming with partisans. We were forced to take shelter in the sewers. We stayed there, ten feet below ground, up to our waists in stinking filth, for the best part of four days. On emerging once again into the open, dripping with slime and half blinded by the brilliance of the daylight, we were snatched up by a company of the SS Reich Division and crammed without ceremony into a Tiger. Never mind that we were weak with hunger after four days roaming about the sewers of Warsaw, the SS needed men to drive a tank, and we were the unfortunates who happened to be on the spot.

They should have had more sense than to introduce a Tiger into the street-fighting of Warsaw. The heavy tank was too big and too clumsy. It was impossible to manoeuvre it through the narrow, twisting passages, and it was not long before it came to grief, with both tracks shattered by shellfire. The Old Man gave the order to abandon the vehicle and destroy it, and once again it was I who had to remain behind to do the job.

I waited impatiently until they had all disappeared, then primed the mechanism and made a breathless dive for the hatch. This time it did not stick. I was up and away and racing across the road to join my companions. We crouched behind the shell of a burnt-out truck and waited for the explosion.

The explosion never came ...

An SS Unterscharführer threatened to shoot me on the spot if I did not instantly return and rectify my mistake. We argued hotly for a few moments as to which was at fault, me or the self-destruct mechanism, but whichever it was I knew I had no alternative but to go back and finish the job. Tigers were still classed as secret weapons. On no account must one be allowed to fall into the hands of the enemy. Even if the Unterscharführer spared my life, I should certainly never survive a court martial.

I crossed the road in a series of nervous jerks and twitches.

Heide was giving me a covering fire, but the rooftops were full of snipers, all of whom were very well aware of my mission and were out to prevent it if at all possible. I rolled beneath the belly of the tank with bullets tearing holes in the road all round me. I attempted to force open the lower hatch, but there was no moving it. I would have to go in by the turret.

I took a deep breath, pulled the pin out of a smoke grenade and sent it rolling across the street. Then I clambered up to the turret under cover of its billowing yellow clouds. Inside the tank, the explosive was still in place. The glass detonator had cracked and the least movement could activate it. Court martial or no court martial, I was going nowhere near it. I shot out again through the turret and scurried across the road like a frightened chicken. The snipers were still at it, but of what danger were flying bullets when compared with the horrors of a seventy-ton tank on the point of explosion? I rolled to safety in the ruins of a bombed house and launched a couple of hand grenades towards the stricken Tiger. The first bounced harmlessly off the outer shell, the second disappeared straight down the turret. I covered my head with my hands and waited.

The seconds ticked slowly by. Every minute seemed like an hour. Cautiously, I raised my hand. I took another grenade from my pouch and tore out the pin. I raised my arm to throw it, and as I did so the tank exploded.

The grenade was snatched out of my hand by the blast. Steel plating was flung across the road. The Tiger disappeared in a sea of roaring flame, and the long cannon was projected forward like an arrow from a bow. It made straight for the open window of a house where a section of German infantry had just taken up position. I did not stay to hear their comments. I took to my heels and tore hell for leather after the Old Man and the rest of them.

The battle for Warsaw continued with unabated brutality. One of Dirlewanger's battalions arrived while we were fighting for possession of the Allée Jerosolimska. They were known euphemistically as the clean-up squad. Himmler had given all such SS groups a completely free hand. Their task was to clear up the city in whatever way would be most effective. And, accordingly, they looted, raped, burnt and murdered from one end of Warsaw to the other. Their latest game was to kick babies about the streets like footballs until there was nothing left to kick. Mothers who had the temerity to complain had their clothes set on fire and were chased in circles at gunpoint. This was all amidst roars of laughter from delighted officers, most of whom were ex-commandants of concentration camps.

The Lieutenant-Colonel, under whose command we temporarily found ourselves, seemed to be a stranger to the ways of the SS. He was an old man, and until this moment had probably succeeded in keeping his blinkers on. But his eyes were now opened, and he stared in horror and disbelief at the sight of a baby being tossed high into the air and caught on its way down on the point of a bayonet. He sought out the Hauptsturmführer in charge of the proceedings and ordered him to withdraw his horde of barbarians immediately. The Hauptsturmführer looked him up and down with cold disdain.

'You are obviously not aware, sir, that this is the Third Battalion, the Dirlewanger Brigade, and that we are under direct orders from the Reichsführer. It would be most ill-advised of you to attempt any interference with our work.'

He pushed the Lieutenant-Colonel out of his way with the butt end of his revolver and led his gallant band of savages further down the street in search of fresh conquests. The Colonel was trembling. His face was grey and puckered, his skin leathery. His eyes seemed to have sunk deep inside his skull in the space of only a few minutes.

'Dear God,' he said. 'Dear God, what a way to fight a war . . .'

The old Prussia had vanished indeed. Gone were the upright generals, the stern disciplinarians. Now it was the turn of the little men. The little men like Heinrich Himmler, Reichsführer SS, Commander-in-Chief of the Army, Minister of the Interior, Minister of Justice, Head of the Police Security Bureau . . . Little men in black uniforms and gold-rimmed spectacles. Men even Hitler himself had cause to fear.

All along the street the houses were alight. People imprisoned on top floors opened their windows and cried for help, but no one could be bothered with them. Not the retreating Poles nor the advancing Germans. They were left to burn. The whole of Warsaw was in flames. The Rue Chlodna was alight from one end to the other, and Germans and Poles alike were caught in the inferno and roasted alive. No one could have escaped through the solid walls of flame. The tar on the roads was sizzling beneath our feet, and the water from the fountains was so hot that it steamed. Warsaw was being burnt to the ground.

We plunged down into the cool depths of a cellar for a few moments' respite, but had been there scarcely ten seconds when a big red-faced staff-sergeant appeared at the entrance and hauled us out again.

'What the bloody hell do you think you're doing, sitting down there on your great fat fannies? Get a move on before I shoot the whole poxy lot of you!'

He drove us down the road at gunpoint before him, and then walked straight into the path of an oncoming grenade and had his head blown off.

'Serves him bloody well right,' said Tiny, pausing automatically in a shower of gunfire to rifle the dead man's pockets.

The Lieutenant-Colonel was seated in the basin of one of the steaming fountains singing hymns. He was surrounded by a circle of encroaching flames, and it was quite impossible to reach him.

'He's gone off his rocker,' said Gregor, fascinated. 'He's gone right off his bleeding rocker ...'

We stood a while, watching the spectacle, until at last a stray shell scored a direct hit on the fountain and the Colonel was buried beneath chunks of masonry.

For the umpteenth time, orders came through that we were to try and recapture the Poniatowski Bridge. I was sick to death of trying to recapture the Poniatowski Bridge. I only wished to God that one side or the other would blow the damned thing up. Then, having nothing left to recapture, we would finally be left in peace. We threw ourselves without any enthusiasm whatever into the attack, and were once again firmly repulsed by Ziemski Wachnowski and his partisans. The Poles were giving no quarter now. Any German who fell into their hands was either burnt alive or beaten to death. I saw a Major, trailing a shattered leg behind him, crawling towards the ruins of the fountain. The Poles also saw him. They turned on a hose and sprayed him with petrol. Then, laughing, tossed a lighted match after him. When the flames died away, the charred skeleton of the Major was still poised on all fours, crawling for sanctuary towards the ruins of the fountain. During the night, we reached the Place Krazinski and found ourselves back with our own Company—or what, at any rate, was left of it. By some miracle they had managed to set up a field kitchen. It was serving nothing but crusts of bread and a dirty grey soup which looked as if it had been wrung out of wet floorcloths. By then we were so hungry we could have eaten fricassée of cowpat and believed it was roast beef.

Gregor and I were detailed for sentry duty at the end of the Rue Krazinski, while the rest of the Company bedded down for the night in the basement of one of the few standing buildings. Shortly before eleven o'clock it began to rain. The chill, melancholy rain of an autumn night, blew across the square and cut around the corner of the street and into our faces. We stood with hunched shoulders, staring glumly ahead, not speaking, while the water trickled down our necks and seeped up through the tattered soles of our boots. After a bit, Gregor shifted his position and I could hear his feet squelching. He swore. He removed both boots and solemnly tipped the water out of them, then crammed them back on again.

'Fat lot of good that will do,' I said.

Gregor sighed.

'It would break my poor old mother's heart,' he said, 'if she could see me like this.'

'Consider yourself lucky to have a mother,' I said, sourly.

249

'The fuss she used to make,' said Gregor, carrying straight on as if I had never spoken. 'Carried on fit to burst a blood vessel ...' He smiled a stupid sentimental smile and gave a wistful little laugh. 'Fell in the river once,' he said. 'Got home dripping wet. Old lady nearly had a fit. Put me straight to bed with hot milk and aspirins. Thought I might catch a cold.' He laughed again. 'Catch a cold!' he said. 'That's a good one, that is.'

'Most amusing,' I said.

The night was silent save for the persistent dripping of the rain off the rooftops. The stillness seemed unnatural, almost uncanny, after the days and the weeks of continuous bombardment. For the moment there was a lull, but tomorrow it would start up again. Tomorrow a few more thousand would die, a few more bridges would be blown, a few more buildings would change hands. All the pawns in the game would be reshuffled and sent to different squares, ready for the masterminds to make the next move.

It was time for the relief, but no one came. There was nothing we could do about it. We could remain cursing at our post, until someone, somewhere, chose to remember us. The rain ceased, and near by a bird sang and almost frightened the life out of us.

'Bloody birds,' said Gregor.

In place of the rain came a stinking yellow mist, which crawled slowly towards us. It unrolled like a thick carpet all along the Rue Lazienkowska and added to the misery of the countless wounded who were lying huddled on the crumbling steps of the church of St Alexander. From where we stood, we could see three dead bodies, two Polish and one German. The German was lying in the gutter with both his legs blown off. One of the Poles was strung up on the barbed wire, hanging limp and shapeless like a puppet which has lost all its sawdust. The other was curled embryonically in a shell-hole full of blood. By the following evening those bodies would be mottled green and yellow and swollen almost to bursting point. They would stay where they had fallen for a day or two, and then they would be trampled underfoot at the next attack, would explode like over-ripe fruit. If their mothers could only see them. The glorious death that they had died for their countries ...

'You wouldn't think,' said Gregor, following my train of thought, 'you wouldn't think there'd be that many people left in the world by now, would you? You wouldn't think there'd be any left to kill.'

'There'll always be people left to kill,' I said. 'Even if they had to breed them specially.'

'They already do,' said Gregor.

The relief arrived at last, almost an hour late. Three motorcyclists from the 104th were in an even worse humour than Gregor and I. They were sick of the war, sick of the Party, sick of the Führer; sick of the bloody British, the bloody Yanks, the bloody Yids, the bloody Reds—

'How about the Poles?' I said.

The bloody Poles, the bloody Wops, the bloody Frogs, the bloody—

'You know what?' said Gregor. 'I'd put a bullet through my head, if I was you.'

Thankfully, we made our way back to the building where the rest of the Company were snoring like a herd of swine. Gregor tripped over a body and woke it up, and the string of oaths which followed woke everyone else up, as well. Then everybody sat up and swore at us in voices full of loathing and contempt. I knew how they felt. Sleep is just about the soldier's most valuable commodity, and precious little he gets of it. Even when he is allowed the luxury of five or six hours' undisturbed rest, it's on a hard floor with a gas-mask case for a pillow and a threadbare coat as a blanket.

I slipped into position between Tiny and Porta. There was a narrow channel of space between them, and I wriggled my way in until firmly embedded. Here I was not only warm, I was also safe, and I could sleep for the short remainder of the night in comparative peace and comfort.

We were woken at dawn by the not unwelcome sound of the

field kitchen. I became suddenly and very acutely aware that the effects of the previous day's floorcloth soup had long since worn off and that the sides of my stomach were gnashing themselves together in angry protest. Mechanically, I picked half a dozen lice off me and crushed them between finger and thumb. Tiny and Porta were already on their feet, clutching their mess tins and their forage sacks. As soon as they had swallowed their travesty of a breakfast, they would be up and away in search of more sustaining fare; and doubtless would not return empty-handed.

'Let's get cracking,' said Porta, giving Tiny a shove up the basement steps. 'Best to get to market before the crowds arrive.'

Porta was one of the earth's natural scavengers. You could set that man down stark naked on a raft in the middle of the Atlantic Ocean and he would sail into port as calm as a cucumber three hours later, dressed in a Savile Row suit, stuffing himself with fresh lobster and washing it all down with a bottle of the best hock. Being in Warsaw in the middle of a battle, he couldn't quite run to lobster and hock, but at the very least he would turn up with a side of horse and a flask of vodka.

They were gone, the pair of them, for the better part of two hours, and when they came back they were carrying half a pig between them. It was wrapped up in a sheet, leaving a trail of blood behind.

'Where the hell did you get that from?' demanded the Old Man, nervously. But for once they were not particularly interested in boasting of their exploits. They had something far more exciting to talk about.

'Sod where we got it from,' said Porta. 'It's what we saw while we was getting it that'll make your hair stand on end.'

'Oh? What was that?'

The Old Man looked apprehensive, as well he might from the expression of evil satisfaction that Tiny was wearing on his face.

'What was it you saw?' he said.

252

'Dorn,' said Tiny, in tones of gloating wonderment, as if even now he could not quite bring himself to believe his luck. 'We saw Dorn, that's what we saw.'

'Dorn from Torgau?' said Gregor.

'The very same,' said Porta. 'The butcher himself.'

'All got up like a dog's dinner,' added Tiny. 'Leather boots, tin hat, P38, all brand-new and shiny.'

There was a stunned silence. Dorn of Torgau, here in Warsaw? Carl Dorn, the Torgau torturer, fighting at the front? It seemed scarcely possible. The war must be nearer its end than we had thought, if even men like Dorn were being flung into battle.

'It was just as we was chopping up the pig,' said Tiny. 'We seen him coming round the corner.'

He turned and began to imitate Dorn's self-important strut. There could be no possible mistaking it. It could only have been Dorn. Slow smiles of triumph began to paint themselves over our faces. Carl Dorn sent to the front, and not a single soldier in the whole German Army who wouldn't shout aloud for joy on hearing the news.

'Did he by any chance happen to catch sight of you?' inquired the Old Man, still uneasy.

'You bet he did!' said Tiny.

'You don't meet an old pal in the street and totally ignore him,' added Porta. 'We naturally turned and waved to him, didn't we?'

I could imagine their waving. I could imagine the two extended fingers, and the jeers and the catcalls which would have accompanied them. So, quite obviously, could the Old Man. He passed a hand across his brow.

'You realise of course,' he said, 'that the first thing he's going to do is come round here in search of you?'

'So what?' said Tiny, indifferently.

'So you're heading straight for a load of trouble!' snapped the Old Man. 'Use a bit of common sense, for Christ's sake! What do you propose to do when he turns up here asking a whole load of awkward questions about half a side of bacon that someone's pinched?'

'Stick a grenade up his arse,' suggested Porta.

'Drown him in a bucket of puke,' said Tiny.

'String him up by the knackers——'

The Old Man stoically heard them through to the end.

'If you're sure you've quite finished?' he said, at last.

'Not really,' said Porta. 'But I guess it's enough to be getting on with.'

'If he survives that lot,' said Tiny, 'we can always think up something else.'

'Are you out of your tiny little birdbrained minds?' demanded the Old Man, impatiently. 'Do you really imagine that Dorn is going to be such a bloody fool as to turn up here without a whole posse of his mates for protection? You really think he'd voluntarily come within ten miles of a couple of cutthroats like you unless he was one hundred per cent sure of his ground?' He shook his head, warningly, at them. 'Just don't try any funny business with Dorn,' he said. 'You'll never get away with it.'

There was a mutinous pause, and then they caught each other's eye and shrugged their shoulders. Tiny and Porta were a law unto themselves, but the Old Man was no fool and they must have realised that he was talking sense. Dorn may have been dragged from his cosy niche in Torgau and sent to the front to do some fighting at last, but he was nevertheless a Sergeant-Major attached to the General Staff, and as such could be classed in the category of privileged persons.

'You lay so much as a finger on Dorn,' said the Old Man, 'and you'll pretty soon find yourselves laughing on the other side of your faces.'

'You mean you want us to let the shit get away scot-free?' cried Tiny, indignantly. 'Not even give him so much as a kick up the arse to be going on with?'

'Some other time,' said the Old Man. 'Some other time.'

'Well, fuck that for a laugh!' said Tiny. He snatched up the bloody bundle of meat and slung it over his shoulder. 'If that's the way you feel, we can always find someone else who'd fancy a nosh-up,' he said.

He disappeared up the steps, followed by a self-righteous Porta. It was the last we saw of them for several days, and the last we saw of the pig, either, except for a few tantalising spots of blood on the floor to remind us of the meal we'd almost had.

Barely seconds after Tiny and Porta had flounced out, we heard other footsteps on the pavement outside, and Lieutenant Löwe appeared in the doorway, accompanied by Dorn, Sergeant-Major Hofmann and three military policemen. All six came down the steps into the basement. Löwe was looking bored and cynical even before he began. Hofmann was leering at us behind Dorn's back. Dorn himself was full of his usual importance. He was dressed up in a brand new uniform, still spotless and uncreased, and his little, evil, deep-set eyes moved unflickeringly in search of his vanished prey.

'Sergeant Beier,' said Löwe. 'Sergeant-Major Dorn has reported to me that earlier this morning he saw two of your men slaughter and carry away a pig to which they had no right.'

'A pig?' said the Old Man.

Löwe turned for confirmation to Dorn.

'A pig, I think you said?'

'Half a pig,' said Dorn.

Löwe turned back apologetically to the Old Man.

'Half a pig,' he said.

There was a pause.

'This is very serious,' said the Old Man. 'Very serious indeed.'

'It most certainly is,' agreed Löwe. 'Looting is punishable by death.' He turned back again to Dorn. 'Well, Sergeant-Major? Are you able to identify the two men?'

Dorn strutted forward. His eyes narrowed accusingly.

'They're not here,' he said.

'How about the pig?'

'Half a pig, sir.'

'Half a pig, I beg your pardon. Do you see it anywhere?'

255

'Of course I don't!' snarled Dorn, suddenly losing patience. 'They've obviously hidden it somewhere!'

Löwe raised an eyebrow at the Old Man.

'Sergeant Beier, I must ask you this question: are you hiding half a pig?'

'No, sir,' said the Old Man.

'Nor any part of a pig? Pig's cheek? Pig's trotters? Side of pig?'

'No, sir.'

'Well, then, Sergeant, that being the case I am sorry to have wasted your time. I bid you good morning. Shall we go, gentlemen?'

Dorn stepped angrily forward.

'You'd don't mean you're going to take his word for it?'

'Why not? I have the utmost faith in Sergeant Beier's integrity.

'But it's a lie! It's a downright lie! I saw them take it, I saw them bring it here!'

Löwe heaved a deep sigh and glanced at his watch.

'Sergeant-Major Holmann,' he said. 'You've known Sergeant Beier a fair time. Have you ever had cause to doubt the veracity of anything he has ever said to you?'

Hofmann stood facing front, not looking at Dorn.

'Never, sir,' he said.

'Then let us go,' said Löwe. He walked up the steps, and turned at the top of the flight. 'Naturally, you will inform me immediately should half a pig or any part of a pig come into your possession,' he said.

The Lieutenant, followed by all his retinue save Dorn, left the cellar. Dorn stood a moment, staring down at the floor. His feet were standing in a pool of fresh blood. He looked up at the Old Man and he curled his narrow lips in triumph over his sharp yellow fangs.

'Nasty accident you've had there,' he said. 'I think I'd better tell the Lieutenant about that. He could find it interesting. Very interesting.'

He clattered back shouting up the steps. I wondered if Tiny

and Porta had left a trail of blood behind them all over Warsaw.

'Roast pork,' moaned Gregor, rocking back and forth on his heels with his arms wrapped round his belly. 'We could have been eating roast pork if they hadn't gone and sent that stupid bastard to the front! Why couldn't they keep him in Torgau where he belongs? Why send him out here to annoy us? Why——'

He broke off in confusion as a shadow appeared in the doorway. It was the Lieutenant come back. There was a silence as he walked slowly down the steps. He stood a moment, thoughtfully studying the pool of blood. Then he looked up, and his eye fell on Heide, the only one of us whose face had seen a razor for well over a week.

'A nasty cut you've given yourself, Sergeant,' he said. 'You really will have to learn to be more careful in the future. It doesn't do to be so careless, you know. It really does not do...'

'It doesn't matter where we are fighting: it doesn't matter who we are fighting. We shall kill when we have to in the interests of our country, and the taking of a man's life shall be no more to us than the slaughter of cattle ... Only with that philosophy behind us can we set out confidently on the path of victory.'

Himmler. In a talk to the Foreign Branch of the SS.

WHATEVER the men of the Dirlewanger and Kaminski Brigades may have lacked in strict military discipline, they more than compensated for in the zest with which they pursued their campaign of terror and torture. Burning, looting, raping, murdering, they advanced on the centre of Warsaw, leaving behind them a long trail of death and destruction. They killed quite indiscriminately. Pole or German, young or old, man, woman or child—anyone who crossed their path was eliminated.

Horrified at the crimes that were being committed daily, General Hans Guderian, Chief of Staff of the German Forces in Poland, told Hitler in no uncertain terms that he could expect his immediate resignation unless both Brigades were withdrawn from Warsaw and their commanding officers put on trial before a court martial.

At the same time as General Guderian delivered his ultimatum, the Commander of the SS Fegerlein Brigade, a relative of Eva Braun, the Führer's mistress, informed Hitler that the men recruited by Dirlewanger and Kaminski were nothing but criminals and psychopaths and that the reign of terror in Warsaw would be an eternal stain on the honour of the Fatherland.

Reluctantly, but far too late, Hitler was forced to take action. He ordered Himmler to withdraw the two Brigades and to replace them by one of the regular Waffen SS divisions. Then, and only then, did General Bor Komorovski agree to surrender.

On 23rd December 1944, Kaminski was shot dead—almost certainly on the orders of the Reichsführer, although this was never proved. As for Dirlewanger, he was captured at the end of February 1945 and met a fitting end at the hands of the Polish guerrillas.

THE END OF THE RACE

WE were gathered outside the Krasinski Theatre, lost in contemplation of a photograph of two naked girls, when Tiny came lumbering excitedly up the road towards us.

'Hey! Look what I've got!' he shouted.

We dragged our eyes reluctantly away from the photograph. Tiny was carrying a couple of squalling, spitting cats by the scruff of their necks.

'Food!' said Porta, his face lighting up.

'Food be buggered,' retorted Tiny. 'These cats ain't food. These is racing cats.'

'Knickers,' said Gregor, making a grab at one of them. 'Why don't we skin 'em and flog 'em to the SS as rabbit? Make a fortune.'

'Piss off out of it!' snarled Tiny.

The cat reached out a claw and slashed viciously at Gregor's face. We all took a couple of hasty steps backwards.

'So what you got 'em for?' demanded Porta, aggressively. 'What you got 'em for if we ain't going to eat 'em and we ain't going to flog 'em?'

'I told you,' said Tiny, tucking an animal under each arm. 'They're racing cats, ain't they? Been specially trained for the job.'

'Who told you that load of codswallop?' sneered Porta. 'Cats don't bleeding race, they're not bleeding stupid enough, you stupid git! You'd believe any old rubbish, you would. You'd believe Adolf was made of green cheese, you would ... Racing cats, my arse! Load of bleeding wank!'

He turned back contemptuously to the two naked girls, and the rest of us turned with him. There was a pause, and then Tiny started up again.

'I seen 'em,' he said, earnestly. 'I seen 'em do it.'

'Do what?'

'Race,' said Tiny. 'They shove dynamite up their arses and they go like the clappers. Jumps and all, just the same as horses.'

Slowly, we turn back again. We looked with grudging interest upon the cats.

'This here one,' said Tiny, jerking his head towards a mangy grey creature with a cauliflower ear, 'this here one's beaten all records over four hundred yards.'

'Yeah? And what about the other one?' said Heide, looking with disfavour upon the bundle of spitting orange fur which had torn Gregor's face to shreds.

'Ah, well, this one,' said Tiny, 'this one's more in the nature of a sprinter, like. Hundred yard dash is more in its line. But it'll still give 'em a good run for their money. It'll still put up a pretty good——'

'Hang on a minute,' said Porta. 'Hang on a minute ... Whose money are you talking about?'

'Them as lays bets with us,' said Tiny, simply.

There was a thoughtful silence, as Porta, the financial whizz kid, scraped his one remaining tooth with a filthy fingernail and considered all the possibilities.

'Yeah, all right,' he said, at last. 'All right, we'll give it a go. There could be something in it.'

We made our way down to the park, where there was a temporary lull in the hostilities, and began clearing an area round the statue of Napoleon. We set up a fine race-course, with a variety of jumps and other obstacles, and prepared the animals for a trial run. Two people held them, while two others tied tin cans to their tails, and on the firing of the starting pistol set light to the fuses. The unfortunate creatures tore neck and neck round the course with the cans clattering and clanging behind them.

'See?' said Tiny. 'They go like a bomb.'

By the time we had set it all up and had a couple of practice runs, a fair-sized crowd of would-be punters had gathered to watch. Porta strode about, self-importantly inviting them to place their bets for the first race.

It very soon became obvious that we were going to need more than two runners if we were to keep alive a healthy interest in the sport. Tiny and Gregor were accordingly sent out scavenging, while in the meantime one or two people turned up with animals of their own which they were eager to pit against the mangy grey and the spitting marmalade tom. Someone produced an enormous black monster which looked as if it had been crossed with a sewer rat. The bets were laid thick and fast, but the creature proved to be a non-starter after all. As soon as the fuse was lighted it turned in a manic feline fury and began attacking the tin can with tooth and claw. Finally succeeding in freeing itself, it set off round the course in the wrong direction and caused havoc amongst the other runners. It was immediately disqualified and its owner fined.

Tiny and Gregor returned with a piebald tom and a small white fluffy creature which showed a quite amazing turn of speed. A sergeant from the Pioneers, who had heard of the goings-on from one of his mates, journeyed half-way across town in order to set his sleek tortoiseshell against our mangy grey. The tortoiseshell was an Italian cat, and it had accompanied the Sergeant all the way from Monte Cassino. The Sergeant's devotion was really quite touching. He carried round a pocketful of stinking sardines with which he kept feeding the beast, and half-way through the first race, when the tortoiseshell was almost two lengths ahead of the rest of the field, he suddenly began shouting about cruelty to dumb animals and had to be forcibly restrained from plunging into the middle of the track and rescuing it. He was a rough, tough, hatchet-faced brute who would undoubtedly have slit his mother's throat for sixpence, but he and his cat were all the world to each other, and after the first race, despite threats and protests, he withdrew from the field, tucking the tortoiseshell under his arm and offering to shoot the first person who attempted to wrest it from him.

Strange how even the most war-hardened of men can develop such fierce attachments to the most curious of creatures. I once knew a corporal who carried a toad in one of his ammunition pouches instead of ammunition. He used to make it comfortable each day on a nest of damp leaves, and sometimes when we were resting it would come out and squat like a gargoyle on his shoulder. It was an ugly little brute covered in pus-coloured warts, but the corporal cried like a baby the day it got loose and was run over by a truck.

Another time, I remember, we captured a Russian motorcyclist and his pet rat. A big, black water rat which behaved like a dog and followed the Russian everywhere he went. They used to eat their meals together out of the same mess tin and sleep in the same sleeping bag. We let them both escape, in the end. It was the only way to save the rat from falling into alien hands and turning up in the evening stew pot. It would have broken the Russian's heart.

After the tortoiseshell cat had been withdrawn from the card we began having trouble with the punters. The big piebald tom beat the mangy grey favourite three times in succession and a cry went up that the grey was being fixed. Someone claimed to have seen Tiny giving it a puff on a grifa* behind the statue of Napoleon. They were probably quite right, and it was on the whole most fortunate that at that point the race meeting was broken up by a sudden burst of enemy gunfire, which sliced the head off Napoleon and sent the mangy grey flying out of Tiny's arms and running for its life. It undoubtedly saved us from being lynched.

An amusing interlude had come to an end. The lull was

* Opium cigarette.

over, and it was back once again to the realities of war. We were on fatigue duty that same night, gathering up the wounded and burying the dead. The wounded we carried to the field hospitals set up in the Sadyba quarter of the town. The dead were laid out in neat rows in communal graves. Some of the bodies were scarcely any longer recognisable as having once been human. Some had been gnawed by rats. Some were minus head and limbs. We had erected a ramp and the bodies were rolled down it into the ditch, where we all took a turn at the receiving end. The worst cases were not those which were still warm, or still wet with fresh blood, but those which had lain undiscovered for a period of days in cellars and basements and were now green and bloated. If you were wise, you manipulated them with the very greatest of care. One incautious move, one impatient moment of rough handling, and the swollen skin would burst like an over-ripe plum, its contents flooding out. And any man caught in the path of such a flood of putrefaction would carry the smell with him for days and even weeks—it would cling to his hair, lodge under his nails, bury itself deep down in the pores of his skin.

We were relieved shortly after dawn, but even now there was to be no sleep. We sat a while on a crumbling bridge in the pale autumn sunlight, listening to the usual early-morning sounds of gunfire and shells, watching the water as it flowed underneath us with its complement of corpses. A few yards further on, an elderly Lieutenant-Colonel from the Medical Corps was leaning far out over the parapet, gazing upstream with vacant blue eyes.

'Stupid old goat,' said Porta. 'He'll get his bleeding head blown off if he's not careful.'

Even as he spoke a shot rang out, and a bullet went thudding into the side of the bridge. The Colonel shifted his position very slightly as a grudging concession to the enemy snipers.

'Hey, you!' shouted Porta, from the safety of his shelter beneath the rusty iron parapet. 'If you want to commit suicide, do you mind going somewhere else and doing it? I've seen enough dead bodies for one night.'

Slowly, the Colonel turned his head. He stared at Porta in undisguised astonishment.

'Are you by any chance addressing me, my good man?'

'That's right,' said Porta.

The Colonel straightened up in best Prussian military manner, shoulders pulled back and chest inflated.

'Do you normally address officers in that fashion?' he said, chillingly.

Porta looked at his white hairs and his pink-rimmed eyes, and seemed suddenly to take pity on him.

'Listen, Grandpa,' he said. 'It's for your own good. Just move away from the edge before you get your brains blown out. OK? It would make us all a helluva lot happier. We've been shoving the stiffs underground all night long and we've had a real bellyful. So just be a good little Grandpa and do what I ask.'

'This is outrageous!' snapped the Colonel. 'I never heard such insolence in all my life! Has the world run mad?'

He took a step towards Porta, and as he did so a second shot rang out. The Colonel gave a sharp cry and staggered back against the parapet. Before we could reach him, he had fallen over the edge and gone crashing down into the turbulent waters of the Vistula below. One more body in the sea of bobbing corpses. Porta shook his head.

'Daft old bugger,' he said.

The Colonel's body disappeared slowly downstream. The sniper retired, satisfied. We settled down again behind the parapet.

We were not left long in peace. The battle of Warsaw had not yet finished for us. The Fifth Company was sent back into the flames at Wola, where the corpses lay heaped in the gutters and from every tree and every lamp-post hung shreds of human flesh.

Early next morning the Germans launched a full-scale attack against the remaining Polish strongholds, which extended from the Rue Kasimira to the Place Wilson. A rain of fire fell upon the old quarter of the town. Twenty-eight batteries were kept in constant action for over five hours. Three regiments of tanks were sent through the Rue Mickiewicz towards the Place Wilson. The last of the Polish resistance was drowned beneath an ocean of blood, and that same evening General Bor-Komorovski knew that the time had come when he must bow to the inevitable. The German forces far outnumbered him. He had few men and even fewer weapons. Warsaw had been abandoned by both Britain and Russia. No help was coming and he must capitulate.

He drove to the Château Ozarow in a Mercedes that was flying a white flag, and there he negotiated the terms of the surrender. There the Germans agreed that all prisoners of war should be treated according to the rules laid down by the Geneva Convention.

On the morning of 3rd October, at eight-thirty precisely, the battle of Warsaw came to an end. A sudden curtain of silence fell over the burning city. All that could be heard was the steady crackling of the flames, and now and then the sound of falling masonry as yet another building collapsed. The Place Wilson, recently filled with tanks and soldiers, was now deserted. Not a man, not a dog, not a living soul. The streets were empty. A sheet of paper was tossed high into the air above a burning house. It hung a moment, suspended, then fluttered back into the furnace and was caught by a licking tongue of flame. The shrivelled fragments fell gently to rest on the burnt-out hulk of a tank, where an obscene travesty of skin and bones, which had once been a German soldier, still sprawled in its death agony half in and half out of the turret.

Down in our basement, where we had spent the night, we crouched in terror as the wall of silence was built up round the city. We could understand the sounds of warfare but silence filled us with a terrible fear of the unknown.

'It can't be the end,' I whispered. 'It can't be the end ...'

No one contradicted me. The end had to come, but surely this could not be it? This silence, this emptiness, this total sense of nothing ... Was this what men had meant when they talked of *the end*?

'Things will start up again in a minute,' said the Old Man, confidently. 'We'd best stay here and wait for orders.'

Things would start up again in a minute. It was a comforting thought. Things would start up again, and we should be back to normal. Meanwhile, we would stay here and wait for orders. That was always best. There must be someone, somewhere, who knew what was happening.

'It can't be the end,' I said. 'It surely can't be the end ...'

'It's a trap,' said Tiny. 'They're trying to trick us into thinking it's all over.'

Another half hour passed. Another hour. The street was still as the grave. The silence, very slowly, was being filled with half-remembered sounds from a long-forgotten past. The creaking of wood, the singing of birds, the ticking of a watch —all the little, insignificant sounds that for so long had been drowned in the chaos of war.

The sudden collapsing of a roof on the opposite side of the street scared us almost into an apoplexy. Tiny let loose a burst of machine-gun fire, and Gregor vomited all over the floor. He wiped his mouth with a trembling hand.

'Jesus, I can't take any more of this,' he said. 'I'm going outside to have a gander. I'm not staying down here to be caught like a rat in a trap.'

'It's a trick,' said Tiny. 'That's exactly what they want you to do.'

Gregor walked to the steps.

'It's exactly what I'm going to do.'

The Old Man made no move to stop him. We remained where we were, every muscle tensed for instant action.

'We'll give him five minutes,' said the Old Man. He ran his tongue over his lips. I had never seen him so nervous. 'Five minutes, and then we'll follow him up.'

Before we could follow him, Gregor had returned. We heard him coming along the street, raving and shouting like a madman. He capered down the cellar steps, followed by Uule and his Finns. It seemed to me that they were all drunk.

'Well?' said the Old Man. 'What's going on?'

'Peace!' shouted Gregor, and fell headfirst down the last six steps.

'Peace!' shouted Uule, raising a bottle of vodka to his lips.

We stared at them, and said nothing at all. Uule came down into the cellar and held out the vodka bottle to the Old Man.

'It's true,' he said. 'They signed the surrender at eight-thirty this morning. It's all over.'

'All over?' I said. For a moment I felt almost a sense of loss. Suddenly they had taken away my reason for living and I was a man without a purpose. 'All over?' I said. 'But it can't be! It can't be! Not after all this time ... It can't be!'

But apparently it was. Peace had come at last, and I couldn't understand it. I couldn't understand why Tiny and Porta were suddenly wrapping their arms round each other and yelling and hooting at the tops of their voices. I couldn't understand why everyone was suddenly hell bent on throwing down their weapons, tearing off their badges, kicking their helmets across the floor.

'It's over!' shouted the Old Man. He turned and punched me in the ribs. 'It's all over!' he said, and the Finns joined in with a chorus of 'Miri, miri!' From further down the street we heard voices calling out in Polish and in German:

'It's over! It's all over!'

'Spokoj! Spokoj!'

And now I, too, was caught up in the general rejoicing and went surging up the steps behind Uule and his Finns, out into the daylight. Heide was still obstinately clutching his rifle, and Uule had his knife pushed down the side of his boot. Other than that, we were unarmed. We had no means of defending ourselves. I felt as if I were walking stark naked through the town.

'Miri, miri!' shouted Uule, but there was unrest in the streets, and I wondered again if the war had really ended.

We seemed the only creatures who had ventured out. There was still no sound, save for the steady crackling of flames from burning buildings. If the Poles came out now from their hiding-places, the Fifth Company would be at their mercy. What a way to end a war.

'Eh, Stanislas!' called Porta. He put his hands to his mouth and shouted, and his voice went echoing through the empty streets. 'Eh, Polaks! Come out and show yourselves! The fighting's all over!'

From a group of ruins twenty yards further on, three Polish soldiers wearing French helmets rose cautiously to their feet and stood waiting for us. Two of them were clutching automatic rifles. Porta gestured with his hands. There was a moment's hesitation, and then they dropped the rifles to the ground and came running and laughing towards us. Suddenly the town was alive with people. They came swarming up from every cellar and every basement, soldiers and civilians, men, women and children, laughing, crying, dancing in the streets. Pole and German alike had laid down their arms, and I saw many uniforms stripped of their Nazi eagles. Of the Fifth Company, only Heide appeared to see no reason for rejoicing. He perched moodily on the edge of the burnt-out tank, with a charred mummy that was lying half in and half out of the turret. He still kept a tight hold on his rifle, and he watched in grim silence as old enemies joined hands and laughed together in the streets of Warsaw.

And suddenly, in the midst of it all, came the sound of an explosion. A hail of grenades fell around us. The tank was blown to pieces, and Heide was flung across the road. Women and children ran screaming for cover. Men who only seconds ago had been embracing each other as brothers now broke apart, cursing themselves for their naïveté.

Tiny came hurtling across the street towards me, and together we dived down the steps of the nearest cellar.

'I told you so!' he panted. 'I told you it was a trick!'

We thought at first that it must be the German artillery who were firing. It was some time before we realised that it was the Russians. They kept up their bombardment of the stricken town for over an hour, in an attempt to finish off Germans and Poles alike. They succeeded that day in slaughtering many thousands of people.

The Fifth Company re-grouped and was pulled out of the area. Uule and his Finns had disappeared, and we never saw them again. The following day we were sent to the Rue Kransinski to supervise the Polish surrender and check that all firearms and other weapons were duly handed over. We felt no jubilation as the long line of soldiers passed silently before us on their way to captivity. They had fought a good fight, and we bore them no ill will.

And so, at last, was it really all come to an end? Not quite. Not yet. The psychopaths of the Dirlewanger and Kaminski Brigades still had one last ritualistic orgy of blood-letting to perform.

That same evening, the executions began. Friend turned against friend, neighbour against neighbour, in frenzied attempts to save their own skins. This man was a Communist, that man was a Jew; this woman had slept with a Russian officer, that woman was known to have Soviet sympathies. One word was sufficient to condemn a person. The executioners were not concerned with evidence.

The terms of surrender had extended only to soldiers of the regular Polish Army. The thousands of others who had taken up arms against the German invader were treated according to Himmler's instructions—they were outside the law and had no right of appeal. They were therefore shot without trial.

What little remained of the civilian population after the night's massacres was rounded up and cattle-herded into an immense concentration camp situated to the north-west of Warsaw. There they were kept without food and water, with no proper sanitary arrangements, with no provision for the sick or the elderly, until transport could be arranged to take them to Germany. Considerable numbers of them died *en route*.

Meanwhile, companies of Pioneers were sent in to begin the task of the wholesale destruction ordered by Himmler. It was not until the end of January that the ruins of Warsaw were finally left alone to die in peace. There was nothing left to burn, nothing left to demolish. The people had all been murdered, the buildings had all been destroyed. Himmler's command had been carried out with typical Prussian thoroughness. Every man, woman and child; every dog and every cat; every street and every building ...

It had finally been achieved. Warsaw had been wiped off the face of the map.

THE END

BLITZFREEZE
by SVEN HASSEL

The Führer's commands were simple − forward to Moscow! And so the mighty Panzer regiments thundered into action − killing, raping, burning their way across the great wastes of Russia . . .

But this was to be the bloodiest of all Hitler's wars − a war where Russian infantrymen threw themselves before the oncoming tanks, where women fought as savagely as men, where German guns killed Germans and Russians alike, mangling them indiscriminately into tattered hunks of meat . . .

And finally Porta, Tiny, Barcelona, all of them − caring nothing for who should win the war − began the long retreat − back through the corpse-littered plains where blood and bodies were already frozen beneath the winter ice . . .

0 552 09761 6

ASSIGNMENT GESTAPO
by SVEN HASSEL

Their more unorthodox weapons were lengths of steel wire and knives with double-edged blades, and some of their most prized possessions were gold teeth snatched from corpses . . .

The 'Disciplinary Regiment', a tank company in Hitler's army − without a tank to its name − was fighting a brutal war against the Russians. A bunch of hardened criminals in filthy rags, stinking to high heaven, this company was worth an entire regiment of freshly laundered troops from Breslau. Guerrilla warfare on the Eastern front was for them a prelude to the bloody massacre of Russian troops who'd attacked the German reserves and occupied their headquarters. Then the 'Disciplinary Regiment' was sent to Hamburg, where their next assignment was guard duty for the bestial Gestapo .

0 552 08779 3

A SELECTED LIST OF WAR TITLES
AVAILABLE FROM CORGI BOOKS

THE PRICES SHOWN BELOW WERE CORRECT AT THE TIME OF
GOING TO PRESS. HOWEVER TRANSWORLD PUBLISHERS
RESERVE THE RIGHT TO SHOW NEW RETAIL PRICES ON COVERS
WHICH MAY DIFFER FROM THOSE PREVIOUSLY ADVERTISED IN
THE TEXT OR ELSEWHERE.

☐ 10808 1	THE WILD GEESE	*Daniel Carney*	£1.95
☐ 10807 3	FIRE POWER	*Chris Dempster & Dave Tomkins*	£2.95
☐ 13273 X	ONCE A WARRIOR KING	*David Donovan*	£3.95
☐ 12686 1	THE COMMISSAR	*Sven Hassel*	£2.95
☐ 11976 8	O.G.P.U. PRISON	*Sven Hassel*	£2.50
☐ 11168 6	COURT MARTIAL	*Sven Hassel*	£2.50
☐ 10400 0	THE BLOODY ROAD TO DEATH	*Sven Hassel*	£2.95
☐ 09761 6	BLITZFREEZE	*Sven Hassel*	£2.50
☐ 09178 2	REIGN OF HELL	*Sven Hassel*	£2.95
☐ 08874 9	SS GENERAL	*Sven Hassel*	£2.95
☐ 08779 3	ASSIGNMENT GESTAPO	*Sven Hassel*	£2.50
☐ 08603 7	LIQUIDATE PARIS	*Sven Hassel*	£2.50
☐ 08528 6	MARCH BATTALION	*Sven Hassel*	£2.50
☐ 08168 X	MONTE CASSINO	*Sven Hassel*	£2.50
☐ 07871 9	COMRADES OF WAR	*Sven Hassel*	£2.95
☐ 07242 7	WHEELS OF TERROR	*Sven Hassel*	£2.95
☐ 11417 0	THE LEGION OF THE DAMNED	*Sven Hassel*	£2.50
☐ 07935 9	MERCENARY	*Mike Hoare*	£1.95
☐ 12659 9	LET A SOLDIER DIE	*William E. Holland*	£2.50
☐ 12419 2	CHICKENHAWK	*Robert C. Mason*	£3.95
☐ 12736 1	THE SPECIALIST	*Gayle Rivers*	£2.50
☐ 10954 1	THE FIVE FINGERS	*G. Rivers & J. Hudson*	£2.95
☐ 11030 2	VICTIMS OF YALTA	*Nicolai Tolstoy*	£3.95
☐ 10499 X	THE GLORY HOLE	*T. Jeff Williams*	£2.50

*All Corgi/Bantam Books are available at your bookshop or newsagent, or can be ordered from the
following address:*

Corgi/Bantam Books,
Cash Sales Department,
P.O. Box 11, Falmouth, Cornwall TR10 9EN

Please send a cheque or postal order (no currency) and allow 60p for postage and packing for
the first book plus 25p for the second book and 15p for each additional book ordered up to a
maximum charge of £1.90 in UK.

B.F.P.O. customers please allow 60p for the first book, 25p for the second book plus 15p per
copy for the next 7 books, thereafter 9p per book.

Overseas customers, including Eire, please allow £1.25 for postage and packing for the first
book, 75p for the second book, and 28p for each subsequent title ordered.